C000185143

THE
SILENT
TWIN

Also by Caroline Mitchell:

Detective Jennifer Knight series
Don't Turn Around
Time to Die

Non-Fiction
Paranormal Intruder

THE SILENT TWIN

CAROLINE MITCHELL

Bookouture

Published by Bookouture

An imprint of StoryFire Ltd.
23 Sussex Road, Ickenham, UB10 8PN
United Kingdom

www.bookouture.com

ISBN: 978-1-910751-92-3
eBook ISBN: 978-1-910751-91-6

This book is dedicated to the parents and families of missing children in the UK and beyond. I hope that one day you find peace.

PROLOGUE

Abigail and Olivia are dressed differently today. Olivia likes soft colours, but Abigail's taste suits her personality; vibrant, bright and bold. It makes her easy to find when they play hide and seek on the farmland, but she never tires of the game. Right now, it's Abigail's turn to hide.

Abigail's blonde hair streams behind her as she runs past the hen house, her siren-red wellingtons contrasting with her soil-dusted yellow dungarees. A sliver of an icy breeze whistles through the rain-rotted wood of the empty cattle sheds, which house freshly hatched spiders and field mice within. It creaks and shivers against the growing gale.

Olivia's voice echoes as the wind whips her words. She is counting through cupped hands, the tips of her fingers lightly touching her forehead as she squeezes her eyes shut . . . *ninety-eight . . . ninety-nine . . . one hundred. Here I come, ready or not.*

Ready or not. The watcher disguises their deceitful expression, but the eyes behind the mask are cold.

Abigail giggles frantically as she searches for a hiding place and runs towards the unused hay barn. There is not a second to spare.

The watcher steps out as Abigail turns the corner, catching her in their shadow, cast by the weakening sun. The outhouse timbers creak, as if to say *we know.*

CHAPTER ONE

Six Hours Gone

Sue patted the chair next to her, keeping her voice low, 'Jennifer, come take a seat.'

Jennifer discreetly returned a greeting before sitting down beside her old colleague. The briefing room at Haven police station was not the time or place for a reunion. Uniformed officers were still piling in, standing with their backs against the magnolia walls. Top brass was present in the form of Detective Chief Inspector Anderson, whose shadow fell like a slender reed against the projection screen. His short grey hair was cut with exact symmetry, his handkerchief folded in a perfect peak as it peeped from the top pocket of his suit. Known for his efficiency, he was the Senior Investigating Officer in the case of the missing twin, which meant police were taking the child's disappearance very seriously. DI Ethan Cole sat across from his superior at the front of the room, looking polished and focused in his charcoal suit.

Jennifer flipped open her black leather pocket notebook and clicked the top on her pen. On the top of the page she wrote the time, date, her name, call sign, and location, followed by her role: Family Liaison Officer. It was the first time she would put her training into use, and she hoped her presence would be worthwhile.

She scratched the back of her head with a perfectly manicured nail. Her mahogany hair had been tied into a professional bun while still damp from the shower, but after ten minutes in the airless briefing room, she longed to set it free. Every inch of her felt uptight at the thought of being thrown into such a high-risk case.

Sue leaned into her, the smell of spearmint chewing gum filling the gap between them. 'How's Will? Honestly, my heart was in my mouth when he disappeared.'

The subject of DC Will Dunston's disappearance had been the talk of the station, and it was with much relief that Jennifer delivered a positive update. 'Much better, thanks,' Jennifer whispered, as they waited for the briefing to begin. 'He'll be back to work soon.'

The door slid shut as the last officer crept in, signalling an end to their conversation. The overhead projector whirred from its mount on the ceiling, and as DCI Anderson pressed the clicker, a series of images came into view. His face was serious, and his eyes held a steely determination Jennifer had seen before – during murder investigations. It was enough to make her sit up and take note, and she worked deftly, scribbling down points of interest in her notebook.

After relaying the background information on the case, DCI Anderson's stretched hand rested on the interactive whiteboard. A map of Blackwater Farm displayed the spot where the nine-year-old child had last been seen at 10 a.m. that morning. A specialist search team had begun searching the house and outbuildings, battling the heavy April showers in their efforts to locate forensic evidence of a potential crime. But there were so many variables. He pointed to the river Blakewater, which ran parallel to the farm, about half a mile down. A request had been put in for the marine unit to attend. His hand swept across the map to Haven woods, thick with forestation and dotted with empty boathouses. Sniffer dogs were being requested, although a local dog handler had already scoped the outskirts of the farm with no luck.

Nobody could criticise the police for a lack of response. DCI Anderson discussed consulting specialist detectives who had worked on high profile cases of missing children in the past. Directions were given with regards to house-to-house enquiries and future press appeals. He pressed the clicker, and an image of an exhibit filled the screen, ceasing the undercurrent of chatter in the room. It was a picture of the little girl's glasses; Harry Potter style circular frames. A smudge of mud blotted a cracked lens, filling Jennifer with a sense of gloomy foreboding.

DCI Anderson looked grimly at the exhibit. 'This is why we're fast tracking enquiries. These were found just outside the farm this afternoon, on a lane leading to the woodlands. Abigail has bad eyesight; she can't get far without them.' His voice dropped as he gazed around the room. 'This information has not yet been released to the press. Given what her parents have told us about their daughter, we do not believe she left the area of her own accord.'

Jennifer glanced at the clock on the wall, painfully aware she had to liaise with the family before evening closed in. She returned her focus to DCI Anderson's voice, her heart faltering as he pointed in her general direction.

'Sue, you've been with the family today, can you provide us with any further update?'

Sue rose, straightening her posture. 'Yes, sir. Well, it's as to be expected, really. Sergeant Duncan, Abigail's father, is devastated. His wife, Joanna, seems to be taking it in her stride. They've only recently moved to the farm, having lived in a townhouse in Haven previously. They don't have any enemies that we are aware of, but enquiries are being made with regards to friends, family and acquaintances.' Sue peeked at her notes and continued. 'Mrs Duncan's an online parenting guru. She runs a blog with over two hundred thousand subscribers, and has an occasional slot on a local TV channel, which places her firmly in the public eye. She's very keen to speak to the press, but I've strongly advised her against it.'

DCI Anderson peered down his nose. 'I see from your report that you've mentioned some unusual activity in the house. Can you tell us about this?'

'Yes, boss.' Sue flushed, the colour rising as her discomfort became apparent. 'There has been unusual activity in the form of light bulbs blowing, banging on the walls, and . . . um . . .' She swallowed hard, throwing Jennifer a sideways glance. '. . . furniture moving by itself.' A rumble of murmurs grew in the room. 'It's a very old house, in need of renovation,' she hastily added. 'DC Jennifer Knight is taking over my role from today, under the remit of Operation Moonlight.'

After a nod from her superior, Sue sat back down.

'Jennifer, please ensure you sign the paper being passed around the room. I want you to approach this family with the mind of an investigator. You are our eyes and ears on the ground.'

Jennifer located the paper and added her details to the list of hastily scribbled names, ranks, departments and mobile telephone numbers before she left. The list would be disseminated to attendees so they could keep in touch with each other during the course of the investigation. Briefing ended with an image of Abigail, looking happy and relaxed as she played in a field of sunflowers with her identical twin sister, Olivia. But the picture seemed drained, and cast a sombre atmosphere in the room as officers filtered out. Jennifer wondered how many of them would be giving their kids an extra hug that night.

Jennifer took the opportunity to question Sue on the strange occurrences at the house, which were part of the reason that she had been allocated to take over as Family Liaison Officer. Operation Moonlight worked in the same way as normal police departments apart from one aspect: Jennifer investigated crimes with an unearthly edge, and she had been kept busy since joining the covert team.

'What's it really like at Blackwater Farm?' she said, cornering her friend in the corridor.

Sue grimaced. 'It's a nightmare. Mum and Dad are at complete discord with each other, and Olivia, that's the twin, hasn't spoken since her sister disappeared. She's so solemn, it creeps me out.'

Jennifer loosened the elastic band around her tightly wound hair. 'It's bound to be stressful, given what they're going through.'

'It's more than that,' Sue said, her voice low. 'It's like the house is alive. Doors slam by themselves, there are footsteps upstairs when there's nobody around, and there's this feeling, like you're being watched.' Sue shook her head, as if struggling to believe her own words. 'This afternoon, the light bulb in the kitchen blew. I don't mean it dimmed, or stopped working. It exploded into a thousand pieces over my head, got in my hair and everything. Frightened the life out of me, it did. I looked across the room and there was Olivia, sitting on the stairs, staring through the banisters with the weirdest expression on her face. It chilled me to the bone.'

Jennifer frowned. Sue was many things, but she was steadfast when it came to her cases. This wasn't like her at all. 'Is that why you walked out?'

'You know me, I'm no quitter. But that house freaks me out. I told the DCI that I was happy to do the investigative work, but someone from Op Moonlight should take the lead with the family.' She sighed. 'I know you probably think I'm over-reacting . . .' Sue said, her eyes searching Jennifer's for reassurance.

'I don't think any such thing,' Jennifer said. 'What do you think is behind it?'

Sue shrugged. 'All I know is that things are taking on a life of their own in that house. I was totally out of my depth.'

Jennifer mentally picked through it all while driving to the farm. Were the incidents Sue described a diversion for what was really going on at the family home? It was doubtful that Abigail had run away of her own accord, but in such a remote area, it was equally unlikely to have been an opportunistic snatch. Briefing made it plainly obvious. After six hours missing, they were not expecting to find Abigail alive.

CHAPTER TWO

Seven Hours Gone

The long imposing track to Blackwater Farm wound like a snake through the desolate marshlands, past the woodlands bordering the river. The countryside consisted of dips and hollows, which scooped up the wind on stormy nights, producing echoing gusts rendered in ominous howls.

Jennifer had once been given a panoramic view courtesy of the police helicopter, as her colleagues had demonstrated their thermal imaging cameras used to locate cannabis factories below. It had been fascinating to see the contrasts in the town she had lived in all her life, all taken in during a twenty-minute trip.

Nature had divided Haven. On one side of the river bridge were the newly developed flats, which housed the commuters to London. This development was embraced by local businesses such as fine eateries, shopping centres and designer retailers. The helicopter had cut through the air to the other side of Haven, over the housing estates, the boarded-up shops and derelict streets you did not walk alone at night. It had then turned away from the town and flown over a plethora of Victorian houses on a pretty tree-lined street. Jennifer had picked out her own home, grateful that none of the neighbouring abodes came up on the expensive heat-seeking equipment. The pilot had taken the scenic route as they returned to base, driving the deer into the forest, which was dotted with Lego-like

wooden lodges, and over the river, where small boats bobbed on
the surface of the unpredictable water, so dark it had earned itself
the name Blackwater. This had since been changed to Blakewater
in an attempt to shake off negative connotations.

Jennifer wondered if there would be any such connotations
attached to Blackwater Farm, which was looming into her vision
as she negotiated her car around the twisty road. People usually
didn't build this far out, as the acres of marsh lands made for a
risky investment. Blackwater Farm had been there as long as Haven
itself. As Jennifer approached the stone farmhouse, she could see
the attraction. It was pretty, in a wild, untamed sort of way.

Jennifer slowed down as she steered her car onto the rough terrain
leading into the yard. A narrow dirt track, it was flanked by strands
of rusted barbed wire, with room for only one vehicle at a time. She
bounced in her seat as her car suspension was tested, driving through
the open gateway past the moss-covered perimeter walls. They stood
strong against the backdrop of the scrub farmland, and surrounded
the old stone house. A leafless vine encrusted the building like
rain-whipped hair. Pulling up between the parked cars, she glanced
around for signs of life as she opened her door, expecting a muddy
dog to come bounding up, at the very least. But the only sound was
the wind whistling through the outbuildings, and a loose sheet of
galvanized metal flapping against a wall. Spring weather was yet to
make an appearance in Haven, and Jennifer shivered as a slice of
cool air crept under her suit jacket. The delapidated building became
less attractive with every step Jennifer took, and her heart felt heavy
as she strode across the foot-worn flagstones. She promised herself
she would not become emotionally involved, or at the very least,
that this was the impression she would portray. But crimes against
children got under her skin. It was the reason she had never joined

the child abuse investigation team. She took in a strengthening breath as she stood before the chipped green wooden door, its age defined by the heavy metal knocker. She gave it three stout raps, then tapped her foot, willing them to hurry up and answer. No response. She took a couple of steps back to look through the old sash windows. Her eyes crept up to the right, and saw a pale-faced girl with large moon eyes fixed directly on hers. It was the face of someone who had lost a part of herself. Wearing the same glasses pictured in briefing that morning, the girl was the mirror image of her missing sister. Jennifer smiled and raised her hand to wave, then paused mid-air as the front door creaked open. She glanced back up one more time, but the child had gone. Stepping forward, she braced herself to cope with the distraught family member and was taken aback to be greeted by a pretty blonde woman wearing a hint of a smile on her lips.

The wind howled, and Jennifer mentally cursed her lip gloss as she pushed back some sticky strands of errant hair.

'I'm DC Jennifer Knight,' she said, flashing her warrant card, before shaking the hand of the woman before her.

'I'm Joanna. We've been expecting you.'

The woman's hand was firm and warm. Jennifer raked her mind as she wondered if she had got the name wrong. Was this happy smiling woman the mother of a missing child? Joanna was toned and well dressed, wearing just enough make up to give her a healthy glow – and not a mascara streak in sight. Her blonde hair was beautifully pinned back in a retro hairstyle, making Jennifer feel underdressed for once in her life. Her clothes were vintage; bright and quirky, perhaps purchased from an upmarket charity shop. Another whoop of wind swept past Jennifer, stealing her composure as particles of dirt flew into her face, making her blink.

'Where are my manners?' Joanna said. 'Please come inside.'

Jennifer's role was to act as a go between, deciphering the police jargon and updating the family on the case. But more importantly, she was also there to observe and gather information, whatever it may turn out to be. She closed the door behind her, pushing it against the wind squealing through the cracks. It was thick and heavy, and as the hinges groaned shut there was a sense of finality, as if she had committed herself to this family. This house. She wondered if her colleagues had felt it too.

Joanna walked briskly down the hall. The oil burners on the small oval table failed dismally to mask the smell of damp plasterboard. Jennifer blinked to adjust her eyes after walking in from the light, feeling like she had entered a long narrow cave. Her sixth sense spiked as she entered the bowels of the house, and other-world whispers streamed into her consciousness.

'You'll have to forgive the state we're in,' Joanna said, bringing her back to reality.

Jennifer was about to reply that it was only natural her emotions would be all over the place, when she realised Joanna was talking about the decor, and not her missing child.

Joanna grasped the brass door handle. 'I'll take you to my husband. I believe you've met.'

Jennifer paused as a floorboard creaked overhead. 'I'd really like to speak to Olivia first, if I could.'

'I'm afraid that's not possible,' Joanna said. 'Olivia hasn't spoken a word since her sister's disappearance.'

'But . . .' Jennifer said, taking a step back as she caught a glimpse of the little girl on the landing. 'I'd like to see her, just the same.'

'All in good time,' Joanna said, leaning against the door and pushing it open. Jennifer masked her expression of disbelief as she entered the spacious kitchen. It was bigger than her hall, kitchen and living room put together. The room was milling with people, huddled together in small groups. It could have passed as a social gathering, if it were not for the attire of muddy boots, duffle coats and wax jackets. Her eyes danced over each group, picking out faces as they glanced in her direction. She immediately recognised Karen Corbett – the latest addition to Nick Duncan's team at Lexton CID, having recently come through her probation.

Jennifer felt a pair of eyes bore into her, and caught the gaze of a bearded man standing on his own in the corner. The tallest person in the room, he was middle-aged, with a weathered face which spoke of the outdoors. Throwing the remnants of his tea into the sink, he pulled up the furred hood of his parka and made towards the door. Joanna gave a blanket introduction to the rest of the mumbling herds of people as 'family and friends', as they knocked back their dregs of tea, ready to recommence searching the lands.

'Who was that man in the parka?' Jennifer said, unable to shake off his mistrustful stare. She had recognised him from somewhere, and hoped it was from a social setting, rather than one of her many arrests.

'That's Charles Radcliffe. Radcliffe, for short. He's been helping out on the farm,' Joanna said. She squeezed past the people to a large oak table, where her husband was sitting.

Nick was a complete contrast to his wife. He sat with his head lowered, threading his fingers through his greying hair. He had barely noticed Jennifer enter the room, he was so engrossed in his misery.

Joanna gently called her husband's name, and he snapped his head up in response. His chair scraped against the black stone tiles as he pushed it back, almost knocking it over in his haste to extend a clammy hand and squeeze Jennifer's fingers in a firm grip.

'DC Knight. Have you any news?'

Jennifer looked into his puffy red-rimmed eyes, wishing she had something positive to give him. 'Call me Jennifer, please. As soon as I hear anything, you'll be the first to know.'

Nick's gaze dropped to the floor, his eyebrows dragging his furrowed brow. This was the response Jennifer had expected; a man barely able to keep it together. Her eyes flicked to Joanna, who was humming to herself as she lifted a whistling kettle from the Aga. Something wasn't right about this scene. The kitchen window abruptly burst open, and a cold breeze rode the goosebumps rising on her flesh. The sudden activity reinforced the urgency of her investigations. Abigail was out there somewhere, lost and scared in the wilderness. That's if she was still alive. At just nine years old, she was blinded by bad vision, with no witnesses to her disappearance. Yet missing children were not an uncommon occurrence in the UK. The figures from morning briefing returned to haunt her, and the fact that over 140,000 children go missing in the United Kingdom each year. She recalled Olivia's face, silent and forlorn as she stood at the rotting timber window frame – waiting for her twin. Jennifer made a silent promise. One way or another, she would bring Abigail home.

CHAPTER THREE

Diary Entry

I wanted to hurt myself today. To slice through my skin and watch the life flow out of me in a red river of madness. It's my madness. I know that. It's why my mother nicknamed me Jekyll and Hyde. One moment I would be calm, serene, a perfect child. Then without any warning I was a typhoon, ripping through the room, upsetting anyone in my path. She didn't understand. And those that did said nothing.

I'm much better at hiding my feelings now. Diaries are therapeutic, a way of bleeding all the poison and frustrations onto the page. What was it the counsellors said? Imagine filling a balloon with all your torment, and watch as it floats up into the sky. But that never worked for me. The only pressure valve to my emotional turbulence was inflicting physical pain. It's not my fault. Besides, I always begin with myself. My body bears the scars to prove it. But some days the slash of a razor or burn from a flame just isn't enough. I try not to allow it to take over, but it builds like a powerful wave. I feel myself being submerged in its darkness, gasping for breath as it consumes me. On those days I can barely recollect what happens.

Being Jekyll and Hyde isn't such a terrible thing. Because if I have two separate identities, then the bad thing happened to my alter ego, not me, and I don't have to take responsibility for what follows. Lately I've been finding it harder to cope. The masses of people coming to the house make me feel dizzy and confused. Oh Diary, I wish you were a real person. Someone I could turn to who would understand without judgement. What made me was an evil so great that I had no choice but to embrace it. There is no redemption for me. And making it my ally has given me the strength I need to survive. Sometimes, when the anger is rising, I fantasise about grasping a poker, white-hot from the fire. I imagine the smell of my burning flesh filling my nostrils as the pain seeps through to every nerve ending. I envision myself striking it down on the people who betrayed me. On those occasions, the pain is good. The strength, the control. But I'm not ready to talk about the past yet. It's like vomiting in your own mouth; tasting the bile that partially digested long ago.

A detective has come to the farm. She is strong and determined. She wants to integrate herself into our lives, like a beautiful dark spider weaving a sugared web. *You can talk to me, tell me how you feel.* Her eyes are hypnotic, and her words lure you in. But I know what she is and I won't allow her a viewing into my soul. I've become an expert at allowing my eyes to glaze over in a disinterested way. Sometimes I blurt out a giggle when nobody is looking – seeing them all running around, crying, shouting, a disgusting outpour of human emotions. I have all the power. Because I know things that nobody else knows. I feel the hysteria bubble up inside me, and I stifle the giggles, camouflaging my response as shock or despair. Am I inhuman, to be without compassion? Devoid of empathy? There was little compassion or sorrow for me. I think of Abigail. So beautiful, and so full of life. Her long flowing white-blonde hair, her loud giggles and whoops as she ran through the house, filling the empty spaces with laughter. But then I think of *my* childhood. And I wonder, is it fair to choose Abigail's life over mine? I remember my pact and know I have no choice.

CHAPTER FOUR

'Are you a tea or coffee drinker?' Joanna smiled. 'I've got some nice pastries from the bakery this morning, I drove into Haven especially. Would you like one?'

'Just coffee, thanks,' Jennifer said, picking a floppy-eared toy rabbit up off the floor and placing it on the table. She returned her gaze to Nick, watching his expression of disbelief as he stared at his wife.

A jagged vein at the side of his forehead began to pulsate as he spoke in cold, hurt tones. 'Make the coffee if that's what you want. We're going into the living room.'

'Of course, darling, you and your police talk. I'm sure it's all above my head anyway.' A dainty laugh passed her lips as she slid out the box of sugar lumps from the cupboard.

'Come with me,' Nick said, taking Jennifer by the elbow, not quite forcefully, but hard enough to take control. He steered her out into the hall, guiding her down the corridor into a door on the right.

Each room seemed more oppressive than the last, and she fought to acclimatise herself to the leaden atmosphere. The ceiling creaked overhead, driving a shiver up Jennifer's spine. In Haven, old houses didn't settle. They carried a life of their own, and Blackwater Farm was no exception. This was a house that would never be a home. The best they could hope for would be to co-exist with the ghosts of the past.

'Take a seat,' Nick said, pointing to an old leather chair. Most of the furniture seemed to have woodworm. A plasma television flashed with the sound turned down, ill suited with the other furnishings.

Jennifer stood, rooted to the spot. She didn't appreciate being manhandled, and was not about to allow him to take his frustrations out on her.

'With all due respect, Sergeant, I'll sit when you do.'

Nick rubbed his hand across his stubble as he breathed a terse sigh. 'I'm sorry. I just . . . I can't handle Joanna right now. Our daughter's missing and she's making tea. Fucking tea!' With one swift kick he sent a spindly coffee table skidding across the threadbare carpet.

Jennifer took two steps forward and grasped his forearm. His sinews were tense in her grip. 'We'll find your daughter. But you've got to stay focused and calm the hell down.'

Nick broke away and turned to face the window. 'I just feel so helpless. I need to be out there, looking for Abigail.'

Jennifer understood his frustration, but to her mind, answers could be nearer than they imagined.

'I was wondering if I could spend some time with Olivia. I know she's not talking, but she might open up to a stranger . . . Nick?'

But Nick wasn't listening. Evening was drawing in, bringing with it the prospect of his little girl being alone in the dark for the very first time.

Jennifer followed Nick's gaze to the bleak fields, and to the left, the array of outbuildings, which had been searched more times than they needed to be. Police did not believe Abigail was in the immediate vicinity, and the search area had widened considerably. Jennifer tried to pick up clues from the energies in the house, but the air was too charged, filled with vibrations of anger and despair. She softened her voice. 'I understand your devastation, I really do. My nephew went missing last year and I nearly went mad with worry. Why don't we sit down and discuss things? Maybe a fresh perspective will help?'

Nick faced her, the anger withdrawn from his eyes for now. 'Your nephew . . .' he said, swallowing to ease the croak in his voice. 'Did you find him?'

'Yes, alive and well,' Jennifer said, leading Nick to an old wingback leather chair.

'Good. And please, call me Nick.' He hitched up his jeans as he took a seat.

Jennifer nodded, inwardly groaning as Joanna entered the room with a tray. Just when I'm making progress, she thought, hoping she would hurry up and leave. Jennifer placed the coffee table on its feet and Joanna put the tray on top, still wearing her plastic smile.

'Here you go. Help yourself to sugar and cream. Oh, and I've put some croissants on the side just in case you change your mind.'

Jennifer smiled a thank you, afraid her words may spark off another bout of anger from Nick. Throughout her career she had to be the bearer of bad news. People would curl up in a ball and wail, would want to attack her, or would just push her out of the door rather than face the reality that their loved one had died. Although no body had been found, the disappearance of a young child was every parent's nightmare. But Joanna's behaviour really was bizarre. Jennifer felt a distinct air of unease as the woman robotically cocked her head to one side and pointed at the television. 'Oh look, there I am.'

Jennifer gasped as an image of Joanna flickered up on the screen. She was flanked by a couple of television presenters from a TV studio in Lexton, wearing sympathetic smiles as they introduced her to the audience. It was the local show where Joanna sometimes made a guest appearance, but Jennifer never expected to see her on screen today.

Nick, who had been staring coldly ahead, snapped up the remote control. 'What the hell?' he said, jabbing the button as he turned up the volume. It was a pre-recorded interview from that day. A few hours after Abigail went missing. 'What have you done?' he whispered, as he watched his wife smiling at the camera. Her perfect white teeth, her beautifully applied make-up, even her blonde hair was styled with precision. She wore a fuchsia skirt and jacket, her legs neatly crossed as she clutched the ears of the toy bunny rabbit on her lap.

Jennifer peered at the screen, recognising it as the same toy she had picked up from the floor minutes earlier. She shook away the uneasy thought that it was being used as a prop, and strained to listen to the interview.

'Abigail has been missing for hours now,' Joanna said, sadly. 'We'd just like her to come home. If anyone knows of her whereabouts, we'd like them to get in touch.'

The presenter nodded sympathetically. 'You mention someone knowing about her disappearance. You don't think she could have run away?'

'Oh no,' Joanna smiled. 'Abigail would never leave her twin sister. They were two peas in a pod.'

She's described them in past tense, Jennifer thought.

The dark-haired interviewer masked her expression, but Jennifer could see the surprise behind her eyes. 'So how do you *feel* about your daughter's disappearance?' she asked, seizing the moment.

Joanna pulled a tissue from her pocket and dabbed the corner of her eye, which was completely dry. 'We just want our little girl to come home. I have a Facebook group, by the way, for anyone that has information, and they can tweet with the hashtag "Find Abigail". I've had some wonderful messages of support.'

Jennifer sighed. Joanna must have sneaked out to Lexton after Sue had left. She was free to go where she wanted, as she wasn't a suspect. But Joanna going against everything the police had asked of her could only hinder the investigation. Jennifer gritted her teeth, willing the show to end. But the interviewers weren't going to let Joanna off the hook that easily. Jennifer stifled a groan as they continued with their questioning.

'Have the police found any leads with regards to her disappearance?'

Joanna uncrossed her legs and looked directly at the cameras. 'Yes. They found her glasses on a track outside our home. She can't see very well without them.'

Jennifer drew her attention away from the screen and back to Nick. His face was red with fury, fists clenched, as his frustrations reached boiling point. 'What have you done?' he shouted, turning to face Joanna, spitting the words backed up in his throat.

It was bad enough that Joanna had gone against their wishes and appeared on TV, but now she had leaked vital information to the press. Jennifer stepped between them, shielding the woman from her furious husband. 'Sit down, Nick, this isn't going to solve anything.'

'I thought it would help,' Joanna said in a small voice from behind Jennifer's shoulder. Jennifer had never been more grateful for her five-inch heels as she squared herself against the man before her. His words came hot and angry as his voice raised another decibel.

'Help? You think the public are going to support us now? You've no idea of the damage you've done! Our daughter is missing and you're sitting there grinning, like you've won the lottery. This is our little girl. How could you be so cold?'

Jennifer planted her hands on Nick's chest, firmly guiding him back. 'What's done is done. There's nothing we can do about it now.' Her phone buzzed angrily in her pocket. It had to be HQ, most likely up in arms at the unannounced interview. She took a breath as she assessed the situation. Nick's face contorted as he tried to control his emotions.

She turned to face an expressionless Joanna, jumping as the tray from the coffee table fell to the ground behind her, the crockery smashing and its contents soaking into the faded rug. I can't believe she's done that, Jennifer thought, reaching for her phone as it vibrated a second time. Nick wrenched open the door and stormed through the hall, disappearing outside. Joanna went in the opposite direction, her vintage couture shoes tapping as she climbed the wide wooden stairs. At least they were apart. Slowly, Jennifer's heart returned to its normal pace. What had she been thinking, volunteering to come here so soon after her last case? All of this had happened, and it was barely six o clock. But there was more to come. The door creaked open and a small pale child tiptoed forward, her eyes pleading with Jennifer's.

It was Abigail's twin. And she had something to say.

CHAPTER FIVE

Joanna stared into the full-length Victorian mirror as she allowed the memory of her husband's anger to seep away. Her outfit had been purchased in that gorgeous little retro shop in Haven, the one with the Portuguese shop assistant. She had chosen the ensemble herself, adding personal touches to ensure its uniqueness. She kept busy in everything she did, because she could not afford to stop, not even for a moment.

She had spoken to numerous police officers since Abigail's disappearance, telling them the same story, over and over again. It had been showery after breakfast, and the twins were going stir crazy inside. As soon as the sunshine peeked through the clouds, they had begged to be allowed out. 'Please, Mummy, we want to play hide and seek,' they chorused in unison. It was their favourite game. It didn't matter where they hid, they could always find each other. They had an inseparable bond.

'Oh go on, then,' she had said. 'Daddy is clearing out the cow shed. Don't go any further than the hen house, all right?'

Living in the countryside meant imposing strict limitations. Their ten acres of farmland was so rugged, so desolate, they may as well have been on the moon. The last ten years of her life had been spent between the city and Haven's busy town. But lost in the jumble of crowds, she had felt so alone.

The girls had responded with giggles, pulling on their welling-ton boots before dragging open the kitchen door and clattering outside. It wasn't much fun for them inside, the renovation work made many of the rooms a no-go area. Of the five bedrooms in the house, four were fit for purpose, and the twins shared one between them. It wasn't easy for her either, when she was used to living in luxury accommodation. But it wasn't just the refurbishment that made living in the house so hard – only hours after moving in, strange things had begun to occur. Cupboard doors swung open by themselves, and there were odd scratching noises, as if someone were clawing the walls. But these strange events usually happened when her husband was out, which was most of the time. Nick told her it was her imagination. The hinges were wrecked, and nothing in the house was straight. He even put a spirit level to the cupboard doors to prove his point. She watched as the bubble edged away from the middle strip, and caught a triumphant glint in his eye as he was proved right.

But she knew better.

Fiona had been baking bread in the Aga while Joanna worked on her laptop at the table. Her housekeeper had been a godsend since they moved in, and at least the kitchen was fully functional. The oven produced a wonderful homely scent, and the twins would be treated to the jam roly polys which were rising on the second shelf. Thick plops of rain had begun to drum on the tin buckets underneath the broken guttering outside. The *tap tap tap* of the rain felt like stiffened fingers on her forehead, like a clock counting down to some god-awful event. Joanna stretched her neck to look through the window for the girls. She had been so carried away working, that time had passed without her noticing.

She had barely opened the front door to call for them when Olivia rushed into her arms. Tears were spilling down her face, and Joanna felt her heart give a little jolt in her chest. 'What's wrong honey?' Joanna said, removing her daughter's rain-dappled glasses and drying them with the corner of her dress. Olivia was a quiet child, but her lack of response was uncharacteristic. She stared at her mother with wide, frightened eyes, her mouth open, a hollow cave devoid of words. Something was wrong. Very wrong. Refusing to speak, Olivia responded to Joanna's questioning with nods and shakes of her head. It was enough for Joanna to ascertain that Abigail had hidden and Olivia could not find her. But they always found each other. Joanna took a deep breath. Calm down, she told herself. Everything is going to be all right. There's nothing to be scared of. Push it down. Way down.

Nick arrived minutes later, red faced and sweaty, rubbing his roughened palms against the back of his jeans. She was used to him looking at her with disdain when he thought she couldn't see. But there was something more in his expression. Something hidden. She pushed away the thought. Abigail was probably hiding in one of the barns, too scared to come out because she had gone further than she was allowed. But Abigail loved her parents. She had nothing to be scared of. They never smacked her. In fact, they barely raised their voices. She never gave them cause to.

With each minute that passed, Nick became more panicked. Joanna, on the other hand, fell back on her coping mechanism. Nick used to find it soothing, her ability to face any crisis with a smile. But not today. Today he looked like he wanted to shake her until her smile became loose and fell from her face. The shower of rain soon became a downpour. She had never seen rain like this when she lived in the city, thick plops of water that could soak you to the skin in the distance between running from your car to the front door. Fiona and Nick searched the barns and sheds while she stayed indoors with Olivia, trying to encourage her to speak. Joanna settled the glasses back onto Olivia's face and, in the absence of words, the child responded with nods and shakes of the head.

'Where is your sister?' Joanna asked.

Olivia replied with a shrug. But the depths of her emotions were reflected in her eyes. Something had frightened her, and she was too scared to say what.

'Do you know where she is?' Joanna said, her voice calm and even.

Olivia shook her head in a 'no'.

'Did you see her go off with anyone?'

Olivia shook her head again.

Joanna recalled her husband's expression; wild, frightful even. She took her daughter by the hand. 'Is something scaring you?'

Olivia bit her lip before fat tears sprang to her eyes, clinging to her long blonde eyelashes until she blinked, setting them free. She didn't need to answer. Her demeanour was answer enough.

'Do you think Abigail's still hiding?'

Olivia shook her head, a sob escaping her lips.

'Oh sweetheart, don't cry, we'll find your sister. She's probably just found a really good hiding place. Now, why aren't you speaking?'

Nothing. Her sob turned into a hiccup and Joanna stood to pull a tissue from the box on the table. Her mother used to keep them up her sleeve, or stuffed in her bra. She was not her mother.

Any further attempt at questioning came back with the same response. Olivia didn't know where her sister had gone. But she was scared. Too scared to speak. But that was okay, because Joanna had enough reassuring smiles for everyone. Unlike Olivia's, her body was relaxed, her words soft and cheerful. Each time she felt a flicker of anxiety she pushed it down, cranking up another ratchet of denial as she told herself everything would be all right. Her ability to push away the worry reminded her of the wind-up soldiers she had played with as a child. She preferred mechanical toys to dolls. She loved the inner workings as *tick tock, tick tock* the cogs fell neatly into each other. Arms and legs stiffly positioned, with a shiny bloom of rosy cheeks, the soldier marched with a rich smile painted on its face. No matter the adversity, his arms and legs kept moving, cogs whirring, in the quiet confidence he would be set back on his feet to complete his journey.

Joanna smiled sweetly, swallowing back the bile. She spun around as the back door opened, and her husband and Fiona walked inside, sodden and shaking from the rain. An hour had passed, with no sign of Abigail. It was a good thing they had tiles on the floor, Joanna thought. She could easily clean up the mud that had been dragged in from the farmyard.

'No sign?' she said, reaching for the mop.

'No, and the rain is coming down hard,' Fiona said, remembering the bread as grey ribbons of smoke rose through the crack in the oven door.

Nick wiped his rain-drenched face with a checked tea towel before plucking his phone from his pocket. 'We need to call the police.'

The mention of the police temporarily seized the cogs in Joanna's heart. She watched Fiona hurriedly slide the burnt bread and pastries onto a tray before easing off her wellington boots. The tips of her thick woollen socks were wet. Focusing on the mundane helped take Joanna out of her world of discord, and the next few hours passed as painlessly as she could make them – the arrival of the police, the endless form filling, the continued search for their daughter and the onslaught of questions that followed. Joanna didn't notice the odd looks from the police officers because she focused her thoughts elsewhere.

The first officer to arrive was the local bobby. Joanna concentrated on the greasy cow's lick that appeared when the officer removed her sodden police hat, and the rivulets of rainwater that trickled from the rim as she rested it on the table. Joanna answered the questions, while the downpour outside drowned her husband's shouts for their daughter.

But something changed when DC Knight arrived. There was nothing mundane to focus upon there. The girl was strikingly pretty, with dark, soulful eyes. Sharply dressed in a designer suit and heels, Joanna afforded her instant respect. She was certainly an improvement on Sue, the previous Family Liaison Officer, all flappy and jumpy. Sue's energy reminded her of Abigail. Whatever she was doing, she had to be moving, tapping her foot, nodding, eyes roving. Her daughter was never still. Abigail . . . Joanna's thoughts floated. She swallowed hard. She could not afford to think about Abigail. Not any more.

CHAPTER SIX

Olivia's footsteps dragged through the puddle of milk leaking from the upturned ceramic jug. Her face was haunted, and deathly pale. The room seemed to close in around the child, who walked in slow motion, as if she were carrying some terrible burden.

Jennifer willed her to come further, fighting the urge to clean up the remnants of the upturned tray underfoot. Olivia had been wordless since her sister's disappearance, and somehow Jennifer knew that her whispers would be precious, secret. But the moment was lost as footsteps approached, and Jennifer stole a glance over the child's shoulder into the dim hall, half expecting to see Nick's sinewy frame.

A woman appeared, smiling gently as she took the hand of the bewildered child. She was slimmer than Joanna, but with softer features, and coffee-coloured hair which skimmed her shoulders in a functional bob. The apron tied over her jeans was covered in a light dusting of flour.

Jennifer's phone continued to buzz, and she silently cursed its insistence.

'I'm Fiona,' the woman said. 'Why don't you answer your phone? I'll take care of things here.'

Jennifer nodded, relief sweeping over her at the presence of a capable pair of hands. 'Thank you,' she mouthed. She could not afford to miss the call, particularly when it was the senior investigating officer for the case – DCI Anderson, or 'Frosty Bollocks' as her colleagues called him. It was not a term of endearment. He oversaw both Lexton and Haven CID, to which Jennifer had been seconded to assist with the case. DCI Anderson was stiff, regimented, and as Jennifer came to realise when she took the call outside, furious.

'I've been trying to contact you. Why haven't you answered your phone?'

Jennifer picked her way through the farmyard as she tried to find a sheltered place to speak. The wind had eased, and the clouds, streaked pink and gold, drifted over the last rays of sun. 'I'm sorry, sir, things are very fraught, as you can imagine.'

'They're not much better here. Just what was that woman thinking, appearing on television like that? Couldn't you have stopped her?'

Jennifer clasped a hand over her ear as she strained to hear him speak. Blackwater Farm was situated in a hollow, and the reception was poor. 'She was interviewed before I got here. And I don't think she *was* thinking. She's not well.'

DCI Anderson huffed, devoid of sympathy. 'She was well enough to promote her business. I want you to watch that family closely, do you hear me? No social media. No interviews. Keep tabs on them at all times. We must work together on this . . .'

Jennifer scanned the landscape, bordered by the peaks of the trees. A team of people were dotted in the far corner of a field, men and women churning the narrow dirt paths as they searched the ditches for clues. DCI Anderson was silent, and seemed to be awaiting a suitable response. 'Yes, sir,' Jennifer said, hoping it was the correct one. Regardless of the question, you did not say no to DCI Anderson. She squinted to make out Nick in the distance. Keeping tabs on him was like trying to control a nest of angry wasps. 'I take it there are no updates?' she said.

'No,' the DCI answered abruptly. 'You've been designated a police issue laptop. Whatever you do, keep it password locked.

The last thing we need is *that woman* going back to the press with our findings.'

'Yes, boss,' Jennifer said. She didn't need to ask who *that woman* was.

'I've requested that you're emailed copies of statements from friends and family so you can familiarise yourself with the investigation. Has the twin spoken yet?'

'I haven't been able to speak to Olivia alone.'

His response was clipped. 'Then make time. I expect a positive update at the next briefing. In the meantime, keep that family under control. We need to draw on public support, not turn them against us.'

'Of course,' Jennifer said, feeling deflated as her DCI terminated the call. Then it dawned upon her. This was why Sue had washed her hands of the family; not because of any suspected ghosts. Joanna's media profile was sure to attract attention, and her unpredictable behaviour turned her into a ticking time bomb. If she handled this badly, it would be career suicide. Her eyes crept to the top bedroom window to see Olivia staring down at her. It was time for some straight talking.

She left a message on Nick's phone telling him to return home. It may have been cruel, because she knew he would think there was an update on the case, but she had no choice. She needed him where she could see him. Jennifer rolled over the possibilities in her mind. Why was he so annoyed with Joanna? Or was he deflecting his anger because he blamed himself? The children were under their care yet neither of them had noticed Abigail go missing. Her phone buzzed with a text, and she felt a warm glow as her partner Will's name lit up the screen. *Saw the TV interview. We still on for tonight?*

Jennifer sighed. She wanted nothing more than to have Will wrap his arms around her and tell her everything would be okay.

But Abigail needed her, and she was in it for the long haul. Quickly she dialled his number, needing to draw comfort from his voice.

'Hello, you,' he answered, in smooth tones.

'Hey,' she replied, feeling her blood pressure lower at the sound of his voice. 'It's all gone wrong here. I don't know what time I'll be able to get away tonight, sorry.'

'I know,' Will replied. 'Have you seen the Facebook and Twitter campaign? It's pretty grim.'

'I've barely had time to catch my breath. I'll check it out.'

'Okay, hun. Look up hashtag "Find Abigail". It's not good.'

Jennifer brought up Twitter on her phone, and it took only seconds to search the hashtag. She gasped as she scrolled through, the hostility rapidly gaining momentum.

You won't have to look hard to #FindAbigail the mum did it.

#FindAbigail before her mum does. Cold hearted cow.

#FindAbigail – mum did it. #SmilingAssassin Arrest the bitch.

We will #FindAbigail even if mum doesn't care, we do.

How can you say that? She's obviously in shock. #FindAbigail

#FindAbigail Shocked at behaviour of Abigail's mum on TV. Hope the little girl is still alive.

#FindAbigail #WickedWitchOfTheWest knows where she is.

On and on the messages went, the supportive ones quickly drowned out by venomous trolls baying for blood. Jennifer turned on her heel and marched inside. This was going to turn nasty, and was bound to disturb the family dynamics. Fiona was in the kitchen, feeding cut timber into the Aga. The heat was stifling, and Jennifer removed her suit jacket and rested it on a chair. She smiled at Olivia, watching her press a cookie cutter into a slab of cookie dough. Hadn't she just been upstairs, looking down at Jennifer? Or was her mind playing tricks on her? The little girl rearranged her features into a faint smile, but the effort seemed to pain her, and she settled back into the haunted look from that morning.

'Where's Joanna?' Jennifer said, directing her question to Fiona.

Fiona dried her hands on a tea towel before returning to Olivia. 'Mummy's in bed getting some rest, isn't she, Olivia? Now why don't you wash your hands and we'll get these in the oven?'

Olivia simply nodded, tightening her lips together, as if to prevent any words escaping.

Jennifer and Fiona looked at her sadly, and then at each other. 'Right. Sorry, I didn't introduce myself earlier. I'm DC Jennifer Knight, from Haven police station.'

'I gathered that,' Fiona smiled, signalling to Jennifer to join her at the back door. Once out of Olivia's earshot, she asked, 'Any news?'

Jennifer deflected the question. 'It's early days.'

Fiona nodded, blinking away the tears welling in her eyes. 'I'm trying to hold it together for Olivia,' her voice quivered. 'She's the one caught up in all of this. You know, she's not spoken a word since Abigail disappeared . . . If we can get her back into some sort of normality, she might just open up to us.'

Jennifer nodded, thinking of the online witch-hunt gathering momentum against Joanna. She doubted things would ever be normal for the family again.

CHAPTER SEVEN

Jennifer was still getting to grips with her developing psychic skills, and coming to terms with her ability to communicate with the other side did not make it any less frightening. The experience she had gained since joining Operation Moonlight had gone only a little way towards developing her understanding. With her open mind and extrasensory perception, she was best equipped to deal with the stream of inexplicable events that were regularly reported in Haven and the surrounding areas. A real life Mulder and Scully, was how Will had described them, although the reality was a lot less glamorous. Sitting at the kitchen table, Jennifer reflected that the Blackwater Farm case had potential for other-worldly involvement too – particularly with Olivia under its roof.

After calling Nick back from the fields, Jennifer managed to persuade him to go down and re-hang a 'No Trespassers' sign and close the rusted gate which led to the farm. Getting Fiona to accompany him was a bonus, providing her with valuable time alone with the troubled child.

Jennifer pulled a fresh sheet of notepaper from her pad and began to draw, using long, sweeping motions. She tuned in to her peripheral vision as she worked, tapping the pen against her lower lip during pauses.

Olivia lingered at her side, resembling a porcelain doll in her blue cotton dress with small white flowers dotted on the hem. They matched the blue wellingtons gracing her feet, and the cardigan now thrown on the back of the chair. She had not been allowed outside since the disappearance of her sister. Not that she'd get far in a summer dress. The wind and rain showed no sign of abating, and Jennifer imagined Nick and Fiona trying to pull across the old rusted gate and fix the flapping 'No Trespassers' sign to the twisted metal.

Jennifer cocked her head to one side as she put the finishing touches to her drawing. She wished she were as talented as her partner Will, but her effort at drawing a horse would hopefully pay off – she had learned that the twins had been promised a pony by their parents, as a reward for leaving their friends and moving to the farm.

Olivia's breath fell on her neck as she crept up to look over Jennifer's shoulder. The little girl's sense of loss was palpable, and Jennifer employed her perceptions to decipher her emotional state. Olivia's deep sense of sorrow wrapped around her like a cold impenetrable fog. Jennifer fought the urge to shudder as the little girl drew near. There was something else . . . something on the periphery that she couldn't quite put her finger on . . . *Why haven't you found me?* The distant words whispered in her ear, making her jerk upwards. Had she heard them aloud or were they from the other side? Sometimes the communications were so clear, it was difficult to tell the difference. She couldn't stop drawing, as it was the only thing keeping Olivia captivated. The voice sounded like it had come from a child, but . . . Jennifer bit her lip. It couldn't have been Olivia. Could it? She wanted nothing more than to drop her pen and question her outright, but she risked frightening her off. This child's trust had to be earned. 'Did you say something, sweetie?' she said nonchalantly, keeping her eyes on the page. She was met with silence. Jennifer finished the lavish mane, and forced herself to carry on as normal. 'This is my aunt's pony,' she said softly. 'I told her I'd help think of a name but I haven't been able to come up with one.'

No response. Jennifer sighed as she stared at the completed picture. 'He's much nicer than this, though, he has a lovely long mane, and he's black and white. There's a name for black and white ponies but I can't think . . .' Jennifer tapped the pen against her mouth once more. 'Oh, what's it called?'

Olivia was facing her now, the look of curiosity replaced with one of slight annoyance, most likely because Jennifer didn't know that black and white ponies were called piebald. Her colourless lips parted to speak, but she paused, the words trapped in her throat.

'Could *you* help me think of a name?' Jennifer said. 'He's really friendly, picks up his feet when he trots, and goes like a dream over the jumps. He's very cheeky too, quite the little rascal in fact.'

She recalled her sister's old pony magazines when they were young, using as many terms as she could think of to ignite the little girl's interest. She rested her pen on the table. Olivia's fingers slowly wrapped around the black ballpoint pen as she pinched a corner of paper and pulled it across the table. With one finger, she pushed her circular gold-rimmed glasses back up her nose, focusing on the paper in front of her. Her fingers gripped the pen as she wrote the word 'Rascal' in wobbly letters, then pushed it across at Jennifer, a smile tugging on her lips. The police had already tried to question Olivia, to no avail. Apart from shaking her head to indicate 'yes' and 'no', she had not given any account of her twin's disappearance. They had not pushed the matter, but it didn't take supernatural powers to figure out there was more to Abigail's disappearance than met the eye.

'Why of course. Rascal! What a brilliant name! Now, you were going to tell me what colour he is, weren't you?'

Olivia opened her mouth, her interest in the horse eroding her vow of silence. She had not heard her father enter until he was upon them. His frown was barely discernible, but Jennifer caught it, and in a fleeting second it passed. Olivia's eyes widened, and she threw the pen on the pad before running out of the room, her thick wellington boots making a *clump clump* noise as they hastily hit the floor.

Nick shied from the question in Jennifer's eyes.

'The gate's closed. You'll need a hand opening it when you leave, though.'

Jennifer nodded, pulling back her sleeve to look at her watch. It was early evening and he was hinting at her leaving already. 'The sniffer dogs are coming over soon. I need some things of Abigail's that carry a scent. Bedding usually works well, something that hasn't been interfered with much.'

Nick led the way to Abigail's bedroom, which she shared with Olivia. It was a typical girly room, with stickers on the doors and fairy lights over the two single beds. The high ceilings carried the heat upwards, leaving a slight chill in the air, and the long sash window provided a good view of the farmyard below. Nick glanced outside before returning his gaze to the bed near the door. 'That's Abigail's bed. Nobody's touched it since she . . .' Nick cleared his throat as the words died on his tongue.

Jennifer snapped on a pair of PVC gloves and removed the pillowcase cover. 'Joanna . . . How is she with Abigail? There's not been any falling out, has there? No reason for her to run away?'

'No. Joanna's a good mum, but since we moved she's been a different person.' Nick stood with his hands on his hips, his gaze on the empty bed. 'I don't mean to get angry with her, but I can't help it. She's barely set foot outside to search, and apart from that TV interview, she's just carried on as normal.'

Jennifer gently folded the pillowcase and placed it in an evidence bag. 'People don't always act rationally in cases like these. Perhaps closing herself off to what's happened is her mind's way of protecting itself.'

'I'm worried that people will think it's disgusting, using Abigail's disappearance as an excuse to get her face on television and plug her business. You know what Haven's like, it's a small-minded community. It won't take long for this to gain momentum.'

Jennifer did not have the heart to tell him it had already begun. 'Has she considered victim support? Counselling?'

Nick shook his head. 'She won't get counselling because she says there's nothing wrong.'

Jennifer picked up a photo album from the bedside table. She flicked through the pages of photos, old and new. 'Can I borrow this?' she asked, slipping it in the bag as Nick nodded his response. 'Has Joanna been acting strangely in the lead up to this? Anything out of sorts? How have you been as a couple? Any undue stress?' Jennifer said, instantly regretting firing so many questions in bullet style. It was a bad habit, born from impatience, and usually served to shut conversations down.

Nick's mouth twitched in a smile. 'You forget I'm a copper too, so I know where you're going with this. As frustrated as I am with my wife, I know she wouldn't hurt a hair on Abigail's head.'

Jennifer reddened. 'Sorry. I'm just trying to get a feel for things, in case there's anything I can do to help.'

Nick picked up one of Abigail's dolls and touched its hair. Like all the toys in the girls' bedroom, it was one of two. He placed it back beside its counterpart and turned to face her.

'If I'm honest, I feel your presence is putting undue stress on my family. But if I don't have you here, I won't get immediate updates. I've asked for full disclosure. Whatever the news, I want to know.' Nick picked up a hairbrush and dropped it into the evidence bag. 'It's Abigail's. Joanna always insisted they have separate things. Take the bed sheet as well. That'll be enough.'

Jennifer turned to the bed, feeling tension creep in the air. Nick resented her presence, and was not shy in telling her so. She thought about Olivia's reaction when he had walked in. She couldn't help but feel that he was the reason behind her silence.

There was something rotten about suspecting a fellow police officer. But *something* was wrong, and she hoped her suspicion was not a sign that Nick would become a suspect in Abigail's disappearance.

CHAPTER EIGHT

It was 10.15 p.m. when Jennifer got back to the station. She was forgiven for missing evening briefing, but it wouldn't be overlooked a second time. An unsmiling DCI Anderson had made that quite clear.

She pushed open the door of DI Ethan Cole's office, attracted like a moth to the soft glow of his lamp. The rest of Operation Moonlight had finished for the day, and with no late shift to replace them, the office was deserted. She found him slumped over his desk, softly snoring into his folded arms. Jennifer gave his shoulder a gentle shake, and bleary eyed, he lifted his head.

'What time is it?' He said, rubbing his face.

'Gone ten. Don't tell me you've been here all day?'

'Um, yeah,' he said, smothering a yawn. 'Have you been down the farm all this time?'

'No,' Jennifer said, a bemused look on her face. 'I left at nine. I couldn't settle at home so I thought I'd come in for an hour, see if I can unearth any clues.'

Ethan cast an eye over her jeans and sweater and smiled. 'I guess I should have worked that out for myself. Have you had any luck?'

'I've been making enquiries with the company that carried out the survey on the house and land. The team have already been on it, but I want to check that nothing's been left out.' Jennifer looked over at the coffee machine, and was disappointed to see the jug was empty. The office was chilly in the evening, another result of recent cutbacks.

'No secret wall panels or hidden tunnels we haven't searched?' Ethan said, shutting down his computer. 'I take it you were a fan of the Famous Five books, growing up?'

'More like *Scooby Doo*,' Jennifer said. 'Although I wouldn't have thought you knew who the Famous Five were.'

Ethan flashed a smile. 'It was something Zoe said. I had to Google it to see what she meant. In the US we had the Hardy Boys, made of much sterner stuff.'

'Well, we could do with them now. I've got a bad feeling about this case,' Jennifer said, her smile fading. Who was she to laugh and joke when a little girl was missing from her bed? She had spent her day making enquiries, liaising with the family, fulfilling tasks and chasing up phone calls, but she still felt no further on.

'Come with me,' Ethan said, rising from his chair. 'I've got something to show you.'

Jennifer followed him out of the office, mildly curious.

'I've managed to secure a room for our investigations. Given the Operation Moonlight slant on things, I thought we'd benefit from having our own separate briefing room.'

'That makes sense,' Jennifer said as she followed Ethan down the corridor. The only difference between their investigation and DCI Anderson's was that theirs would also take into consideration any possible supernatural element. Jennifer blushed as she realised which room he was pointing out. The PIRS room, where witnesses used to be taken to ID photos of suspects; the same room where they'd had a drunken fumble at the Christmas party last year. As Ethan shoved his key in the lock, he paused, gave her an awkward smile, then pushed the door open.

Jennifer's embarrassment was forgotten as she took in the contents of the narrow room. A whiteboard had been attached to the wall, and was filled with a timeline of events, beginning from the first report. Images of family, friends and relatives of Abigail were pinned to the wall on the other side. On the table were photocopies of the investigation to date, as well as history of the area and a list of items seized.

'I'm impressed,' Jennifer said, peering at the timeline. 'When did you do this?'

'I started after briefing with DCI Anderson. It didn't feel right, you know? Going home to my nice warm bed when that little girl was still out there somewhere.'

Jennifer nodded. It was an insight into Ethan she hadn't seen before.

'You need to add another person to the wall,' Jennifer said, pointing to the sea of faces. 'Karen Corbett. She's been spending time at the house.'

'As in Karen Corbett of Lexton CID?' Ethan said. 'I knew she was helping the family, but so are a lot of police officers.'

Jennifer had watched her with interest when the group of searchers returned to the farm. 'She seems very close to Nick. She has a brother too, Matt, who's a few years younger than Nick. Apparently, they socialise sometimes, all three of them. I just find her a bit . . . clingy.'

'Right,' Ethan said, his hands on his hips. 'I'll see that they're added. Anyone else?'

'Well, Joanna had a sister but she committed suicide last year. Jumped in front of a train,' Jennifer said. 'Whereas Nick's sister . . .'

'Is homeless and has a record as long as your arm,' Ethan said, finishing her sentence. 'It's hardly any wonder he doesn't mention her.'

'They've not spoken in years,' Jennifer said. 'I'm hoping she doesn't make an appearance at the farm.'

'Quite the troubled family.' Ethan patted his pockets for his cigarettes. 'Still, we're not here to pass judgement. Anyone else missing from the board?'

'No, you've got everyone here. He's a bit odd.' She pointed to the picture of Charles Radcliffe. 'I earwigged him having a conversation with Nick earlier. He's quite well spoken for a handyman, and judging by his accent, he's not a local either.'

'He's already on the radar,' Ethan said. He didn't need to elaborate. Anyone who had attended the farm in the last couple of weeks would be under scrutiny.

Jennifer frowned as realisation dawned. 'All these faces . . . this is more than a missing child investigation. Do you know something I don't?'

Ethan pointed to the evidence picture of Abigail's broken glasses. 'Finding them was enough to set alarm bells ringing. That, and the fact that she's not the type to wander off. If she's not discovered soon, this will be elevated into a murder inquiry.'

CHAPTER NINE

Diary Entry

Our story has spread and is bringing with it a wave of hatred and finger pointing. How I wish I could meet with the online trolls who make it their business to despise people they know nothing about. They are ignorant of real hatred, real pain. To them, this is just entertainment. I wanted to lash out today. I wanted to cut, stab, and pierce until my boiling rage subsided. For a few brief seconds, I caressed a carving knife in the kitchen. Gliding my fingers along its sharp edges, I dreamt of the possibilities. *The next person . . .* I thought. *The next person that says another word to me will feel its force.* But the fantasy was quickly forgotten when the detective walked in, and I reluctantly slid my hand from the cutlery drawer, keeping a lid on my emotions long enough to leave the room.

At what point in my development was I marked out as different from everyone else? Was it from birth? My childhood? And did my family ever notice? We would have these stupid dinnertime discussions about how our day went. On the bad days my words just wouldn't come. My throat felt too tight to swallow, as I fought to dam the tears. Some days I chewed the same mouthful of food, over and over, hoping my mother would get bored and stop asking. School was no better. The older kids noticed my misery, and when nobody else was looking, they pushed me around.

While the other children had school dinners, I tucked into my lunch, packed in an old Quality Street tin. Food became my comfort. My only friend.

My tormentors were experts in sneaking up behind me. I never felt the hands on my back until it was too late, and one day my face made contact with the concrete as I landed on all-fours. A string of blood-tinged spit dribbled from my mouth, and my right knee took the brunt of the fall. I sat back in utter shock as they danced around me, their chants hurting more than the pain in my knee. *Loser, loser,* they mocked, making 'L' signs with their fingers against their foreheads. The rest of my lunch ended up in my hair, and smeared in my face. When they were done, they left me there, my loosened tooth producing a dull throbbing pain, my right knee feeling as if it were on fire.

My injuries provided a welcome distraction. When the spit balls landed in my hair during class, I'd put my hand under the table and feel my scab. Its bumps and ridges brought me comfort, as my body fought to heal itself. But I didn't want it to heal too soon. Picking the crust gave me something to focus on, and silenced the chants in my head. Sometimes I would sit in my room as I picked, watching the beads of blood form, the sharp sting providing release. That day I found a new ally in pain.

CHAPTER TEN

A cold streak of moonlight flooded through the blinds, casting the kitchen in a monochrome hue. Insomnia crawled over Nick like a nest of spiders, slowing his thoughts and driving his body into a jerky autopilot. He pulled open the cupboard door and closed it again. He wasn't even hungry. It was two in the morning, and he needed sleep, not food. But sleep was a memory, and the best he could hope for these days was catching an hour or two before dawn. He bumped against the chair, drunk with fatigue. It was nights like this that he could actually feel the weight of his skull.

No sleep for the wicked, he thought, pulling up a chair. He rested his cheek against the cool plastic table cloth, and the faint aroma of bleach and lemons rose up to greet him. He thought of Fiona, keeping house while the rest of them fell apart. He allowed her to linger in his mind, wondering what she would say if she could see him now. He poked the doily with his index finger. Joanna had bought them when they first moved in, her head full of plans of restoring the farm to its natural beauty. As always, he had abandoned rational thinking and allowed himself to be swept up in her enthusiasm. But now it was difficult to see a way back to normality. Since moving to the farm he had not just lost his daughter, but his wife too. Although there in body, the fun-loving, impetuous woman he had fallen in love with was somewhere out of reach. Even Olivia walked around the house in a daze. Poor little Olly, too grieved to speak since her sister's disappearance. What had she done to deserve this? What had Abigail? Hot tears threatened to spill, and he swallowed back the pain. A hard lump passed down his throat, and he wondered how mental anguish could be manifested as something so real. Night-time was the worst, when he was left alone with his thoughts. But his suffering had begun long before Abigail disappeared. Abigail . . . His heart ached for his little girl, and the loss of his family drove like a blade through his heart. His head jerked up as the creak of a timber echoed overhead. If only they hadn't come to this godforsaken place.

His eyelids grew leaden as his body screamed for rest, but each time sleep came close, his limbs jerked in an involuntary spasm, shaking his thoughts loose from their resting place. Accusations rushed around his brain like a pinball machine, hitting off the sides with nowhere to go. Guilt, disgust, fear, longing. Nick rubbed his face, wishing he could unplug his mind and settle for numbness as his wife had chosen to do. But his brain ticked on like the hands of a tightly wound clock.

By 4 a.m. he was staring up at the sky through the open kitchen window, allowing the soothing night air to wash over him. He had fallen into a fuzzy pre-sleep standing up, but when a low moaning sound crept through the pipes he jerked, and sought sanctity outside. Somehow, the open air made him feel closer to Abigail, and the sky was beautiful just before dawn. Blue-grey clouds stroked the underbelly of the moon, and sounds of the forest echoed in the distance, reminding him that, somewhere, creatures were coming to life. He thought of the river, running purposefully through Haven. What it would be like to wash himself away. Would he see Abigail then? Or would he go somewhere else, a darker place, fitting for his crime? His footsteps carried him out to the sheds, down the well-worn path past the hen house where Abigail had played the day she disappeared. He stood outside the barn, bathed in moonlight. Where it happened. Shame washed over him. What had he been thinking? He loved his daughters. He would never purposely cause them pain. His shoulders shook as a guttural gasping sound broke free. Shuddering sobs wracked his body and his knees thudded against the broken soil as he finally succumbed to his tears. He hung his head, hiding his shame from the world. Even the moon rejected him as it hid behind the clouds, banishing him to a world of loneliness and despair.

As his sobs subsided he began the merry-go-round of 'what ifs' and 'if onlys' – the tormented game that grieving people play. *If only* the children had stayed inside like they were meant to. *If only* they hadn't bought this place. And *what if* he and Joanna had never met? At least then they would have been spared the pain. It wasn't as if he hadn't the opportunity to settle down with someone else, but his courage had always escaped him. Why had he agreed to marry her? Deep down he knew why. He was attracted to her vulnerability, and taking care of her made him forget his own problems; helped him turn his back on the life he knew was wrong. Now he wasn't so sure. She was different to anyone else he had dated, and his friends had warned him, tried to make him see sense. But it was easier to go along with it, set up home and have children. Isn't that what you were meant to do? And he had wanted children. Abigail and Olivia were the only good thing to come from this whole sorry mess . . . and now . . . His stomach cramped as the realisation hit him again, winding him like a hammer blow. Abigail was gone.

The night chill crept through the crevices in his coat, seizing his body in an involuntary shiver. He clamped his hand on the back of his neck, rubbing the hairs that had begun to rise. The feeling of being watched had stayed with him since he left the house. Damp with dew and exhausted, he turned and headed back for home.

He took the stairs to check on Olivia, gently pushing open her bedroom door. She was in the room she shared with Abigail, the darkness softened by the glow of the night light. Olivia's blonde hair spilled over the lace pillow, and Nick straightened her duvet, which was rucked from restless dreams. She looked so tiny, her face bare without her glasses. He thought of Abigail's glasses, found in the yard, dented and cracked, and a fresh wave of pain took his breath. Olivia would always serve as a reminder of what he had lost. Huddled under her duvet, the sight of her sucking her thumb brought fresh tears to his eyes. Abigail's school uniform hung neatly on the door of the wardrobe. Joanna had wasted no time in cleaning up the room, and as he gazed at the board games stacked neatly in the corner, Nick wondered if Olivia would have to learn how to play alone. It must feel as if half of her has been amputated without anaesthetic, he thought. Fresh guilt overtook the pain. It was wrong, asking her to keep his secret . . . but what choice did he have? Everything would fall apart if it came out now. He couldn't cope with seeing the disgust in his family's eyes. And as for his parents . . . it would devastate them. What's done is done, he thought. Nick stepped out of the bedroom and closed the door, But he was denying the inevitable. The truth would come out in the end. As sure as the sun would rise in the morning, the truth would come.

CHAPTER ELEVEN

One Day Gone

Tying Nick down seemed to be a battle in itself. Rather than sticking together in their grief, the family members were like magnets, set to repel. Gathering them in the same room was next to impossible, and given the last outburst, inadvisable. Fiona had taken on the role of matriarch and Jennifer was damn glad of her. As she placed the tray of tea and sandwiches on the rickety coffee table in the living room, Jennifer was grateful to have someone in her corner.

'C'mon, sausage,' Fiona said, taking Olivia gently by the hand. 'Let's leave the grown-ups to it.'

Jennifer sipped her tea, wishing it were coffee. Morning briefing had produced no new developments, despite the teams of police working on the case. Pressure was mounting for the safe return of the little girl, and police were working through the hundreds of calls, emails and social media messages produced in the wake of the news report on Abigail's disappearance. So far, they were a mixture of hate mail, false leads and mistaken sightings. Jennifer gently placed the cup back on the saucer and stared at Nick long enough for him to return her gaze.

'I know it's hard. When my nephew went missing, it felt like my world was caving in.'

Nick's shoulders sagged as he listlessly picked at a ham sandwich. 'Multiply that by a hundred and you'll get an idea of what I'm going through.'

Jennifer nodded. 'Will you do something for me? Put your sergeant hat back on and imagine the tables have turned. Say it's my child that's gone missing, and that so far I've disappeared for hours, had a domestic with my partner and thrown a tray against the floor. What would you say to me?'

Nick exhaled, and wearily threw the uneaten sandwich back on the plate. 'I didn't throw the tray.'

Jennifer blinked, trying to get his words into context. 'What?'

'You said I threw things around. I didn't.'

'Yesterday. The tray with the coffee and pastries, you upturned the lot.'

Nick shook his head vehemently. 'No, I didn't. I walked straight out the door.'

Jennifer was too tired to argue, and let it go. Worries about taking on this case had left her with little sleep, and as each hour passed, she regretted it even more.

Completing the paperwork was easy, given Nick's experience in the police. Approaching the subject of his daughter's behaviour was another matter altogether. The fact Olivia had refused to speak was worrying enough, but Jennifer was bothered by the look in the child's eyes each time Nick entered the room.

Car tyres scrunched in the gravel drive outside. It was soon followed by three heavy raps, which reverberated around the house. Nick stiffened, his face struck by a panic that hit him every time there was a knock at the door. You couldn't fake that kind of fear. But was it fear for his daughter or himself?

Jennifer rose to answer the door, but Fiona had beaten her to it, and she groaned as a strident voice filled the hall. DCI Anderson gave her a curt nod, before following Fiona and Nick into the kitchen. Jennifer's spirits lifted as Will stepped in behind him, smartly suited, with his beard neatly trimmed. He must have bagged the job as the DCI's driver to see her. She stood at the door, her attention drawn to a van in the distance. She glanced past Fiona as the white Transit van abruptly pulled over onto the side of the road.

'I don't suppose you know who owns that van, do you?'

Fiona squinted, pulled her glasses from her pocket, and then stared outside. 'Oh. It's Radcliffe, the local handyman. He probably doesn't want to intrude.'

Jennifer recalled the man in the parka, who had glared at her with mistrustful eyes. 'He can come if he wants. I'm going to have to speak to him at some point anyway,' she said, before closing the front door. 'Could you do me a favour and tell Joanna we have guests?'

Fiona nodded and took the stairs.

Jennifer followed everyone into the kitchen. Will's suit had been dry cleaned, which meant he must have had fair warning he'd be driving for the DCI. So much for recuperation, she thought, pulling out a chair at the table and sitting down. Now was not the time to catch his eye. She was all too aware of her DCI, standing stiffly as he waited for Joanna to join them. Nick took a seat, straining to keep a professional front. His fingers were tightly clasped together as he stared stoically ahead, but Jennifer knew that inside he was crumbling.

'You didn't have any problems opening the gate, then?' Jennifer asked, more to break the silence than anything else.

Will shook his head. 'We drove straight through. It was wide open.'

Nick looked at him, confused. 'But we closed it last night, and hung the "No Trespassers" sign to keep the journalists out.'

'I didn't see any sign,' Will replied. 'The press have been all over Haven, but they've been turning up at your old address.'

'Who left the gate open, then?' Nick said, his head swivelling as Joanna walked into the kitchen.

Jennifer would have expected her to look wretched, with puffy eyes and hair askew. Instead, her morning lie-in had afforded her a refreshed face, her colourful vintage clothes adding a splash of glamour. If her demeanour surprised DCI Anderson, he didn't show it. Joanna took a seat, the question on her face not urgent enough to reach her lips: had they found her daughter?

'I'll keep my visit brief,' DCI Anderson said, taking a chair. 'As you know, DC Knight has been assigned to provide updates, but I'd like to speak to you both about conducting a press appeal.'

'They haven't found any evidence yet, have they?' Nick asked, drumming the table with bitten-down nails.

'Helicopters have scoured the area since first light. It's difficult with the woodlands, of course.' His gaze returned to Joanna. 'The technology picks up heat sources but the trees block their radars.'

'Oh, so that's what the noise was this morning,' Joanna said, smiling politely, with all the interest of someone discussing servicing their car.

Jennifer caught Will's puzzled expression. Even the sight of him gave her a little tingle inside. He glanced back, and she flushed as she dropped her gaze to her notepad. The last thing she wanted was their DCI cottoning on that they were seeing each other. He'd have them on opposite shifts at the drop of a hat.

Over the next thirty minutes, DCI Anderson brought them up to date on the numerous enquiries taking place. Jennifer monitored Nick's gaze as he drew upon every word, the DCI trying to provide what little comfort he could.

'I wouldn't give up hope just yet. Abigail is unfamiliar with the area and may have become disorientated. The woods are quite dense, and the search teams are very thorough.' He turned to Joanna. 'I know things have been fraught for you.' He paused.

Joanna smiled weakly at the DCI, as if unsure just what mask she should wear for this particular scenario.

He continued. 'However, we must draw on public support and use the media to our full advantage.' He threaded his slim fingers and rested his hands on the table. His left eyebrow dropped, as he gave Joanna a stern stare. Jennifer recognised the look. It was the face he used when he gave people a bollocking. 'Unfortunately this has not been the case to date. Your unannounced television interview has not helped the situation, much less the constant tweeting and use of social media as a vessel to promote your business.' Nick groaned loudly and the DCI silenced him with a stare.

Jennifer swallowed as quietly as she could. The silence was stiff and awkward. But it all appeared lost on Joanna, who sipped her tea. She placed the cup back on the saucer and smiled politely at the DCI.

'I didn't realise there was a law against it.'

The DCI pulled a face as if someone chopped a lemon in half and shoved it in his mouth. He sucked in a sharp breath, his diplomacy exhausted. 'Mrs Duncan, I am at a complete loss as to why you do not grasp the seriousness of this situation. Your daughter is missing, and despite a full operational search, she appears to have vanished without a trace. Public support is imperative at this time. If you are not careful they'll turn on you, and make your life a living hell.' DCI Anderson stared at her intently before continuing. 'It's very important we move fast on this, and engage assistance from all available outlets. I need you to attend a press appeal today. DC Knight will explain what is expected of you and will escort you to the venue. I expect you there in one hour. I'll see myself out. DC Knight, may I have a word?'

'Of course, sir,' Jennifer nodded, sidling alongside Will as they left the room. Nick was shaking DCI Anderson by the hand, offering his thanks in hushed tones.

Jennifer took a deep breath as she got outside. Keeping her voice low, she gave Will's arm a squeeze. 'What are you doing here? I thought you weren't due back for another couple of days.'

'I'm not, but the DCI's driver is out sick and I volunteered to cover. How are you getting on?' He nodded towards the house. 'She's a bit of a cold fish, isn't she?'

Jennifer took a step back and stared up at the bedroom window. It was empty. 'Walls have ears,' she whispered, feeling as if she were being watched. 'Get in the car.'

Will took the driver's seat as Jennifer slid in the back. It smelt of new car leather, and was a significant improvement on the vehicles she was allocated for work. 'It's all a bit weird,' Jennifer said. 'She's acting like nothing's happened, and he's devastated. I just wish they'd find the poor little mite. Olivia's floating about like a ghost but the only one keeping it together is Fiona, the hired help.'

Will chuckled softly and Jennifer gave him a quizzical look. 'What are you laughing at?' she said, wondering what was funny about such a grim situation.

'You, the cleanliness queen, working out of that ramshackle farmhouse. I thought I'd find you at the sink, scrubbing your fingernails with a wire brush.'

'Give me time,' Jennifer said. She thought about it, and rephrased her response. 'Actually, I've been OK. I haven't had time to think about it.' It was true. Since being accepted as part of Op Moonlight, some of her old anxieties were melting away.

'I was expecting the Amityville house,' Will said. 'Zoe's been working around the clock digging up its history.' Operation Moonlight's newest detective Zoe was a transferee who also happened to be a qualified exorcist. It was comforting to know her colleagues were approaching it from a different aspect, when traditional methods had failed so far.

'It's creepy, and not the most welcoming of places, but nothing's really jumped out on me yet.'

'Look out, here he comes,' Will said. 'Do you think you can make it to mine tonight? I could run you a bath, provide a bit of stress relief.'

'Oh, is that what we're calling it now?' Jennifer said with a grin.

The smile fell from her face as DCI Anderson slid onto the seat beside her. She had forgotten he always insisted on taking the back seat, like he was royalty or something. He shook a handkerchief from his breast pocket and patted his pasty forehead. 'So, DC Knight. What do you make of it all?'

Jennifer inwardly glowed. It was nice being taken seriously again, in a case where her opinion mattered. She just wished she had something valuable to impart.

'I've only been with the family a day, but there's something strange going on. The fact that Joanna is so calm would suggest she's in shock at the disappearance of her child, but I believe there's more to it than that. I'm also concerned that Olivia may have witnessed more than we realise. She was about to open up to me when her father came in, then she clammed up and ran out of the room.'

'I was afraid you'd say that. Do you think he's hiding something?'

'The grief he's displaying is hard to fake. But I do think someone has told his daughter to keep quiet, perhaps threatened her if she speaks. Olivia is the key. I just need some time alone with her in an informal setting.'

DCI Anderson folded the handkerchief and placed it neatly in his breast pocket. 'I don't need to remind you that every minute is precious. Abigail has been gone twenty-four hours now. It doesn't bode well. Don't let your loyalty to a fellow police officer cloud your judgement. You know the statistics.'

Jennifer knew of the stats he was referring to; and that in most cases of abduction, the answers lay close to home. Missing and abducted children were rarely victims of murder, and just one in every two thousand children reported missing in the UK would be a victim of homicide. But the stats on familial involvement were chilling. Over the past few years nearly two thirds of those victims were killed by a parent or step parent. With each hour that passed, the likelihood of finding Abigail alive became increasingly remote.

'Sir, I assure you – my priority is that little girl and the safety of her sister. If she *does* know something, she could be in danger too.'

'In that case I think it's best if officers try again with a video interview.'

Jennifer kept her composure, knowing a hint of disagreement would go against her. 'Of course. But if pressured, Olivia may clam up altogether. I believe I'll have much more luck if I'm allowed to spend some time with the family.'

DCI Anderson paused to give it some consideration. 'Very well, I'll give you time. But there's something I need to divulge, and it's not to be shared with the family.'

CHAPTER TWELVE

Jennifer focused on her superior's words as the car ambled up the drive. Their departure from the house wasn't to inspect the gate which had been disturbed, but to impart some vital information.

'We're interested in Charles Radcliffe. I believe he's been helping them renovate the house since they moved in.'

Jennifer took a subtle intake of breath. It felt icy cold. 'Yes, that's right, although he seems to be avoiding me. Is there evidence against him?'

'None yet, but he's got previous. A common assault offence from when he was a minor, and some recent intelligence reports about him approaching children in the area. He's been spoken to informally, but we're monitoring his movements to see if he'll lead us anywhere.'

Jennifer's stomach churned at the thought. Approaching children may have been a confidence builder, leading up to something bigger. She paused, reluctant to release the words hanging on her tongue. 'Do you think Abigail's dead?'

DCI Anderson sighed. 'I sincerely hope not. But if we're looking for a murder suspect, I don't think we'll need to look far.'

A cold chill ran down Jennifer's back. The locals of Haven had seen many things since the decline of their town, but child abduction and murder was unthinkable. 'I'm surprised there haven't been more locals searching the area,' she said, staring out the window at the barren lands.

'There were, but we've appealed to them to call off the searches as they were hampering the investigation. They're looking for a live child. What they don't realise is that we are looking for evidence. Of course we want to find her alive, but we're realistic about it. And if you have any concerns for Olivia's welfare, I want you to call it in. I'd rather see her placed into temporary care than have her put at risk.'

'Yes, sir,' Jennifer said, although she hoped it would not come to that. 'So do you have any special instructions with regards Radcliffe?'

'Don't breathe a word of our suspicions to anybody. If a family member disappears, make a note of it. Be discreet, but keep an eye on them. They may just lead us to Abigail. Of course, if Joanna wants to make an unscheduled public appearance then dissuade her. I don't want her opening her mouth at the press appeal today, we'll leave that side of it to Nick. And for God's sake make sure she's not sitting there grinning like a fool. We desperately need to claw back some public sympathy.'

But Jennifer was already thinking ahead. 'I have an idea that may help to get Olivia talking.' She explained about the child's love of horses, and her aunt Laura's stables. She knew without asking that Laura would only be too happy to show Olivia and her mother around. It would give her precious time together with Olivia and hopefully help her get closer to Joanna too.

DCI Anderson gave it three seconds of consideration before responding. 'I'll authorise that. If this continues we'll be bringing in a child psychiatrist, but I think it would be good to get them away from the house. Just clear it with your aunt and whatever you do, don't have the child galloping about, the last thing we need is her getting hurt.' The DCI reached for his seatbelt and drew it across his chest. It clicked into place, signalling the end of their conversation. 'DI Cole will update you on briefing. I expect you to have something to share with us soon.'

Jennifer nodded, hoping it would be the case.

'Off you go,' he said dismissively.

Jennifer nodded, briefly casting a glance over Will before exiting the car. Radcliffe's possible involvement put a whole new spin on things. She needed to find out what the family thought of him, and if they suspected anything. Her head was buzzing with possibilities.

She glanced down at the tasking sheet her DCI had given her, as she walked back towards the house. Some of the questions were very personal, and would need to be handled with a great deal of sensitivity. Jennifer held tight to the paper as the wind tried to snatch it from her grasp. Thank God for computers, she thought, preferring the neatly typed list to the pages of scrawl she received in the past. There was nothing on the list that she had not already expected. She needed to question the family further on possible suspects, whether they could think of anyone acting suspiciously, or if there was anyone they had suddenly stopped hearing from. If so, a full statement would have to be taken. She needed to record what they were wearing on the day of their child's disappearance, and their exact whereabouts. Video footage of Abigail would have to be requested. Despite her young age, she had to ask if Abigail had a boyfriend, a bank account, and if any of her belongings had gone missing. The officer filling out the missing person enquiries would have already covered questions such as what she last ate, her doctor and dentist's details, what she was wearing and her favourite places, to name a few. Not all parents realised that the question regarding the last meal was to cover the eventuality of a post mortem later on. But Nick would. Jennifer's questioning would focus on the family, listing immediate and extended family on both sides. Radcliffe was currently a person of interest, but a shady past did not necessarily mean he was responsible for Abigail's disappearance. Public opinion seemed focused on blaming Joanna. But blinkered vision was bad for the case.

Jennifer returned to the house feeling the weight of responsibility. If the press appeal went wrong, it could damage the investigation, delaying Abigail's return. And the blame would lie solely at her feet. She couldn't put it off any longer. She had to draw on her skills and attempt communication with Abigail.

CHAPTER THIRTEEN

An impromptu prayer session was something Jennifer was loath to interrupt, and having already made Nick's parents' acquaintance, she was keen to avoid their company. Bob and Wendy made no secret of their religious beliefs, although little was said about their errant daughter, Nick's sister. She was proving hard to pin down, and part of Jennifer's role was to complete a family tree, tracing the family history of the parties involved.

Slipping into the empty living room, Jennifer closed the door behind her and took a seat beside the unused fireplace. This was where the tray had flipped up, spilling its contents on the floor, and the room where Sue had reported some activity. It was time for Jennifer to tune in, and seek Abigail's presence. She would always put regular police work first, but right now the investigation needed every bit of help it could get.

Given that paranormal investigation was part of her Operation Moonlight remit, she felt compelled to attempt communication. She powered up the police laptop and watched the egg timer making up its mind as it flickered on the screen. It was only a matter of time before Fiona knocked on the door offering tea, and she could not afford to waste another second.

Laying the computer to one side, she tried to relax in the creaky wingback chair. Despite the large window, the room was dark and dreary, and held a strong echo of the past. Jennifer glanced up at the high ceilings and mould-stained covings. The cobwebs that Fiona had dusted away had made a reappearance, and Jennifer shuddered to think how big the spider would have had to have been, to cover half the ceiling so quickly.

It was a large room, and perhaps Joanna had seen potential when they had bought the property, but to Jennifer the atmosphere was so oppressive she may as well have been in a darkened cupboard. Forcing all thoughts of dust and spiders away, she closed her eyes, and her lids flickered a couple of times before finally giving in to her intentions. Taking a few deep breaths, she allowed herself to become immersed in the house, soaking in the energies past and present. She felt herself fall, deep into the past, until she was surrounded by sounds of life; the crackling of a fire, the clatter of busy footsteps. The dull *tick tock* of a grandfather clock kept time in the hall, and the smell of paraffin lingered as the rustling of petticoats swept across the floor. In the distance, someone was coughing. A child. Jennifer absorbed their symptoms, feeling a hot flush across her brow. There was fever in this house. Jennifer took a deep breath. She had gone too far, allowing the ghosts of the past to drag her into their story. 'No,' she said, quietly. 'I need present times.' A cold hand of regret brushed against her cheek, and then they were gone. Jennifer gasped, blinking the experience away, like wispy cobwebs on her skin. Many children had died in this home, due to a plague, or fever of some kind. They were taken with such ferocity that some occupants still remained in spirit. But their fate was not connected to this case. She had to move on. She took a deep breath, closed her eyes and waited. A floorboard creaked from underneath her feet as the darkness closed in. Whispers grew, scratching noises like rats' claws tapped along the floorboards. They were drawing near. A noxious smell rose in the ether. Gone was the soft glow of a paraffin lamp. The only light rose and flickered from the fireplace, where a boiling pot produced the stench of rotten meat. Jennifer wanted to put her hand to her nose, but to do so would bring her to the present. Steadily she breathed, focusing on the whispers growing around her as the room darkened from behind her eyelids. This was not a welcoming energy.

'Leeeeave,' a deep disembodied voice drawled. 'Be gone, all of you.' It sounded like a recording being played back on slow, and impossible to tell if it were male or female, or even human at all.

'Where is Abigail?' Jennifer asked, remaining steadfast.

A low moan was followed by a growl, a presence casting a shadow over her closed eyes. A darkness enveloped her, and the rotting smell grew, forcing Jennifer to break contact. She fought to shake off the presence, like a heavy coat of tar crusting on her back and shoulders. Whatever it was, it had no interest in helping the family, but fed off their discord.

She opened her eyes, rubbing her arms as she grounded herself. If Abigail had passed on, it was too soon for contact to be made, and the dark, thick energy that claimed ownership of the house was too strong to allow anything else through. Jennifer shook off the remnants of its presence.

'Leave this family be,' she whispered. 'They've been through enough.'

But she had closed the door to communication. She picked up her computer and powered up her emails. It was time to contact Zoe and see what secrets she had uncovered on the history of Blackwater Farm.

CHAPTER FOURTEEN

Joanna lay back on the bed and inspected the cracks in the ceiling. Her bedroom was her refuge, the confines of the four walls keeping a lid on her emotions. But at night, four walls became five, when her husband slept with his back to her, flinching if she touched him in the night. As if she were something bad. Something dirty. She thought of another ceiling, with polystyrene tiles and yellowed walls. Where nobody could hear you scream. Her eyelids fluttered closed and she was back there . . . back with the hailstones tapping their icy fingers on the window, and the acrid chemical smell that enveloped her every cell.

The heavy thump of the front door made her jolt, and she gripped the duvet, gasping for breath. She had been falling, deep into a nightmare. She couldn't push away the army of thoughts invading her brain. Not without help. Alighting from her bed, she sat in front of her vanity table, plucking the clots of mascara knitted between her eyelashes. Her reflection stared at her in triplicate, and she practised her smile. *Be strong. You can do this.* The voice whispered inside her head. Her voice. It was the only one she should be listening to. Her fingers wrapped around her bracelet and pulled as far as the band of elastic would allow. It was a cheap piece, picked up in Spitalfields market. She had told Fiona she bought it because the bright beads matched her outfit. The truth was, it was a prop to clear the fog in her head. Her heart flickered as she released the tension. It snapped hard against her narrow wrist, and she gasped in satisfaction at the sudden sting of pain. Her reset button was switched, and she was back in control.

The wardrobe door creaked on its hinges as she rifled through her clothes. Just what did you wear to a press conference? Nick's shirts dangled on wire next to her dresses on their pretty padded hangers. She held his shirtsleeve to her cheek. It smelt of fabric conditioner. Fiona had ironed it far better than she ever could.

The last time Nick had worn the shirt was at a dinner party, when he had introduced himself as her long-suffering husband. It had started out as a joke, but after a few years of marriage the words were delivered with an ugly edge that only she could hear. People would laugh, saying he had the perfect family; a beautiful wife, two children, and a career in the police. Nick would raise his glass and smile, toasting his good fortune.

Joanna dropped the sleeve, trying to understand why her husband had grown to despise her so much. Perhaps despise was too strong a word. At best he tolerated her. At worst . . . he frightened her. She had gone over it so many times in her head. She had rushed him into marriage, just like she had railroaded him into having children. But he could have said no, he could have changed his mind. He was a police sergeant, and it wasn't as if she was holding a gun to his head.

She looked beyond the vanity table to the window, where a gentle breeze billowed against the nets. Closing her eyes, she inhaled the smell of the countryside. Abigail was out there. Her baby. Joanna's hand dropped to her stomach, where she bore the faded stretch marks of her twin pregnancy. And now the police were invading her house, with their constant questions and buzzing radios, issuing press releases for her child's safe return. But Joanna knew from their guarded expressions they didn't believe that would happen. A vision of Abigail rose in her mind, the edges soft and blurry. She was just a little girl, who couldn't sleep without a glass of milk before bedtime. She called a hug a 'huggle', and had a cute way of mispronouncing her words. And she was oh, so beautiful, the brighter spark of the two. Pure and innocent, she didn't understand the concept of stranger danger, because she saw the good in everyone. Particularly in people that didn't deserve it. 'God help me,' Joanna groaned, her chest tightening as a cold flood of dread spread throughout her senses. It brought with it crushing physical pain, and she caught her breath to accommodate it. Abigail, her marriage, everything was crumbling. Her world was crashing down around her and there was nothing she could do about it. Her breathing quickened as the onset of a panic attack threatened to overtake her. She stretched the bracelet back, further than the elastic would allow, and it snapped hard against her wrist. Coloured beads spilled on the floor as it broke, and Joanna gratefully lost herself in the distraction.

CHAPTER FIFTEEN

The press appeal passed without event, and Jennifer could at least breathe a sigh of relief that Joanna had left the talking to her husband. Her expressionless gaze was an improvement on the smile she had worn during her last interview, and Jennifer wondered if she was thinking of Abigail, or the vicious online hate campaign launched against her. Apart from some probing questions about how Joanna was feeling, the press conference focused on Abigail's disappearance, rather than the gaudy headlines published in the local rag. Jennifer watched from the sidelines as Nick sweated under the glare of the lamps, flashbulbs popping, choking on his words. He took Joanna's hand and squeezed, a small show of support, which elicited a flurry of camera flashes. Jennifer felt a ripple of sympathy for them both, as they sat under the microscope. But she couldn't help but feel that Abigail deserved better. Thoughts of the little girl made her heart wrench, and it had taken all her strength to focus on the investigation and not go searching herself. She slid her phone from her pocket, checking Twitter as the press conference wrapped up. Most of the #FindAbigail tweets were pointing the finger at Joanna. Their farmhouse address had become a tightly guarded secret, and police were able to intercept the hate mail making its way to their townhouse in Haven. Jennifer hoped the press conference would go some small way towards repairing the damage done by Joanna's previous flippancy. It seemed crazy, all the focus on Joanna's personality rather than her missing child.

As Joanna and Nick returned home, Jennifer stayed on for another round of police briefing. But by the time she saw them off, she had missed the first ten minutes.

Sliding in between the bodies standing at the back of the conference room, relief washed over her as she discovered that DCI Anderson was not leading the briefing, DI Ethan Cole was. His accent, a mixture of American and British, had never been more welcome as she tried to squeeze in without being noticed. DCI Anderson must have been asked to cover the murder that had just been reported in Lexton. A gang-related stabbing over territory, it was part of the unrelenting drug-related crime wave flooding the area. Not that she would have any involvement. It was good to have a break from that side of things, and investigate crimes where her real talents lay. She was pinning a lot of hopes on being able to speak to Olivia after briefing, and being able to encourage her to release the secrets she so tightly concealed.

The stark white projection screen complemented DI Cole's honeyed skin as he brought them up to speed on the investigation to date. He was easier on the eye than DCI Anderson, and a lot more impassioned.

'The diving team will be searching the river Blakewater, although there are no leads to indicate we're going to find anything in the water. Additionally, we've been scouring the land surrounding the farm and, as many of you are aware, numerous items have been seized. Now I know some of you think we're just collecting litter, but I *must* impress the importance of early evidence. Abigail is nine years old. You may have children of your own, nieces, nephews, neighbours.' Ethan gesticulated, his hands conducting his words. 'Keep them in mind as you search for this little girl. She could be lying somewhere, cold, vulnerable and alone. Or maybe we're already too late. And if this is the case then we must catch the person responsible, before they strike again. If it means going over the same patch of land three or four times, then so be it. We're leaving no stone unturned.' He paused to take a sip from a bottle of Evian.

'Hundreds of items have been seized, from sweet wrappers, to scraps of fabric and discarded chewing gum, but the only one directly tied to Abigail is her glasses. We cannot get complacent. We must continue to bag up anything we feel may be of relevance, until we can determine if there is any connection to the case.'

He clicked the screen to a map of Haven. 'Right, moving on. The key area is where she disappeared, but I also want the Community Support Officers to concentrate their efforts on the local community. That involves the continuation of house to house enquiries in both the town and rural areas.' He paused to regain eye contact with the uniformed officers. 'You may be the person in the community that finds answers. Speak to holidaymakers, dog walkers, joggers, kids down the skate park. Don't forget the risk assessments, folks. Haven has its moments, particularly in the more isolated spots. We don't want you encountering any angry farmers with guns, or amorous bulls.'

Jennifer rubbed the back of her neck as an ache developed. What she really needed was a strong cup of coffee with two large sugars. Her mouth felt as dry as a sand pit, and she forced herself to concentrate on the tasking and updates Ethan relayed. Footprints and car-tyre print analysis had taken place on the well-trodden land, the usual checks had been made with local hospitals, and visits to the local sex offenders by the public protection team were underway. CCTV was under review in the town, and ANPR – the automatic licence plate notification system – was being matched up with the intelligence system to see if there were any vehicles of note entering or leaving on the day of Abigail's disappearance. There seemed to be no end to the enquiries, and forty minutes after she entered the room Jennifer was beginning to flag. She shifted from foot to foot, wondering if anyone would notice if she dropped a few inches and slipped her feet from her shoes.

She had just wriggled her feet in preparation for escape when she found all eyes on her. Her update was requested, and she relayed her notes, wishing she had more information to impart. 'I believe Abigail's twin, Olivia, may be key to the investigation. She has what's often termed as "selective mutism" since the disappearance of her sister, and as we know, she was the last person to see Abigail alive. I'm beginning to bond with her and I hope she'll open up to me soon. The difficulty is getting her alone, but I hope to overcome that today as I've organised a trip out. Sanctioned by DCI Anderson, of course.'

'Thank you,' Ethan said. 'What do we know about extended family?'

'Nick's parents have been spending a lot of time at the farm, and they live relatively nearby. They have a good relationship with the family. Joanna's relations are more of a mystery, and I've not yet made their acquaintance. Her mother passed away years ago, and she and her father are estranged. For the last few years he's been living in a local care home. A couple of weeks ago he had a stroke, and he remains critically ill in hospital. Joanna's got a housekeeper that she heavily relies on, but her only network of friends seem to be online.'

'That's something for you to get your teeth into, then,' Ethan said, turning back to the board. Jennifer made some notes as he ran through a section of calls that had come in since the press appeal. After a round of questions and answers, he finally called it a day.

Jennifer was pleased Ethan had called her into his office, as he strode into the room. She liked spending time there, away from the chaos of the regular office, with its strewn coffee-ringed files, over-stuffed bins, and jammed shredders. The filing system in her DI's office was organised with military precision, the chairs were comfortable, and she was pleased to see the percolator had been replenished as the welcome smell of recently ground coffee hung in the air.

'Sorry I was late, boss,' she said, gratefully taking the cup of Columbian roast from his outstretched hands.

'No problem. The DCI asked me to jump in at the last minute. It's not my remit, to be honest, but given your involvement in the case I couldn't say no. How are things going from an Op Moonlight perspective? Have you picked anything up since we spoke last night?'

So this is why he called me over, Jennifer thought, to ask the questions that couldn't be discussed in regular briefing, or 'vanilla briefing' as Will called it.

'It's very early days. I've only been there a few hours,' she said, wrapping her fingers around the glass cup, embracing its warmth. 'The house holds a lot of history, and there's plenty of spirit attachments, but I don't know . . . I don't think her disappearance has much to do with the building itself. I think the family are key.'

Ethan nodded. 'It's difficult with Nick being a fellow copper, isn't it? But you've got to put that aside for now. Tell me, what's your gut feeling? Using your insight, do you think Abigail is still alive?'

Jennifer sighed, wishing her answer was yes. 'There was something. When I was in the house, I thought I heard the voice of a little girl, asking why we hadn't found her yet. It seemed to come from very far away, which would suggest she has passed on. But it's not cut and dried. Sometimes thoughts can transmit to me if I have a connection, or have a conduit . . .'

Jennifer's eyes widened.

'Maybe that's it.'

'What?' Ethan said.

'Olivia was standing behind me at the time. Perhaps she's a conduit to her twin.'

'In that case, I suggest you get back there. Take her out as planned and see what you can find out.'

Jennifer wasted no time in finishing her coffee and getting back to the farm. Right now, Olivia was their only hope of speaking to Abigail.

CHAPTER SIXTEEN

Diary Entry

It seems ironic that now, when I am finally rid of my old life, I am trapped by the prison of my mind. For all the years I dreamt of being free, I never imagined that I would spend every day tortured by the past. Back then, everything I did revolved around the weight of the depression. These days, I kid myself that I'm normal but I know that, deep down, something is terribly wrong. It's as if a part of my memory has been disassembled and put back incorrectly. For now, I can only go with my instinct, because I don't know what normal is.

I visited Abigail today. I had to see her, just one more time. She was lying there, caked in mud, her blonde hair hanging in dirty strings on her face. I can still see her dead-eyed stare. It's engraved on the back of my eyelids when I close my eyes. I tell myself it's not my fault, but her presence bothers me. I think about moving her. It's unsettling, her being so near the farm.

It's bad enough that her face is all over the newspapers and online. And as for the phone calls – *RING RING RING* they torture my brain, making me rake my skin with my nails until they draw blood. The scratches invoke memories of my childhood, and the whole cycle begins again.

It wasn't just my self-harming that made me different to the other children – I positively reeked of desperation. Never, in the whole of my sorry life, had I one person I could truly call a friend. I hung around limply, straggling behind the other kids, thinking that a pity friend was better than no friend at all. But they didn't want some fat kid in secondhand clothes embarrassing them, and I was soon told where to go.

Everything changed at my ninth birthday party, when I suffered the acute embarrassment of being the butt of their jokes. My mother decided to hold a party in my honour, and I was thrilled that so many people came. I thought perhaps it was a turning point, and I gratefully tore through the presents. I got one of those fat Bic multi-pens, and someone even gave me a Rubik's Cube. Not that I could ever get the better of it. But my joy was short-lived as my mother left us to buy some more crisps.

For some reason they thought that bringing me plates of leftover cake was funny. *One more slice, one more slice*, they chanted, stopping only when I had scoffed the lot, my salty tears intermingling with spoonfuls of sticky butter icing as they shovelled it down my throat. I told myself that being the centre of attention was fun. But all I felt was shame and disgust.

That's when my father walked in. He found me in the bathroom, crying. I felt physically sick as I retched into the bowl. But no, my body decided to work against me, holding on to the fats and carbohydrates to pile on even more weight than before. Food brought me comfort and pain in equal measures. Yet here was a man I trusted, telling me not to cry, because I was perfect just the way I was. It made me feel grown up to call him by his first name. That's when he said I should have my photo taken. I snorted, waiting for the punch line. He went as far as listing my redeeming features: my striking eyes, my healthy complexion, and my shiny hair that carried many hues. Like petals of a flower opening for the sun, I bloomed under the glow of his praise. He cast all my self-aspersions aside. I was a perfect model, he said, *because* I was different from the others, not in spite of it. I wanted to believe him, because he described me as if I was something special, something good. So I smiled. The kind of foolish, fragile smiles that predators love.

CHAPTER SEVENTEEN

One Day Gone

The timing could not have been better as Jennifer offered to take Olivia to Laura's stables for a treat. Joanna's fresh coat of make-up did not disguise the fact that the press appeal had taken its toll, and cracks were finally starting to appear. Jennifer hoped that time away from the gloomy house would draw Olivia out of herself long enough to find some answers. She also wanted to help the little girl, who was at risk of being traumatised by the whole awful situation.

Joanna marvelled at Laura's home. Like hers, it was set on several acres of land, but no renovations were needed for this country abode. Unlike the shadowy dampness of Blackwater Farm, Laura's house was bright and airy, each room as large as Joanna's but tastefully decorated with country charm. Paintings of thoroughbreds lined the walls, alongside pictures of Jennifer and her sister Amy growing up. Daily housekeepers ensured the house was clean, even to Jennifer's standards, and the grounds that housed the stables were beautifully maintained. Jennifer had nothing but fond memories of growing up in her aunt's care, and was happy to show Olivia around the paddock.

'This is Toby,' Jennifer said, introducing the thirteen-hands pony. 'My sister Amy used to ride him in pony club. He's retired now, but he still loves to be taken out for a jaunt. Would you like a ride?'

Olivia's face lit up for the first time, then clouded over as she gazed at her mother for permission. Joanna hesitated, and Laura intervened.

'He's very well behaved, and he loves children.'

Joanna nodded and Laura gently steered her inside to sample the scones she had made that afternoon. Jennifer sighed with relief, and patted Toby on the neck before tying him up next to some steps.

'C'mon then, Olivia, let's get this hat on,' she said, adjusting the straps around her cheeks.

Olivia beamed in response, her eyes resting on the pony before her. Jennifer pointed out all the parts of the saddle and bridle. She used to watch her sister clean the tack at night, the room smelling of aniseed oil and leather. It was an improvement on the beer-and-cigarette smell that had tainted their childhood when their father had been in charge. They had gone from having absolutely nothing to having everything, and even now, Jennifer wasn't sure if she had ever fully adjusted to it.

'Are you ready?' Jennifer asked. Olivia nodded more times than she needed to, and tentatively placed a hand on the pony's rounded belly. 'Good. Just climb up these steps and hold on to the saddle. Toby will take good care of you.'

But the little girl's excitement evaporated as her eyes misted over, their spirit withdrawing into itself. Jennifer felt the change in the air, and time seemed to stand still. She knelt down, touching Olivia's hand. Her skin was deathly cold, and her chest rose and fell in an effort to breathe.

Jennifer had seen it before, when her nephew Joshua had allowed himself to be used as a transmitter for voices on the other side.

'What's wrong, sweetheart?' she said, afraid to break the spell.

Olivia stared into nothingness, her hands hanging numbly by her side. 'It's cold here. It's cold and dark and I want to go home.' Her voice was hollow, as if coming from very far away.

Jennifer's heart skipped a beat. But she couldn't jump to conclusions. Children were highly suggestible and the last thing she wanted was to put words into the girl's mouth. 'Don't be scared, Olivia, it's just the stables. It's not dark, not really.'

But the child stood frozen to the spot. 'I'm not Olivia. I'm Abigail. I don't like it here. It's dark and I can't see.'

Jennifer crouched until she was eye-level. There was no time to wonder if Abigail was really coming through. Such links were tenuous, and very short-lived. 'Abigail? Describe it for me. Where are you?' Jennifer whispered, praying for something, anything that would provide her with a clue.

'I'm in a d . . . dark tunnel. With a l . . . light at the end.' Olivia's face screwed up and she shuddered a tearless sob. She was a puppet, and the ventriloquist controlling her was crying. 'Somebody's at the other end, but I . . . I don't want to go with them, I'm *scared*. I want to go home.'

There was no time for platitudes. Jennifer needed answers.

'Did someone take you? Are you lost?'

But as Olivia took a sudden breath and blinked, Jennifer knew that contact with Abigail had broken. It was as if she had emerged from underwater, and she took a few more breaths before returning her attention to the pony.

'Are you okay?' Jennifer asked.

Olivia nodded, climbing the steps to mount. Jennifer could not ignore the sense of unease creeping up on her. There was change ahead. She could feel it in the air. She had watched her nephew emerge from the same type of trance, and his was not the only case. He had also returned to normality quickly, with no desire to discuss what had happened moments before. She wondered if it was because the children had no recollection, or because it was such an unpleasant experience. It didn't matter. There would be more to come.

Jennifer helped her into the saddle, adjusting the stirrups before leading the pony forward. She glanced up at Olivia's face, alight with happiness. A different child, she was pink-cheeked and smiling with delight. Olivia clicked her tongue, coaxing the pony to walk a little faster across the neatly clipped lawn. Normally the horses would be ridden in the fields at the rear of the stable, but Jennifer had already gained permission to ride on the lawn, within sight of the house.

Jennifer tried gently to question Olivia on what had just happened, but even in her silence she seemed to have no recollection of the words. Had she really spoken to Abigail? And if so, did it mean Abigail had crossed over from the other side? A dark tunnel, seeing a light, someone waiting on the other side. It had all the hallmarks of a death experience. Or was Olivia trying to communicate her secrets in the only way she could think of? Pretending to be her sister in order to get the message across? Jennifer let go of the bridle, allowing Olivia more control. The pony chewed on the bit between his teeth, plodding contentedly beside her. As she had discovered in her own childhood, animals had an ability to heal, just by their presence. She took a note from Toby, and stayed quiet for the remainder of their session.

'Did you have a good time, darling?' Joanna asked as she joined them.

Olivia nodded, flashing a toothy smile as she dismounted.

Joanna returned her smile. 'That's wonderful. Guess what? Laura and I have been talking. She's going to loan us Toby, once we fix up a stable for him. Would you like that?'

Olivia emitted a gasp of delight, nodding until her over-sized riding hat peaked on her nose. Joanna hugged her daughter tightly, tears prickling her eyes as she mouthed the words *thank you* over her shoulder. The sight of real emotion crossing Joanna's face, combined with Olivia's excitement, brought a lump to Jennifer's throat, and she wrestled with her conscience for not disclosing that Olivia had spoken earlier that day.

Jennifer soaped her hands in the kitchen sink as she mulled over Olivia's words. Working in Operation Moonlight was a huge step forward, and she would be able to disclose full details of the case without fear of ridicule. She dried her hands and gave them a squirt of sanitiser for good measure. Aunt Laura would not allow Jennifer to leave without sampling her homemade scones, and she sat on the patio with a pot of tea brewing in a china teapot. Laura showed Olivia how to groom Toby, before releasing him into the field. She had come up trumps this time, giving Jennifer alone time with both Olivia and Joanna without making it obvious that this was her intention all along. Jennifer tucked in to the scone, allowing the homemade jam and clotted cream to intermingle on her tongue. She washed it down with a sip of tea before patting the corners of her mouth.

'They're lovely scones, aren't they?' Joanna said. 'Even nicer than Fiona's.'

'Don't let Fiona hear you say that,' Jennifer smiled. 'Do you bake at all?'

'Oh no, I'm not allowed,' Joanna said, blushing as soon as the words had left her mouth. 'I . . . I mean, I don't need to, not with Fiona on the payroll.'

'Joanna, may I be frank with you?'

Joanna sighed, her eyes never leaving her daughter. 'Of course.'

'You've never once asked me about the investigation into Abigail's disappearance. Is it because it's too painful to think about?'

Joanna shrugged, toying with a length of her hair, twirling the blonde strands around her finger.

But Jennifer was not ready to give up yet. 'Some people deal with stress by keeping it pushed down. You could call it a coping mechanism.' Jennifer pressed down on the loose crumbs of scone with the pads of her fingers and placed them on the saucer. 'I think it's a perfectly understandable way of dealing with things. I've done it myself.'

'I wish Nick did,' Joanna said. 'He knew what I was like when he met me, so why should I be any different now?' She looked at Jennifer, a wealth of longing behind her cool eyes. 'But how can I change? It's just the way I am.'

She finished the sentence with her usual smile, and Jennifer understood. She thought of her own past, the childhood she repressed for so many years.

'I don't get why you were so flippant in the interview, though. Why would you act like Abigail doesn't matter, when inside you're falling apart?'

Joanna didn't reply straight away. She returned her gaze to Olivia, watching as she groomed the pony's mane. Jennifer had given up hope for an answer when Joanna eventually replied.

'It's hard to explain, but . . . sometimes I can't stop the words coming out of my mouth.'

Jennifer nodded, allowing the silence to fall between them as she composed her words.

'Sometimes people say things they don't really mean. It's like they want to be punished, but they don't know why,' she said, feeling more like a therapist than a police officer.

Joanna rubbed her wrists, as if she was searching for something that was no longer there. 'Oh, listen to me, talking about myself. It's nothing really, I'm fine.'

'But you're *not* fine, are you, Joanna? Have you thought about getting help?'

A pained expression crossed Joanna's face, as if she had sat on something dirty, and she jumped up from the chair, clapping her hands together. 'Olivia, are you all done now? We'd better get home. Daddy will be wondering where we've got to.'

Jennifer bit back her frustration. Nick was well aware of where they were, and had told them to take their time. Joanna turned to face her. 'Oh, and thank you. You didn't have to do this. I feel like I'm getting my little girl back.'

But what about your other daughter? Jennifer thought, as she nodded in response. She swallowed back the words, too judgemental to say aloud. Nick's aggression towards his wife was inexcusable, but she could see how Joanna's lack of sensitivity would ignite the flame. Why did she use memory repression as a coping mechanism? That, paired with the possibility she was punishing herself, could suggest there was something very wrong. It would take time to find answers, and time was a luxury they could ill afford.

Olivia beamed as her mother recounted the arrangements she had made for borrowing the pony. It was a one-way discussion, but the journey home was filled with hope: Olivia's message was a breakthrough, and Jennifer clung on to the belief that there would be more to come.

She drove on autopilot down the pot-holed country lane, inhaling the sweet smell of the rapeseed as it drifted through the car window. The fields lit up the landscape in patches of vibrant yellow, but their beauty was lost on the occupants of the car. Jennifer's mind was crowded with thoughts. The fact that tomorrow would be the second day following Abigail's disappearance weighed heavy, and even the farmhouse seemed to have slumped since she last left it. Olivia's stolen whispers replayed in her mind. *Somebody's at the other end, but I . . . I don't want to go with them, I'm scared.* Where could Abigail be? Sue had reported footsteps on the landing and a smashed light bulb. She had heard the tray hit the floor. Was the spirit of Abigail making her presence known? Or was this activity caused by human hands? The spirits invading the home carried a strong negative energy, amplifying the family's discord. It seemed likely that they were at the root of the activity. Her email to Zoe was yet to be answered, as her colleague dug deeper into the history of the house.

Sinister intentions appeared far from Joanna's mind as she knocked on the door, and breezily called that she was home.

'Don't you have a key to the front door?' Jennifer said, scraping the mud from her shoes.

Joanna shrugged, evading the question as she slipped past Fiona, who allowed them inside. Nick was slouched on the leather sofa, too exhausted to respond. His boots were wet with mud, and his hands scratched from searching thickets. The group of volunteers was growing by the day, meeting in Haven to search woodlands, sheds, crops, ditches and dykes. It was good to get the search underway while hope was still alive, but well-meaning locals were trampling all over what could be valuable evidence. Spent cigarette butts thrown in the woods. Discarded chewing gum wrappers. All transient evidence. Its worth minimal unless found on the body. *The body.* Jennifer caught her thoughts. She was imagining Abigail as deceased. The words that had escaped Olivia's lips were similar to the ones she had heard so many times in the still of the night, when the whispers of the dead were at their strongest; spirits trapped in a cold, dark place, wanting to come home. Tortured souls looking for answers that weren't hers to give. She squirted alcohol gel on her hands, the scent a soothing balm as old anxieties fought to rise within her. She wanted to go home, to the clean, cool worktops of her kitchen and the spotless floors. Where everything was level, organised and regimented.

Fiona placed a tray of salad sandwiches and a pot of tea in front of them, urging Nick to eat.

He nodded his thanks, brightening only when Olivia bounced over to the sofa, her eyes bright with a sparkle that had been absent far too long. His eyebrows shot up as she giggled, and Jennifer warmed to the sound. It was a beautiful song after what felt like a lifetime of silence.

'I hear we're bringing home a pony,' Nick said, washing down the remnants of his sandwich with a mouthful of tea from a fat blue mug. Olivia nodded fitfully, dancing on her toes, barely able to contain her excitement.

'Be a good girl and we'll soon have him here,' Joanna said, leaving Olivia with her father.

Jennifer turned to follow the women back out to the kitchen, feeling like an intruder.

Olivia planted a kiss on her father's stubbled cheek. Almost as an afterthought, she leaned forward, her whisper just within Jennifer's earshot. 'I'll be a good girl, Daddy. I promise I won't tell.'

CHAPTER EIGHTEEN

'Are you sure that's okay?' Will said, refilling Jennifer's glass as she ate the reheated food. 'I can make you something else if you like.'

Jennifer wound the pasta around her fork. 'It's delicious. I'm just sorry I'm late, especially after you went to all this trouble.'

'Don't be daft,' Will said, smiling. 'A spag bol and a bottle of plonk is hardly going to trouble.'

It was a novelty to be met with such understanding. But then Will was the first police officer she had dated. Well, apart from Ethan. But a quick fumble at the Christmas party was hardly what you would call dating. Being in a relationship with Will was the best thing that had ever happened to her. While past boyfriends complained about her inability to finish work on time, Will accepted it with calm understanding. She knocked back her wine, her eyes drawn to the defined chest muscles under his sweater. Her day had been stressful to say the least, with no real leads. It was heading towards a murder inquiry at breakneck speed. All they needed was a body . . .

A myriad of thoughts demanded her attention, and she silenced them without guilt. She needed this. She craved intimacy with Will, absorbing his affection instead of the anger, frustration and fear which had encompassed her over the last few days. Just a little while, she promised herself, then she would think about work.

But peace did not come quickly. Will's phone constantly buzzed with texts from Zoe. There was a rumour that more people would be joining the team, and Jennifer was beginning to feel more like an outsider with each day that passed. Will turned off his phone and settled back into the sofa.

'Sorry,' he said, with an apologetic grin. 'I think she's a bit lonely. She was asking if we could go out for a drink tonight.'

Jennifer stifled a yawn. 'I'm too tired. How's it been, working with her?'

'I couldn't possibly say. We're frontline detectives on Op Moonlight, you know, and seeing as how you're just a lowly FLO . . .'

Jennifer moved in close and blew in his ear as she snaked her hand against the ridge of his trousers. His stomach tightened as her fingers found his skin, and she teased him by running her nail inside the waistband of his boxer shorts. 'Oh, but I have ways of making you talk,' she said huskily.

Will groaned, wrapping his hands around her waist as she sat astride him. 'In that case, I'm ready for my interrogation.'

Intimacy followed by a hot bath was all she needed to feel human again. Satiated, she lay back in Will's arms, allowing thoughts of work to return.

'So how are you getting on with the case?' he said, kissing the side of her head as she lay back on his chest. Her hair was damp from the water, and he tucked a strand behind her ear. Steam rose around them, and the gentle flicker of candlelight reflected against the bathroom window.

'We don't have to talk work,' Jennifer whispered as she dipped her chin into the water, trying to push back the nagging questions demanding an audience.

'I'm interested. A different perspective might help.'

Jennifer sighed. There was no getting away from it. She was doubtful other boyfriends would be as accommodating, although she would never have been able to speak to them about cases anyway. Keeping it to herself had made it all the harder. Not that they had understood any of that. She filled Will in on the case to date, bringing him up to Olivia's behaviour around her father.

'I took the opportunity to question Olivia again,' Jennifer said. 'I heard her whisper something to her dad, about keeping a secret. But she's been mute ever since, and somewhat spooked. I didn't want to push things too far.'

'You don't think he's abusing her, do you?'

Jennifer shivered as their bathwater began to lose its heat. The words sounded ugly as they hung in the air.

'I asked if her mummy or daddy had hurt her, or made her do anything she didn't want to do,' she said.

'And?'

'No. Well, at least she shook her head, which implied no. I watched her face closely for a reaction. I couldn't see anything which would suggest that they were abusing her.'

'Best you document it just the same,' Will said, handing her his bathrobe as he stepped out of the water. 'Here. I'll make you a coffee, get you warmed up.'

Will wrapped a thick white towel around his waist and rough-dried his hair. Jennifer admired the contours of his body, and looked forward to the rest of their night together. A night in his arms was long overdue.

'Want to know what I think?' Will said, as Jennifer joined him in the living room. She had just finished cleaning the bath, and was now eyeing the dishes piled up in the sink.

'Yes,' Jennifer said, taking the coffee from his outstretched hand.

'Olivia's keeping a secret, and she's too scared to tell you what it is. It might not be related to her sister, but it seems too much of a coincidence that all this is happening around the time of Abigail's disappearance. I think she knows what's happened to her sister, but it's too horrific a prospect for her young mind to contemplate.'

He closed his eyes briefly as he took a sip from his mug, then placed it on the newly purchased coasters now gracing the coffee table.

'The bulbs blowing, things being thrown, that's all coming from Olivia. Her emotions are so pent up, she's making things happen, whether she knows it or not. She needs a child psychiatrist, to help her work through her issues.'

'I've tried. They won't allow it.'

'Who won't?' Will asked, cocking his head to one side.

'Her mother. Nick is all for it, but Joanna's flatly refused.'

'That's interesting,' Will said. 'I expected you to say her father. I thought Joanna was withdrawn.'

'She is. That's what makes it so strange. It's the only thing she's insistent on.'

'Have you asked why?'

'She's not given a proper reason. If any child needs help, it's Olivia. I hope we find Abigail soon, so they can get on with their lives,' Jennifer said.

'Do they think she's still alive?'

'They're clinging on to hope. Well, you would, wouldn't you? Because the alternative . . .'

Her words trailed away. Jennifer placed her cup beside Will's, turning them until the handles faced the same way. Will rubbed her back, and she lay back into the crook of his arm. Will had known her long enough to notice her signals, and after some comforting murmurs he pointed the remote control at the television and selected an inoffensive movie; something to take their mind off work, at least until they got lost in each other again.

But Jennifer didn't see the movie. Instead, she replayed snatches of her visit to Blackwater Farm, the bits that had been bothering her long enough not to evaporate into the ether. Natives of Haven, both Nick and Joanna had moved away a couple of times, only to return. They used to live in London, while Nick commuted to work in Lexton every day. Moving to their townhouse in Haven had made sense for them both. She had a good job, was financially secure. But everything had changed dramatically in the last few months. They had sold up to live in a creepy derelict farm and Joanna had given up her job to work online, going from mixing with lots of people to being a recluse. Her friends were all virtual, and quick enough to desert her when the allegations came to light. Jennifer thought of the farmhouse, hollow and empty, crawling with a negative energy that would send most people packing. But there was something niggling at the back of her brain. When they came back after their trip to see aunt Laura, Joanna had been locked out. Why didn't she have a key to her own house? The doors were old and battered, but the inner locks had all been filled in. The only door that had a key was the bathroom, and she had never seen Joanna use it. Jennifer remembered Joanna's throwaway comment about not being allowed to bake, and the embarrassment that followed. There was something about the way Joanna spoke, that made her think she wasn't allowed to cook either, or even to touch a knife. But she wasn't imprisoned in the house. Joanna was able to go to the local TV studios after all. It was as if there was an unseen rule. It was one Jennifer would be keeping a very close eye on.

CHAPTER NINETEEN

Two Days Gone

It was a welcome relief to return to the CID office a couple of hours early to catch up with outstanding work. Two suspects for a previous case had failed to answer their bail, and Jennifer now had the pleasure of updating them on the police national computer system as 'Wanted'. But mundane tasks like updating the PNC didn't bother Jennifer, because as stressed as her job got, it was nothing compared to the repressive mood pervading the Duncan household.

She pored over an email from her colleague Zoe. Her digging on Blackwater Farm had produced some interesting insights about its history. In the 1880s the building had been used as what could only be described as a workhouse. Orphans and unwanted children had tilled the land until an epidemic of scarlet fever wiped them out one by one. Makeshift graves were discovered close to the house, and the remains removed to Haven children's cemetery, where they were given a proper funeral. Several children were never traced. Jennifer thought of the paraffin lamp, and the sorrow emanating from the woman in the long black petticoat as she gently nursed the sick. Enough sorrow to keep her walking the corridors, tending to her charges long after her death. For a few brief seconds, she had shown Jennifer her world. She only hoped that, having done so, the woman would be able to move on.

Jennifer scrolled down, her heart skipping a beat as she digested the second paragraph. Zoe stated that in the 1960s, teenage squatters had regularly frequented the house. That in itself was not unusual, but the email contained pictures of the interior after their departure. Pentagrams were crudely daubed on the floors, the carcass of a dead goat was found in the basement, and dozens of half melted candles lay throughout. Jennifer's stomach heaved as she gazed at the image of an abandoned pot in the filthy living room, animal bones sucked dry, strewn beside a mattress on the floor. Had the teenagers invoked something evil? According to Zoe's research, the farm had been plagued with misfortune ever since. Suicides, failing crops and dying animals followed over the years and, given recent events, the spate of bad luck wasn't changing any time soon.

She clicked off the email, as much to dismiss the thoughts of her earlier encounters as anything else. To allow them to linger would be to give them power, and she had come far too close to such entities in the past to want to go there again.

She studied copies of the Duncan family's statements for the third time, trying to glean some clues. Nick had stated that he was at home, clearing rubbish from the outbuildings and throwing it in the trailer on the back of his tractor for burning. At least he hadn't lit the fire. The thought of going through the charred timbers in search of a body was too grizzly to imagine.

Joanna had said she was working from home on her computer with Fiona, who was baking cookies in the kitchen. The handyman Radcliffe had stated that he had been helping Nick but had left to attend a job. Jennifer's thoughts lingered on his van. She had only seen Radcliffe twice, and each time he had seemed keen to avoid her.

Jennifer dry-washed her hands as an internal clock started ticking in her brain. Hearing Abigail's voice had heightened the sense of urgency, and she wondered if her DI, Ethan Cole, had been asking too much of her, throwing her into such a harrowing case so soon after the last one. She gave her desk a critical gaze before straightening her monitor, keyboard and mouse mat with strict precision. As long as she was in control, she would get through this. She had to.

Will's desk told a different story altogether. Coffee-ringed paperwork lay skewed in an order only he would understand. His computer screen was framed by yellow Post-it notes with illegible scribblings, and a half eaten sandwich lay beside empty sweet wrappers which had not yet found their way into the bin. But her constant source of irritation also brought a wistful longing. She missed their banter, the work-fuelled days, and the satisfaction of a job well done.

Working with the Duncan family was draining, and deciphering their emotions was like wading through a web of chewing gum. She glanced at her watch and sighed. It was almost 8 a.m. and time for her to go to the farm. DI Ethan Cole's well-groomed head bobbed up from his office, and signalled her in for a catch-up. She couldn't get used to the fact that he was her superior, particularly given that he was several years younger than her. By the time she entered the office, he had poured her a fresh cup of coffee from the percolator and placed it on the desk. It was becoming an agreeable habit, and she inhaled the welcome aroma as it mingled with the light spice of his aftershave. Ethan was lucky enough to have a window in his office, and the slice of morning sun brightened the sterile room. Jennifer smiled in appreciation as she took a seat across from him.

'Hello, boss. You're looking well.'

He flashed her a smile. 'Thanks. I thought it would be good to have a catch-up, discuss what's happening up at Blackwater Farm. Any closer to answers?'

Jennifer crossed her legs. Will would have asked her how her family was, or how she was settling into work after such a horrific experience with her previous case. But Ethan was not Will, and he had her back at work as quick as her legs would carry her. Will may be a scruff bag, she mused, but he was *her* scruff bag, and had a caring nature beyond the realms of her DI. Still, at least he made good coffee. She took a sip and cradled the cup in her hand.

'The family are distraught. They're all dealing with their own issues. Fiona, the housekeeper, seems to be the strongest, and I've been very grateful for her support.'

'I've read your reports to date. Is there anything you're leaving out? They've not been giving you a tough time, have they?'

'No more than you'd expect. Getting them in the same room together is like trying to herd wild cats. Between us, I'd be surprised if their marriage survives this.'

'Sue's said as much. But I want to get to the crux of this case. Dozens of officers are investigating, but you're the one making that connection with the family. Tell me, with whom do your suspicions lie?'

Jennifer bit back her dimpled smile. Ethan's formal tone took some getting used to. She wondered if he had to try very hard to prove himself; prove that he was all grown up instead of a young man finding his feet. His designer suit, his authoritative tone, they hid his vulnerabilities well. But she saw right through him, because that was exactly how she had been before she met Will. She straightened her spine and looked him in the eye. 'I have my suspicions, but it's early days.'

'Go on,' Ethan said, his long slender fingers toying with the rim of his cup.

'Nick's hiding something, and his daughter is scared. He resents my presence, and tolerates me only because he'll get quicker updates. But I've no solid evidence yet, nothing that would warrant a formal investigation.'

'Mmm,' Ethan said. 'Sue's been investigating Joanna's family, what's left of them. I'd like to know why she's estranged from her father, particularly given he's her only surviving parent. She certainly doesn't seem too concerned by his condition.'

Jennifer swallowed the dregs of her coffee. 'Yeah, but that's how she is about Abigail. I've tried asking her about her father, but she won't say.'

'Then ask Nick. Suggest taking Olivia to see her grandfather. That might get him talking.' Ethan arched an eyebrow. 'Are your psychic skills giving you anything?'

Jennifer squirmed. She hated being called a psychic. The term covered such a wide range of people. The word had been tarnished by fraudsters, as far as Jennifer was concerned, taking advantage of the vulnerable and exploiting the lonely.

'It's very hard to get some quiet time, with so much going on. But you're aware of what I've picked up on so far.'

'Yes, that was good work with the child. Do you think you'll get any more out of her?'

Jennifer thought of the little girl with the pale face and spectacled moon eyes, lost in the absence of her sister. She wouldn't use her as a pawn. The family had been hurt enough. Not that she was going to tell Ethan. She wouldn't put it past him to take her out and put someone else in her place. Someone cold-hearted enough to extract what they needed, with little thought for the child.

'Yes. I hope to. I just need more time. What she's picked up so far . . . it's not very hopeful.'

'Yes, I know.' Ethan shook his head. 'But we have to focus on catching the person responsible. Olivia could be at risk. That's why I need you to hang on in there as long as you can.'

Jennifer wanted to ask Ethan how he *really* was, running a new team with such a high profile case hanging in the balance. Reporting to such a strict taskmaster as DCI Anderson would not have been easy. But now was not the time. She straightened her skirt as she stood, painfully aware she was needed at Blackwater Farm, where a drama of some kind most likely awaited her.

'I'd best get a wiggle on.'

'If you need anything, just give me a call. You've got my mobile.'

Jennifer returned to her desk, checking her emails as a ruse to wait a few minutes longer for Will. He and Zoe were already out on a job, an early start attending the graveyard where an occult group had set up camp and were allegedly decapitating dogs. Intelligence had stated that they were on the lookout for a human sacrifice, and the mention of Will attending a job where machetes and cults were involved had made her bristle. It didn't help that he was with Zoe, who was all of seven stone. What good was she going to be, if they got into trouble?

An echo of laughter floated through the air as footsteps approached the office. Pulling up her sleeves, Jennifer began to clean Will's desk. The thought of him working in such a mess bothered her, and she wiped over the coffee stains with a quick spray of antiseptic before shuffling his papers into a neat pile.

Zoe burst through the door, sniffing the air. 'Ah, the antiseptic queen is back.'

'Behave,' Jennifer replied with a grin. She warmed at the sight of Will. Despite his crumpled tie and plodding apathy, she had missed spending the morning with him. 'How was the graveyard?'

Will dropped his briefcase on the desk, frowning at the disappearance of his chaotic filing system.

'Disappointing. There was nothing but a few meth heads. They were cooking up some roadkill over a fire.' He shouted over at Zoe. 'Oi, Danger Mouse, I'm parched here. Stick the kettle on, will you?'

'Already done,' she said with a twinkle in her eye, shuffling off to the kitchen with the dirty mugs.

Will returned his glance to Jennifer and gave her a wink. 'That's how you do it.'

Jennifer laughed. 'It'll take a bigger man than you to house-train Zoe. How's it going? You feeling all right?'

'It's like I've never been away. Zoe's a nice enough girl. Weird, but nice.'

'Weird is a prerequisite for the job, isn't it?'

Will smirked. 'Speaking of weird, how are things going down at the crazy farm?'

Jennifer glanced around before lowering her voice. 'It's difficult with Nick being a sergeant. I had to prevent a domestic between him and Joanna on my first day. He's so bewildered, I don't think he knows whether he's coming or going.'

Will rolled his eyes. 'Well, if he gives you a hard time I'll be having a word with him. You're only trying to do your job. He should know that more than anyone.'

Jennifer contemplated Will's words during the drive back to the farm. She knew from previous run-ins with Ethan that he meant what he said. She hummed as she tapped the steering wheel, feeling better for seeing her colleagues. There was still a chance Abigail was alive. Perhaps today she would find answers. The short trip to the office had done her good, clearing her mind and setting her priorities. Because now she knew what she needed to do. It was time to confront Nick.

CHAPTER TWENTY

What is it about this place? Jennifer thought, stepping out of her car. She had been hopeful just moments before, but a gloom descended as she walked towards the old grey farmhouse, sapping her good mood and replacing it with a heavy sense of resignation that things were not going to end well. The farm had the cold stillness of a graveyard, dotted with clusters of purple-headed thistles affording splashes of colour in an otherwise bleak landscape. Once filled with livestock, the fields were now barren, dotted with ramshackle galvanized huts. The sky resembled a sheet of dirty white cotton, casting a dull filter over the fuzzy radiance of the sun. Abandon all hope ye who enter here, Jennifer thought wryly, surprised to find the front door unlatched.

She blinked to adjust her eyes to the dim corridor, silencing her steps by walking on the balls of her feet. She preferred not to announce her arrival. At least not yet. The smell of freshly baked bread and melting cheese filtered down from the kitchen, and her stomach grumbled in response. She hadn't eaten breakfast, but now was not the time for food. Nick's low murmurs confirmed his presence in the living room. She leaned in to the door to listen, but his words were unintelligible. Her hesitation weakened her resolve and doubts began to creep in. What if confronting Nick put Olivia in danger? Could she live with that on her conscience? Jennifer dismissed the thought. Nick was a police officer, not a killer, and there was probably an innocent explanation. *I'll be a good girl, Daddy. I promise I won't tell.* Olivia's words replayed in her brain, more damning each time they were repeated. She had to confront him now, before she lost her bottle. Hoarse murmurs drifted through as she slowly pushed open the door. Nick was having a one-way conversation with Olivia about the pony.

Jennifer caught Nick's furtive glance as the door creaked to announce her presence. His jeans were stained with dried mud, and his hair was in disarray, as if he had been running his fingers through it backwards. Tiredness had finally caught up with him, days without sleep taking their toll.

Nick jerked up, turning to his daughter. 'Tell you what, why don't we go out and have a look at the stable now?'

Jennifer bit her lip, assessing the situation. It was clear he was avoiding her, but she couldn't allow Olivia to get caught up in their confrontation.

'Food's ready,' Joanna said, walking in behind her. She was wearing a peach 1940s-style dress, making her look like a bit part in a low-budget stage show. 'Oh hello, Jennifer, I didn't realise you were here. Would you like some pizza? It's homemade.' She tittered behind her hand as if sharing some private joke. 'Olivia loves pizza any time of the day.'

'I was just hoping for a quick word with Nick,' Jennifer said, observing Joanna's expression to see if she too would notice just how haggard her once handsome husband had become. But the eyes behind the smile were unconcerned.

Joanna reached out for her daughter's hand. 'C'mon, sweetie, Fiona's made your favourite.'

Olivia gave her father a pleading look.

'I said we'd go outside to see about stabling the pony,' Nick said, clearing his throat.

Joanna stretched an insistent hand towards her daughter. 'Later. You don't want your food getting cold, now, do you?'

Joanna and Olivia left, sealing Jennifer and Nick in the room. His eyes darted to the floor as he shifted on his feet, his hands deep in his jean pockets.

'You missed the drones,' he said, his voice scratchy from calling for Abigail. 'The helicopter came over briefly too. They couldn't find any heat sources, but it's difficult with the woodlands.'

'What did she mean, Nick?' Jennifer asked bluntly, locking on to him with her eyes.

'What did who mean?' Nick said, barely having the strength to return her gaze.

Jennifer took a step forward. 'Olivia. What did she mean when she said she wouldn't tell?'

'When did she say that?' Nick said, his voice rising an octave.

'I heard her whisper it before I left yesterday. She said she'd be a good girl and she wouldn't tell.'

'You must have misheard. She hasn't spoken a word.'

Nick put his hand on the door knob but Jennifer blocked his path. He was so close she could feel the heat radiating from his body, heat derived from an inner anger he had carried since Abigail's disappearance. She stood firm, a tightness forming in her throat.

'If you're in trouble, I'll do everything I can to help.'

Nick bore down on her, his stale breath heavy on her face. 'If you're insinuating that I've hurt my daughter, then you are way off the mark.'

She resisted the urge to let him past as his grip tightened on the door knob. 'I'm not insinuating anything,' Jennifer said, her tone taut. 'I'm trying to help. You'd do exactly the same in my shoes.'

Nick pressed his face inches from hers, his voice low and rumbling. 'How could you think I'd hurt my children? They're my whole world.'

Their standoff was interrupted by a scream from the kitchen. Nick barged past, and Jennifer followed, barely having time to register what was happening as she burst through the kitchen door.

Fiona was clutching Olivia tightly in the corner of the room, and Joanna was pointing to the floor. Jennifer's gaze fell on the blood-red splatters on the kitchen tiles and gasped with relief as she spotted the Heinz label clinging to fragments of glass. It was ketchup.

'What happened?' Nick asked, checking Olivia over.

Fiona cleared her throat to speak, her expression one of disbelief. 'It . . . it just flew off the table by itself.'

'Again?' Nick said, shaking his head. 'It's okay, sweetheart, the table's crooked, that's all. Eat your pizza. Everything's all right now.'

Jennifer assessed the room, sensing a charge of static electricity. Sue had mentioned things moving by themselves, and judging by Nick's reaction it was not the first time. Olivia nodded glumly as she slowly pulled in her chair to sit. Her eyes nervously darted around the room as she nibbled the pizza crust, like a small bird waiting for a predator to pounce. Jennifer's heart plummeted. This was the last thing Olivia needed.

Nick left the room, mumbling something about getting a bath. His blistered feet had prevented him searching any longer, and he plodded heavily up the stairs, hitting each step with a laboured thump. Nick's anger seemed to have evaporated in a puff, but Jennifer grew fresh concerns about Joanna's relationship with her husband.

'Are you OK?' Jennifer said, glad to get Joanna alone as Fiona took Olivia to the living room to watch TV.

'Of course. I'm fine,' Joanna replied, delivering her usual smile.

'I mean with Nick. He's a bit aggressive. Is this something I need be concerned about?'

Joanna gave a short laugh. 'Nick? He's a big softie. He's just stressed, that's all.'

'Because if you're worried, I can try to get you and Olivia into a women's refuge for a few days, give you some time apart.'

Joanna's retort was firm. 'I appreciate your concern, DC Knight, but I'm perfectly safe. I'm not a battered wife. A refuge is the last thing we need.'

Jennifer noted the coldness in Joanna's tone and decided to leave it at that. She was right. Staying at a refuge might only add to Olivia's trauma, and she was probably worrying over nothing.

'There is one thing you can help me with,' Joanna said, running a mop over the kitchen tiles.

Jennifer raised an eyebrow. 'I'll do my best. What do you need?'

'I want you to contact Abigail.'

Jennifer recalled her earlier contact, and a wave of guilt fell over her. She cleared her throat as she constructed a suitable response. 'We're doing everything we can to find her.'

'I don't mean that. Your colleague Sue, she said . . . well, she said you're psychic. I want you to speak to Abigail. See if she's on the other side.'

Jennifer inhaled sharply, cursing Sue under her breath. How dare she act so unprofessionally?

'I think Sue's got her wires crossed. I'm a detective, first and foremost. Granted, I sometimes deal with unusual occurrences. Haven is different to other towns. It hasn't moved on from the days of superstition and folklore. It doesn't mean I'm psychic, sorry.'

'Then you must know someone that can help,' Joanna said, her smile loosening as her voice became frayed. 'You hear about psychics helping the police all the time.'

Jennifer thought of the last psychic she had had contact with and it made her shudder.

'"Help" is the operative word. After all this family's been through, the last thing you need is someone making it worse. Besides, you're making the presumption that Abigail might have passed away. It might not be the case, and to presume such would be very upsetting for Olivia, don't you think?'

Joanna shrugged, returning her attention to the floor. 'She's her twin. She already knows.'

The conversation took a surreal turn as Jennifer watched Joanna casually discuss her daughter's death while mopping the floor. She wanted to throw the mop to the other side of the room, and ask her to at least have the decency to grant her daughter her full attention. She was beginning to experience the frustration and disbelief that Nick felt.

'What do you mean, she already knows? Has she said anything to you?'

Joanna dipped the mop into the dented metal bucket and pumped the handle up and down. 'No. And believe me, I've tried to get her to open up. But I can tell. Twins pick up on things.'

Jennifer grasped the handle, temporarily gaining Joanna's attention.

'I may have . . . an insight, but I don't class myself as a medium. Perhaps I can speak to Olivia alone. I might be able to help her come to term with things, at least until the child psychiatrist gets here.'

Joanna smiled, but her eyes were icy cold. 'I'd like that. But under no circumstances is a psychiatrist coming into my home.'

Jennifer dropped her hands, splaying them palms upwards. 'But they only want to help . . .'

'We've given the police free rein on our farm. But just this once, I'm putting my foot down. I'm happy for you to speak to Olivia, but I'm not having any counsellors involved. If you have a problem with that, you can call social services.'

'God, Joanna, I don't have a problem. I'm just surprised, that's all.'

Joanna smiled, calmness restored. 'That's okay, then. I think she's just gone upstairs, if you'd like to speak to her now. Nick's in the bath, so you won't be disturbed.'

Jennifer did not need to be asked twice. She gripped the thick wooden banister as she climbed the stairs. The bulb on the landing had blown, and grim shadows filled the empty space. The need for cleanliness and order began to rise, and she could not contemplate spending a night in the unwelcoming farmhouse, let alone live there. Somewhere in the depths of her senses Jennifer could feel ghosts of the past brushing against her skin, their icy whispers raising goosebumps on her flesh. A cold, sickening sensation arose as each step brought Jennifer further up into the gloom. Whatever she had encountered previously in the living room hung like a ghostly fog upstairs. Her eyes crept to the damp speckled ceiling, and she tightened her grip on the banister. She couldn't help but wonder what had possessed the family to leave their luxurious townhouse and set up home in such a desolate, unwelcoming abode. The air was thick with moisture, and as she ascended a humming noise played an eerie tune. Jennifer's heart froze as she reached the landing and saw a pallid child in a white linen dress, facing an open bedroom door. A whisper rose in Jennifer's throat.

'Abigail? . . . Is that you?'

The child turned, her blonde hair no longer shadowing her face. She was wearing glasses. It was Olivia, who had clearly changed out of her ketchup-stained clothes. Jennifer exhaled a little sigh of relief as she approached her.

Soundlessly, Olivia raised her hand and pointed into the bedroom. The source of the humming noise was slowly dying away.

Jennifer took a step towards it, her body tensing as she wondered what she would find. She was reassured by sounds of splashing rising from the bathroom end of the corridor. At least for now, Nick was preoccupied.

Olivia took Jennifer's hand as she entered the room. Light filtered in from the generous sash window, bouncing onto the wooden floor. The low hum subsided, and the spinning wheel which had produced it rattled onto its side. Olivia's dolls and teddies made up an audience, surrounding it in a perfect circle.

'Did you do this?' Jennifer asked.

Olivia shook her head.

'Do you know who did?'

Olivia paused, before shaking her head again.

'It's OK,' Jennifer said. 'Do you want to help me put them back?'

Olivia toed the floor with her shoe before nodding.

Jennifer wondered if Joanna's reluctance to call in a psychiatrist was more to do with her own issues than her daughter's. The child needed help, and further recommendations would be made.

'Olivia, do you remember when we went to see Toby, and we spoke about Abigail?'

Olivia looked down at her hands, small and delicate as they fingered the ear of a stuffed rabbit. She nodded in response, pursing her lips.

'Well . . . I'd like to speak to her again. Do you think you could do that for me?'

Silence. Olivia's head dipped as she pulled the stuffed toy close to her chest.

Jennifer felt a pang of guilt as she awaited a response. She should have had an appropriate adult present. But Abigail's life was at stake, and it wasn't as if Jennifer was formally questioning her. One more try, Jennifer thought. One more try and I'll let it go.

'Can you remember anything about the last time she spoke? . . . Olivia?'

Suddenly a voice erupted, tearful and anxious. 'I'm Abigail. I'm alone in the dark. Please, can't you find me?'

Jennifer's heart pounded as she measured her words. 'We will find you, sweetheart. I need you to describe where you are. What does it feel like?'

'Dirt. I can feel dirt between my fingers. It's wet. I . . . I want to come home.'

Jennifer touched Olivia's hands. They were cold to the touch, and trembled in her grip. 'We're looking for you. How did you get there?'

The words were punctuated by heart-rending sobs. 'They left me here . . . I don't like it. I'm scared.'

Tears slid down Jennifer's jawbone, dappling her shirt collar. Abigail's fear had infiltrated her senses, and she wiped the tears away with the back of her hand. Time was running out, and she was no further on.

'Who, Abigail? Who left you?' Jennifer whispered.

Olivia jumped as the bathroom door slammed in the hall, and her glazed eyes became sharply focused as a look of terror streaked across her face.

Hearing her father's footsteps, Olivia jumped from the bed and over to the far side of the room. Raising her finger to her lips, she climbed into the wardrobe, pulling the doors shut.

'Hide,' she whispered urgently. 'Hide, or Daddy will be cross.'

CHAPTER TWENTY-ONE

A gentle morning fog skimmed the banks of the Blakewater river, rising like steam over the divers who had been there since sunrise. Jennifer picked her way across the dewy bank. It felt odd having the soles of her feet firmly on the ground. Downsizing by five inches to squeeze into wellington boots unsettled her, and she craned her neck to look up at Sergeant Mike Stobart as he directed his team of divers. Jennifer had come to know Mike well over the years. He had begun his career at the age of eighteen, working in various roles until he found his place as the head of the diving team. It was a position he had been in for over ten years, and he was not shy when it came to sharing his experiences. He was a competent officer; Jennifer could relax knowing he was overseeing the search. There were five other divers on the bank, and it was obvious by their determined expressions that they had been fully briefed on the situation.

'Mike,' Jennifer said, offering a nod of respect.

'Well, if it isn't me old mucker. How the heck are you?' Mike said, throwing an arm around her shoulder in a half embrace.

Jennifer laughed, cutting her joviality short as she took in the scene. It felt wrong somehow, laughing on such a sombre occasion. She was painfully aware that at any second a signal could be raised, and Abigail could be found. She was a professional, and she had faced some horrific things in her career, but it didn't make it any easier. 'I'd be a lot better if we could find Abigail,' she said. 'I take it you've not found anything?'

Mike gave her a wilting look and Jennifer blushed. 'Sorry. Stupid question.'

He smiled. It was a patient smile; the kind you would give one of your kids. He had a large family, with five children under ten. Patience was something he had cultivated over the years. 'The water's murky, although thankfully the last few days have been cool, and the river's not moving very fast.'

The divers were in full dry suits with face masks. These were a given when searching the river Blakewater, due to the risk of pollution and the presence of rats. Jennifer shuddered at the thought of groping her way through its hidden depths. She was far too claustrophobic to submerge herself in the murky waters.

She watched as one of the divers disappeared into the depths of the river, leaving an eruption of bubbles on the surface. His rope attachment resembled a yellow umbilical cord, his lifeline to his colleagues on the surface. Jennifer stared, fascinated, as the officers on the ground communicated with him through their two-way equipment. She did not envy his task. Most of the team were mature in service and had children of their own, and a solemn atmosphere fell as they spoke in hushed tones.

'Wouldn't the body be floating on the top?' Jennifer said, never afraid to ask questions.

Mike shook his head. 'Bodies don't tend to float until after a few days, when the gases build up. The warmer the weather, the quicker the process.'

More bubbles broke the surface of the water as the diver arced across the river, his colleagues releasing another metre of rope as each section was searched. Most of their work was nil visibility underwater. Submerged in darkness and chilled to the bone, they groped their way through the rising silt, weeds and debris, never knowing what was going to appear before them. So far the process had turned up some car tyres, an old safe, bottles and other unwanted souvenirs.

It had been Jennifer's job to assimilate a list of new questions to put to the family. A full background of the incident had been requested by the diving team: exactly where Abigail was last seen, and by whom. What sort of mood was she in? What she was like around water, was she foolhardy or cautious? Could she swim, and if so, what was her level of capability? What was the weather that day? What had she been wearing? Was her hair tied up or down? On and on the questions went, and given the lack of cooperation from her parents, Fiona had answered the bulk of them. Although there was nothing to suggest that Abigail had gone as far as the river, drowning could not be ruled out. The search was centred around the most likely point of access from the house to the river bed. Abigail and Olivia had walked the crooked path with their father a couple of times in the past. Neither of them were confident swimmers, and would not have got into the water on their own. Jennifer discussed what Abigail had been wearing last. It was not for descriptive purposes. Her clothing could have been caught in the riverbank. Wellington boots could be submerged with water and act as weights unless she could wriggle free. Dungaree straps could get stuck in low-lying branches and foliage. The thought of Abigail floating in a watery grave sent a sick feeling through Jennifer, but she discussed it all with her usual professionalism. She never met Abigail, but felt like she knew the little girl, because Olivia was worming her way into her heart.

Mike left to speak with one of his divers and re-joined Jennifer at the bank.

'That's Ian,' Mike said, making scant effort to hide his grin as he buried his hands into the pockets of his police jacket. 'He made a bit of a schoolboy error when we recovered that suicide victim last week.' He gave a little chortle. 'I've told him a hundred times. Never grab a body face-on when asking to be pulled in. It wraps itself around you, and that's when you drop it. Which is exactly what Ian did. We had to send another diver in to start the search all over again.'

Jennifer shuddered as she imagined the weightless body enveloping her, its cold bloated face looming in on hers. Black humour was a coping mechanism used by the police to deal with such incidents. Nobody cared more about their victims than they did, but to an outsider listening in, his laughter would have been difficult to understand.

Jennifer stared, mesmerised by the water. 'I don't know how you do it. It's not my cuppa tea.'

Mike, who was enjoying her discomfort, carried on. 'You have to be careful when you grab things like a trainer, because quite often there's a foot attached. And then there's the thermoclines. They take a lot of young lives in the summer.'

'Therma what?' Jennifer said.

'Thermoclines. Different levels of water as you descend. One minute you're having a nice lukewarm dip, and the next you come into a pocket of freezing cold water. It can literally shock the breath out of your lungs.'

'From what the family have said, I don't think Abigail would have entered the water voluntarily.'

Mike's chest heaved in a thick heavy sigh. 'No. Neither do I.'

Jennifer wondered if it would be better for Abigail to be found, just to put an end to the misery. Her words replayed in her mind, like an earworm that refused to go away. *'Dirt. I can feel dirt between my fingers. I want to come home.'* She was lost in a pit of darkness, lying in a bed of soil. Was she naked and dumped in a shallow grave? Or was the dirt in the depths of the river bed? The Blakewater river had claimed many lives over the years; tormented souls searching for peace. Or maybe . . . just maybe she was alive. But how? Where? Jennifer had tried reaching out, but there was nothing but a void. She cursed the powers that chose the worst possible time to desert her. Abigail needed her, and all she was doing was playing referee between the family and trying to coax whispers from a traumatised child. *Hide, or Daddy will be cross.* The urgency of Olivia's words had startled her. She was beginning to regain her speech, and Jennifer wished she could whisk her away and talk to her alone. She knew from the beginning there was something special about the little girl. A vibrational energy afforded only to children with certain abilities. Yet Olivia seemed unaffected by the spirits that roamed the house. Was her energy tuned in to that of her sister's, like an old transistor radio that could only pick up one channel? And if so, was Jennifer's slow, gentle encouragement the right way to get her to open up? A midge landed on Jennifer's neck, its bite bringing her sharply back to reality. Mike had walked up the bank to talk to his diver, and she hadn't even noticed. She bade him goodbye. There was no point in staring mournfully into the water when there was so much to be done. As she trudged back up the path, Abigail's words repeated in her thoughts. She walked away from the cold unforgiving river, and was just out of earshot as the diver's hand speared the water, beckoning his colleagues to his find.

CHAPTER TWENTY-TWO

Diary Entry

It's been two days now and the police are still here. The longer they stay, the tighter my old, destructive emotions wrap themselves around me. But there's no getting away from it. The press appeal has placed Abigail's name on everybody's lips. I can't walk down the street without hearing about it, and if I see one more yellow ribbon tied to a lamp post I will scream.

I was upstairs last night, when Olivia's grandparents called. Good old Bob and Wendy, with their rosary beads and whispered prayers. Downstairs, they mumbled their usual platitudes about Abigail, and how the fires of Hell awaited whoever was responsible for her disappearance. I came out of the bathroom to find Olivia, pale-faced and ashen, taking it all in. Not once had they mentioned her, or asked how she was feeling. It was as if she had become the house ghost, and I thought, just for a second, that perhaps it would be better if she was. I stood behind her at the top of the stairs, and had this incredible urge to shout *Boo!* in her ear. What a hoot that would have been! Instead, I uttered some comforting words, and asked if she wanted to join me downstairs. I rested my palm on her back, and for a few delicious seconds I felt the urge to push. But Olivia stepped forward and the moment was lost.

My childhood is as much a part of my present as it was my past. I have tried to leave it all behind, to be normal; but doing so has resulted in my mother's prophecy coming true. She was right. I *am* Jekyll and Hyde. I wonder whether, if she had taken a little more notice, I would be any different now. Mother didn't notice my disappearances when I was Olivia's age; she just presumed I was out playing with the other children. It was a close-knit community. Someone should have known if there was a wolf in the village, shouldn't they? Only the wolf wasn't in the village. He was living in our home.

Slowly he groomed me, and made me grateful to have him as my first and only friend. We even had our own private jokes; rude names for Mother's cats, that we used when she wasn't listening. For the first time in my life, I woke up with a smile on my face. Father had never paid much attention to me before, but now we were the very best of friends. And the most exciting thing of all was that I was going to be a model. At first, I didn't believe it either. But grown-ups didn't lie. He was a good man, because Mummy told me so. He was my friend.

At first, they were simple photo shoots: smile for the camera, cross your hands on your lap, make it natural. It was the usual rubbish taken by amateurs. He said that he would make a portfolio, get me some modelling work. I was nine, not old enough to understand that grown-ups didn't always tell the truth. I imagined my face on the cover of the fashion magazines that Mother used to read. He said most famous models started off when they were children. But it had to be our little secret. Lots of people would be jealous, and we weren't to tell a soul until the contracts were signed. Then I would be rich, and everybody would want to be my friend.

Sometimes he would catch my eye and wink, and I would wear my secret smile. He even sorted out the bullies so they would not bother me again.

We developed a routine. Every Sunday, I attended my photo session. The studio was heated by a two-bar electric fire, and kept under lock and key. Anyone that dared interrupt his session by knocking would bear the brunt of a temper that could change in a millisecond. One Sunday he said his contacts had come back to him. They wanted something different, something to make us stand out above the rest. He told me how grown up I looked and gave me some clothes to wear. It didn't matter if the trousers were too small. Tight-fitting clothes were all the fashion, he said. I changed in the studio, and he returned when I was done. He didn't mind when my rolls of fat peeped out from under my vest. When the magazine signed me, I would go up to London, and wear proper clothes that fit. For the first time in my life I felt valued. I could not have been happier. Little did I know what was ahead.

CHAPTER TWENTY-THREE

Jennifer made it back to the house just in time for the news. Nick had provided police with a short video clip of Abigail and Olivia playing in a field of sunflowers. It was the same image that had been displayed on the first day of briefing. It would soon be Abigail's signature, aired worldwide for all to see. An entrepreneur mother and police officer father, the case was certainly worthy of media attention. Jennifer hoped that the video would help draw focus away from the poisonous trolls hounding Joanna and back to Abigail. She wondered, not for the first time, how people could be so venomous.

The family sat in silence as the video aired on Sky News, scattering the images to the far corners of the world like freshly potted billiard balls. The only sound was the girl's laughter, as she danced between the long stalks, touching the petals in amazement. Seconds later, the presenter moved on to the story of a disgraced politician, and the family stared motionless, not taking in a word.

Their grief filled the room, their combined energies reaching breaking point. Joanna shot up to her room without a word. Nick trudged back outside, and Fiona planted Olivia in front of the smaller television in the kitchen while she mopped the floors. Jennifer set up her laptop on the kitchen table, to catch up on some police enquiries. Minutes later, a plate of shortbread was pushed in front of her. 'You're as bad as my sister,' Jennifer said, biting into the buttery pastry. 'She's a feeder too.'

Fiona smiled, joining her as she laid two huge mugs of tea on the table. She had unremarkable features, the sort of person who could blend in with a crowd. She padded around in thick woollen socks rolled over her jeans when indoors, pausing only to dip her toes into her wellington boots when she had to venture outside. From her blunt bobbed hairstyle to her make-up-free face, everything about Fiona was practical, functional, homely. Which, given Joanna's erratic behaviour, was just what the Duncan family needed right now.

Jennifer pushed down the lid of her laptop as Fiona pulled up a chair. There were times when you knew when to talk, when to ask questions, and when to thrash things out. This was not one of these times. This was a time to listen.

Fiona wrapped her fingers around her mug, probably more for comfort than for warmth. 'It was me,' she said absentmindedly.

Jennifer opened her mouth to speak, but Fiona's wistful expression told her she was thinking of happier times, rather than making an admission of guilt. Jennifer had begun to roll around thoughts of suspects in her head, and it left a bitter taste to imagine that one of the people who professed to love Abigail the most could be responsible for hurting her.

Fiona tapped the cup with her neatly cut nails. They made a clinking sound as she spoke, and her head leaned to one side as she stared into the distance.

'I recorded them with the sunflowers,' she said, smiling at the memory. 'We were driving past when we noticed the field. There was me and Joanna, and Abigail and Olivia. Everyone was fed up because the house was damp and miserable. Nick was working one of his long shifts and the girls were bored. I packed a picnic basket and took Joanna and the kids out for a few hours. It was really warm, for the time of year. The kids were chatting in the back about ponies, and that was when I saw the field. We pulled up alongside and shot some footage of the children dancing with the sunflowers.' Fiona gave a short laugh. 'I was waiting for some shotgun-toting farmer to tell us off but he never came. The girls were mesmerised by the bright colours, and they looked so beautiful with the sun reflecting off their hair. Afterwards we had our picnic on the riverside. It was perfect.' A sob caught in her throat and she swallowed it down. 'Now it's all gone.'

She looked at Jennifer for reassurance but it was not hers to give. 'We're doing our very best. Something is bound to come up soon.'

'That's what scares me. I've only known the family six months, but I've really come to care for them. I don't want something awful to be unearthed by the police. I want Abigail to come home of her own accord. But every hour that passes makes the chances of her coming home unharmed more and more remote.'

Jennifer slowly nodded, her eyes downcast. She wanted nothing more than to tell Fiona that Abigail was alive, but she knew that any second now the phone could ring with devastating news. It was easier to change the subject than it was to make promises.

'Radcliffe . . . Have you seen him about today? I need to have a word.'

'He's been here every day, as part of the search party.' Fiona sniffed, taking her cup to the sink and throwing away the remainder of her tea. 'I'll tell him to hang around when he comes tomorrow, although he's already spoken to police as far as I know.'

Jennifer thought she saw a shadow cross Fiona's face at the mention of his name, but it was fleeting, and she wondered if she had imagined it.

'Why *did* Joanna and Nick buy this place? I've seen their townhouse. We're still collecting mail from there. Why would they move from luxury into this?'

'Joanna got it into her head that she wanted a project. She had planned to renovate the house and turn the land into a petting zoo for inner-city children. She had it all set up, and was working with a charity to make it happen.'

'That's some undertaking. And now?'

'Whatever was driving her just upped and left. I've no other way of describing it. I just hope she finds her inspiration again . . .'

'Otherwise?' Jennifer said, gently coaxing for more.

'Otherwise I'm out of a job. I was taken on as a live-in house-keeper while Joanna got on with things. If they end up selling . . . that's the end of my job.'

'I'm sure it won't come to that,' Jennifer said. But the truth was, she wasn't sure of anything. Joanna, Nick, they were embroiled in something beyond her understanding. And it was up to her to find out what. She held her breath as the ringtone of her phone played out. It was Ethan. Without a word, she took herself away from Fiona's questioning eyes and jogged down the path to her car. Heavy rain had been forecast, and the sky had changed dramatically in the last couple of hours, with storm clouds rolling in from the east. The first droplets of rain splashed against her jacket, and she swiftly slid inside the driver's seat of the old Ford Focus, in case her phone call took her back to the station.

'Hello,' Jennifer said, slightly breathless. 'I take it you've got an update?' It wasn't usually how she greeted her DI, but something told her the small talk could wait.

'Yes, I do. The divers have discovered a body. It's not been identi-fied yet, but a journalist turned up just as they were removing it, so I need you to inform the family before they hear it elsewhere.'

Jennifer's heart plummeted. 'Are there any indications . . . is it?'

'We just don't know. We believe it to be female with blonde hair, but she's been snagged by some debris and the body is pretty bloated. That's all I know for now.'

'Mmm,' Jennifer said, her face creased in a frown. 'I'll tell them that a body's been found and we'll update them as further information comes in.'

She didn't notice the rain pelting on her face as she returned to the house with the news. Shoulders heavy, she tried to take what she could from the update. She had to accept the truth. The communications with Olivia, the body in the water . . . it had to be Abigail. But if it was, at least they were bringing the little girl home. She pushed the heavy front door open. It was time to tell the family.

CHAPTER TWENTY-FOUR

Two Days Gone

Joanna fastened the flower-shaped buttons on the front of the pretty summer print dress. It had been a steal at seventy-nine pounds, and she had bought it from an online shop which specialised in 1940s clothing.

She checked her appearance in the mirror before sliding the iPad from underneath a magazine in her bottom dresser drawer. Her Twitter feed was alight with notifications, and almost none of them good. The red circle flashed to show that there were 142 tags for her username, and her heart sank as she scanned the poisonous messages, many of them orchestrated by the user @Truth00Seeker. His image displayed a hooded faceless man, and his profile listed him as someone searching for answers. It didn't list his location. But there was something about his tweets that made Joanna believe this was personal. The fact he had tagged her into the posts suggested he wanted them to be seen. Was he goading her into a response? Hundreds more tags were attached to #FindAbigail, and she gasped to see that the hashtag had gone viral. It was ironic. She had tried for months to get her online business viral on Twitter, and it took something like this to come up in an instant. She raced through the messages, resisting the temptation to reply. Police would be monitoring the account, although she could not see anything of value in the hate-fuelled bile.

She turned off the app, switching to her emails. Joanna pored over the messages of sympathy and hate, wishing her email address was not broadcast so publicly on her parenting site. It had only been a few days, but her website was losing revenue as advertisers cancelled their contracts, and her online supporters were dropping off as the trolls attacked them without mercy. She searched for the email she was looking for, her eyes growing wide as it pinged up on her screen. It was from Marcella Kelly, clairvoyant psychic – a woman known for her contact with the dead. Famed for a string of books and her travelling performances, Marcella could be just what she needed. She greedily scanned the message. Marcella would be happy to attend at a moment's notice, just name the time and she would be there. No fee involved. Joanna snorted. No fee indeed. Psychics were lining up to come to her home since Joanna leaked the paranormal activity to the press. No doubt Marcella would already be penning the title of her next book. Joanna typed up a quick response, telling Marcella things were up in the air but tonight should be fine, pending developments. She pressed the send button without hesitation. Her nail polish cracked as she bit into her thumbnail, trying to work out the best social media strategy for what was ahead. Somewhere deep inside, she knew her actions were wrong. A memory played, as if hidden behind a thin fog, cast away by a sudden breeze. *Half a pound of tuppenny rice, half a pound of treacle.* Joanna stared entranced as she absentmindedly hummed the tune. *Wrapping her fingers around the steel handle of her Jack-in-the-box, her heart gave a flutter. She knew what was coming but was excited just the same. Tomorrow was her birthday. She was a big girl now. Soon she would have ten candles on her cake . . . her hands dropped from the Jack-in-the-box and it fell on the floor.*

Joanna snapped back to the present as a commotion erupted downstairs. Had they found Abigail? No, she thought sadly. That wasn't very likely to happen. She swallowed hard, returning her attention to the computer. If they wanted her, they'd call her. Everything was just fine and dandy, she thought, typing pleasant responses to the hateful online campaign.

'Joanna.' Jennifer knocked gently on the door. 'Can I come in?'

She huffed with impatience. She had yet to update her blog.

'Very well,' she said, sliding the iPad under her pillow. 'Come in.'

The detective's face told her that there had been a significant development. And it was not good news. 'Can you come downstairs and join the rest of us?'

'Can't you tell me now?' Joanna said, unsure if her legs would support her. A war was waging in her head and she fought to remain in control.

Jennifer shook her head grimly. 'It's best if you come downstairs.'

'Very well.' She interlocked her fingers and stretched them out before her. 'I'll be with you in a second.'

The detective nodded, her inquisitive eyes sweeping the room. As if Joanna couldn't see the suspicion they held. Her bed, the wardrobe, the open en suite door. She caught Joanna's gaze, and had the decency to look embarrassed before she retreated through the door.

Joanna sat at her vanity table and undid the clasps of her hair. She fingered her long blonde locks, allowed them to slide through her fingers. Her hair was soft and untangled, her pride and joy. Her fingers found the nape of her neck, and she began to comb. She touched a tender spot of skin, before winding her index finger around a bunch of hairs. On she wound, until the tip of her index finger turned blue. Gritting her teeth, she pulled sharply until a handful of hair broke free from her scalp. Muffling a yelp, she savoured the sweet sting of release. It took only two calming breaths before she could face herself in the mirror again. Smiling, she picked up the old-fashioned paddle brush and worked it through her hair with long sweeping strokes. A quick squirt of hair spray, an application of lipstick, and she was ready. She smiled for the mirror, running her tongue over her teeth as she leaned into her reflection. *Tick tock, let the cogs turn, wind me up and off I go.* The words rebounded in her head like a mantra. It would be all right. Keep winding until you could not stop. Everything would be all right.

But each step down the stairs felt like crossing a chasm, her legs taking her somewhere she did not want to go. But they carried on, bringing her closer to what she already knew. Abigail was dead. And it was all her fault.

CHAPTER TWENTY-FIVE

The clock in the kitchen seemed to pause between each tick as Joanna's leather shoes tapped on the stairs. *Tick . . . tick . . . tick . . .* It felt as if the house was slowing down, allowing them time to digest what lay ahead. Jennifer stared at the white linen tablecloth. She had gradually adjusted to the heavy oppressive cloud, but she felt like an outsider as she ushered extended family and friends to wait in the living room. They had regarded her with some suspicion, as if she was responsible for the pain she was about to inflict. Good news would have been shouted from the rooftops, but bad news was spoken in quiet tones, away from prying eyes. They must have known that, but it didn't stop them searching her face for clues. Avoiding eye contact, Jennifer kept her expression neutral.

Around the table were Fiona, Nick, his colleague Karen Corbett, and the young man Jennifer had seen on her first day to the farm. Brother and sister, both had come up squeaky clean during police background checks. It was hardly surprising, given that Karen was a trainee investigator from Lexton CID. Her tresses were a couple of shades darker than her brother's tousled auburn hair, but they both shared the same striking green eyes. She was barely out of her probation, and working under Nick in CID. Nick's voice softened when he spoke to her, as if it were a relief instead of a strain. Jennifer would rather have spoken only to Nick and Joanna, but Nick had asked for Fiona, Matt and Karen to be there too.

Joanna appeared sombre as she joined them at the table. The fragrance of her floral perfume overtook the sweet smell of damp timbers burning in the Aga, and the only sound was the crackle of the range and the wind whistling through the cracks in the back door.

Jennifer stared, seeing rigidity behind Joanna's expression – her eyes glazed, as if she was somewhere else.

Joanna wrapped her fingers around the solid oak chair before robotically sitting down. Every movement came under Jennifer's scrutiny, and cracks were starting to show in her veneer. Nick coughed to clear his throat, and Jennifer could feel his eyes boring through her skull as he awaited the news.

'We've had a significant update,' Jennifer said, seeing no point in delaying the news. 'As you know, the divers have been searching a stretch of the river.'

A whimper came from her left and Fiona clasped a hand over her mouth to contain it. Nick bowed his head, and Jennifer watched as Karen wound her hand around his back, rubbing in circular soothing strokes. They seemed oblivious to Joanna, whose eyes were on Jennifer, waiting for her to continue.

Jennifer took a deep breath, the words distasteful as they rolled onto her tongue. 'They've found a body.'

She quickly followed up the words with reassurance, trying to offer them the little hope she could. 'There's been no identification yet, so it may not be Abigail. But you've asked to be updated every step of the way.'

'Right,' Joanna said, clasping her hands together. 'Well, in that case we wait to find out more.'

'Of course. There was also a journalist in the area of the search. We didn't want you hearing it from anywhere else.'

Joanna's face lit up at the mention of journalists. Jennifer bit her lip, holding back the scolding on her tongue. This was about Abigail, not Joanna, or some poxy publicity.

Jennifer took a deep breath. 'Obviously we recommend you don't speak to journalists just yet. We're just starting to claw back public support, and you don't want to do anything to jeopardise your relationship in the community long-term.'

Nick spoke a flat drawl, as if someone had just stamped on the last spark of hope. 'So what you're saying is that you think the body is Abigail.'

Jennifer reddened, realising that her comment about settling into the community long-term didn't offer much hope.

'I'm sorry if it came out like that. I . . .' Jennifer sighed, considering her words carefully. 'I meant that, whatever happens, even if Abigail is returned to the family safely, people will remember what was said in the press. I know as much as you do right now. I'm just advising caution as far as the press is concerned.'

But Jennifer's thoughts were racing ahead. If the body in the river was Abigail, Jennifer could be pulled away from the family very soon. How were they going to pick up the pieces after this? If the police didn't catch the person responsible, Olivia could be in real danger. It was possible she had witnessed the whole lot, and her attacker could be in the home, just waiting for the opportunity to silence her. She needed to speak to Olivia, to see if she could glean any further clues.

Nick grabbed his car keys from the hook on the wall as he made towards the front door.

'Where are you going?' Jennifer said, wondering why *she* was asking the question and not his wife.

'To the mortuary. They'll need someone to ID the body. If it's Abigail, then I should be with her.'

Jennifer followed him into the hall, keeping her voice low.

'I don't think that's a good idea. There's . . .' She lowered her voice as she approached him. 'The body's decomposed. I think they're going to ID by other methods, probably dental records.'

The instruction was to wait for further updates with regards the identification procedure, but Jennifer knew it was a waste of time trying to stop him.

'I'm a sergeant,' Nick said. 'I'm more than capable of dealing with this and I'm not waiting around for any dental records.'

He turned on his heel and left. Karen paused at the door.

'It's OK,' she said, glancing back into the kitchen. 'I'll go with him. Matt, you may as well go home. I don't think there'll be any more searching tonight.'

Jennifer waited for the front door to close before calling Zoe and arranging for her to be there to greet them. Zoe was a lot nearer to the mortuary, and the last thing they needed was Nick turning up and creating a scene. That taken care of, she plugged her feet into her wellingtons to go outside and speak to Olivia.

The little girl had been brought outside by her grandparents in an effort to distract her from everything going on in the house. The rain pitter-pattered against her umbrella as she checked her phone. Twitter was already streaming with suspicions of a body being found, and it didn't take long for it to be linked it to Abigail's disappearance. She glared at the tweets in disbelief, as @Truth00Seeker spewed their hateful messages.

Police found a body in the river. Mum needs to own up NOW. #FindAbigail
Body found? Is it Abigail? Has her mom been arrested? #FindAbigail
Only a matter of time. She did it. We want answers. #FindAbigail
I'm a friend of the family & you shouldn't be saying this stuff. Who are you @Truth00Seeker
The clue is in the name. Seeker of truth. Bringer of justice. #FindAbigail

Olivia didn't have a phone, but Jennifer didn't want to take the chance of her hearing the news from anyone else. Joanna had given her permission to speak to their daughter alone, and she was going to make use of it.

'There you are,' she said to Olivia, who was standing with her hands on her hips, surveying the inside of the barn. Nick had done a good job converting it into a cosy stable and tack room for the pony that was coming on loan. 'Wow. This looks great, doesn't it? Fit for a king,' Jennifer said, happy to see a smile on Olivia's face, even if she didn't reply.

Heavy rain hammered on the galvanized roof, and Jennifer folded her umbrella. The sweet smell of hay filled the barn. Nick had replaced the rotten bales with fresh ones, and cleaned the cobweb-laced timbers overhead. She signalled to Olivia's grandparents Bob and Wendy that it was okay to leave her with the child. Their grief was painfully prominent, and with each day that passed the elderly couple looked increasingly gaunt.

'Have you found her?' Bob asked, his voice thick with emotion.

Jennifer followed them to the front of the barn, keeping her voice low. 'We don't know. They've recovered a body in the water but there's not been any identification yet. We just have to wait and see.'

'You want to tell Olivia? Is that wise?' Wendy whispered sharply. Her tightly permed white hair made her look more like Nick's grandmother than his mother, and Jennifer had heard that she was quite forthright with her opinions.

Jennifer glanced over at the little girl, who was busy stuffing a hay net in the corner. 'Yes, I think she deserves to know what's going on.'

Wendy grasped Jennifer's hands, holding them tightly in hers. Her skin was cold as she squeezed hard. Inhaling a sudden breath, she pulled them towards her.

'I know why you're here. It's because you think they did it.'

Jennifer gasped, desperately wanting to pull her hands away. She opened her mouth to speak, but Wendy carried on, determined to have her say.

'Joanna's a good girl. I know she acts odd, but she would never hurt the children, and Nick . . .'

Bob placed a hand on her shoulder and shot her a warning glance. 'C'mon now, love, the officer doesn't need to hear this.'

Wendy squeezed Jennifer's hands, as if her husband had never spoken. 'Nick . . . he's made mistakes in life, wicked ones at that. But he's putting things right now. He loves those girls, we all do.'

'Wendy,' her husband said, squeezing her shoulder. She blinked twice before releasing her grip.

'I just thought you should know. That's all.'

'Know what?' Jennifer said, none the wiser.

'Just what she said,' Bob said. The couple turned to leave, their faces devoid of hope.

Finally alone with Olivia, Jennifer sat down on a bale of hay. She pulled a loose strand and threaded it between her fingers. Wendy's comments had given her food for thought, but right now her priorities lay with Olivia.

'It looks so cosy,' she said to the little girl. 'Do you want to sit down? You must be tired after all that work.'

Olivia had only taken a few steps before her face clouded over. It was as if she was in a hypnotist's stage show, and someone had just clicked their fingers.

'Why haven't you found me?' she said, her words distant and hollow.

'What?' Jennifer shuddered, as an icy shroud formed around her. 'Is that you, Abigail?'

'Yes, it's me. Why aren't you coming to get me?' the voice responded, with chilling lucidity.

It *was* Abigail. It *had* to be. Jennifer's heart began to pound as the sense of urgency hit home. She resurrected the questions she had planned to ask.

'Were you in the water? Please, Abigail, describe where you are.'

'I'm deep in the ground. The water's coming in and I can't get out. I'm so hungry. Why have they forgotten me, why?'

'Who, Abigail?' Jennifer said. 'Who took you?'

Olivia took in a sharp breath and tears began to prick her eyes. It was heartbreaking to watch her connection with her sister. Olivia's fingernails dug into the flesh of Jennifer's hands.

'I . . . I don't know . . . You've got to find me, pleeease.'

'I'm trying, sweetheart, we all are,' Jennifer said. But the life left Olivia's hands as they dropped to her sides, and she gave a small jolt before returning to herself.

'Olivia?' Jennifer said, testing her reaction. 'What just happened, sweetheart?'

Olivia shrugged, maintaining her usual silence. The connection was gone. And was she any further on? Frustration bit into Jennifer as thoughts ran riot in her head. Storm clouds rumbled overhead, and in the distance Jennifer could see the headlights of the police search teams drive away. There would be no more searching this evening, not in this weather. But what did she mean, the water was coming in? She tried to elicit further communication, but Olivia stared blankly, taking Jennifer's hand and showing her around the newly converted stable. After a few minutes, she sat her down on a bale of hay.

'I've got something to tell you, but I don't want you to worry, because it might not mean anything.'

Olivia nodded, pushing her fingers under the blue strand of baling twine as she sat on the hay.

'You know how the police divers were searching the river? Well . . . they've found somebody in there. I need you to be a brave girl until we find out who it is. Can you do that?'

Olivia nodded, a sad half-smile on her face. She stood up and stared mournfully at the rain-soaked wastelands. Jennifer didn't know if Olivia's thoughts were seeping through to her, or if it was empathy that brought her to the conclusion, but she felt that Olivia wanted to search for Abigail herself. The little girl's eyes were wide and pleading through her gold-rimmed glasses as they met Jennifer's, who instinctively responded, despite the lack of a question.

'You can't go looking, sweetie. What would happen if you got lost too? Who would look after Toby?'

Olivia nodded, visibly wilting before her. She really was a pitiful sight. A lone twin, with no knowledge of her counterpart. Jennifer had tried gently coaxing her for information, but all she could come up with were the occasional snatched whispers meant only for her.

Jennifer wanted to tell her that there were no promises that they would find her sister alive, that she needed to prepare herself, and she would meet her again, one day. But as she stared into her haunting blue eyes, the words formed a lump in her throat. She had no right to utter them . . . and the truth was too harsh for a little girl to face. All she could do was nod. Jennifer was loath to bring Olivia back inside while her mood was so low. Instead, she called her aunt and, putting her on speaker, talked about the arrangements for the pony's delivery. Pony nuts, tack and mucking out: such topics were enough to temporarily brighten Olivia's mood.

Jennifer was grateful for the confines of her car when Olivia was finally called inside. Waiting for an update on the identity of the body was torturous, because she knew she would be the one to deliver the news. She needed respite from the cloud of despair weighing heavy on the Duncan family home. She pushed back the driver's seat, stretching her legs and easing off her heels. She had gained new blisters from walking over the uneven ground, but she

couldn't substitute her beloved high heels for flats every day. They
bolstered her confidence, strengthening the professional image she
strived so hard to maintain as a woman in the police force. Without
them, she was the same as everyone else: fallible, emotional, and
susceptible to mistakes.

She pulled out her notebook and scribbled down the stolen
words. Hope was cruelly both given and taken away in each sentence. Deep in the ground would suggest a burial. Not a shallow
grave but deep. But then, a child's perception of deep could be
different to an adult's. Where else could she be? There were no
bunkers or basements in the area, but her connection with Olivia
was strong, so she couldn't be far from home. In the same breath
she had mentioned food, being hungry. All human emotions. The
wants and needs of a living child. A flicker of hope reignited in her
chest. Surely this was a good sign? Spirits didn't get hungry, did they?
Unless they didn't know they were dead. Jennifer stared hard at the
words, as if they were going to rearrange themselves into answers.
Abigail had asked why they had forgotten her. But to whom was
she referring? She slipped her hand into her jacket pocket and
pulled out her mobile phone, calling up Ethan's number. Even if
she wasn't in the office, having a temporary connection with work
grounded her and staved off the risk of emotional involvement,
which was growing by the minute.

'DI Cole speaking,' he said, even though her name would have
flashed up on his phone. She passed on Abigail's message, and they
discussed the possibilities. Ethan came up with the conclusion that
it could be Olivia finding comfort in pretending to be her sister, or
the voice of a lost soul trapped in the torment of being abandoned
in the earth. Either way, they had to keep digging for more.

'I just don't know,' Jennifer said. 'It feels like wading through
treacle with this case. We're all on tenterhooks waiting for the
identity of the body in the river.'

But Ethan was distracted by whoever had just entered his office. Muffled voices followed as a hand masked the receiver, and Jennifer slid her feet back into her shoes, sensing an update was on its way. Ethan returned to her call with a renewed sense of urgency.

'Your information may be more valuable than you think. We've identified the body.'

CHAPTER TWENTY-SIX

A noisy flock of geese flew over Jennifer's head, their necks stretched, feathers merging with the pearl grey sky. Keep flying, Jennifer thought, as the perfect 'V' formation drove onwards. Haven didn't accommodate many migrating birds. The menacing stillness acted as a deterrent to both wildlife and strangers who passed through the lands. She watched as the birds disappeared into the clouds, envying their freedom. She should have been relieved; she had delivered good news, but a gnawing dread told her it would not be long before the family's hopes were dashed for good.

She walked across the car park of Haven Police Station. It was a relief to get away from the farm, even for an hour. Abigail's disappearance was all-consuming, keeping her awake at night and on the edge of her nerves during the day. The discovery that the body was not hers was a minor victory. But any minute now, the family's world could come crashing down. Jennifer knew that, despite appearances, Joanna would be physically sick inside, enduring a surreal kind of hell until her daughter was returned. *Unless she was responsible for her disappearance.* The words took her by surprise as they flashed in her mind. Was the child being held captive? Could this be some bizarre publicity stunt? Jennifer stood before the police station with her hands on her hips, feeling like she was about to go into battle. But against whom? Abigail had been taken by someone she knew. She sensed it in her words. There was no fear there, just disbelief at the betrayal. But each attempt at contact was cut painfully short. It came in intermittent bursts, like clouds passing over the sun. Was it due to her weakening mind or her soul? Thanks to her latest report on Olivia's nervousness around her father, and his denial of their secret, he was deemed a 'person of interest' and would be spoken to formally with regard to Abigail's disappearance. If he refused to attend the police station to speak on tape, consideration would be given to his arrest. It was slim pickings evidentially, but if there was any chance Abigail was alive, then they would do whatever it took to find her. Zoe had used every ounce of her diplomacy to calm Nick down and get him out of the coroner's office. He had come close to being arrested for a public order offence, due to the amount of swearing taking place. He'd then been given the choice of being interviewed about his daughter's disappearance, with or without being arrested first. He had agreed to the latter.

Jennifer had not come to the police station just to get away. She had plans for how to spend her time: researching Joanna Duncan. But she was rewarded with very little information. The woman was swiftly becoming an enigma. Rather than being puzzled by her behaviour, Nick's parents treated her like she was some sort of saint. Yet Joanna's relationship with her husband was strained. And as for her father . . . Jennifer glanced up at Mr Hines's picture on the wall. It was a blown-up image taken from a newspaper article. She looked across at Nick's father, Bob. His picture had also been taken from an article. In fact, it seemed to be the same one. Rifling through the file on the table, she found the printout of the original clipping. It was a piece on Haven's first photographic club, set up in the late 1990s. So Bob Duncan and Joseph Hines were both members. But their relationship shed little light on Mr Hines's fractured history with his daughter, and the broken home she had come from. Just what happened between them? He lived on the outskirts of Haven, just a couple of miles from Blackwater Farm. Why hadn't Joanna moved in there, instead of renting his house out to strangers? It wasn't as if he was going to move back. Jennifer turned back to her computer and clicked on the image of the house portrayed on the letting site. It seemed quite nice by all accounts, a damn sight nicer than Blackwater Farm anyway. She had been tempted to pay the new tenants a visit, but what would she say? *Excuse me, I'd like to have a look around in case I can pick up some terrible history from the walls of your home?*

'I'm really grasping at straws now,' Jennifer mumbled under her breath, shutting down the site. What good was delving into the past, when Abigail was missing right now? Unless . . . She trotted out of the office to see her DI, and he instantly waved her inside. Ethan looked surprised to see her back so soon.

'I thought you'd be at the farm,' he said, clasping his hands together.

'I was. But I was thinking . . . would it be possible to have Joanna's father's house searched? I don't think it's been checked properly, has it?'

'Enquiries were made with the occupants, but not a thorough search, no. Abigail's never been there, and it's being rented by strangers to the area.'

'It's worth a shot, though, isn't it?' Jennifer said, casting a glance over the piles of paperwork on his desk. 'I know you're busy, but . . .'

'Finding Abigail takes precedence over all this,' he said, waving his hand over the paperwork. 'Leave it with me. I'll speak to DCI Anderson today, get the necessary authorisation.'

'Oh,' Jennifer said, crestfallen. 'But I'd like to conduct the search myself.' She glanced through the office door at Will, who had returned from custody with interview notes in hand. She envied his productivity. At least he was dealing with a suspect. If only Abigail could be located safe and well, and she could get on with the business of investigating her abductor.

'I need you back with the family,' Ethan replied. 'Nick's being interviewed as we speak. I can't see him making any admissions of guilt, so I'd like you back at the farm before he's released.'

Jennifer sighed. It was getting late, and her shoulders were heavy with the weight of her concerns. 'Oh, OK then. But you'll keep me informed?'

'You have my word,' Ethan said, picking up the phone.

Jennifer mumbled her goodbyes. Two days since Abigail went missing. Two long days. And soon it would be three. Even if Abigail were trapped or lost, there was no way she could survive much longer without food and water. How could Jennifer return to the farm, knowing all the odds were against her?

CHAPTER TWENTY-SEVEN

'I can't believe this,' Nick said, the veins throbbing in his neck like blue cables about to snap any minute. 'You should be out looking for Abigail, not questioning me. Don't you realise? I'd never hurt my daughter, never!'

'We're not saying you have. You're a sergeant, you know we're only doing our jobs.'

The police officer across the small square table was a stranger to Nick, but he looked not long off retirement. Greying hair, eyes pouched from lack of sleep, DC Kelly had the look of a man who had spent too long in the job. Nick vaguely recognised the female sergeant. Her name was Baxter or something. Her long brown hair was scraped back into a bun, making her face appear pale and pinched. Nick decided that anyone with that many frown lines was not to be trusted, and he regarded her with casual unease. They had met him at the morgue and offered to take him further afield to prevent any professional embarrassment. But Nick, protesting his innocence, had not wanted to be far from his family in case of further developments. Lack of sleep combined with stress over the discovery of a body had made him bad tempered and snappy, and he barely recognised the man he had become. He rubbed his chest as it tightened, feeling as if he was being squeezed in a vice-like grip.

'Are you all right?' DS Baxter asked, tilting her head in concern.

A glut of gas rose in Nick's stomach and his cheeks puffed as he belched into his clenched fist. The chest pain eased. Indigestion.

That's all it was. Brought on by stress and eating snatches of food at odd hours of the day and night.

'Excuse me,' Nick muttered, gathering his composure. 'Can we just get on with this? Just do what you've got to do.'

The windowless interview room was small and poky, smelling of recycled air. Haven CID churned out suspects as if they were on conveyor belts: drug dealers, domestic abusers and small-time shoplifters. Officers queued to use one of the four interview rooms which were more like broom cupboards. Unlike the modernised police station in Lexton, where Nick worked. He wished he were back there, overseeing criminal investigations instead of being the suspect in the case of his missing daughter. They could dress it up all they wanted, a person of interest was one step away from being arrested if the right evidence came to light.

DS Baxter's voice cut into his thoughts, her voice soft and coaxing. 'I understand this is an upsetting time, but we'd like to get some ambiguities cleared up. Can you tell me, what were you doing on the day of . . .'

'I was in the cow barn, clearing it out,' Nick said, pre-empting her question. What other day could they be talking about, if not the day of Abigail's disappearance?

A faint smile touched DS Baxter's lips, but her eyes remained cold. 'I take it by the tone of your voice this isn't something you particularly enjoy?'

Nick sighed. 'Renovating a shitty cow barn isn't on my list of fun things to do, no.'

'So whose idea was it to buy the property?'

'What are you trying to imply?' Nick said stiffly. 'I was unhappy about renovations, so I abducted my own child?'

'I'm not implying anything,' DS Baxter said. 'I simply asked you a question.'

'It was my wife's idea. One of her many projects.'

Nick folded his arms, which suggested that this was all he was going to say on the subject. He glanced over at DC Kelly. Pen poised over his notebook, he was giving nothing away. But Nick's emotions had taken control. Exhausted and stressed, he lacked the capacity to keep them in check, and each one emerged on his face, giving his audience a full viewing. He shifted in the hard plastic chair, knowing they would take full advantage.

DS Baxter crossed her legs and clasped her hands on the table. 'Where were the children on the morning of Abigail's disappearance?'

'You know where they were,' Nick said. 'We've already answered these questions a hundred times over.'

'I know,' DS Baxter replied, with a slow sympathetic nod. It took Nick by surprise, and he wondered if she had children of her own. 'Please. Humour me.'

'They were meant to be in the house. I'd told Joanna not to let them out because the ground was all churned up from the tractor.'

'Did you *see* them outside?'

Nick dropped his eyes to the desk, the memories exposed too painful to share. 'No. The last time I saw them was at breakfast. Look, I don't see the point behind this interview if you're going to go over old –'

DS Baxter interrupted with a quick rebuke. 'Why is Olivia frightened of you, Nick?'

Nick's head snapped up. 'Frightened? Who said she was . . .? Ah. Jennifer Knight. She's behind this, isn't she?'

DS Baxter locked her gaze on Nick in an intense stare. 'You know as well as I do that she has an obligation of duty to report her findings.'

Nick opened his mouth to speak but DS Baxter continued. He had seen officers like this before. Her sympathetic mumblings had been a ploy, and when he wouldn't give her what she wanted, she would rebuke with a vicious attack. He folded his arms, wondering if he should request a solicitor after all.

DC Kelly joined in on the questioning, and Nick had two pairs of stony eyes upon him instead of one. He felt the weight of their stares, and swallowed back the lump in his throat.

'I don't think you're in any position to disapprove,' DC Kelly said. 'Olivia is so traumatised that she's refused to speak. You've blocked our offers of a visit by a child psychiatrist, and she was overheard whispering to you that she wouldn't tell. Would you like to enlighten us as to what this secret is?'

Nick laughed incredulously. The hollow, bitter sound seemed to rebound off the four walls. His resolve to stay strong was crumbling. He wished the ground would swallow him up and take him somewhere dark, away from the pain, the bitterness and the accusations.

'This is outrageous. Kids say stupid things all the time, it doesn't have any bearing on Abigail.'

'I'm not so sure. When DC Knight questioned you on it, you became very defensive.'

DS Baxter joined in, 'And when she was alone with Olivia, the girl became so frightened of you discovering her talking to the officer that she hid in the wardrobe. Does this seem like normal behaviour to you?'

Nick inhaled a slow soothing breath. He knew how the police worked, and he shouldn't allow them to get the better of him. He closed his eyes as a wave of tiredness overcame him, and allowed the tension to leave his shoulders.

'You know if I was at all worried by your questioning, I'd call a solicitor right now.' Nick opened his eyes, and returned the officer's gaze. 'But I'm not. Because as far as Abigail is concerned, I've done nothing wrong. So you can say what you like.'

DS Baxter jumped in with a response. 'I'm not saying you *planned* on harming Abigail. I just think something happened to her, and you were there at the time. It's a farmyard, full of machinery and old buildings. An inquisitive child playing hide and seek, anything could have happened. Perhaps you knew it would be too much for your wife to bear. So you decided to cover it up, in the hope of sparing her the pain. But Olivia found you, and you warned her not to tell a soul.'

'Bollocks. Utter bollocks,' Nick said, the words ending in a yawn. It wasn't that he didn't care. He hadn't slept in days and his body was shutting down. The officer's voice seemed to be coming from far away, and he rubbed his eyes with the heels of his palms to focus. DS Baxter was still speaking, back to her 'good cop' routine. Nick was able to see right through her, and her method of interview did not impress him at all.

'If something happened, then we can help. Just tell us where she is. She deserves that much.'

Nick licked the dryness from his lips. His throat still felt scratchy from shouting over the last couple of days, and the dry stale air in the poky interview room didn't help much.

'You think she's dead, don't you? It's why the search teams don't call her name any more. Because the dead don't answer back.'

DS Baxter had the gall to look affronted. 'I'm merely pointing out . . .'

'You're talking utter shite. How dare you tell me what my daughter deserves? I live for my kids, I'd give up my life for them,' Nick said.

DS Baxter leaned forward as she fired off the last few barrels of accusation. 'Nick Duncan, did you kill your daughter Abigail?'

'No.'

'Do you know where she is?'

'No.'

'Have you hidden her, dead or alive?'

'No.'

'Do you know who has?'

'No. Now I'm done answering your questions. If you want to question me any further, I want to exercise my right to a solicitor,' Nick said.

'What happened to "I've done nothing wrong"?'

'It got bored and left the interview.'

Nick was thinking of Abigail, of all the time wasted in this interview when he should have been looking for her – that's if her waterlogged body wasn't lying in the morgue. He shook off the thought. He couldn't afford to fall apart right now.

'You're hiding something,' DC Kelly said, having found his voice for the second time.

'It's nothing to do with Abigail,' Nick snapped. 'Now, I'm done here. I've answered your questions, and you can take your Family Liaison Officer out of my home.'

'Which will result in you getting updates only when necessary. Is that what you want?'

'Fine. In that case she can stay. But . . .'

'But what?' DS Baxter replied. 'She can stay, but she can't do her job? It's all or nothing here. There are to be no repercussions for DC Knight. We want to find Abigail as much as you do, and if it means asking some unpleasant questions then so be it. I want you to think of Abigail. What she's doing right now. Is there anything you can tell us that will bring us to her?'

Nick took a deep breath, his eyes swimming with tears as he pictured his daughter's face.

'I'm so tired. I thought I could do this, but I can't.' He shook his head, wiping away his tears with his fingers. 'I *was* at the farm that day but . . .'

A knock on the door interrupted their conversation and DS Baxter rose from her chair.

'This better be good,' she mumbled tersely under her breath as she left the room.

DC Kelly announced her temporary departure, leaving the tapes running to negate any accusations later.

'Please, carry on,' DC Kelly advised.

But Nick was too caught up in what was happening the other side of the door. 'There's been a development, hasn't there?' He swallowed back the bitter taste rising in his throat as panic rose in every cell. 'Oh God, they've confirmed it, haven't they? They've found Abigail.'

CHAPTER TWENTY-EIGHT

DS Baxter's face was set in a mask of composure as she took her seat. 'They've identified the body taken from the river. It's not Abigail.'

Nick blurted out his relief in a string of nonsensical words, tears running unbidden down his face. 'Oh God, Abi . . . Abi, my little girl . . .' Shoulders shaking, he crossed his arms over the desk and wept into them like a baby. The room was silent, apart from the squeak of the tape machine as the tape cogs turned ominously, picking up every sniffle, every tear of despair.

As much as DS Baxter tried to bring Nick back to the line of questioning, the moment had been lost, and Nick was only interested in the recent developments.

'If it's not my Abi, then who is it?' he asked, accepting the offer of a tissue from DC Kelly.

DS Baxter spoke in clipped tones. 'A young homeless girl who disappeared in Lexton. It's believed she may have jumped off the bridge and been carried downstream.'

'What age was she?'

'Nineteen.' DS Baxter pre-empted Nick's next question. 'She was a heavy drug user, very waif-like.'

Nick frowned. 'Abigail was just a child. How could they have thought it was her?'

'We never said it was. You asked to be kept abreast of *every* development,' DS Baxter said, in a pitiless voice. It was plainly obvious she thought he was responsible, and being on the wrong side of a police interview was opening Nick's eyes in more ways than one. He turned his focus to DC Kelly, deciding to ignore Baxter from now on. 'Well, at least for some family the nightmare is over. But what about us? What next?'

DC Kelly cleared his throat. 'We keep looking. Nick, hundreds of officers have been drafted into this. Your colleagues have come home from their leave to get involved in the search. Officers are working on enquiries around the clock, many of them over their rest days. We won't let go until we find your daughter. That, I can promise you.'

Nick nodded, blowing his nose one last time before shoving the tissue into his back pocket. 'Does this mean we're finished?'

DC Kelly began to nod, but was swiftly interrupted by DS Baxter.

'Just one more thing.' She glanced over their notes. 'Before we were interrupted, you said you were tired, "you thought you could do this but you couldn't". What were you going to say?'

Nick shrugged. 'That I blame myself. I should have been watching her. I'm meant to be there to protect my children, and I let them both down.'

'And Olivia? Why is she scared of you?'

'She's not. She's just traumatised by the loss of her sister. Talk to her if you want. It's my wife who refused help for her, not me.'

'And Joanna? How does her reaction strike you?'

'I'm a copper, not a psychiatrist. It's unprofessional of you to ask me to assess her reaction to all of this.' Nick stood, and leaned his hands on the back of his chair. 'Now, seeing as I'm not under arrest, I'm going home to be with my family.'

The news of the identity of the body had been met by a wave of relief when Jennifer passed it on to the family. For her, it brought mixed reactions. She had felt all along that Abigail was in soil, not water. Logic told her that if this was the case, she was most likely dead. Yet something held her back. A small wisp tugged at her senses, something she could not share for fear of giving them false hope. Dare she believe that Abigail was alive?

Jennifer's phone beeped with a text informing her that Nick was returning home. She downed the cup of tea that Fiona had made her and finished her ham sandwich. Like her, Fiona was staying on late to help the family. She had given up telling her that she took coffee with two sugars rather than tea with none. It was hardly surprising that Fiona was distracted, and the drink washed down well with the slabs of homemade soda bread that she presented fresh from the oven. They had all found different ways of coping with Abigail's disappearance: baking and making hundreds of cups of tea seemed to be Fiona's. Jennifer would watch her staring vacantly out the window, only to jump when the oven timer emitted a shrill ring. Jennifer wondered why the woman had never had children herself, as she was so good at looking after everybody else's.

Jennifer brought her mug to the sink and followed Fiona's line of sight to the fields in the distance, now bathed in darkness.

'Do you see your family at all?' Jennifer said.

Fiona smiled. 'Not as often as I'd like. My mother's in Canada and my father passed away last year.'

'I'm sorry to hear that,' Jennifer said, observing Fiona for a flicker of regret, or a change in expression. Full background checks had been made on all persons of significance, and Fiona's words rang true. The scrunch of car tyres on gravel snapped Fiona out of her daydream, and she busied herself setting the table she had cleared minutes before. Her role seemed like an endless round of tea- and sandwich-making. If she was unhappy about it, she never gave any indication.

Nick pushed open the kitchen door, beckoning to Jennifer from the hall. His hair jutted up at the sides, dishevelled and unkempt, and he seemed oblivious to the state he was in. Lack of sleep had brought him to his knees, and Jennifer wondered how long he could keep going. She followed him into the living room, which held the sweet smell of damp logs that hissed in the recently lit open fire. She had been informed about how the interview had progressed, but remained on her guard in case he wanted to admonish her for her distrust.

Nick ran his fingers through his hair, his face looking haggard in the glow of the flickering embers. 'I don't want any bad feelings between us. I've never been a FLO, but I know how hard it must be, coming into all of this and having to take on everyone's frustrations.'

Jennifer nodded, relief sweeping through her. The last thing she wanted was another confrontation. 'Thanks. I'd be lying if I said it hadn't concerned me. But I'm here as an investigator, not to make tea. I have to follow up every concern, no matter how small.'

'I know,' Nick said. 'I've not given up hope, though. She might still be out there, alive.'

Jennifer nodded. 'That's why it's important you pull together as a family. You know, underneath all that bravado, Joanna's suffering too.'

Nick's lips thinned at the mention of his wife, and Jennifer sensed he was swallowing back his words. He would not trust Jennifer now, not even with the slightest throwaway comment.

'You look terrible. Why don't you try to get some sleep? I'll let you know if there's any development this end.'

A bitter laugh escaped Nick's lips. 'If only I could. I'm an insomniac. Sleep doesn't come easy, and lately . . . it doesn't come at all.'

Jennifer chewed the lipstick from her bottom lip, wishing there was something she could say to make things better. 'Why don't you get some food down you? Fiona's prepared supper. I think she enjoys fussing over everyone.'

Nick reached for the door knob. 'I could do with a coffee . . . will you be joining me?'

'I've just eaten, thanks, and I've got some phone calls to catch up on.'

She watched him plod down the hall, his body giving off all the signals of a man fighting a losing battle.

Her colleague's updates brought nothing new. The police hadn't ruled out the possibility of a kidnapping, and efforts were being made to investigate all traffic passing in and out of Haven that day – including the movements of the elusive handyman, Radcliffe.

Picking her way through the darkness, Jennifer retraced Abigail's last known steps as she took the call, and by the time the conversation ended she found herself under the lights of the outbuildings where Nick had been working that day. Closing her eyes, she tried to pick up the vibrations running through the farm. But the ancient mutterings and whispers had little bearing on the little blonde girl who had disappeared. Then out of the background, a man's voice filtered through, but this one was very much alive. Jennifer stole a glance from inside the shed. It was Nick, having a heated phone conversation he clearly didn't want shared.

His tones were hushed but aggravated, and he kicked the dirt as he approached, too deep in conversation to notice her hiding behind the shed door.

'I told you, as long as you act normal and keep your mouth shut it'll be fine . . . No . . . I didn't say anything . . . Well, you'll have to take my word for it . . .'

Jennifer held her breath as Nick's voice grew louder. She should find a hiding place and keep out of sight. But as Nick's voice grew more aggravated, she knew this was a conversation she couldn't afford to miss.

'Listen, you need to get your shit together,' Nick said, leaning against the shed door. 'No, you listen to me. I've lost everything . . . my home, my family . . .' His voice cracked, 'No . . . now isn't the time. I've told you before, I'm not interested . . . Olivia won't say a word . . . because I know.'

Jennifer leaned back, her heel kicking the galvanized metal lining the wall. The sound seemed to echo around the farmyard, and she bit her lip as she ducked down behind a stack of hay bales.

Nick spun around. 'I've got to go. Just act normal. All right . . . all right . . . I'll speak to you later.'

Jennifer strained to hear Nick end the call and take slow, steady steps inside the barn. The sweet smell of the hay tickled her nose, provoking a sneeze. I don't believe this, Jennifer thought, pinching the bridge of her nose as she stemmed her breath.

'Hello?' he called out, his footsteps getting nearer.

Jennifer crouched down as far as she could go. She was going to feel very stupid if she got caught hiding in the shed. Nick would surely kick her out for spying on him, or worse. Every day the stress strengthened his anger, and he wouldn't believe that her presence was coincidental. She was well within her rights to challenge him. His comments were damning, and she committed them to memory, feeling more like a spy than a Family Liaison Officer. But she didn't want to confront him. The information would go in a report, rather than compromise her relationship with the family.

Nick's footsteps lightened as he tiptoed around the shed. He had stopped calling out, and warning lights began to flash in her head. What if she had heard too much? She thought of the pitchfork lying against the shed wall. He could be standing on the other side of the straw, ready to strike at any second. The thought made her pulse quicken as she worked out a strategy. She was too far away from the house to shout for help. She thought of her phone, nestled in her pocket. Any minute now, Will would be calling her, wondering where she was. Nick's footsteps grew louder as he searched the shed, and she closed her eyes and sent a plea for help. A gust of wind hit the walls, sending a loose sheet of galvanized metal clattering in response.

Jennifer mouthed silent thanks as Nick turned and left the shed. She quickly punched in a text to Will. She wasn't coming home just yet. She had work to do.

CHAPTER TWENTY-NINE

Diary Entry

I wanted to laugh, to allow my authentic self to come out to play. But instead, I pushed everything down, no time for playing, at least not today. So I played with Olivia instead. Well, when I say played, I mean I watched her mope about and drew some pleasure from it. It makes me question the value of her existence. If Abigail is gone, then isn't it kinder to let her go too? Such thoughts came to me as I stood in her shadow, watching her stare mournfully from the bedroom window, eyes half open, with her hands by her sides, while everyone else gathered downstairs. Lost. Alone. Forgotten. Emotions I know too well. As if someone had scooped out her soul and promised to come back for the rest later.

It's been two days now. Two days of watching the household become turned on its head. I've enjoyed it so much, I've decided I'm not ready to let her go. Not yet. Last night I paid Abigail a visit. On the way over, I had the feeling I wasn't alone. That creepy-crawly feeling you get, like spiders on your skin. I wandered through the undergrowth, my boots sticking in the mud. The darkness provides a much bigger challenge, and I depended on the light of the moon to guide my path. I was at the point of giving up when I found her, sleeping in her pit. A strange stirring squirmed in my gut as I stared down at her from my vantage point. I was holding her life in my hands. And I liked it. A mole in a hole. Helpless and blind, completely at my mercy. I threw her some scraps and she took them gratefully, calling for Mummy, Daddy, or whoever she believed me to be. The power was all mine, at least until they found her. And they would. And I can't have that. I can't have that at all.

CHAPTER THIRTY

Two Days Gone

The relief that the body had been identified as some other poor soul was short-lived, as psychic Marcella announced her arrival and invited herself in. Joanna hadn't seen fit to tell anyone of her arrangements for a séance. Jennifer was aghast, and Nick furious. It did little to dissuade the attending psychic, whose presence caused an argument within thirty seconds of her arrival. Jennifer's suggestion of an evening with friends seemed to be the best solution all around. A couple of hours in a quiet pub would ease Nick's frayed nerves, and give Joanna a break from his disappointed looks. Matt drove over to pick him up, and with a resigned shake of the head, he braved the rain and jumped into his friend's car.

Marcella took in the room, her eyes alight. A small gold-spangled woman in her sixties, she was followed by a reedy young man no more than sixteen or seventeen years old. Marcella pushed off her hood, revealing a shock of frizzy blonde hair. No doubt the black-hooded cloak was something she used to great effect, Jennifer thought. Underneath she was dressed in a long black flowing skirt and a puffy ivory satin blouse. Her fingers were lined with rings and the bracelets on her arms jangled as she walked. This was the stereotypical view of a psychic in Haven, but in Jennifer's experience people with gifts could take many forms: an innocent child, or a well-heeled detective. She had come into contact with Marcella for ten minutes and the woman's croaky voice was already getting on her nerves.

'Ooohh, I sense great sadness within these walls,' the psychic said, her head swivelling left to right as her fingers teased the air. 'There is much unease in this home.'

No shit, Sherlock, Jennifer thought, her jaw tight. People like Marcella were the reason she hated to be labelled a psychic, and her communications with the dead were nothing like the theatrical performances Marcella had in store. She had watched her in action when she investigated one of her stage shows, and although no wrongdoing was proven, Jennifer had doubts about her abilities.

Jennifer had wondered why Joanna arranged for Olivia to go to her grandparents' house for a couple of hours. It was doubtful they would have been happy, had they known the reason why.

'Did you know about this?' Jennifer whispered as Fiona leaned her weight against the heavy door to close it.

'I knew about Olivia going out, but nothing of this . . . this psychic,' she said, pronouncing it as if it were a dirty word.

'You don't think it will do any good?' Jennifer asked.

Fiona's brows creased in a disapproving frown. 'It's not done much good so far, has it?'

She was referring to Nick walking out. And that led Jennifer nicely into questioning her about Nick's friendship with Karen, who happened to be in the car when her brother picked Nick up. She had already texted Will, hoping he would conduct some off-duty surveillance on her behalf. 'What about . . .' Jennifer began to say.

They were interrupted by the flow of voices coming down the stairs. Joanna was wearing her usual counterfeit smile. Her manicured fingers slid down the banister as she spoke animatedly to Marcella about the history of the house.

Fiona eased her coat from the hook on the wall. 'I'll leave you to it. See you tomorrow.'

Joanna's face fell. 'Oh. I'd like you to stay. I'll pay you overtime.'

Fiona groaned, still holding her coat mid-air. 'I'm not really a believer . . .'

'Please,' Joanna said. 'Just for an hour. We need three or more people for the séance.'

Sighing, Fiona rested her coat back on the hook and followed them through to the kitchen.

If Marcella picked up any line of communication with Abigail, she didn't show it. She seemed more interested in communicating with the spirits of the past that still walked the corridors. They were nothing new to Jennifer, who had caught their whispers the first day she arrived. So many spirits occupied this space. The old man who had died in the living room, age-worn and tied to the lands. The woman who passed through the walls with an oil lamp, checking her fevered children. Such were merely echoes of the past, and not capable of hurting anyone. But there was one ugly presence which seeped into the walls of the home. The more time she spent there, the more convinced Jennifer became that the dark entity she had encountered had taken residence, and was not leaving any time soon. But malevolent beings were not responsible for Abigail's disappearance. To her, the answers lay much closer to home.

Joanna struck a match, igniting a tang of sulphur in its wake. It touched the wick of one of the candles that made up the centrepiece of the small circular table dragged in from the living room. Next to the candles was a photo of Abigail, and a plate of soda bread; an offering to encourage the spirits. According to Marcella, they were attracted to the warm glow of the candlelight and comfort of food.

Enticements were never needed, as far as Jennifer was concerned. She took her place at the table, her eyes skimming over the young man sitting behind Marcella. Mystics often had a silent helper ready to jump into action should anything go wrong. His old-fashioned cardigan and corduroy trousers were hardly weekend wear for a young man his age. But something told her he did not socialise with his peers. His dark hair was tightly cut, and he had the same delicate unlined hands and pale skin as Marcella. Jennifer tried to catch his eye, but he stared expressionless into the distance. She could sense it. His presence was like a poultice, drawing out the spirits that lurked beneath the shadows. As the candles danced and flickered, the temperature began to chill, raising a row of goosebumps on Jennifer's arms.

'Gather around, please,' Marcella said, placing her hands on the tarnished wood. 'Place your palms flat on the table, until our little fingers are touching.' She lowered her voice as she leaned forward. 'Whatever happens, you must not break the circle.'

Despite her misgivings, Jennifer's heart fluttered in her chest. She wanted contact with Abigail more than anything, but communicating in this way was akin to inviting a stranger into your home. Malevolent spirits often lied to gain the trust of their host, and once the door was open, it was very hard to close. She directed her focus solely on Abigail, touching fingers with Marcella and Fiona either side. Fiona was looking very nervous for someone that claimed not to believe. Joanna completed the circle, and they sat around the dancing candlelight, waiting for Marcella to begin.

Closing her eyes, Marcella took in a whistling breath through her nose and out through her mouth.

'Our beloved Abigail, we bring you gifts from life into death. Commune with us, sweet child, be guided by the light of this world and move among us.'

Marcella's slow, rhythmic chanting brought the darkness ever closer as the words rolled off her tongue. The boy closed his eyes, his pale lips moving slightly, but producing no sound. They were near. The army of the dead. Marcella fell quiet, opening herself up to the spirit of the little girl.

Jennifer shuddered, a sense of dread falling upon her. It's all right for them, she thought, her eyes flicking across the table to

Joanna and Fiona. *They don't feel what I feel.* A pang of guilt cut her short as she remembered Joanna's less than enviable position. She switched her focus, trying to draw comfort from the sounds of the kitchen. The tick of the clock. The crackle of the logs burning in the Aga. But there was nothing. She was being plunged into the netherworld and she was helpless to stop it. And slowly they came. She could hear the steps of the barefooted ghosts, padding down stairs and creeping through the corridors; the creak of a floorboard, the opening of a door. Jennifer's eyes flickered open and closed. They were here. Without knowing it, the trance had drawn her in, and her sixth sense had taken over. Her eyes crept around the room as she watched with second sight. A blue-tinged haze had crept in like a fog, forming shapes and outlines of the dead long gone, shoulders hunched, huddling around the table, desperate to have their say.

The figure of an old lady materialised before her, staring pointedly in Jennifer's direction. Her misty eyes narrowed in disdain, as if Jennifer had no right to be there.

Jennifer drew in a chilled breath, before dropping her gaze to her hands. She could feel them closing in around her. But she didn't want to speak to them, and her heart skipped a beat as she built up a mental barrier, closing herself off to the hungry spirits.

'My, the spirits are keen to speak tonight.' Marcella's eyes flickered and she shook her head. 'I'm sorry. We are here only to speak to Abigail. Don't be scared, child. Come talk to us.'

Jennifer kept her eyes cast firmly on the table as an icy coolness seeped in behind her. Soon all she could hear was the swoosh of blood as her heartbeat pounded in her ears. It felt as if a cube of ice had been rubbed on the nape of her neck, and other-world fingers slowly caressed her skin. Tiny hairs prickled on the back of her neck and she fought her natural instincts to run. Jennifer risked a glance upwards. The candles flickered, then one by one snuffed out. One, two, three . . . the darkness was closing in. Marcella chanted under her breath, urging Abigail to come forth.

Jennifer's breath quickened as fingers stroked her face. They held the coldness of the graveyard, festering in a world they should have moved on from decades ago. Her heart was beating wildly now, and her eyes locked on the pallid face of Marcella's companion, pleading with him as she held in a scream. She couldn't break the circle now, even if she wanted to. She was rooted to the spot. *If only she could get to the light switch. Then everything would disappear.*

'Be gone,' the boy said, breathing out the words in a whisper. 'You are not welcome. Go now, do you hear?'

Just for a moment, Jennifer felt as if the air were being sucked out of her lungs. They had been trying to enter her body, to use her as a voice to the outside world. But as soon as the boy's words were uttered, the spirits withdrew. She dragged in a sharp breath, and Marcella raised her head.

'Are you all right?' she asked, as all eyes turned on Jennifer.

She bobbed her head in three sharp nods, not trusting herself to speak. She wanted to scrub her skin, to wash away the feeling of the insistent bodies crowding in around her.

'I'm afraid Abigail's not speaking,' Marcella said, 'but I *can* sense a child's presence . . .'

Joanna glanced around. 'Oh, the candles on the mantelpiece have gone out. Will I light some more?'

'Do not break the circle,' Marcella said, her tone dour. The centrepiece candles illuminated her displeasure. 'Are you listening to me? I said I sense your *daughter.*'

Joanna apologised, squirming in her chair.

Marcella drew her attention inwards. 'Your child . . . She's buried under the ground. She will not rest until you bring her home.'

'Where?' Jennifer said, with sudden belief in Marcella's powers. 'Where is she?'

'She is not in the woodlands, or the river, but it is somewhere vast. Somewhere near home . . .' Her eyelids fluttered shut as she tried to delve further. 'I . . . I see a "V" sign. Two blackened fingers.'

'Yes?' Jennifer said, gnawing her bottom lip. Two blackened fingers meant nothing to her, but right now she would take whatever she could get.

'I'm picking up the energy of a man. He has done things . . . things he has come to regret. He seeks forgiveness.'

'Forgiveness for what?' Joanna asked, taking the words out of Jennifer's mouth.

'He's too ashamed to say. There's a strong family link.'

'Who is it?' Joanna said.

A cold breeze chilled the air as Marcella's features softened, and she began speaking through pursed lips. The childish voice that carried on her breath made Jennifer's spine crawl.

'Please, Daddy, not that, don't make me do that.' The room fell silent as the meaning became clear. 'I'll be a good girl, please Daddy, no, I don't want to.'

'Who is this?' Marcella said, breaking away from the voice inhabiting her body. 'Who is this speaking?'

The voice mocked, as Marcella's features turned upwards in a smile. 'Half a pound of tuppennny rice, half a pound of treacle. That's the way the money goes . . .' She grasped Joanna's wrist, digging in her nails as she screeched the line, her face sneering, a weathered hag. 'Pop! Goes the weasel.'

A scream rose in Joanna's throat as she pulled away from the table, knocking the candles and leaving the circle in a pool of darkness. 'Get away from me, get away!' Tripping over herself, she stumbled in the darkness to reach the light switch, flicking it on before finding the door and slamming it behind her. Heavy footsteps pounded the stairs and another door slammed above them.

'She should have left it alone,' Fiona murmured, before going after her.

There remained only Jennifer, Marcella and her helper, who was sitting calmly in his chair. 'I've given many readings over the years and this has been one of the most difficult,' she said, picking up the spilled candles. 'There are too many conflicting energies in this house, and not all of them have passed on.' She picked at the candle wax beginning to solidify in a white puddle on the table. 'This house . . . or perhaps the land of this house . . . is not a positive energy. It does not bring love, or joy, but desolation and sorrow. It will drag this family down into the depths of despair.'

A stifled sob leaked in from the doorway. Jennifer swivelled around, taken aback by Joanna's naked expression. Gone was the plastic veneer and the robotic smile. Her neatly pinned hair fell loose in strands around her face, and tears ran in rivulets down her cheeks, dragging black mascara trails in their wake. Her words came staggered, as if each syllable caused her pain.

'What you said about the man . . . Daddy . . . and the voice of the little girl . . . was that Abigail? Was she talking about my . . . husband?'

'I'm sorry,' Marcella said, taking Joanna's hand as she took her seat at the table. 'I cannot say. I left myself an open vessel. The messages could be from many years ago, or present day. It's like tuning in to a radio. You don't know what you're going to get. But you *should* get your family away from here. I feel there is worse to come if you stay.'

'Worse? How . . . how can there be worse?' Joanna said, sobbing and hiccupping as her emotions ran free. Marcella's hand hovered over her back, and she patted her a couple of times, murmuring something about being in touch. Fiona appeared, mouthing that it was okay, and she reached across to put the kettle on, signalling at them to leave Joanna to her.

Jennifer was torn. Did this mean Joanna had suspicions about her husband? Was this the secret he was trying to hide? It would be something she would have to tackle later. She followed Marcella out to the front, having formed some respect for the woman. Her companion, seemingly unaffected by the experience, was waiting beside Marcella's blue Toyota Yaris, parked in the yard. He seemed unaffected too by the rain, which had eased, due to a break in the showers.

Marcella touched Jennifer's arm lightly, keeping her tone low. 'You have the gift. I see it in you.'

'I have something,' Jennifer said, as if she was talking about an infectious disease. 'It's not wanted, though.'

Marcella emitted a soft chuckle. 'My dear, the gift of insight is indiscriminate. But you shouldn't be scared of it. They can sense your fear and will use it against you.'

Jennifer stared out into the yard. The fullness of night had closed in, camouflaging the fields in a sheet of metal grey. An owl screeched in the distance, flapping as it broke free from a tree, its white feathers tearing into the fabric of the night. 'I try to keep my distance from spirits,' Jennifer finally said. 'My interests lie in the police.'

'But for you they come hand in hand. You are a carer and a giver. A protector of people who is unable to defend herself,' Marcella said, her eyes following the owl's journey. 'Remember, not all spirits are here to hurt you.'

'Perhaps,' Jennifer said, not wanting to dwell on her inadequacies. 'He looks like you,' she said, her gaze on the boy. 'Are you related?'

Marcella smiled. 'He's my son. He doesn't leave my side.'

Jennifer frowned as she worked out the age gap. 'Your son? But . . .' She froze mid-sentence, her eyes growing wide as the truth dawned.

'You are fortunate that he chose to show himself to you. I don't always see him, but I know he's there.'

'But he looks so real . . .' Jennifer said, returning her gaze to the silent figure. Embodiments of the dead were nothing new to her, but she had never witnessed one appear so tangible, so completely human in appearance as this young man.

'He *is* real. Perhaps now you understand what I meant about help being there if you need it. You also have guides. You need to open up to them.'

Jennifer stared at the young man, at the gentle hint of a smile on his lips. A silent *thank you* passed between them before he faded into the ether. That was why Fiona and Joanna had never acknowledged him. They couldn't see him.

She followed Marcella out to the car, holding open the door as she pulled the seatbelt around her. 'This case . . . Is there anything more you can help me with?'

Marcella leaned forward and whispered croakily. 'This family is immersed in secrets, but the answer lies near. And the child . . .' Marcella shook her head. 'I feel she's dead, or very close to it. There's a strong energy in that house, a hate born of anger.' She turned the ignition, and revved the Yaris into life.

Jennifer didn't care if she was begging. The woman had proved herself and she was going to accept help anywhere she could find it. She leaned into the open door, her eyes wide and pleading. 'From whom? Please. Can't you give me anything more to go on?'

Rain danced in the car headlights as Marcella thought her words over. After what felt like a lifetime of silence, she spoke. 'The person responsible for Abigail's disappearance is connected with the family. Abigail knew the last person to see her alive and she left with them willingly.'

CHAPTER THIRTY-ONE

Joanna

Joanna awoke, foggy and disorientated. Had she really heard a door slam downstairs or was she imagining it? Groping in the darkness, she clicked the small plastic light switch next to the bed. The bedside lamp cast a jaundiced yellow hue, doing little to enhance the murky room. She sat up in the bed, unease creeping over her. High ceilings and damp covings sucked any heat generated from the Aga and the smell of rotting wood never left. It was no wonder the estate agent had snapped her hand off when she offered the full asking price. Just what possessed her to take on such an enormous undertaking? The surveyors had warned her, but once she set her mind on something . . . Her chin dipped as her body returned to a drug-induced sleep, and she jolted as the rumble of a storm erupted outside.

Rubbing her eyes, she peered around the room. Where was Nick anyway? She rested her palm on his side of the bed. The sheet was cold. The last thing she remembered was him popping two sleeping tablets from the foil pack and handing them to her with a glass of water. There was no point in them both being awake, he said. She knew all about his wretched insomnia. She squinted at the bedside clock, the display screaming 3 a.m. in bright red numbers. He couldn't be searching for Abigail at this time of the night. The rain was hammering against the mossy slate roof, and didn't sound as if it was going to let up anytime soon.

It wasn't the first time she had awoken to find herself alone. She walked across the cold wooden floorboards to peep through their bedroom window, and was rewarded by a flash of light. The heavy rain bounced against puddles in the yard. The Land Rover was gone. *Where's he gone at this hour? And who is he with?* A small voice played out in her head as she withdrew from the window. *He's having an affair. You've got to confront him.* She gave it fleeting consideration. No, it was easier to push it away. She reached over to the brass bedpost and pulled on the long grey cardigan that used to be his. She had commandeered it after their first night together, when they got up for cigarettes and coffee in the frosty winter night. He had wrapped the cardigan around her shoulders, gently kissing the back of her neck. But any remnant of comfort from the worn garment had evaporated long ago. She delved her hands into the sagging pockets, wrapping her fingers around the foil pack Nick had given her earlier with great insistence. Six tablets left. There were enough to send her into oblivion. She popped two and dry swallowed them, producing enough saliva to ease their journey. Nick's not gone far, she thought, pulling back her covers. I'll just go back to sleep and . . . she froze as her bedroom door slowly creaked open.

'Nick?' she said, stiffening as a cool breeze wrapped around her shoulders like an icy scarf.

No answer. The door gaped open, and she peered into the gloom, wishing they had replaced the landing bulb. 'Olivia? Is that you?' she asked weakly, slowly stepping towards the door.

A wave of drowsiness overcame her, and her body fought with the recently ingested drugs to stay awake. 'Nick?' she said. But a cold realisation dawned. It wasn't Nick. She would have heard the car pull into the yard. She clasped a hand to her chest as a loud creak echoed on the stairs. It was the wonky step, the third one up. But who was treading on it? And were they coming up or going down?

Her heart beat like a hammer from under her thin cotton nightdress. She was not a wind-up toy; she was flesh and bone and scared out of her skin. She gripped the bedpost as she heard a scuffling noise from downstairs, and fought against the drowsiness invading her body. Something or someone was out there. The tinkle of a Jack-in-the-box echoed through the air, each pin plucking an eerie note as the handle cranked forward. But who was turning it? She held her breath as she stepped forward into the landing, peeping in on Olivia, asleep in her bed. Heart pounding, she tentatively descended the stairs, her fingers gripping the worn banister for support. Staring into the darkness, she cursed whoever had turned off the downstairs light. The absence of streetlights left the house in inky blackness as the haunting melody played. Olivia didn't have a Jack-in-the-box. But *she* did. Once. The words of the rhyme replayed to the tune playing in the hall.

Half a pound of tuppenny rice, half a pound of treacle. That's the way the money goes – the tune paused. Joanna stiffened as she descended the stairs. *Pop! Goes the weasel.*

She blindly grasped for the light switch, her body fighting the drug-induced stupor. Gasping with relief, she clicked on the switch and spun around to greet her tormentor. But the villain was a vintage Jack-in-the-box, lying in the middle of the floor. Eyes vibrating, it had been propelled from its rusty metal tomb. Joanna stared at the grinning, evil thing, as if it were ready to pounce. Yet there was something familiar about it, and she recoiled as a long buried memory filtered through the fog. She pressed her palms flat against the wall, sidling past the small rusted toy.

'Who's there?' she said, pushing the kitchen door open.

She flicked on the light, agog at the empty room. There was nobody there. Nobody human. The cold grip of fear clutched at her throat as a flash of memory returned . . . the tinkle of a Jack-in-the-box. She stumbled back to the hall, staring in disbelief at the unmoving toy. 'No . . . you're not real,' she gasped, tripping on her nightdress as she bolted upstairs.

Her heart froze as a flash of lightning revealed a ghostly white figure standing on the landing. It was Olivia, staring with empty eyes, her nightdress billowing in the breeze. Wind and rain whooped in through her bedroom window, causing her door to swing back and forth. Muggy and confused, Joanna ushered her little girl into bed. With great concentration, she closed the rain-drenched window before stumbling into her room to grab her phone. She must ring Nick, she thought, as another rumble of thunder passed overhead. She needed him here.

Rubbing her eyes in desperation, she tried to focus on the blurred screen. A cold chill ran over her, and she climbed under the bedcovers as her heart raced. Had she taken three sleeping tablets tonight? Or was it four? The phone fell from her hand onto the bedroom floor, the whites of her eyes rolling upwards before her eyelids flickered shut.

Olivia stood in the doorway, watching her mother as she fell into a thick black sleep.

Her pillow felt moist on her cheek as Nick's fingers dug into her shoulder, shaking her awake. His voice was edgy and cold.

'How can you sleep when Abigail is missing? Wake up, will you? People are wondering where you are.'

Nick pulled across the heavy curtain, and dazzling sunlight spilled into the room.

Joanna crossed her forearm over her eyes as the light beamed over her face. 'What? . . . What time is it?'

'It's almost eleven o'clock. Mum and Dad are expecting us at mass. Everyone's going to be there.' A pang of regret crossed his face, and his voice softened as he sat on her side of the bed. 'I know you're dealing with this in your own way, but you need to get dressed and go down there.'

Joanna tried to swallow, and her throat clicked in response. Bob and Wendy had railroaded them into holding a mass for their daughter, assuring her it wasn't a memorial, simply a place where people could come and pray for her safe return. She had had no choice but to agree. But why wasn't Nick there already? And how had she slept in so long?

'Where were you last night?' she croaked, an uneasy feeling of distrust creeping in.

'What do you mean?'

'I woke up and you were gone.'

Nick frowned as he rose. 'I was here all night.'

'The Jack-in-the-box. Did you see it?' Joanna said, fighting for clarity.

'What *are* you on about?'

'Last night I heard something downstairs. The Land Rover was gone. *You* were gone. I heard a Jack-in-the-box in the hall.'

Nick looked at her as if she had gone mad. 'A Jack-in-the-box? You must have been dreaming.'

'No, I wasn't,' Joanna said firmly. 'I woke up and took more sleeping tablets. It's why I slept in. Pass me your cardigan,' she said, pointing to the garment she didn't remember taking off. 'The foil pack is in the pocket, there're four tablets missing.'

Nick reached over to the bedpost, the sleeve of his shirt rising up.

'Your arms . . . they're all scratched,' Joanna said, as Nick unhooked the cardigan from the bedpost and threw it on the bed.

Nick unrolled his shirt sleeves, buttoning them at the wrist. 'Of course they are. I've been through every bush and thicket this side of Haven.'

Joanna pulled out the foil pack from the pocket of the frayed cardigan. She blinked, her face frozen in disbelief as she stared at two puncture holes. 'There should be four missing. I swear. I took four tablets last night.'

Nick threw her an exasperated look before turning on his heel. 'I'm sorry, Jo, I can't deal with this right now. Just . . . just get dressed and go to mass. Fiona's already gone with Olivia.'

Joanna stared at the pack trembling between her fingers. Her throat felt sore and raw. She hoped she wasn't coming down with something. That would be too bad. But thoughts of an illness weren't enough to block her rising anxiety. Unable to move, she felt a black tide rise from within, threatening to engulf her. Her breath quickened as the beginnings of a panic attack flooded her system. She grasped the sheets between her fingers as she fought for breath. She was losing control. Releasing the sheets, she slapped her right cheek hard. Her breath faltered. Good. That was good. She slapped with the left hand, harder this time. She gasped, as sweet release was delivered with each stinging blow. Her breath slowed, and her focus returned to the room. The breeze from the open window, the sound of muffled voices carried from downstairs. Her eyes crept to her phone on the bedside table. She recalled hearing the clunk as it hit the mat when she fell asleep. So what was it doing there? Pulling back her right hand, she slapped her cheek hard, sending her head rocking to the left. She rose effortlessly from the bed and walked into her en suite. An icy cold shower would take away the redness, and she would welcome the stinging pain. It was the least she deserved.

CHAPTER THIRTY-TWO

Three Days Gone

'Thanks for coming,' Jennifer said.

Mr Struthers stood at the front of the house, leaning on his granddaughter's arm. Her name was Danni, and she was twenty-four years old. It had taken some persuading to get Danni to bring her grandfather, but not many people could turn down the plight of a little girl in trouble. His lined face stared at the building for a long while, sadness reflected in his eyes.

'Let's get you inside, Granddad,' the young curly-haired woman said, easing him forward. They were both of the same tall, slim stature, and Danni had warned Jennifer that her grandfather wasn't as good on his legs as he used to be. But given his age, Jennifer was just grateful he could get around.

'I said I'd never come here again,' Mr Struthers said, emitting a deep sigh of resignation. His feet seemed rooted to the spot, and he glanced back at his granddaughter's car, perhaps wondering if it wasn't too late to change his mind and go back home.

'Danni got in touch after I posted on a forum about Blackwater Farm. Mr Struthers is one of the previous occupants,' Jennifer said, as Nick came outside.

'Mr Struthers,' Nick said, outstretching his hand. 'I'm Abigail's father. I really appreciate your time.'

'I know who you are,' he said. 'I only wish I could have stopped you buying this damned place before you did, then none of this would have happened.'

'Why don't we go inside and talk about it?' Jennifer said, painfully conscious of the time. Joanna had left to attend mass and,
despite Jennifer's assurances, Nick had insisted on staying behind
to see what Mr Struthers had to say. Not that she could blame him.
Jennifer's faith lay in being productive. Each second that passed was
another second Abigail remained in the cold unforgiving ground.
Prayers could come later.

Mr Struthers sat uneasily at the table with a cup of tea in his
hand. Jennifer knew from their communications that he had had
his own experiences with the dark entity that lurked within the
walls of Blackwater Farm.

'I can't say the place has changed much,' he said, raising the
cup to his lips.

'We have plans to redecorate,' Nick said, opening his mouth
to continue.

But Mr Struthers cut him short, his voice flat and disparaging.
'Don't. This place has caused nothing but grief. It should be burnt
to the ground.' Mr Struthers took in the room, his neck shrinking
back into the collar of his shirt, like an aged tortoise. 'Can't you feel
it?' he whispered, his eyes widening. 'It's still here . . . the darkness
is all around you.'

Jennifer caught her breath, her fingers finding the small silver
crucifix around her neck. *The darkness is all around you.* Such words
had been spoken to her before. And at that time, it had not ended well.

'We were young when we moved in here, my wife and I,' Mr
Struthers said. 'We had big plans too. We didn't know what the
symbols were at first, but the more we stripped back this old house,
the more we found. Pauline – my wife – she took pictures and
brought them to the library. They told her they were satanic. That
was the day it all began.'

The light bulb rattled overhead. Mr Struthers glanced up at the
ceiling and frowned at the interruption.

'The doctors said it was post-natal depression. But our baby was nine months old. Pauline doted on him up until then. All of a sudden, she became withdrawn. She had no time for anything or anyone,' he said, his voice growing thin. 'She told me things were happening in the house, but I said she was being silly. It wasn't until I saw it for myself that I knew something else lived here with us. Something evil.'

Jennifer realised she had been holding her breath, and let it go. She wished she had discussed his experiences somewhere neutral, and not at the farm. An icy prickle touched her senses. The darkness Mr Struthers spoke about was aware of his presence. She could feel it, drawing near, feeding off the attention. Nick rubbed the back of his neck, a puzzled expression on his face. He turned to Jennifer.

'I don't understand. What's this got to do with Abigail?'

'It's got everything to do with your daughter.' Mr Struthers banged the table with his fist, before she could respond. 'Don't you see? When I moved here, I was just like you. But I soon learned such things existed, and paid for it dearly.'

'Don't go upsetting yourself,' Danni said, patting his arm.

'I'm all right, love' he replied, resting his hand on top of hers. But he didn't look all right. He seemed to have aged since he entered the kitchen, each word a struggle to deliver. 'I couldn't save your grandmother,' he said, with a tremble in his voice. 'Maybe I can do some good now.' He took a deep breath as he addressed Nick. 'Mr Duncan, I know you most likely think I'm senile, but think on this. This house has been the ruin of every family that lived here. Move away. You'll never be happy at Blackwater Farm.'

'I can't. Not until I've found Abigail.'

'I lost my wife to this house,' Mr Struthers mumbled under his breath.

He was drifting into the past, and Jennifer needed him to focus. 'I know how hard it's been for you, returning here. But I wanted to ask you about the land. Are there any sinkholes or wells that you are aware of?'

'I know every inch of this land,' he said. 'I used to roam it at night, when I couldn't sleep.'

Word of the man's insomnia was enough for Nick to start taking him seriously. 'We had the land checked by a surveyor. There's no well on the plans.'

'There wouldn't be,' Mr Struthers said, easing into a standing position. 'They don't know about it. But I can show you where it is.'

'Best we not waste any more time, then,' Jennifer said, turning the handle of the back door.

CHAPTER THIRTY-THREE

Jennifer's earlier research had made for grim reading. Wells could be up to fifty feet deep, with water averaging at six feet. If Abigail had fallen into one of those, she wouldn't have stood a chance. Some dried out over time, or were filled in by previous occupants. In a place as old as Haven, some were likely to have never been recorded. Jennifer had no way of knowing about the condition of the well Mr Struthers was referring to, or if there was one at all. She had simply put out a plea on the internet forum, asking for information from previous occupants of Blackwater Farm. It was a primitive way of enquiring, given police had already investigated the land registry and the recent survey, but one that appeared to be paying off.

After twenty minutes of walking, Jennifer's heart began to sink. They were going around in circles. The land was drenched from the storm the night before. She hadn't called for back-up for this very reason. Too many false leads had been generated for police, and this was proving to be one of them. She took a breath as she gathered her wits, and when Mr Struthers stumbled on the churned up soil, she suggested that they call it a day.

'It's around here somewhere,' Mr Struthers said, with Nick on one side and Danni on the other.

Jennifer followed the old man's gaze past the rusted gate. She paused mid stride, and stared incredulously at the landscape to see an old burned out tree, split in half from the lightning storm.

Gnarled and deadened, it reached into the sky. That's it, she thought. Two blackened fingers, jutting out from the charred earth in a 'V' sign. The landmark the medium had forecast. She was here. Abigail was here.

'Wait,' Jennifer said. 'Mr Struthers, do you see that tree? It wasn't always that way. Is that what's putting you off?'

The man turned and peered in the distance. 'Yes . . . Near the tree. That way.' He pointed a withered finger to the left of the burned out wooden carcass at the foot of the field.

They followed the tyre tracks as they wound around the tree, cautiously picking their way through the mud that had clearly been searched before them.

'Here,' Mr Struthers said. 'Next to the trailer.'

It was little wonder that police had not found the well, if it was buried under the rusted trailer. But recent tyre tracks suggested the trailer had been moved.

'I've found something,' Nick said, testing the ground with his boot.

Throwing the rope he had brought to one side, he dropped to his hands and knees and the whites of his eyes flashed as he clawed manically at the loose soil. Jennifer fell to her knees and joined him in digging. She could almost feel Abigail's fear as the little girl fell into the muddied tomb. But when she called her name, she was met with silence. Her fingernails scratched against tarpaulin, and she paused only to text Will in a confusing babble of words. Abigail in a well at farm. Call ambulance and fire. Seconds later her phone buzzed, but she didn't have time to answer. Will trusted her enough to do as she asked. Help would soon be at hand.

Red-cheeked and panting, she pushed back the earth, aware of Mr Struthers in the background, whispering a quiet prayer.

'Be careful,' she said to Nick, 'come back to the edge, don't fall in.'

Grunting with exertion, Nick heaved back the layers of mud, and wrapped his fingers around the corner of the tarpaulin. 'Pull back the other side,' he said, sweat trickling down his face as he stood back from the edge.

'Perhaps we should wait for the –' Mr Struthers began to say, before Jennifer butted in.

'She's waited long enough.'

Nick nodded, taking up the far corner and pulling the tarpaulin across. A look passed between Nick and Jennifer, an exchange of understanding. They were both on the same side. And they weren't going to wait another second to set Abigail free. In the distance, a siren screamed. It was barely discernible as it sped through the country lanes to their location. *They're not quick enough,* the thought resounded through her mind each time she considered waiting. Her brain told her to wait for back-up, and allow the experts to plan a proper entry into the muddied hole. But her heart won out. Abigail could be dying down there. They could not afford to wait for strategies and pre-entry briefings. She was going in. But as she approached, her expression was a mixture of apprehension and regret.

CHAPTER THIRTY-FOUR

Nick joined Jennifer at the edge of the hole and stared into the gaping darkness. It was black as the night, and encased in rough circular brick. The stench of rotting soil and brick rose up, and Jennifer realised that there was something else intermingled with the smell, something not born of the land. As Jennifer and Nick leaned further forward to inspect the inside of the well, Mr Struthers and his granddaughter backed away, heads lowered in respect.

'Abi,' Nick called. 'Sweetheart, can you hear us?'

His words echoed in the hollow void, returning no response. Suddenly the wind dropped, the birds stopped singing, and there was nothing but perfect silence. As if Haven was waiting for what lay below. Sensing his discomfort, Jennifer gently placed a hand on his back.

'It's okay, Nick,' she whispered. 'Whatever we find . . . If she's down there, we're going to bring her home.'

Jennifer stood with her hands on her hips as she peered into the well, mentally preparing herself for what was to come.

Nick pulled off his coat and shone the torch on his phone. 'I'm going down there,' he said.

She followed the beam of light into the gloom. It did not reach the bottom.

'Oh no, you're not,' she said. 'The last thing we want is you landing on Abigail.'

She plucked a stone from the ground and held it between finger and thumb. Dropping it into the depths of the darkness, she held her breath until she heard the splash. The hole was surely no more than fifteen feet down, but they had no way of telling how deep the water was.

'Thank you both,' Jennifer said, giving Mr Struthers a nod of gratitude. 'Can you find your way back to the house and direct the emergency services to our location?'

A look of relief spread over Danni's face at the prospect of getting away. 'Of course. C'mon, Grandad, let's get you inside in the warm.'

Mr Struthers didn't argue. Neither of them wanted to see what lay ahead.

'I'm going to climb down,' Nick said, handing one end of the rope to Jennifer. 'I'll lean against the wall, so you shouldn't have to take my weight.'

'Are you serious?' Jennifer said. 'I'm not strong enough to take your weight. What if you fall? I'm lighter than you. Let me do it.' She placed a hand on his tensed shoulder. 'Please, Nick.' She wanted to say that they did not know what faced them. If Abigail was dead, then Jennifer would prefer to take the memory of finding her body than allowing the little girl's father to. Nick nodded solemnly, his face dark with emotion.

'Whatever happens, I need you to stay up here,' Jennifer said firmly. 'It's a narrow space and it could cave in. If it does, just wait for the emergency services. There's been enough tragedy.'

The cold wet mud had numbed her fingers, and she forced them to grip the bristled rope. Dirt patches stained the knees and arms of her suit, but it was the least of her worries as she squeezed into the narrow space. She looked regretfully at the trailer. If only it had been nearer, she could have anchored herself to the metal. But she needed every inch of rope, and would have to trust Nick to take her weight. But if he let her fall . . . it didn't bear thinking about.

Her tongue clicked against the roof of her mouth as she swallowed back her nervousness. Descending into the filthy hole was her worst nightmare, but the thought of Abigail drove her on. Yes, she should wait for the experts, but she knew from experience that risk assessments and safety equipment took time to set up. Abigail's life could be hanging in the balance and she couldn't afford to wait. She took one last breath of the clean outside air before shuffling down into the claustrophobic gloom.

Thin-lipped, Nick gripped the rope, his heels dug solidly into the ground. Jennifer ignored the manic palpitations of her heart. *Left, right, left, right,* she focused on her hands as they moved down the rope. With each step, she delved deeper into the confined space. A slow intake of breath brought another burst of stench rising up to greet her. She balanced her feet against the crumbling brick circle.

'Abigail,' she shouted, her voice echoing against the circular walls. 'If you can hear me, make a noise, a movement, anything.'

But all she could hear was the sound of her own breath. The air was thick and heady; the sort of climate people ran from the second they encountered it. Taking her weight with one hand, she plucked a pebble from her pocket and dropped it into the abyss. She felt like Alice in Wonderland as it slid down the well, but rather than a wonderful adventure, she was faced with a horrific task. The pebble plopped into the water beneath. She prayed that Abigail was somehow alive, and had her head above water. But given the lack of response, it wasn't looking likely. Insects scuttled out of the moss-lined bricks. She took a steadying breath, forcing herself to continue focusing on her hands as they carried on working their way down the rope. But the further she was plunged into the darkness, the more uneasy she became.

Using one hand, she pulled her phone from her pocket and jabbed the torch button, casting the narrow beam below.

'Can you see anything?' Nick's voice echoed all around her.

Jennifer cleared her throat as she stared at the water a few feet below. 'No. Just water.' She gazed up at the light from the entrance hole, and Abigail's words came back to haunt her. It was just like she had said when she had spoken through Olivia: a tunnel, with a light on the other end. And somebody was waiting on the other side. But instead of it being a death experience, it was a traitor, leaving her to die. Jennifer craned her neck to make out Nick's blurry outline, and became painfully aware that her life was in his hands.

She hung, helpless in the silent depths of the well. All hopes of saving Abigail disintegrated. She had done all she could, and the instinct to escape was rising like a tide within her. She reasoned with her decision. If Abigail *was* in the water, there was nothing Jennifer could do for her now. 'Pull me up,' she shouted, ready to hand it over to the professionals. But there was no response, just Nick's outline, staring down as he blotted out the light from above. She tried shouting again, but cold fear restricted her throat, turning her plea into a warble. Why wasn't Nick answering? Gritting her teeth, she willed her body to climb, but holding the phone, the rope and balancing her weight was proving too much, and her limbs trembled in protest.

'No!' she gasped, as her phone slipped between her fingers. She reached out to grab it just as the rope jerked from above. Fingers numbed from the cold, the rope slid between her hands, and she was plunged into the water with a sickening splash. Icy cold water invaded her body, dragging her into its depths. It thundered in her ears, flooding her nostrils, the silt stinging her eyes. She kicked furiously in an effort to break the surface. An image of Abigail flashed in her mind, falling into the water, watching in horror as it rose. Had she died in this underwater tomb? Jennifer scratched the dampened brickwork as she grasped for purchase, her fingernails bending backwards, while she spluttered for air. Helplessly, she slid down the wall, grasping for a rope she could not see. Then it came; a sense of dread that told her she was not alone.

The dark and foreboding presence loomed all around her in the narrow enclosure. Within seconds, she knew it was the same creeping menace she had encountered in Blackwater Farm. But now it was upon her, embedded in the heart of the land. Her search for answers had led her to this place, and Haven did not give up its secrets easily. A deathly presence settled in the well.

Cold hands tugged her ankles, and she fought back the rising panic as her head bobbed beneath the water a second time. Drawing on her police training, she forced herself to think rationally. It wasn't hands. It was the rush of the water streaming through the weakening brickwork below. But where was the rope? She reached blindly in the darkness, spluttering as she swallowed the tainted water. *Don't leave me down here*, she thought, blinking in the darkness as a shadow descended overhead. 'Take my hand,' a male voice said. His strong warm hand gripped her forearm, dragging her upwards into his embrace. It was Will. He had climbed down the rope and he wasted no time in pulling her onto dry land.

'What the hell do you think you're playing at?' he said, pulling off his coat and wrapping it around her.

Jennifer retched as she coughed up dirty water. She waved away the paramedics, as an assortment of emergency services piled in. 'I couldn't find her,' she said between chattering teeth. 'It's too late. She's gone.'

CHAPTER THIRTY-FIVE

Diary Entry

To say it's been eventful would be an understatement. By the time I went back to the well, it was almost too late. The water was just a puddle when I first saw Abigail, sitting at the bottom, staring upwards through eyes from which she could barely see. She had even dug a hole, and sat on the mound as the water trickled in. I hadn't expected to see it rise so sharply. An underground stream, perhaps, dislodged from the movement above land. Any later and she would have drowned. She mewed, weakly like a kitten, her puny arms reaching up to the light. To her, I was nothing but a blur. Why couldn't I have left her there?

I am at war with myself. It's too late for anything else now. But I won't be rushed. And I can't risk her discovery. That's why I moved her. The rain has been both a curse and a blessing. I've had to work hard to keep the police off my back, and was grateful that it was washing away my tracks. But the mud and water made her extraction all the more difficult. Like plucking a tooth out of a diseased gum, I pulled her, pale and feeble from the stinking well. The water had risen to her chest. I climbed back up the rope ladder I had hitched to my car, pulling her up by the straps of her dungarees. All that time, I fought a battle in my head. Why didn't I just leave her there? Why did I have to return? But the compulsion was too strong to bear. So, I took her somewhere more fitting. Somewhere she can die in peace, and take my tortured memories with her.

CHAPTER THIRTY-SIX

Recovery from her ordeal came all the quicker when news filtered through to Jennifer that Abigail's body was not in the well. A hot bath and a change of clothes later, she was ready to face the world. But there were so many questions to be answered, and her concern for Olivia grew. She could be the only living witness to her sister's abduction. And if the police didn't find Abigail soon, Olivia could be their only lead. Something Abigail's abductor would also be aware of – if such a person existed.

The seriousness of the situation had warranted further briefing and, humiliated after being told off by DCI Anderson, she was not in a hurry for a repeat performance as she entered the office of Operation Moonlight. But DI Ethan Cole was not going to allow her off the hook that easily.

Office chairs were wheeled into a circle and the team were invited to take a seat. Ethan rolled up his shirt sleeves, the endless shifts drawing dark circles under his eyes. The office smelled of last night's takeaway, and Jennifer wrinkled her nose as she picked the most comfortable chair.

'What was it, curry?' she whispered to Will.

'Yeah, we've worked long hours this week. I had the leftovers for breakfast this morning,' Will replied, smirking at Jennifer's disgusted reaction.

DI Cole stood in the centre of the circle, silencing their conversation.

'I know you've got your own workloads to be getting on with, but if you'll pull up a seat, I'd like you to join in with a quick brainstorming session.'

Claire, Jennifer's sergeant, wheeled in beside her, across from Zoe and Will. Jennifer flashed her a smile. It was nice being back in the bosom of her team, if only for a few minutes.

Ethan clapped his hands together, making Claire jump.

'Right! DCI Anderson has been working with some highly regarded criminal profilers on this case. I've condensed their reports. Although some of the information is conflicting, I've taken the main points from each one.' Picking up a manila folder, he slid out some paperwork and handed the sheets around.

'When children under five are missing feared dead, in most cases one of the parents is responsible. They could be suffering from a mental health illness, post-natal psychosis, or, more commonly in fathers, it involves a domestic incident in which they kill their children then commit suicide.' Ethan glanced at the paper, although the words seemed committed to memory. 'Where the missing children are aged five years and over, outside intervention is also probable. The reports profiled the suspect as likely to be male, between the ages of eighteen and forty-five, with past criminal convictions. He may be known to the family, and could have had direct contact with Abigail, or been in a trusted position, for example a friend of the family, work colleague, relative, or someone the parents know.'

Jennifer nibbled her bottom lip as she followed her DI's words on the sheet of paper. The suspect was sounding more like Radcliffe by the second.

'The abductor may be shy, withdrawn, living alone or with a parent, socially inept, and have a powerful imagination. They may take refuge in fantasy. In this imaginary world, they are a powerful person, admired by others. The more time they spend in this fantasy, the less satisfied they become with their everyday existence. They retreat into their imaginary world, making it so vivid, so real, that it eventually takes over their real life. '

'But aren't we in danger of making the personality fit the profile?' Jennifer asked. 'The first example sounds like Radcliffe, but the second paragraph sounds more like Joanna.'

'Perhaps,' Ethan said. 'Remember, it's just there to guide us. And if it sounds like two, or three, or five people, then they are the people we need to be putting under the microscope. The report also states that the individual could be shy, anxious and reserved, someone who feels inferior to their peers. That sounds like both parties again, doesn't it?'

Jennifer nodded, scanning the rest of the page. *In their fantasy world, they become omnipotent and powerful. But the more they take flight into the imagination, the more real it becomes. As a result of this secret inner world, family, neighbours and friends may never guess they are capable of such a crime.*

She tuned back in to Ethan's voice, which carried back and forth as he continued to pace the room.

'We've also investigated the possibility of a revenge plot, given that Mr Duncan is a police sergeant, and we've toyed with the idea of a failed ransom abduction, given his wife's success. However, there's nothing to suggest either at this time. It's also unlikely that Abigail made acquaintance with the offender online and arranged a meet.'

'From what Olivia has said, and my experiences in the well, I agree,' Jennifer said.

Ethan slid the paper back into the folder. 'Can you fill us in on that?'

Jennifer nodded. 'Up until recently, a trailer had covered the well – which means someone's been there and moved it to one side.' She stretched her legs, her body stiff from her exertions. 'DCI Anderson said the well could have been discovered by a local who, finding nothing inside, covered it back up for safety reasons.'

'And you disagree with his findings?' DI Cole said.

Jennifer nodded. 'From what Abigail's said through her sister, I feel she was there. But there's something very dark attached to the farm. It wasn't a very pleasant experience down there.'

'Thoughts, anyone?' Ethan said, opening it up to the team.

'Do you think this dark energy is responsible for Abigail's disappearance?' Claire asked.

Jennifer was quick to answer. 'No. But it's possibly influencing the actions of people involved.'

'It's related to the house,' Zoe said. 'Blackwater Farm was used to practise the dark arts years ago. It's like a . . .' Zoe squinted one eye, constructing her words. 'Call it a negative energy if you like . . . There are lots of spirits attached to the house, but this energy is malevolent. It can't directly harm us, but it *has* depressive qualities.'

Jennifer turned to her colleagues to explain. 'Whatever was invoked back then has a strong presence now. I felt it when I was in the well too. I don't think it can do much, other than draw out what's already there, but there was a moment when . . .' She tailed off.

'Go on,' Ethan said. 'It won't go beyond this office.'

'Well,' Jennifer sighed. 'Nick was standing over me, holding the rope. I shouted for help, but he was staring at me with this weird expression on his face. I hate to distrust a colleague, but . . . I couldn't get back on dry land quick enough.'

'You said the rope jerked, making you lose your grip. Do you think he let you fall on purpose?' Will asked, a mixture of anger and concern darkening his face.

Jennifer recognised that look. Will could be fiercely protective, and she wouldn't put it past him to confront Nick for not taking better care. It was better to put her reservations to one side than to start some sort of feud. 'No, not at all. You know, thinking about it, I just freaked out. You know what I'm like in confined spaces.'

'What I don't understand is,' Ethan said, displaying his characteristic hand gestures, 'why would they take the chance of going back and removing her? You said yourself, the well was filling up fast with water. They risked a lot, going back there.'

'But did they?' Jennifer replied, having already mulled it over in her head. 'If it was a member of the family, or even a local, all they had to do was to say they were looking for Abigail and had just come across her. They would have been the hero of the day. Who's to say any different?'

'Unless the kid was still alive,' Zoe said, crossing her legs.

Jennifer nodded, smiling at the purple Harry Potter socks peeping out from Zoe's trouser legs. 'Yeah, but without her glasses she can't see very much anyway,'

'Joanna's media hungry. What if this is some weird publicity stunt?' Claire said.

'She definitely likes the publicity,' Will said, 'but chucking your own child in a well is too extreme for that. I think it was someone more sinister, like Radcliffe. He's a weird loner, a bit funny with kids, and – you said yourself – in no hurry to speak to police.'

Jennifer nodded, but more in acknowledgement than agreement. 'There's got to be human involvement in Abigail's disappearance. She hasn't got lost or been hurt. I think someone knows exactly where she is. But Radcliffe? . . . I don't know. There are too many secrets in that family. I can't help but feel they're somehow involved.'

'Radcliffe's been voluntarily interviewed today. So far, he's denied any offences,' Ethan said, spreading his hands wide in a non-committal gesture. 'Has anyone any suggestions as to progressing from here? C'mon, guys, I really want Op Moonlight to crack this case. Getting a result would secure our future.'

Jennifer should have been shocked at Ethan's motivations. To her, finding Abigail was all about getting the little girl safely home to her family. According to Ethan, it was a case that could secure future funding and the respect of his peers. But she hadn't forgotten his earlier comments about not being able to sleep while Abigail was out there, lost and alone. It was a tiny glimpse into his persona. In private, he was caring and considerate, but here, in the driving seat of the Op Moonlight investigation, he was a hard-edged professional. The room fell silent, and a thought entered her mind.

'I've got an idea,' she said, looking in Will's direction. 'But you might not like it.'

CHAPTER THIRTY-SEVEN

'Just remind me why you've volunteered us for this again?' Will said, sliding out a stick of chewing gum from silver foil and throwing the paper on the floor of Jennifer's car.

'Excuse me,' Jennifer frowned before leaning forward and picking it up from the footwell. 'Just because you drive a wheelie bin with an engine doesn't mean I want my car the same way.'

Will's fingers crept up the back of her shirt as she leaned forward, sending a pool of warmth into her stomach. 'And less of that, DC Dunston, this is meant to be a stake-out.'

Will withdrew his hand and gave her a cheeky grin. 'That's a shame. We've not christened the car yet, have we?'

Jennifer straightened in her seat. 'And we won't, either. Can you imagine the mess? Now, can we get back to the matter in hand?'

'Aye aye, captain, whatever you say. But you didn't answer my question. Why are we doing this in our own time? I thought the family were already under surveillance.'

'Cutbacks. They're keeping a close eye on Radcliffe, but can't afford anyone to watch the house. To be fair, they don't have the justification, given that I'm there all day. I would have offered to stay over, but I think I'm wearing out my welcome as it is.'

'She's been three days gone, babe. I hate to say it, but if she's been dumped somewhere it's unlikely she's still alive.'

'But don't you get it?' Jennifer said. 'If she was in that well, then someone's moved her. Our best hope is that they're looking after her and she's alive.'

Jennifer peered out her car window down the moonlit path. It was fortunate that it was a clear night and she had managed to find a good spot to park the car where it would remain unseen. She would have some answering to do if she was caught by a member of the family, and had planned to say they were covert in case anyone presented a threat. Not that Joanna would care. Nick, on the other hand, would present more of a challenge. He was currently on sick leave from the police. But feelings were running high, and she would not have put it past him to ask his colleagues to update him on the investigation. It was another reason why her visit had not been recorded. She would forgo being paid overtime if it meant nobody knew of her visit but the Op Moonlight team. It was hard enough keeping tabs on members of the public. But when it was one of their own police force, it presented a whole new set of challenges.

'So who are we expecting to see?' Will asked. 'Mum, Dad, or both?'

Jennifer shrugged, the memory of Nick standing over her in the well still fresh in her mind. 'God knows. But whoever moved Abigail must have done it under the cover of night. It's only a matter of time before they lead us to her.'

Will's jaw cracked as he yawned. 'Can I ask how long you're expecting to stay? It's gone two-thirty and we both have work in the morning.'

'You didn't have to come,' Jennifer snapped. To her, one sleepless night was a small price to pay if it brought them to the missing child. Will's silence brought forth guilt, and she squeezed his knee. 'I'm sorry, I do appreciate you being here. Give it until three, and then we'll call it a night.'

'I'm not complaining,' Will said. 'I want to find her as much as anyone else, you know.'

Jennifer arched an eyebrow. 'But you think we're wasting our time.'

'It'll be a miracle if she's alive.'

Jennifer returned her gaze to the farmlands. Mercifully, the full moon illuminated the footpath leading to the woodlands beyond. A gap in the thicket gave them a decent view without giving away their location. From her vantage point, Jennifer could see if anyone passed by. There were other routes they could have taken, through hedges, or off to the fields at the back of the house, which eventually led around to the woods, but it was a long hike and if anyone was sneaking out in the dead of night, they would take the quickest route so they could get back quickly without being seen. Jennifer tapped her fingers on her lips as she mused the possible direction of travel. It was doubtful they would return to the well, as it had now been filled in, so the woodlands were the best bet. They provided thick cover, but it was not a good place to visit at night unless you knew where you were going. Although it had been searched by locals and police, large patches would have remained untouched because of the vast density of the woodlands. Hordes of volunteers would have trampled out any scent for the police dogs to find, and, like the helicopter and drones that flew overhead, they had drawn a blank. A terrorist incident in another area of the country had killed off any headlines in the news on Abigail's disappearance, but the social media hate campaign raged on. Will had theorised that if the girl had gone missing from a well populated town, the coverage may have been better. Children went missing all the time. What made one more newsworthy than the other? The surveillance was a last ditch attempt at a resolution. Soon Jennifer's time with the family would come to an end. Police work didn't stop coming in just because there had been a tragic incident involving a child. There would be more cases, more victims piling up and no extra resources to deal with them.

Jennifer realised she was becoming grim and switched her focus. She had come so close already. Perhaps tonight would be the night they would find Abigail.

'I walked in on Nick having a right old barney with his dad today,' Jennifer said, breaking the silence.

'Oh yeah? What about?' Will said, reclining his car seat a notch.

'I think it was because he didn't go to mass. I get the feeling they don't see eye to eye . . . Hang on, I think I can see movement,' Jennifer whispered, ducking down.

A glimpse of white caught her attention. It flickered in the distance, and Jennifer made out a figure in a billowing dress. Or is it a nightdress? she thought, peering through the night. Jennifer could see that the ground was broken and uneven, but the white figure walking towards them seemed to glide.

'What the hell is that?' Will said as they eased out of the car.

'Shh,' Jennifer said, 'keep your voice down, she'll hear you.'

The slim figure of a woman approached, and she recognised it was Joanna, completely oblivious to the outside world. Devoid of make-up and her usual colourful clothes, she resembled a marble statue come to life. The night breeze played with strands of her long blonde hair, and her eyes shone with an ethereal quality as she gazed into the distance. Jennifer noticed she was barefoot, but she wasn't walking with care, as you would over such terrain, but rather passing calmly over the surface.

'I think she's sleepwalking,' Jennifer whispered. 'If she goes too far, we'll have to wake her up.'

'Listen,' Will whispered as she passed them on the path. 'She's talking to herself.'

'I can't make it out. What is it?' Jennifer said, creeping up the path from the other side of the thicket.

'I think she's humming a nursery rhyme,' Will said, struggling to keep his balance on the chewed up terrain.

Jennifer grabbed the sleeve of his jacket to balance herself. She hadn't had the benefit of nursery rhymes when she was young, unlike Will, whose family was comparable to the *Little House on the Prairie*. 'I should have known you'd know that. But why's she singing it?'

'Hold up, she's stopped,' Will said, pulling Jennifer into the thick gorse as Joanna looked to her right.

A yelp escaped Jennifer's lips as thorns embedded themselves into her jeans. She strained her neck to watch, as Joanna looked left, then right, as if she were lost.

'Daddy?' Joanna said. 'Daddy, is that you?'

She looked unsure, and began to cry with child-like sobs. Her sobs subsided into sniffles as she made faltering steps over the rough terrain.

Jennifer was about to blow her cover when she was alerted to heavy footsteps pounding the track from the direction of the house. The beam of a flashlight speared the night as the heavy-footed figure gained ground.

'What do we do now?' Jennifer mouthed to Will as they both crouched down. Will put a finger to his mouth and gestured at her to be silent. It was Nick, out of breath and bewildered.

'What are you doing out here?' Nick said, throwing off his wax jacket and placing it around his wife's shoulders.

Joanna spun around, unblinking as she reached out in the darkness. 'The party . . . Have you seen Daddy?'

'Babe, you're dreaming. Wake up,' Nick said, giving her a gentle shake.

'What?' Joanna said, stumbling on the path. 'Where am I?'

Nick took her by the arm. 'Steady, now. You're sleepwalking. Anything could have happened.'

'I . . . I don't understand,' Joanna said, wincing as she took a faltering step forward on the stony ground.

'Look at your feet.' Nick's voice echoed his pity. 'They're bleeding. Here, put your arm around my shoulders. I'll carry you home.'

Joanna did as she was instructed, and leaned into her husband as he swept her off her feet and carried her up the path. It was a scene reminiscent of an old Mills & Boon novel, and Jennifer wondered if there was hope for their marriage after all.

Jennifer and Will tracked them back to the house, staying until the bedroom light had been extinguished. It was a quarter past three by the time they returned to the car, wondering if they could gain any clues from Joanna's mysterious behaviour. 'What was that all about?' Will said, clicking his seatbelt into place.

'I've no idea. But my arse has got a few battle scars from you pushing me into those brambles.'

'Sorry. I didn't want her to see us,' Will grinned, looking anything but sorry. 'Are you going to turn on your lights or what?'

Jennifer peered up the lane as the car crept along. Dawn was in no hurry to break, but the small country road was well lit by the cool night sky. 'In a minute, I don't want them to see us. Do you think she was really sleepwalking?'

'If she wasn't, it was an Oscar-winning performance. What was the mention of a party about?' Will said.

'Well, it's the twins' birthday soon,' Jennifer responded.

'But why would she be calling out for her daddy?'

'I wish I knew,' Jennifer said. 'It's a touchy subject. She was probably just having a bad dream, a kickback from the psychic's visit. When I think of some of the weird dreams I've had . . .'

Will smirked. 'I know. Last night you were talking in your sleep about cleaning my flat. I presume it was a feather duster you were looking for when you grabbed hold of me?'

Jennifer choked mid-yawn. 'Well, I won't be grabbing your feather duster tonight, I can assure you.'

Will grinned. 'If you change your mind and feel like any . . . cleaning, I'm at your service.'

'I'll bear that in mind,' Jennifer grinned, her eyes flickering to her rear-view mirror.

She switched on the headlights as she approached the junction, her thoughts back at the farm. Just where had Joanna been going? And as for Nick . . . it was the closest she had seen the couple since she'd met them. With her and Will, what you saw was what you got. But Nick and Joanna's relationship was fractured. Was the rift related to their daughter's disappearance, or did the problems lie deeper? Something told Jennifer she was just touching the surface of the Duncan family's secrets.

CHAPTER THIRTY-EIGHT

Four Days Gone

The rain dictated their meeting place, and as she crouched behind the thicket, Jennifer accepted getting soaked in exchange for some much needed information. Her stake-out the night before had been disappointing, but her snooping during an early visit to Blackwater Farm had revealed a secret meeting, away from prying eyes. Or so Nick and Karen had thought.

Jennifer shuddered as the rain trickled down her collar onto the back of her neck. At least she had had the foresight to wear her jeans, trainers and puffa jacket, rather than her usual suit and high heels. She only hoped that Nick wouldn't see her, crouched like an idiot behind a shelter in the children's playground.

Karen arrived just seconds after Nick, and Jennifer peeped out from behind the shelter, to spy on the clandestine meeting.

They hugged tightly as they met on the path, breaking to enter the shelter together.

'We shouldn't be meeting like this,' Nick said. 'If anyone sees us . . .'

'If anyone sees us, we're just two colleagues who bumped into each other. And besides, who'd be crazy enough to come out in this rain? Now, how are you doing? You look like shit,' Karen said.

'What do you expect?' Nick replied, flatly.

Jennifer held her breath as the conversation came through loud and clear. She didn't need to be able to see them, to know that Nick and Karen had a close bond.

'Sorry, I'm only trying to . . .' Karen said.

'No. I'm sorry, I shouldn't have snapped,' Nick replied. 'You're only trying to help. I'm still getting over being interviewed by the police. It was weird, being on the other side of that table.'

'I know. You've got to expect that. How's the wicked witch of the west?' Karen said.

'You know I don't like it when you call her that,' Nick said, grimly.

'Sorry. How's Joanna? Still as mad as ever?'

'Karen . . .'

'What? It's the truth, isn't it?' she said petulantly.

Nick sighed. 'I don't know how much longer I can keep up the pretence.'

'Then don't. You don't owe her anything. All you have to do is leave.'

'I can't leave, not with all this going on. What would people think?'

'Anyone that knows her will understand why. How you've stayed with her this long, I don't know.' Karen's words seemed cold and well-worn. Nick's lack of response brought forth another question, but this time her voice was unsure. 'You don't . . . you don't still love her, do you?'

'God, Karen, you're so naive. It's not that simple. Life isn't one of those chick flits, you know.'

Karen chuckled. 'Chick lit. If you're gonna disrespect my reading material, then at least get it right.' Silence fell between them as the rain pattered on the roof of the shelter. 'It's not doing Olivia any good, you know, watching you argue all the time.'

'Argue? Joanna barely raises an eyebrow. It's as if Abigail never existed.'

'Then leave. Just pack your bags and walk out the door.'

'What will people think? What about my job?'

'It's the twenty-first century, Nick. You're not the first person to have an affair.'

Jennifer's thoughts raced as she tried to comprehend the revelation. It shouldn't have come as a surprise, but hearing the words aloud seemed wrong. She pulled out her notebook and shifted her feet to evade the pins and needles gathering in her legs.

'It's not just the affair, though, is it?' Nick said, his voice uneasy. 'What if people find out . . .'

'They won't, not unless you tell them. God! I hate to see this turn you into something you're not. Leave now before she bleeds you dry, or you'll end up a zombie just like her.'

'I know you're right, but I'm scared. Scared of the consequences when it all comes out.'

'Then just say you're taking a break. What's done is done. It doesn't make any difference now. Life is short, you owe it to yourself to be happy.'

Nick sighed. 'I don't think I'll ever be happy again.'

'You will. It won't always be like this. One day you'll look back and you'll be free. I promise you.'

'Thank you. I don't know how I would have got through this without you.'

'You can thank me by leaving your wife. You deserve to be happy. Sod the lot of them.'

'And Olivia? What's she going to think of me?'

'She hasn't said anything, has she?' Karen said, an edge of concern in her voice.

'No, but . . .'

'Then it's OK. Honestly, you're going to worry yourself into an early grave. Stay strong, otherwise you won't survive it. You'll always have me, remember?'

Jennifer edged away. She had heard enough by now, and needed to get off before they discovered her presence. She also needed time to process what she had just heard. Were Nick and Karen carrying a bigger secret than their affair? She remembered something Will had told her. Clues are like a jigsaw. Solve the easy pieces first, get your edges in order. The difficult middle pieces will slot together eventually, and bring you to the very centre of the crime. So the obvious clues were that Nick was having an affair, and Karen couldn't wait for him to leave his wife. The wicked witch of the west . . . she'd heard that somewhere before. Shaking the droplets of rain from her hands, she slipped out her phone and logged on to Twitter.

Jennifer cursed under her breath as she looked at her watch. Ten past nine. DCI Anderson was a stickler for time and wouldn't approve of her late arrival. But it wasn't without reason, and there was no way she could go to work looking like something that had been pulled out of the river Blakewater.

She knocked on his office door and murmured an apology for being late.

'You missed briefing again,' he said. 'I'll fill you in, but as an integral part of the investigation you should have been there.'

'I'm sorry, boss, but I took the initiative and it paid off. I've got some information that may be of use to you.'

But as Jennifer filled her superior in on Nick's possible affair, she got the distinct feeling it was low down on his list of priorities. She pulled down the hem of her black shift dress and crossed her legs.

'. . . and it was something that Karen said. I've got a feeling I've heard it on Twitter. There's hundreds, maybe thousands of posts under that hashtag, so I need some time to look through them all. I've got the feeling she could be our troll, or at least one of them.'

'Hmmm,' the DCI said, taking a sip of his coffee. 'Hang fire on that for now. Nick may well be having an affair, but it doesn't make him our suspect. Keep doing what you're doing, monitor the situation, and report back to me. I don't want to jeopardise our relationship with the family. The last thing we need is them withdrawing their support.'

'But, sir . . .'

'Trust me,' the DCI said, 'and don't go stirring things up just yet. We've got another suspect we're interested in, someone close to the family.'

CHAPTER THIRTY-NINE

Fiona opened the door, greeting Jennifer in hushed tones and signalling for her to come in. The hall flickered with light from candles of every shape and size, and chanting . . . no – Jennifer listened intently . . . praying filtered through from the living room.

'It's Bob and Wendy,' Fiona whispered. 'They're having mass.'

Jennifer followed her through to the kitchen, dropping her coat and bag onto the table for her second visit of the day, as Fiona poured her a tea. The portable radio played soft music next to the stove, and Jennifer took a seat.

'They just turned up with Father Murphy and some of their church friends,' Fiona said, wearing a weak smile. 'They got wind of the séance and came straight around, dragging that poor priest after them. There's no stopping them. Nick and Joanna're in there now.'

Jennifer nodded. The term 'a force to be reckoned with' had been invented for Nick's parents. 'And Olivia?'

'She's gone to school. The teachers recommended she try to get back into some routine. Perhaps they'll be able to help her come out of herself, to speak a bit more. I only hope it's not too upsetting for her.'

'I'm surprised Bob and Wendy didn't insist you attend mass as well.'

Fiona gave a sideways grin. 'I told them I had to answer the door, take calls, attend to visitors, and if the school rang . . . Well, I've been on tenterhooks, hoping she's getting on okay.'

Jennifer welcomed the cup of tea, and took it in both hands. 'You really care for this family, don't you?'

'I've come to, yes. Goes with the territory, I suppose,' Fiona said, taking a butter knife from the drawer. 'Can I make you anything? I've been so busy looking after everyone else this morning, I've not had a chance to eat.'

'No, thanks, I'm fine. You work away.'

'One thing about Joanna,' Fiona said, pulling out wafer-sliced ham and a tray of butter from the fridge, 'she always insists on having plenty of food in the house. Eats like a bird herself, mind.'

Jennifer watched as Fiona skimmed a layer of butter across a thick wedge of bread. 'How did you meet?'

'I was in between jobs when I saw the ad online. I have a diploma in complementary therapy, but there's not much call for that around Haven. I worked as a nanny in Canada for a few years, so I thought I'd fall back on that until something turned up. It's worked out well so far.' The smile fell from Fiona's face. 'Until now.'

Jennifer took a sip of tea. 'A nanny, eh? Would you say Joanna's maternal?'

'She's not everyone's idea of maternal, but she loves her girls. I don't think she's capable of hurting anyone,' Fiona said, bringing her tea and sandwich to the table.

Jennifer nodded her understanding. 'I never said she was. I'm just trying to understand her. That way I can answer any awkward questions in briefing, like why she appeared on TV with a smile on her face after Abigail went missing.'

Fiona plopped heavily into her chair, as if her legs had decided they couldn't take her weight any more.

'How can I explain without sounding disloyal? Joanna . . . she doesn't handle stress well. When things get tough, she closes herself off to it.' Fiona rubbed her mouth, as if the words were distasteful. 'She handles things her own way. She likes working for herself, because she can focus on her business twenty-four hours a day if she wants.'

'And we've effectively taken away her business, so . . .'

'She's had to come to terms with what's happening, with no safety net to fall back on when things get tough. She's a good person, they both are, but this has hit them very hard.'

'But don't you mind, feeding everyone and caring for the children while she's sitting at the kitchen table? Doesn't it bother you?'

'Not at all. Joanna pays me well and I enjoy it. Being at the heart of the family is lovely, to feel needed . . . I wouldn't want to be anywhere else.'

'Has she always been so troubled?'

Fiona glanced around the empty room. 'This isn't an official line of questioning, is it?'

'God, no, I'm just interested,' Jennifer replied.

'Joanna told me once that she had a troubled childhood. It wasn't until she met Nick that things began to improve. He was her knight in shining armour. Marrying Nick turned her life around.'

'You said earlier that Joanna wouldn't hurt anyone . . .'

Fiona chewed her sandwich and muffled an 'uh huh'.

A mellow tune played on in the background, and Jennifer was grateful for the meditative effect. It softened the question she had been waiting to ask, and she waited for Fiona to finish her food. 'How did Joanna get the scars on her arms? Self-harm?'

Fiona nodded slowly, as if an unspoken secret had been exposed. 'So you've seen them . . . It's something a lot of teenagers go through, isn't it? Teenage angst? I can't say I could go through with it myself . . .' Her voice trailed away.

Jennifer wasn't surprised to have her thoughts confirmed. She had only glimpsed one faint scar on Joanna's wrist, but had a feeling there would be many more. Another piece of the puzzle locked into place, and suddenly everything made a little more sense.

'It's part of the reason you're here, though, isn't it?' she said to
Fiona. 'It's not just the children you're babysitting, it's Joanna.'

Fiona's lips turned upwards in a smile. 'There's not much that
gets past you, is there, DC Knight?'

'Please, call me Jennifer. And to be honest, it didn't take a lot
of figuring out.'

'I suppose not,' Fiona said. 'She sometimes has mood swings,
and she's prone to paranoia. Nick imposed the house rules for her
own good. She uses her en suite toilet, and the cabinets are clean.
There's no lock on the door, so she can't be tempted to hurt herself.'

'And what about the main bathroom?' Jennifer asked, although
she had already figured out the answer.

'It's out of bounds. Nick keeps his razors there, and there's
always a concern she could lock herself in and get tempted to use
them. It's not a prison here – if she really wanted to harm herself,
she could – but she wants help. And it's all worked well, up until
now. She has little tics, signals when she's getting stressed.'

Jennifer took a sip of her tea, which had now gone cold. 'Have
you ever tried to draw the truth out of her?'

'She doesn't like talking about her feelings, and I don't like to
stir things up.'

'I'd say things are already stirred up,' Jennifer said. 'Could you
try to find out what's bothering her? It may give us the answers
we're looking for.'

'I don't know. I'm her employee. It seems disloyal to spy.'

'I'm not asking you to incriminate her, Fiona, I just want to
make sure we've explored every avenue.'

'In that case, there might be a way . . .' Fiona said, looking
thoughtfully at Jennifer. 'Sometimes we meditate together. It helps
her de-stress, and stops me becoming de-skilled. Perhaps if I could
get her to relax enough, she might open up. See what's blocking
her psyche.'

'It's worth a try.'

Footsteps echoed in the hall, and Fiona rose, empty plate in hand.

'Heaven help me, I'll do it. I don't want to cause trouble, but if it helps you find Abigail, then it's worth a shot.'

Jennifer smiled her thanks. The DCI had advised her to lay low, so he didn't need to know about this latest line of enquiry. His focus was elsewhere, although he wouldn't tell her with whom. Her latest adventure down the well had cast her in a bad light, and his earlier promise of full disclosure had now been withdrawn. All in good time, Jennifer thought, knowing that if an arrest were imminent she would find out soon enough. In the meantime, she would pick through the family secrets slowly unravelling before her. The door opened, and Jennifer cast her face in a neutral expression, disguising her knowledge of Nick's affair.

CHAPTER FORTY

Diary Entry

Abigail sleeps soundly in her sleeping bag as I watch. Nobody seemed to miss the clothes I took from her wardrobe. Her dungarees smelled so bad I burned them. I stood over the flames as they singed the damp clothes, and I nurtured the idea coming to life. Abigail's reprieve had eased my troubled conscience. My alter ego had been particularly vocal, and my uncharacteristic act of compassion had, at last, silenced the fracas in my brain. But as I absorbed the heat of the flames, the fire also seduced me, appealing to my darker side. Afterwards, when the clothes were nothing but embers, I picked among the remnants, pocketing the buckles and buttons of what was once the yellow dungarees. They clinked in my pocket as I walked, making me smile for the very first time that day.

The sound takes me back to a time I clinked glasses with my tormentor. I can talk about it now. Even writing about it doesn't seem as painful, because soon all of this will be over. It was Saturday, and I was meant to be helping out in the allotment. I was wheeling my bike when Father called me into the studio and handed me a glass of fizzy wine. His eyes were alight; I'd never seen him so jovial. He said his contacts had agreed to sign me up. I believed him, because I wanted it to be true, and I felt ever so grown up, drinking alcohol for the first time. The bubbles went up my nose, and I didn't like the taste, but I sipped it just the same, holding my pinkie finger up just like they did in the movies. After two glasses, he insisted we do a photo shoot for my portfolio. But when I waited behind the camera, he asked me to take off my top. At first I thought I was wearing the wrong clothes, and it took a few seconds for the meaning to sink in. He wanted me to pose with no top at all. It made me go cold at the thought, and small alarm bells began to sound a warning.

I gathered my courage and refused. I remember stuttering as he towered over me, ranting and raving about how let down he felt, how he would have to go back to his contacts and tell them they would have to find someone else. I cried, saying I was sorry, but it was just too embarrassing, standing there half-naked, with nothing but the tiny pair of shorts he had passed me. His features turned into cold, hard stone. Didn't all models get undressed for the camera? Then, when I was getting ready to leave, he revealed dozens of photos of me getting changed. Perhaps he should show these to my school friends and get their vote, he said, his face twisted into a smile. There was something about the way he leered as he said it, that scared me more than when he was angry. He laughed as if it was the funniest joke ever. But the joke was on me. So slowly, reluctantly, I agreed, clasping my arms against my rolls of fat to cover my shame. I did not understand what it meant to be blackmailed. But I knew I was in a far worse position than when I was being bullied in school.

Things were taking a frightening turn, and I wondered how I ever got myself into this situation. Perhaps he was good at hiding what he was, or perhaps I just didn't want to see it. I tried talking to my mother, but when I mentioned the photographs she produced an envelope from the drawer and said that I was lucky to have professional shots. I was agog. She had been collecting the snaps all along. Not the sordid ones he bullied me into posing for, but the first innocent shots that were taken. I knew then that she would not believe anything I had to say. If only someone would catch him, I thought, at least then I could leave the responsibility of reporting him to someone else. But there was no one to tell. My step sister was in boarding school, and regarded me with little more than plodding apathy. Having a ready-made sister to look out for me had been all of my dreams come true. I used to fantasise about us having midnight feasts, as we stayed up late and talked about music. She was slim, pretty, clever. All the things I was not. We were even born the same day. But she had her own friends in boarding school, and she was not interested in me. Father had never asked to take her photo. Only I was afforded that privilege. Every time she came home I tried to pluck up the courage to tell her, but every time his threats blocked the words. I couldn't see a way out of the hell my life had become.

CHAPTER FORTY-ONE

Jennifer steeled herself as the young slim priest entered the room, flanked by Nick and his parents. Father Murphy was not at all what she expected. New to Haven, he seemed too green to take on the role of spiritual counsellor. He seemed pleasant, polite, and in a hurry. Pulling on a pair of black leather driving gloves, he'd no sooner arrived than he made his farewells.

'Can I make you a cup of tea?' Fiona said, as she worked her way through a pile of ironing.

'Not for us, thank you,' Wendy answered for both herself and Bob. 'It goes right through us.'

Wendy was about a foot smaller than her husband. Not that it held her back; she was quite forthright with her opinions. Jennifer was yet to see any affection pass between her and her son.

Bob, on the other hand, was more like Nick. Tall and well-built, he had a kindly, age-worn face. She wondered if his parents' religious views were the reason Nick felt the need to remain in a marriage where he was not happy. As if reading her mind, Wendy peered over at Jennifer, catching a glimpse of her jewellery.

'I see you wear a crucifix. Are you a Catholic?'

Jennifer's hand rose to her collar bone, where the silver cross lay. She did not wish to lose favour with Wendy and Bob, and thought how best to answer the question. 'I have a strong belief,' she answered, not saying what that belief was, or that it was none of her business anyway. Wendy gave a satisfied nod of the head.

'You should have come to mass. We'll include you on the next one.'

Jennifer hoped there wouldn't be a next one. She wanted to get this case wrapped up as soon as she could, and return to normality. Although Wendy was deeply religious, Jennifer did not feel that the woman was altogether good. There was something about the strength of her glare that made Jennifer squirm. 'I'm afraid I'm here in my capacity as a police officer. But thank you for the offer.'

Wendy sniffed, mildly affronted. 'Oh. Nick is a police officer too. He still has time for the Lord. And I don't think police should have to work Sundays either, that should be reserved for devotion and prayer.'

Jennifer stifled a laugh as she realised the woman was deadly serious. 'Unfortunately the criminals of Haven don't give such consideration to religion. My boss would have me work every day if he could.'

Wendy cast an eye over her ring finger. 'You're not married, I take it.'

Jennifer was about to say that it was none of her business when Nick made a show of looking at his watch.

'Is that the time? Best we get you back, I've got a meeting with DCI Anderson.'

'You never said . . .' Wendy replied. 'I thought we could –'

'The DCI is coming here. He wants to speak to us about the case,' Jennifer interrupted, not interested in whatever Wendy had lined up for them that day. Nick shot her a grateful smile, and escorted his parents to the door.

'You'll telephone if you hear anything?' Wendy said, as she shuffled through, her husband obediently following behind.

Jennifer and Fiona exchanged glances as the door closed, and Fiona bit back a smile.

'Blimey, she's a bit full-on, isn't she?' Jennifer said, wondering if Wendy had been waiting for the right opportunity to pounce on her all along.

'That's nothing,' Fiona said, as she smoothed out the shirt sleeve she was ironing. 'She was going easy on you. I've had the full interrogation. She wanted to check I wasn't a fallen woman before allowing me to care for her grandchildren.'

'And what do you have to do to qualify for that category, then?' Jennifer said with a grin.

'Sex outside of marriage for a start . . .'

'That's the best kind, isn't it?' Jennifer said, thinking of Will.

Fiona laughed, quickly covering her mouth to stifle the sound. 'Oh don't, you'll get me into trouble. You're not gay, are you? Because she has a massive problem with that too. And don't get me started on children outside of marriage.'

'I think I'm going to hell.' Jennifer shook her head in mock despair.

'Oh, I know,' Fiona grinned. 'I'd like to say she's a nice woman deep down, but she's not. Looks like I'll be joining you in hell.'

The living room door creaked open and Joanna popped her head through the gap.

'Is she gone?' she said, ready to flit back upstairs any second.

'I can go and call her if you like,' Fiona winked across at Jennifer.

'Don't you dare,' Joanna said. 'I'm all prayed out. If I ever see that woman again, it'll be too soon.'

'She can't have been pleased about the medium, then,' Jennifer said, hoping to gauge her reaction.

Joanna's eyes glazed over, and she seemed to withdraw into herself. 'They don't know anything about the medium, apart from the fact she turned up and I sent her away. And you mustn't tell them otherwise.'

'I'm not going to say anything,' Jennifer said, the smile falling from her face.

For a short few moments it had been good to lighten the mood, but the inevitable guilt set in, and the fact Abigail was now gone a whole four days hit home. She checked her phone, and seeing it was free of calls or texts, shoved it back in her pocket.

'So what about *your* father?' she said, seeing Fiona shaking her head just too late. 'Is he a religious man?'

Joanna frowned. Her words were steely cold, as if imparting something Jennifer should have known. 'Don't ever mention my father in this house. He's nothing to do with me.'

'I'm sorry,' Jennifer said. 'I didn't mean to . . .'

Closing her eyes, Joanna took a deep breath, and when she opened them again she was smiling. 'That's no problem, Jennifer. You'll know the next time. Now excuse me, I feel like some fresh air.'

Fiona lowered the iron, all joviality evaporated from her face. 'I'm sorry,' she said to Jennifer. 'I tried to warn you.'

CHAPTER FORTY-TWO

Joanna rarely ventured outside. So when she slipped out the back door, Jennifer grasped the chance to get her alone. Nick's parents had fitted a holy water font next to the front and back doors. Abigail's disappearance had taken its toll on them too. The lines on their faces were etched with worry and concern, their eyes watery with tears waiting to be shed. The loss of a child spread many ripples, and they leaned on their faith to get them through it. Jennifer couldn't blame them. She had expected some animosity from them towards Joanna, but it was far from the case. From what Jennifer had seen, Wendy had seemed comfortably at ease in her daughter-in-law's presence.

Together they walked the landscape, which was spoiled only by the pylons tethering electricity to the farm. Jennifer relayed what Nick called 'another non update', but she didn't tell Joanna everything. The value of reconstructing Abigail's disappearance for *Crimewatch* was being brought into question. How did you re-enact a child disappearing into thin air? Twitter had finally shut down the accounts spewing the worst of the abuse, but for every account that was closed, two more popped up in their place, their demands for the truth twice as venomous as before. It was like trying to hold back the tide, and when the trolls got bored of blaming Joanna for Abigail's disappearance, they attacked the police. Nobody ever tweeted when it was a job well done. Being a detective was thankless, and Jennifer had never been recognised formally for her good work. But every now and again, she received a card or a thank you letter from a victim of crime. She treasured those more than any commendation.

Jennifer matched her pace to Joanna's strides as they walked through the farmyard towards the open fields. A heavy shower had moistened the path, and Joanna seemed oblivious to the mud seeping through her art deco shoes. In her back-seamed stockings and couture dress, she looked more like a 1950s pin-up girl than the parent of an abducted child. Jennifer thrust her hands deep into her coat pockets, biding her time. Her eyes danced over the rusted farm machinery lying scattered on the land like old dinosaur bones. The yard was dotted with a number of sheds, all of which had been checked. Some of them were demolished, while others stood elderly and creaking against the bitter winds. A haunting tune echoed through the tubular steel gates as the breeze pushed forth, whistling underneath the galvanized roof, trifling with Jennifer's senses.

'Can you hear it?' Joanna said. 'Sometimes it creeps in through our bedroom window. It used to keep me awake, until I realised what it was.' She stopped to listen to the mournful tune. 'It sounds so sad.' The two women fell silent as the wind gathered around them, playing its melodious song.

'Why did you buy this place?' Jennifer finally said, leaning over the gate. 'You strike me as a city girl.'

'I am. At least I was, deep down. Our townhouse was nice, but just too perfect. And Haven isn't London. It's quiet, but without any of the benefits of the country. I decided to either go back to London or go completely rural. I found the farm for sale online, and put in an offer that day.'

Jennifer noted an absence of 'we' in her decision-making. 'So you tend to make your decisions on impulse?'

Joanna pushed down her dress as the wind tried to take it. 'I've never thought about it like that before. If I see something I want, I take it.'

Jennifer trudged stoically on, head down, picking her way through the path. 'But don't you find that you don't really appreciate anything when things come easy? Don't you tire of it quicker?'

'I don't know what you're getting at,' Joanna said, her smile fading.

'I'm not getting at anything. I'm just interested in why you took on such a massive undertaking.'

'Because I could. There's your answer.' Joanna lifted up her foot. 'Oh, look at my shoes. They're ruined. I'd best get back and clean them off. I might be able to save them.'

But Jennifer was not ready to change the subject just yet. 'So when did the activity start?'

Joanna swiped her shoe in the grass in short, jerky movements, her eyes darting to her house. The expression *cat on a hot tin roof* came to Jennifer's mind.

'What activity?' Joanna eventually asked, increasing her pace as she turned back for home.

You're not escaping me now, Jennifer thought, ready to lay hands on her if necessary. She had waited long enough for answers, and was not about to allow Joanna to slip through her fingers. 'You know, stuff being thrown, banging noises, things like that. Has it been going on long?'

'The psychic said it was an uneasy spirit,' Joanna said, now walking so fast she was almost breaking out in a trot.

Jennifer caught her by her arm as she brought her to a standstill. But despite the force, her words were calm and reassuring. 'And what about Olivia's abilities? How long has she been telepathic?'

For a split second Joanna's mask dropped, and a tumult of emotions glazed her face.

Jennifer held her gaze. 'It's okay, I'm not going to tell anyone. I know what it's like, growing up with abilities that don't fit in the modern world. You've been trying to protect Olivia all this time because she's different, haven't you?' Jennifer held her breath, hoping her theory was right.

Joanna seized Jennifer's arms, her face set in a thunderous glare. 'You mustn't tell anyone. Do you hear?' A maddened panic surfaced behind her eyes as she dug her fingers into Jennifer's biceps. 'I can't have my daughter being treated like a freak. This has got to stay between us.'

'It's okay, I won't make it public,' Jennifer said. It was as close to a promise of confidentiality as she could get. Her reports to Operation Moonlight were not for public consumption.

Joanna dropped her hands and attempted to recover her light-hearted demeanour. 'I'm sorry . . . I don't know what came over me.'

But Jennifer didn't mind. She wanted to see the true Joanna, the protective mother she knew had been lurking under the surface all along. And she could not waste a single second.

'What age was she when it began?'

Joanna sighed; the sort of sigh someone gives when they've had enough of being strong.

'I first noticed it when they began primary school. Abigail was at home sick one day and Olivia was able to tell the teacher what programme she was watching on TV. It became like a game to them, and they'd do it any time they were separated. How did you know?'

'The first time I met Olivia, I knew that she was a very special girl.' Jennifer paused, slowing her footsteps so they didn't reach the house too soon. 'Is that why you didn't want a child psychiatrist? Because you were afraid they'd find out?'

Joanna averted her eyes, but she could not hide the emotion in her voice. 'Yes. I was scared they'd label her as mentally ill. I've tried to broach it with Nick, but he's refused to discuss it.'

Jennifer was not surprised. Nick did not seem the type to consider anything beyond the norm; like Will, he was stoic and down to earth.

'It's more common than you think. There's a lot more understood about it now.'

'That's why I don't talk about Abigail. It pains me to think about her, so I can't imagine what it's doing to Olivia. Not being able to find her sister . . . it must be eating her up inside.'

'So you think that not talking about Abigail is keeping a lid on things? In my experience this rarely works.'

'It works for me,' Joanna said, in a small voice. 'In everyday life, I mean.'

The grey clouds parted overhead, allowing streams of light to dapple their path. Jennifer took in a soothing breath as she composed her words. The smell of the rain-dampened soil brought peace as the winds began to calm at last.

'I really want to help, Joanna. But I feel you're holding out on me.'

Joanna crossed her arms. 'My personal life is none of your business.'

Jennifer sighed. It was one step forward and two steps back. Jennifer gave her a firm stare, having no qualms about getting her point across. 'I'm sorry if my questioning makes you uncomfortable, but let me get one thing straight. My number one priority is finding Abigail. Not getting a conviction, or setting anyone up. She's just a little girl. I'll ask as many uncomfortable questions as it takes, if they lead me to her.'

Jennifer glanced at Joanna, whose neutral expression gave nothing away. They had just one more gate to pass through before they reached home, and she would dart up to her room as usual. Jennifer took a deep breath and continued. 'Have you considered that you may know more than you're aware?'

Joanna stopped dead in her tracks. 'What do you mean?'

'What if you hurt Abigail unintentionally, or witnessed something take place? I think you cope by repressing your feelings, but you still feel the need to punish yourself.'

'That's ridiculous. I'd remember something like that.'

Jennifer recalled the months of therapy she had been forced to endure in the early days, when occupational health had treated her as if she had a mental illness, instead of being psychically gifted. If nothing else, she had come away from that with a better understanding of the psyche.

'The mind is a very complicated thing. Sometimes when you repress memories they come out in different ways, either by projecting your feelings onto someone else, for example your husband, or subconsciously. How long have you been self-harming?'

Joanna's mouth gaped open. 'What? Where did you get that from? I don't self-harm,'

'C'mon, Joanna, I've seen the scars. And it's not just self-harming, is it?' Jennifer paused to take a deep breath. 'How's your memory? Have you ever woken up in the morning with dirty feet and no recollection of how it happened? Or found yourself wearing different clothes? Has that ever happened to you?'

'No . . . I . . .' Joanna stuttered, her uncertainty providing the answers.

'There's more going on than you're willing to admit. Don't you want to know what it is? No matter how awful? Wouldn't it be better to know the truth?'

'You're wrong . . .'

'Perhaps I am, but something's not right. I can feel it.'

Joanna flung back the last gate and barged her way through. 'I didn't hurt my daughter.'

'Then who did?' Jennifer said, pushing back the gate as it rebounded against her. 'Was it Nick? Are you protecting him? What happened that day?'

'I can't remember,' Joanna said, arms swinging by her sides as she marched up the path.

Jennifer closed the gate and trotted up behind her. A stone had rolled into her shoe but she couldn't afford to stop. The house was in sight and soon their conversation would be over. 'You can't remember or you're too scared to? Whatever's happened is in the past. You need to allow Abigail to rest now. It's time to bring your daughter home.'

Joanna clenched her fists, turning on Jennifer one last time. 'You're wrong. I was in the kitchen with Fiona the whole time. Nothing happened.'

'That's what you're telling yourself, but is it true? At least think on it. Consider seeing a psychiatrist, or a hypnotist. See if they can get to the root of what's bothering you,' Jennifer said, trying to ignore the pebble digging into the sole of her foot. 'Perhaps it's something further back, from your childhood. We have to face our demons if we've any hope of fighting them.'

Joanna laid her hand on the back door handle. 'It's all right for you. You're strong. I can't go back there. If I start delving into the past . . .'

Jennifer placed her hand on Joanna's, her voice calm now. One last parting shot before their conversation came to an end.

'You'll do it. Because you love Abigail, and opening old wounds is a small price to pay if it brings her back to you.'

Joanna responded the way she always did, breezing into the house with a smile plastered across her face.

'Goodness, it's nippy out there. Anyone fancy a coffee? I've got some nice Columbian from Starbucks. Can I get you a cup, Jennifer?'

Jennifer nodded and took a seat at the table. It was as if their conversation had never happened. But as Joanna reached for the kettle, Jennifer detected a shake in her hand. Joanna's wall of defence was slowly crumbling. And Jennifer wouldn't give up until every brick had been pulled down.

CHAPTER FORTY-THREE

Joanna

Joanna slumped onto the vanity chair, the last of her strength evaporating. Her head felt weak, still carrying the melody of the Jack-in-the-box. Round and round it played, threatening her sanity as her world unravelled around her. In the sanctuary of her bedroom, the mask of indifference fell. She picked a ladder in the knee of her tights, forcing the thoughts back down. But she was trying to retreat back into a shell that couldn't accommodate her any more. There was one way to ease the pressure. The thought lingered. She owed it to her family to stay strong. But it was so hard. The psychic's words intermingled with the tune, taunting her unease. 'Please Daddy, not that, don't make me do that.' Was the psychic talking about her husband? Was he capable of hurting Abigail in that way? It couldn't be true. And yet . . . those words were strangely familiar. Somewhere in the back of her mind a cog whirred, then clicked into place as the response came forth. 'Shh, be a good girl for Daddy and don't tell.' She had heard it before – and the memory brought the sensation of unwelcome hands. She lunged towards the en suite, the contents of her stomach hitting the floor before she could make it to the sink.

But then with each pump of cleaning fluid, she gathered her senses. It would take something bigger to help her carry on now. A slap on the face or pull of hair was not going to do it this time.

She wiped her forehead with the back of her forearm and threw the tissues in the toilet. A sickly tang of lemon hung in the room, and she opened the small box window, closing her eyes as she breathed in the purity of the fresh air. The air really was different in the country.

Another horrific image flashed before her. Abigail buried in the ground, her soul trapped, crying for peace. No. It wasn't real. It was just her mind playing tricks on her. She blinked, inhaling sharply as a voice outside snapped her back to reality. Peering through the crack in the window, she caught sight of DC Knight. Head bowed, she was speaking intently on her phone as she walked to her car. It was where she went to have private conversations, because in Blackwater Farm walls had ears. Joanna swallowed back the burning sensation lining her throat, and turned to the sink. A waxy face stared back from the mirrored cabinet door. God, she looked old. Joanna swung it open and reached for the toothpaste. She could fix her face. But inside she was festering, and the sense of guilt hung on her shoulders like a leaden cloak, getting heavier by the day. She splashed cold water onto her skin, the act strengthening her resolve. As long as she played the part of the entrepreneur, the home-maker, the pretty wife . . . as long as she was all those things, everything would be all right. Her eyes rested on the box of Andrex tissues. Her special hiding place. A single razor blade lay hidden underneath the wad of double ply. It was her insurance. Knowing it was there helped calm her breath when it came quicker than she could manage it. She stared at the blue and green box longingly. *No.* She had promised her family . . . but did they really care? And besides, whose business was it anyway? It wasn't as if she was hurting anyone else . . . 'No,' she whispered, taking a step towards the tissues. But the nagging whispers promised quick release, and as she drove her hand into the oval gap, she knew what she had to do.

With ceremonial grace, she placed a towel on the closed toilet lid, then rolled her stocking down past her thighs. Lifting her skirt around her waist, she sat on the towel, and placed a smaller one between her legs to catch any excess blood. She was returning to the dark place. She felt it like a black moth fluttering up in her chest, and the old justifications sprung free. Some people smoked to relieve stress, others drank or took drugs. At least this way, it wasn't harming anyone but herself. The silvery scars seemed to smile up at her. Nick wouldn't notice a fresh one. Intimacy was a thing of the past, and the few light cuts and strokes that patterned her body were hardly life threatening. Fat tears blurred her vision and she blotted them away. 'Pull yourself together,' she whispered under her breath. A hard ball of anxiety had lodged in her throat, and this was the only way to set it free. Calming breaths steadied her right hand as her left clamped the towel against her thigh. A light slice, that was all it would take, and she sucked between her teeth as she brought the razor blade two inches in a horizontal line. The kiss of the blade brought relief as her nerve endings screamed and the blood trickled down her thigh along with the pent up stress. She gazed at her handiwork. It was like welcoming back an old friend. She gently wrapped the towel over her leg, soaking up the excess blood before applying a small strip of sterile gauze. She would not need to cut again. Just pressing on the wound would bring instant relief. Yes, she thought, feeling calm for the first time that day. She had done the right thing.

She eased off her stockings and stepped into black high-waisted trousers. The fabric would absorb any blood, and the chaff of the gauze against the material would provide relief. She watched from her window as DC Knight exited her car and paced the yard, still on her phone. She admired her ability to wear heels in such conditions. And she was one of the few people who still wiped their feet at the door. She doubted the group of people downstairs would bother. They had gathered in the kitchen this afternoon, planning on redirecting their search. There were so many people traipsing in and out of their house she had given up asking them to use the doormat. What was the point? It wasn't as if they had expensive woollen carpet like in their townhouse in Haven. That house situated beyond the bridge, near the designer shops and the delightful chic cafes . . . She allowed her mind to wander until she noticed a convoy of police cars coming over the hill. DC Knight shielded her eyes with her hand and hurried inside.

Joanna met her in the hall, the welcome sting of the cut keeping her on her toes. 'What is it?' she asked her.

Jennifer's face was alight, and she spoke with an urgency Joanna hadn't heard before.

'I need you to watch out for Olivia. When she comes back with her dad, you need to take her out of here. I've tried to ring him but I think he's out of range.' She glanced back at the police cars filling the yard. 'I've tried to put them off, but they said it can't wait.'

'What? What can't wait?'

'There's been a development. I need you to stay calm.'

Calm? Joanna thought. She was the queen of calm. She shoved her hands into the pockets of her trousers and pinched where she had sliced her skin. The sharpness brought her back to ground, and she smiled as she nodded in response.

Three officers bundled into the house while Sue, the original FLO, and a uniformed officer waited outside. Joanna guessed that the two officers in plain clothes were detectives, although she didn't recognise them from Nick's work. They barely afforded her a glance before following Jennifer into the kitchen. 'Be quick,' she heard DC Knight whisper. 'Nick and Olivia are due back from school any second.'

A quick nod affirmed their understanding. Joanna peeped over their shoulders as the crowd of twenty or so people parted to allow access to the person in their sights. The realisation made her stomach clench, and she began to feel sick all over again. They had come to her home to make an arrest.

CHAPTER FORTY-FOUR

'What's going on?' Nick asked, his body rigid and unyielding as Jennifer tried to escort him inside. Her hand was quickly shrugged off his shoulder, and disbelief flashed across his face. 'Why have they arrested Radcliffe?'

'Zoe's fresh from briefing,' Jennifer said firmly, her emotions locked behind her eyes. 'Why don't we go inside for an update?'

Nick's gaze trailed over the police cars snaking up the twisted road. He rubbed his chin, rough with two-day stubble. He reached into his jacket pocket, the jangle of his car keys announcing his intentions.

'You can go after them if you want, but they won't tell you a damn thing,' Jennifer said, giving him a hard stare. 'And when you come back from wherever they're bringing him, we'll both be off duty.'

'Look,' Nick said, 'I'll go inside as long as you're completely upfront with me.'

Jennifer's nod relayed her agreement.

The divide between family and police was evident, as Zoe and Jennifer sat one side of the kitchen table, and Nick and Joanna on the other. It wasn't that long ago that Nick had been working on police cases himself, but lack of sleep and growing anxiety skewed his perceptions, making him paranoid and mistrustful. The dynamics of the house had changed since the incident with the well, and for once there were no cups of tea or slices of homemade cake on offer. The kettle was cold, and the Aga lukewarm. Fiona placated Olivia in her bedroom, and Joanna took a seat beside her husband as they spoke of arrests and forensic evidence downstairs.

'First,' Zoe said, in her most diplomatic voice, 'DC Knight wasn't aware of Radcliffe's arrest until seconds before we arrived. The decision was made pending anonymous phone calls received by Crimestoppers, along with past intelligence and Radcliffe's lack of an alibi when questioned.'

Joanna piped up. 'You've only just finished interviewing my husband, for goodness' sake. Who's next? Me?'

Jennifer raised an eyebrow at the uncharacteristic outburst. What had got into her? And why was she so quick to defend Radcliffe?

Nick reached across the table for his wife's clasped hands, unknotting her fingers and giving them a squeeze. 'Shh, it's okay, let the officer tell us what's going on.'

Joanna nodded, withdrawing her hands and shoving them deep in her trouser pockets. Jennifer watched as a shot of colour bloomed on her face, her pupils dilating as the imitation smile found its way back to her lips. She recognised the inner struggle as the woman became calm once again. Whatever had fuelled Joanna's outburst had returned to its box.

Zoe gave Jennifer a knowing look before bringing her attention back to the investigation. 'We're all on the same side.' She turned to Nick, shooting one of her bullet stares from under her jagged black fringe. 'There shouldn't be any animosity. We're your colleagues, and we're working around the clock to find Abigail. You get that, don't you?'

Nick sighed, a long tired exhalation of breath. 'Sorry. Yes, we know you're doing your best.'

'As I was saying, Radcliffe was in the area prior to Abigail's disappearance, but he's failed to provide us with an alibi for the rest of the afternoon. Today we received an anonymous call stating that he was seen driving around the edge of the woodlands, acting in a suspicious manner.'

'Does this mean they'll continue with the search?' Nick said, making Jennifer wince as he cracked each of his knuckles. Every inch of him was tensed, and she wondered how much longer he could carry on without sleep.

Jennifer decided not to push Nick any further, and made an excuse to get Zoe outside. Sitting in the comfort of her car, they parked outside the gate, making the most of the opportunity to talk freely about the case.

'I don't envy you there,' Zoe said, nodding back at the house. 'I'd make a useless FLO.'

'I'm just grateful to be allowed in. They've knocked back all other offers of help. I understand their frustration but Nick's reaching breaking point. It feels like he's going to snap any minute.'

'He wasn't too bad once we got him inside the house.'

'That's what I don't get. Maybe it's just tiredness, but . . .'

'What?' Zoe said.

'Well, he's just been told that his friend, a man he trusted, may be involved in his daughter's disappearance. The Nick I know would have kicked off, knocked some furniture over, or got in my face. Even Joanna piped up. But he just sat there and took it. That strikes me as odd.'

'Huh!' Zoe said. 'Everything about that family is odd. A daughter who doesn't speak, an insomniac father, and a ghoul for a mum. You've got your work cut out for you there.'

'Don't I know it,' Jennifer sighed. 'But these are horrible circumstances. Who knows how any of us would react? Anyway, how's work going? I'm itching to get back to the team.'

'Oh, you know, the usual,' Zoe said, pulling out two sticks of chewing gum. 'Want one?'

Jennifer waved a hand to decline. 'No, thanks. Fill me in, then. Anything interesting?'

Zoe offered up a teasing grin, speaking between chews. 'Hmm, I'm not sure. I reckon you'll owe me a drink if I tell you.'

'Do I have to give you a Chinese burn?' Jennifer said, only half joking. The case must have been juicy, or Zoe would have told her by now. Every case that Operation Moonlight investigated was on a strict need-to-know basis, but that wouldn't stop Jennifer questioning her colleagues if she thought she was missing out. And lately she felt she was.

'Shouldn't you be getting back?' Zoe said, glancing at the farm in her rear-view mirror.

She was right. Jennifer had just dropped a bombshell and then left the family to it. But she was too caught up in Zoe's investigation now to let go.

'They'll be all right for a minute. What have you got?' Jennifer said, with a glare that suggested she wasn't leaving until she got answers.

Zoe chewed a couple more times before clearing her throat. 'There's been whispers about the Reborners case. I heard you're going to be reassigned to it.'

The very mention of the cult sent a chill down Jennifer's spine. The case involving Bert Bishop, otherwise known as the Raven, still gave her nightmares. But it was her case, and a spark ignited inside her at the prospect of reopening it.

'I don't understand. We closed them down.'

'Ethan thinks the cult is still active. Remember that bust we carried out? He thinks it was just a front. The real meetings have gone underground. They knew we were onto them and they set us up to see if we'd bite.'

'We closed them down,' Jennifer repeated. The box she had firmly shut away in her mind had sprung open, its contents crawling like maggots on her skin. The Reborners were a terrible prospect for Haven; a cult which left a trail of dead bodies in its wake. But the ringleader had been taken out of the equation. It couldn't be true.

'Well, I'm sorry, hun, but that's the word on the street. I'm slowly building up some contacts in Haven, but it's going to take time.'

Jennifer nodded, her thoughts in the past. Zoe's previous experience as an undercover officer would not go to waste in her new role. 'You have my number. Call me if anything significant comes up.'

'You owe me a drink first, remember?' Zoe said, shaking her feet from her kitten heels and throwing them on the back seat. 'Ohhh, that's better.'

Jennifer smirked. No matter how stressed she was, Zoe's quirky ways always made her smile. 'You're not seriously gonna drive barefooted, are you?'

'Of course,' Zoe said, wriggling her purple painted toenails. 'And don't go changing the subject. Mine's a vodka and coke.'

Jennifer opened the car door and stepped out into the breeze. 'Play your cards right and I'll get you a kebab too,' she said, laughing at her colleague's disgusted reaction. 'See you later. Be careful driving in your bare feet.'

'Chill your beans, babe, I'm all good.'

Zoe turned over the ignition of the unmarked Ford Focus, revving it into life. Jennifer watched as the car hared up the winding lane. This would be her first and last FLO job. She couldn't stand to be away from the beating heart of the investigation any more. She was yet to admit it was because she also missed working with Will. She cared for him far more than she could afford. Life had changed beyond recognition in the last year, and it was time to put her foot on the brake. Her childhood had taught her some valuable lessons. It didn't pay to invest too much in one person, and life had a way of letting you down.

She stared into the distance, until the silver car was a dot on the landscape. It was typical that Radcliffe turned up to the house on the day he was to be arrested. She had been just about to speak to him when she received a call telling her to hang fire. But an arrest was good news, wasn't it? Radcliffe fitted the profile as Abigail's abductor. So why did she feel so uneasy? Unanswered questions niggled the back of her brain, and she couldn't help but wonder if they had arrested the right man. There was one person she had yet to speak to – and her visit would not be welcomed.

CHAPTER FORTY-FIVE

The door opened only a fraction before Karen caught sight of her on the other side. Feeling like an unwelcome salesman, Jennifer flashed her warrant card as a reminder of the importance of her visit.

'I'm DC Knight . . .' she began, her voice low so as not to disturb the other residents.

'I know who you are,' Karen said, giving her a frosty glare. 'You'd better come in.'

Karen's flat was small and cosy, and the welcome aroma of sandal-wood incense lingered in the air. Jennifer cast her eyes over the sofa littered with mismatched sofa cushions, and the outdated television decorated with family photos and cat ornaments. A probationer's wage did not stretch very far, and she guessed that Karen's family had furnished the flat with their unwanted furniture and knick-knacks. A small black kitten mewed as it scurried towards her, and Karen scooped it up as if Jennifer was a Rottweiler that had prowled into the room.

'What can I do for you?' Karen said, stroking the kitten protectively.

'I'd like to ask you some questions. Nothing to worry about. I just thought we'd have more privacy if I came to you.'

Karen frowned. 'Why do we need privacy?'

Jennifer shifted on her feet. She had hoped to be able to sit down with Karen and draw out whatever trouble Nick was in, to come to a resolution; but as Karen stood stiffly before her it soon became apparent no such invitation would be forthcoming. 'I want to talk to you about your relationship with Nick . . . because I believe it may have a bearing on Abigail's case,' Jennifer added hastily, justifying her intrusion.

Karen snorted. 'So you're saying my friendship with Nick has something to do with Abigail's disappearance? It's not just you being nosey now, is it, DC Knight?'

'Of course not,' Jennifer said, affronted. 'We're all professionals here. If Nick's in trouble, I'd like to help. He's not been forthcoming with the police, and when this comes out it might make him look bad.'

'You don't need to tell me how the police work, I've spent the last couple of years having it drummed into me. In which case, I don't see the relevance. It's getting late. I'd like you to leave.'

Oh sod it, Jennifer thought, taking a deep breath. 'I heard you talking down by the playing fields. I know you're having an affair.'

Karen paled. The kitten mewed for her to resume stroking, as her hand froze mid-air. 'You were spying on us.'

'Never mind me, what about you? What secret is Olivia keeping for Nick? As you said, people have affairs all the time, but there's something else, isn't there? What's he holding back?'

'I . . .' Karen's lips tightened, as if to stifle the words. Her bravado fell away, and she visibly squirmed under Jennifer's gaze.

'I'm not here to get anyone into trouble. I'm trying to help.'

'You'd better sit down,' Karen said, gesturing to a beanbag in the corner.

Jennifer raised her eyebrows at what resembled a giant marsh-mallow. 'Thanks,' she said, taking a seat next to Karen on the sofa instead.

'We're not having an affair. Nick's been like a brother to me,' Karen said, moving to the other end.

'But you said –'

'I've known him for ages. I had some problems with my ex-boyfriend and he sorted it out for me. Even helped me get an attachment on CID. I owe him a lot.'

Jennifer frowned, unconvinced. 'Then why did you tell him to leave his wife?'

Karen rolled her eyes at the mention of Joanna's name. 'Because she makes his life hell. Call it mental abuse, but she's not all sweetness and light like she comes across.'

Sweetness and light was not how Jennifer would have described Joanna. Distant, troubled, even spaced out, but she was happy to let the description slide if it brought her nearer the truth.

Karen kissed the kitten on the top of its head and gently placed it on the floor. It instantly jumped back on her lap. 'Joanna's very manipulative. Right from the beginning she wanted Nick all to herself. Why do you think she's bought that farm in the middle of nowhere? And when people do visit, she sets herself up to look like the victim.' Karen widened her eyes in an effort to convince her. 'It's just another form of control, turning his friends against him, so he's more reliant on her.'

'She didn't seem to mind you,' Jennifer said, recalling Karen's presence at the table when she gave an update. Stroking his back, patting his hand, and then there were the phone calls. 'Have you ever thought that Nick could be exaggerating the facts? I've borne the brunt of his temper. He's very quick to react.'

'Of *course* he's upset, his daughter's missing,' she said, stating the obvious. 'I wouldn't be surprised if Joanna was behind the whole thing.'

Jennifer lowered her hand to stroke the kitten, now rubbing up against her tights. She shifted in her seat, hoping Karen would hurry up and get to the point. But Karen was fully engrossed in her tirade.

'You don't like her very much, do you?' Jennifer said.

Karen almost spat the words. 'I can't stand the bitch. She's a leech. Don't you see? It's all about her, how much she can syphon from someone or something. She's never cared about Nick or the kids. It's the attention she craves. If you want to see who's taken Abigail, start looking at her, because I can guarantee that's one big publicity stunt too.'

'Then why isn't she acting the grieving mother and gaining public sympathy? She's not done herself any favours in the press.'

'Because she's devoid of emotion. Why do you think she has a housekeeper raising her kids when she's at home all day herself? If there's a hate campaign against her, then it's all she deserves. She's hurt Abigail and she'll hurt Nick too.'

'For someone that's not in a relationship, you seem very passionate about it all.'

'As I said, Nick's my friend.'

'But I heard you say he's having an affair.'

Karen's glance flickered across the room and back to Jennifer. 'If you want to know any more, you'll have to ask Nick. I suppose you'll put that in your little report and get him into more trouble,' Karen said, petulantly.

Jennifer brushed off her trouser legs before rising to leave. She was tired, feeling like a dog chasing his tail and getting nowhere. 'No. I don't think I will. But if you know anything about Abigail's disappearance, you have to tell me. Even if she's dead, we've got to bring home her body. She won't be at rest until we do.'

'I would never withhold information, especially not involving the disappearance of a child. I can see what it's doing to Nick. The only good thing that's come out of this is that now he can see what his wife is really like, and leave her.'

Jennifer cast her eyes over the photos on the mantelpiece as she slid her card from her jacket pocket. She rested her card on a coffee table.

'Here's my mobile. Call me if you hear anything.'

'I won't need to,' Karen said.

'Oh, and Karen – I recommend you stay off Twitter for a while.'

Karen opened her mouth to speak, then shut it again. Her cheeks flushed as she showed Jennifer to the door. 'I never really liked Twitter anyway,' she mumbled.

Jennifer sat in her car, trying to piece together the puzzle. So many different pieces, she thought, working with the analytical side of her brain. If Nick wasn't having an affair with Karen, then who was he with? The two places Nick spent his time were at home, and at work. Home . . . she thought of Fiona, their shared glances, hushed whispers as she entered the room. It wasn't the first time the thought had entered her mind. Was Fiona a cuckoo trying to shove Joanna out of the nest? But there was no spark between them, nothing to suggest feelings of a romantic nature. Karen's words replayed in her mind. She had let down her guard as she spoke of Nick. *The only good thing that's come out of this is that now he can see what his wife is really like, and leave her.* She could imagine her on the phone now, ringing Nick to warn him. Why did she have such an interest in his marriage if she wasn't dating him? And what about Abigail? Could Karen be capable of snatching her in an attempt to expose Nick's wife as the heartless woman she believed her to be? She wished she had taken notes of their conversation in the park. But the rain had blotted her notebook the second she had flipped back the cover, sending ink trails running down the page. They had said something about a secret, she was sure of it. But Karen was a young woman with a career ahead of her. Surely she couldn't orchestrate something so heartless. Jennifer groaned in exasperation. Too many what ifs and not enough evidence. But she was not ready to lay this at Radcliffe's door.

She rolled it all around in her head as she drove back to the farm. She could have reported Karen for her part in the online hate campaign against Joanna, but what good would that do? The young woman had her career ahead of her, even if she was blinded by loyalty to Nick. Loyalty. Karen said Nick had been like a brother to her, not a lover. She recalled Karen's reaction as she had challenged her for the second time about the affair. Her gaze had flitted away, over the mantelpiece and . . . Jennifer recalled the ornaments and the framed photo where Karen's attention lay. The photo . . . surely not? She drew an involuntary gasp as another piece of the puzzle slotted into place.

CHAPTER FORTY-SIX

Diary Entry

So an arrest has been made. Radcliffe, of all people. Hopefully he won't bore them to death with his talks on climate change and the future of the economy. If there was ever a more unlikely handyman, I've yet to make their acquaintance. And yet it got me thinking, because Radcliffe tends to more than the farm. Plans continue to hatch in my brain. The voice of reason has been pleading for mercy, telling me that once Abigail dies, there's no coming back. But, you see, there is. And I know just the person to take the blame for her demise.

The more time I spend watching her in captivity, the more I remember myself at her age, gripped by anguish, all wide-eyed and suspicious.

The photos became a routine, and I learned to retract from my surroundings as the flash bulbs lit in quick succession. Off came my clothes, all of them now, and if I didn't beg or plead I could cut down my time in the studio to fifteen minutes flat. My silence seemed to worry him more than my tears, and sometimes I could hear him, mumbling to himself as he justified his actions. He was a photographer, that was all. I was his model, just like the models you see on the catwalks and on TV. Except that I was nine years old. White-hot anger built up inside me as I ran the gamut of emotions. I had gone from tears, to trying to reason, to complete numbness, before I fell into the realms of bitterness and hate. Although he never touched me, the weekly humiliation made my life a living hell. I began to fantasise about hurting him. About putting an end to him for good. He saw it in my eyes because he began to act shifty, and come up with even more excuses, even managing to turn it around. He was acting as my guardian, he said. His clients were keen for more, and wanted to meet me in private. What if they knew where I lived, where I went to school? He was my protector, keeping the information from them. Really, he was doing me a favour, because the pictures were the only way of keeping them satisfied. If he didn't continue . . . who knows what would happen? He was bigger and stronger than me, and had me cornered. There was nothing I could do. So I became reacquainted with my old friend the razor. My compulsion to self-harm had lain dormant in the days when my 'father' had pretended to be my friend. But now it emerged with new relish, and this time, the relief was immeasurable.

CHAPTER FORTY-SEVEN

The thought of getting involved in a colleague's love life made Jennifer uneasy in her skin. She reasoned that it was only relevant to the investigation because Nick had made it that way. If he had told the truth from the beginning, then she would not have had any reason to suspect him in the first place. Secrets were damaging, particularly if the person keeping them was a serving police officer. Jennifer wrung her hands as she prepared to confront him. Stress had been the root of his chronic insomnia. His nocturnal outings produced nothing of interest apart from him pottering around the farm, unmasking the emotions he denied an audience during the day. She guessed that night was when the tears came, and she could not help but feel sympathy for the man whose life was falling apart. She hoped that by getting his secret out in the open things could move forward.

She wasn't thrilled about luring him away with the promise of an update, but it was the only way of getting him alone. Meeting at the police station was a bad idea. Instead, she chose her favourite coffee shop, where the atmosphere was warm and homely. Nick entered, showered and wearing a change of clothes. The dark rings under his eyes had aged him, and he looked gaunt and withered as his weight slipped away.

'You said you had news?' he said, taking a seat across from her.

Jennifer pushed a cappuccino across to him. 'Here. You look like you could do with it.' Nervousness bubbled up inside her, taking her by surprise. She was never shy when it came to dealing with victims of crime, but Nick was different. He was a superior officer, and the last thing she wanted was to offend him. 'I know about your affair,' she blurted, wondering what had happened to taking things slowly.

Nick spluttered, almost spitting out his coffee. 'There's nothing going on between me and Karen, she's already told you that.'

'I agree. But I'm not talking about Karen, am I, Nick?'

Nick dropped his gaze to his coffee, his Adam's apple bobbing as he swallowed hard.

'I don't know what you mean.'

'It was something that Karen said, about you being like a brother to her, someone she'd known for years. It was only when I saw the photos of you with Matt that I realised she meant brother-in-law. How long have you been seeing each other?'

Jennifer took no pleasure from the revelation. She had seen evidence of Nick's strict religious upbringing, and his parents' disapproval of anything that deviated from the norm. His mother's comments about her son's wicked mistakes, and her adoration of the less than perfect daughter-in-law Joanna all made sense now. Only now, with the benefit of hindsight, did Jennifer recall Matt and Nick's secret glances across the room.

'Nick,' Jennifer said, resting her hand on his wrist. 'It makes no difference to me. But it's relevant to the case when you're asking your daughter to keep secrets. Just let it go. The worst has already happened.'

Nick's calloused finger toyed with the wedding ring on his left hand. It was white gold. A sign of their commitment. A deep sigh passed his lips, carrying all the pain and hurt of the last few days.

'I'm not . . .' He leaned forward to whisper the tainted word '. . . *gay*. I'm a married man. I've got children, for God's sake.'

Jennifer stirred her coffee, watching the frothy swirls absorb the sugar she had deposited on top. 'Nick, it might be a big deal to your mum, but it's not to me . . . I wouldn't even be asking you if it wasn't for the investigation.'

'Wendy's my stepmother,' Nick said, the corners of his mouth turned down in a scowl. 'My real mother's dead . . . for all the good she was.' Nick stared at his coffee, his face growing dark.

'So you've got this all wrong . . . I love my wife.'

'I'm sorry, but I can't let this go.' Pushing her coffee aside, Jennifer rose to leave.

'I suppose the whole station knows,' Nick said, stilling her departure.

Jennifer sat back down. 'What do you take me for? But I think you're doing your colleagues a disservice. It's not like the olden days. There are plenty of gay people in the police force.'

'I can't go public. I've got my marriage to think of,' Nick said.

'And Olivia?' Jennifer said, relieved to be unwinding the truth from the tightly bound spool of lies.

Nick glanced around before responding. 'I was wrong to ask Olivia to lie for me. I know that now. But I panicked.'

Jennifer nodded in understanding, but in truth she was bluffing. She had no idea what he was going to say. All she could think about was the photo on the mantelpiece in Karen's home. A picture of Karen, Nick and Matt, cheek to cheek as they held up their pints and beamed for the camera. The reason that Joanna wasn't jealous of Karen was because there was nothing to be jealous of.

'Joanna knew about Matt when we met. My parents . . . they had disowned me, but Joanna got us back together again, at the expense of my friendship with Matt. Meeting Joanna seemed right. I wanted to start a family, and for a few years everything was good.'

'But?' Jennifer said, wrapping her fingers around her mug.

'I bumped into Matt on a night out. We started seeing each other, and I knew I'd been living a lie to please my family. I'd decided to get a divorce when Joanna announced she was pregnant.'

Jennifer nodded, relieved that Nick was opening up to her at last. She thought about Joanna, and her previous comment that if she wanted something, she just took it. 'Had the pregnancy been planned?'

Nick nursed his coffee cup. 'When we first got married, it was all I ever wanted. Joanna said she'd stopped taking the pill, but months later I found a pack under the mattress. I decided to say nothing, as I was questioning my own motivations by then. Then she fell pregnant. She must have found out about the affair and stopped taking them.'

'And neither of you mentioned him?'

'I thought if we had any future as parents I had to come out in the open. I told her about my feelings for Matt. I presumed she'd want a divorce, and I made it clear I wanted to be a father to our children. But instead, she started self-harming. She said she'd cut herself and end the pregnancy if I left her. It was superficial cuts, but I couldn't take the risk. So I decided to make a fresh start.'

'And Matt?'

'We broke all ties. But then Karen, his sister, came back into my life through work. Matt came to see me on the farm . . .' Nick swallowed, his discomfort evident.

'And that was the day Abigail disappeared?' Jennifer said.

'Yes,' Nick said, his eyes glistening. 'He said he was going to confront Joanna, get everything out in the open. I persuaded him to give me some time. Things got . . . well, we got carried away . . .' Nick reddened at the memory. 'Well . . . anyway, we were half undressed when Olivia ran into the hay shed. I told Matt to leave. I was furious at myself for allowing it to happen, and I shouted at Olivia, telling her she mustn't say a word. She nodded that she wouldn't, and went looking for Abigail. I presumed they were playing hide and seek. Only later did I discover Abigail was actually missing. After searching the yard, we went inside to check with Joanna. The police were called and the whole thing snowballed from there.'

'And Matt kept ringing you?' Jennifer said, sheepishly. 'I heard you on the phone.'

'Remind me to offer you a place on my department,' Nick said, relaxing enough to offer her a slight grin. 'Matt phoned every day. He was upset, angry. In truth, I was scared. I didn't want anyone to know, least of all my colleagues.'

'What I don't get is why you've been so angry with Joanna when *you're* the one cheating on *her*. You risked being implicated in your daughter's disappearance rather than tell the truth.'

Nick looked around the coffee shop. The barista was out of earshot, collecting cups from empty tables. 'I'm not proud of my actions. My parents are very religious, as you know. When I met Joanna, she was a breath of fresh air. I wanted to be in a normal relationship, and accepted by my parents. I loved her – just not in that way. But every time I tried to leave, she'd self-harm, or threaten to tell my parents.' He shook his head at the memory. 'It's been a difficult few years. I thought it couldn't get any worse. And then Abigail disappeared.'

'So what next?' Jennifer said.

Nick stared hard at the dregs of his coffee, wrapping his fingers around the cup, which had grown cold. 'I need some time to come to terms with Abigail's disappearance. Maybe now I've spoken to you I'll be able to get some sleep.'

'And what about Olivia? She's been through so much. She doesn't need the burden of keeping your secret.'

'Yes,' Nick said, doubtfully. 'I'll talk to her. Soon.'

Jennifer tried not to grimace. 'Well, make sure you do. All this self-flagellation isn't getting you anywhere.'

Nick's eyebrows shot up at the comment, but Jennifer spoke again before he could come up with a response. Her thoughts had returned to Abigail, and it felt fitting that their last words should be about the little girl.

'Have you told me absolutely everything, Nick? You really didn't see Abigail on the day?'

'Go and ask Matt. He'll confirm our story.'

Jennifer nodded. Matt was a potential witness and she would be taking a statement from him very soon.

'You mentioned Joanna taking extreme action when she found out about you and Matt in the past. How do you know she hasn't orchestrated Abigail's disappearance?'

'The thought did occur to me. But she was with Fiona the whole time. And I don't think she'd actually lay a finger on the children. She's never even smacked them.' Nick's face clouded over. 'Besides, the police think it's Radcliffe.'

'True,' Jennifer said. 'Although it's difficult to know, there's still a grain of hope that she's alive.'

Nick nodded. 'Up until now, I've been clinging on to that hope. She was always shoving biscuits and juice boxes into the pockets of her dungarees. But if she was trapped somewhere, it's unlikely she could survive much longer.'

'Your relationship with Matt was a vital piece of information. You shouldn't have hidden it from us.'

Nick sighed. 'We all do things we regret.'

CHAPTER FORTY-EIGHT

Another evening, another round of briefings, and the full extent of their enquiries were revealed as DCI Anderson made a short appearance in the briefing room. Up until now, the evidence had been kept close to his chest. The justification for Radcliffe's arrest had come after the press appeal produced an anonymous call. The witness had stated that Radcliffe was seen carrying something to the woods. Something wrapped in a blanket. According to DCI Anderson, the house search had unearthed vital evidence, such as a browsing history on his computer displaying an interest in children. Nothing illegal, but numerous images from Facebook, downloaded for darker intents. All they needed was a body – or a confession – but neither was forthcoming. The Crown Prosecution Service had authorised bail, as Radcliffe's van was seized for forensic testing.

'We'll be able to curtail your time at the house when we get a charge, at least until the court case,' the DCI said, with the hint of a smile on his lips. 'Hopefully this will help the family get on with their lives. The search has been resumed in the woods, and I'll leave it to you to update the family.' He paused, noticing Jennifer's glum expression. 'You don't seem very happy, DC Knight. What's the matter with you?'

That's rich, Jennifer thought, coming from someone whose face was set in a permanent scowl. 'Sorry, sir, I just find it hard to believe Radcliffe is responsible. I think our suspect is closer to home.'

DCI Anderson's eyes narrowed. 'Have you any evidence to back this up?'

'No,' Jennifer said, wishing she had engaged her brain before her mouth.

'Well, then I suggest you return to the family and update them on our findings. Oh, and keep your opinions on the case to yourself, unless you have anything to substantiate your claims.'

Jennifer reddened, feeling like a schoolgirl as she was chastised in front of her colleagues. 'Yes, sir,' she muttered, keeping her eyes to the floor.

But as she drove into the yard of Blackwater Farm, the nagging voice returned. Her eyes alighted on Nick, and he quickly glanced away, shoving his hands deep in the pockets of his wax jacket as he made his way down the dirt track to the woodlands.

'Nick,' Jennifer shouted, flinging open her car door. 'We need to talk.'

The four words stopped him dead in his tracks, but he didn't turn around.

'Let's walk,' Jennifer said, taking her place beside him on the rugged track. 'It was you, wasn't it? You made the anonymous call.' Her words were met with silence, conceding the truth of her assertion. 'You said the woodlands was the one place that couldn't be searched properly.'

Nick ploughed down the track with little regard for Jennifer trying to keep up in her unsuitable designer heels. 'Don't you ever get tired of being on my back?'

'You know me by now,' Jennifer said.

'Does it matter who made the call?' Nick said coldly. 'Looks like it was him after all.'

'Does it?' Jennifer said. 'Yes, he's a loner with a fascination for children, but the only evidence is circumstantial.'

Nick kept on walking, his brow furrowed as he worked things over.

'Nick, I'm all for catching whoever's responsible. But not like this. You know it's wrong, don't you?' Jennifer said, the wind stealing her words.

Nick tilted his head in her direction, shouting over the gusts. 'They were pulling back the search. And if DCI Anderson believes Radcliffe's responsible, then it's good enough for me.'

'They're bailing him while they carry out forensics on his van. Promise me you won't go near him.'

He lowered his head against the rising wind. 'Of course,' he replied, his voice cold and even. 'Justice will prevail in the end.'

Jennifer slowed, allowing him to carry on without her, until he disappeared from view. She tilted her head to the sky, inhaling the scent of the countryside.

'Come back to us, Abigail,' she whispered to the wind. 'Come back to us soon.'

CHAPTER FORTY-NINE

Diary Entry

The most mundane things often trigger memories. Strawberries evoked my latest recollection. The sticky red juice poured from my helping of pie, lacing my fingers and dripping onto my plate. It brought forth an image of her blood, rich and red, pooling onto the wooden floor. It's been a long time since I dusted off that memory, but I recall it with pristine clarity.

The photo sessions carried on for another whole year, tapering off when I hit puberty. But instead of going away, my hatred grew, blooming like a bitter poison in my chest. Relief came when I began to turn the hurt outwards, releasing the frustration with each sharp slice of the blade. I began to experiment, using mirrors, glass and broken bottles to gouge my flesh. Mother caught me one day, engraving the word 'dirty' into my stomach with the knife she used for peeling potatoes. I had only got as far as 'dirt' when she forced me into the car. A whole year of therapy followed, which was a complete waste of my time. As if I was going to lead them to the photos I tried so hard to cover up.

It was little wonder I reacted by pushing Mother down the stairs. She had tried to help in her mealy-mouthed way, but I wasn't ready to go back there again. Not then. She wanted to have me committed, because the therapy was not working. She said I was impossible to live with, but I knew that all my family wanted was to turn their backs on me. I remember my heart feeling like it was punching its way out of my chest as I stole a glance downstairs. The deathly cracking noise of Mother's skull hitting the lino reverberated in the sunlit hall, and shockwaves passed through me as reality dawned. The mundane things in life merged with my horror; the bin man whistling as he passed our gate, the low rumble of the lorry trundling by. The world hadn't stopped spinning, despite the fact my mother was dead. And I had killed her. There was no way she could lose that much blood and still be alive.

I smile to myself now, as I recall just how shocked I was, and how far I have come. Her skirt had risen ungraciously to her thighs, exposing her pasty white flesh, and her arms and legs splayed in right angles like a human swastika. A wave of nausea passed over me and I grasped for the banister. I took a few deep breaths to calm down, but I couldn't stop shaking. Then came the primal urge to run. Acting on impulse had always been my downfall. But not any more. Somewhere in the chaos and panic in my brain was a slow sensible voice telling me to wait. In a way, my entry into killing was gentle, easy. But I had to be quick. Delays would raise suspicion. I paced the landing as I worked out what to do next. Purdy, the tortoiseshell cat, narrowed her green eyes at me while Maggie mewed downstairs, making footprints in the blood. I smiled as Panther lapped at the bright red liquid. He was the only one of all her damned cats that I liked. *My babies,* she called them. They even had their own birth certificates, in a special silver frame. Mine was kept in a brown leather bag, with a grocery list hastily scribbled on the back. *Beans, eggs, bread, milk.* Ah, treasured moments. Mother found solace in her cats, and I found solace in a razor blade.

I tiptoed back to the landing, staring in wonderment. I was fourteen years old and had changed the course of our lives with a simple push. She was badly broken, her leg coming back upon itself as if she was trying to kick herself in the mouth. A wild giggle erupted in my throat, startling me as it escaped my lips in a puff of air. It was only then that I realised Purdy was in my grasp. My mind had been busy plotting my survival, but my fingers had reached out to touch her treasured cat. As if sensing my intentions, Purdy flattened her ears and released a mean growl. I wrapped my fingers around her collar and, with some satisfaction, flung her down the stairs. Legs flaying, eyes wide, she bounced against the steps until she landed on Mother's backside and ran skidding out to the kitchen. I kicked the mat into a ruck on the upstairs landing. It was a stupid place to have it anyway. She had tripped, that was all. It wasn't difficult to let myself out the back door then make a big show of having found her. Having to play the mourning offspring was exhausting, but as it turned out I had little time for grief. It wasn't long before I could move on to something new.

CHAPTER FIFTY

He should have stayed away, Nick thought, as he circled Radcliffe's home. The cottage was nestled on the outskirts of Haven, down a dog walkers' country lane. It had taken every ounce of Nick's strength to reach it. He showed no mercy to his body as it cried out for sleep, forcing it to walk the three miles through the back roads so he would not be seen. He would not have put it past the police to have him under surveillance, although he had seen the yearly budget and he knew they couldn't afford it. He thought of DC Knight, her eyes full of conviction when she talked about following correct procedures, and doing things the right way. But contrary to his comment earlier, he knew more than anyone that justice didn't always prevail. He had closed enough unsolved cases to know of the pain that families carried when the perpetrator of evil was free to roam at will. Life was unfair, but he would not be a victim. If Radcliffe would not tell him Abigail's whereabouts, then he would die.

As time ticked mercilessly by, it was a case of his daughter's life or Radcliffe's. He didn't want to believe it, but it had to be him. He had interrogated the police system on Jennifer's laptop, when she had been distracted by talking to Joanna. Radcliffe was a loner, and police intelligence stated he had an interest in children, photographing them in the town. A police search at his home had produced hundreds of pictures on his computer and more hung on the walls. Why the fascination unless he was building up to something? He vaguely remembered making an anonymous call, in the middle of the night when sleep wouldn't come. But he had never imagined it would lead to all this. He had only done it so they would keep searching the woods.

Nick's stomach churned in a mixture of disgust and hunger. When was the last time he had eaten? He couldn't remember. His shirt collar felt damp as he rubbed the back of his neck. It felt strange to be on the other side, to be the person about to commit a crime. He pushed his fist into his jacket pocket and ran his fingers over the cable. He had thought long and hard about how he was going to do this. Any form of blood spilling was messy, and left a trail of forensic evidence. No, he would enter like a ghost, catch Radcliffe off-guard while he was asleep. Then he would wrap the cable around his neck, demanding he reveal where Abigail was. A balaclava would protect his identity, and his gloves would prevent the damning fingerprints that would bring police to his door. He had never been to Radcliffe's home, which now struck him as odd. He was a police officer. How could he allow this man in their lives without knowing how he lived? And now Radcliffe had been bailed. Surely the police would have advised him that returning home would leave him open to vigilante acts? Perhaps he felt he deserved it. Or perhaps it was arrogance. Nick settled on the second reason, because it would make it easier for him to do what he needed to do. Lately he felt as if his masculinity had been called into question, as if somehow he was less of a man. Coming out to DC Knight had been a test for what lay ahead, and he didn't know if he was strong enough to go through with it. Since Abigail's disappearance, his pride had taken a battering. What sort of man allows someone to take his daughter and does nothing about it? He knew what his parents would say: that he wasn't a man at all. Charles Radcliffe wasn't going to confess. And even if he were sent down, he'd be somewhere that Nick couldn't get to him. It would eat him up inside, and he'd never truly be free. He needed to confront him; to watch the life leave his eyes.

Satisfied there was nobody watching, he pulled on his balaclava and gloves. The thick wire cable felt clumsy in his hands. Radcliffe was strong. What would happen if the tables were turned and Radcliffe tried to kill him? Would it be such a bad thing? At least he would be with his daughter. It was an option he would have surrendered to, if it were not for the tiny spark of hope that she may still be alive. He thought of his Matt, and his own fractured family, Joanna and the girls. What would become of them? He gritted his teeth. He could either turn back now or get on with it.

He rammed his weight against the back door and it flew open with a shudder.

Nick was surprised. He hadn't expected entry to be that easy. It couldn't have been bolted because there it was, gaping open in front of him. The yellow torch beam jittered, exposing his tattered nerves. He clicked the off switch and stowed it in his jacket pocket. The cottage was not bathed in the glow of street lamps, like many homes in Haven. But he had been walking at night for so long now, his eyes were accustomed to darkness. Nick took a breath, trying to calm his galloping heart. A scrawny-looking mouse hopped over the dishes in the kitchen sink, stopping him in his tracks. Nick slowly twisted the door knob.

CHAPTER FIFTY-ONE

Nick froze at the sight of Radcliffe's sleeping silhouette. He had expected him to be in bed, not asleep in an armchair, a crocheted blanket over his lap. It was 3 a.m., and this was not a social visit. The hall light guided his path as he picked his way through Charles's litter-strewn living room, and Nick raised his nose to detect the sweet tang of cannabis in the air. He wasn't here for that. This was not police business. Each step inside transported him further towards the wrong side of the law, and his breath came thick and heavy as his heart pounded in his chest. Beads of moisture gathered around the mouth hole of his balaclava, and an itch began to form. He wanted to pull the thing off, to wake up Radcliffe and ask him what he'd done with his daughter. He sidestepped the empty coffee mugs and overspilling ashtrays, licking his lips to ease the dryness in his throat. Days of shouting for his daughter had made it raw and painful, but it was the least of his concerns. A voice in the back of his mind whispered that this was all too convenient, that nobody left their doors unbolted any more, especially not someone accused of child abduction. But there was no turning back now. This bastard had taken his little girl, probably done unspeakable things to her and disposed of her like a piece of rubbish without a backward glance. They had allowed him into their home, fed him, paid him. And he had been eyeing her up, watching her run around the farmyard. The thought repulsed him. Had he intended on taking Abigail all along? Their bright spark? Their livewire? Or was he going to settle on Olivia? Quiet, trusting Olivia, ready to take anyone's hand. He had allowed this man to hurt his family. It was time to make him pay. Blind hate rose up inside him as he approached the slumbering figure. Radcliffe slept with his legs crossed, wearing the same blue pullover which had become snagged from the briars paving the entrance to the woods. Nick's jaw tightened as he remembered that day; Radcliffe insisting on pushing through the thorns to investigate an old plastic bin liner. Had he been putting himself at the scene in case his forensics were found later? Or was he a leech, feeding off their pain?

A voice whispered in his consciousness. It was the voice of his wife. *You're not a violent man. Come home. We'll find another way.* The voice was an act of self-preservation. If he were caught . . . Being in prison was every police officer's nightmare, and he would rather be dead than face the people he had put away. He shuffled behind Radcliffe, jostling against a coffee table. Radcliffe's snore came to an abrupt halt. *Clumsy stupid idiot,* he admonished himself, preparing to bolt for the door. Gradually Radcliffe's breathing returned to a slow, steady pace.

Nick steeled himself for action, every muscle in his body tensing as he gripped the wire flex. The voice piped up again with more urgency. *Stop and think about what you're about to do. This is murder.* It wasn't difficult to counteract, because his justification had been playing in a loop since he left the house. What about Abigail? She's just a child. Did he stop and give her a chance? Standing behind the chair, he thrust the cord over Radcliffe's head, tightening it around his throat.

Radcliffe's eyes snapped open, and his body slackened as Nick overpowered him.

Nick expected him to cry out, to clutch at his arms, to scream, to fight. But he sat there, immobile, blinking in the shallow light. As if he wanted to die. Nick pulled his bulk from the chair as he tightened the grip around his neck. Radcliffe was muscled from physical work. He could take Nick if he wanted to, but he made no effort to defend himself. 'Where's Abigail?' Nick rasped. In the darkness the two figures were bonded by the loss of a little girl.

Eyes bulging, Radcliffe gurgled a whisper, but Nick couldn't make out the man's words. He eased his grip slightly, aware it could be a trap. Radcliffe's hands fell to his side, making no attempt to grasp the cord threatening to end his life. A trickle of sweat fell into Nick's eye as he fought to support the dead weight. He blinked back the stinging salt liquid and growled in Radcliffe's ear.

'I said, where is Abigail? Tell me now or I'll kill you. I mean it.'

'Make it quick,' Radcliffe whispered hoarsely.

Nick loosened his grip. He had not planned for this. Was that why Radcliffe had left his door unlocked? Why he was sitting in his chair? Had he been waiting for Nick to come along and administer his punishment? He released his grip and threw the man across the room. He would not grant him his wish. Radcliffe choked and spluttered as he was released, his words tinged with disappointment.

'Why didn't you finish it, Nick?'

Nick ripped the balaclava from his head, anger and bitterness coursing through him.

'Because it's what you wanted. What have you done with my daughter, you bastard? Is she here?'

Radcliffe rose to his feet, one hand around his neck. 'I've not touched Abigail, I swear.'

'Why did you come back?' Nick said, slightly dizzy as a wave of sickness took his breath. He had almost committed murder.

Radcliffe approached him warily, an eerie calmness in his voice. 'I've been waiting for you. I can tell you the truth, if you want it.'

'So you're ready to confess?' Nick said, flexing the cable in his hands. But it was all for show. Deep down, his resolve was fading.

Radcliffe sighed, shaking his head. 'Your DCI has been lying to you, Nick.'

'If you're trying to delay . . . have you called the police?' Nick said, peering out the dingy window for flashing lights.

'And what good would come from that?' Radcliffe said, switching on the living room light. 'DCI Anderson is trying to frame me.' He brushed past Nick and flicked on the light switch. 'Here, let me show you.'

Nick blinked as the glare of the one-hundred-watt bulb stung his eyes. It threw the room into sharp focus, and Nick glanced around as his police brain searched for clues. A picture of dogs playing cards around a table hung over a coal-darkened fireplace, and next to the padded chair lay several stacks of books.

Radcliffe caught his stare. 'It's *Tsundoku*,' he said, with perfect pronunciation. A smile caressed his lips, as if the word invoked a memory of long ago. 'It's Japanese for out of control book piles.'

He pushed his hand into his jeans pocket, pulling out a piece of red string. On the end was a key. Gesturing at Nick, he took it to a door at the back of the room, and undid the bolt. Nick's mind was working overtime. He slid his hand into his jacket pocket and wrapped his fingers around his torch. It was solid, unyielding, and a useful weapon if things went awry. Radcliffe could turn on him at any minute, and for all he knew Abigail could be behind the locked door. He patted his jacket pocket with his left hand and felt the outline of his phone. He could call the police if he needed to, say that Radcliffe invited him there, and as for the cable . . . that was easily disposed of. But by God, if Abigail *was* behind that door he would kill the bastard and fuck the consequences.

The bolt sprang open with an audible clunk, and Nick's eyes widened as the door opened before him.

CHAPTER FIFTY-TWO

'Now do you see?' Radcliffe said, casting his arm wide. 'What's left of my life is within these four walls.'

Nick's mouth gaped open as he took in the array of colourful oil paintings of children at play. There must have been two hundred works of art, in varying shapes and sizes. What could not be hung on the walls was stacked in the corner, laced with cobwebs. Half-finished paintings sat on easels, the canvases daubed with a big red X as the artist's frustration became evident. Only the most beautiful pictures were framed and hung on the main wall. And they were enough to take Nick's breath away.

'Did *you* paint these?' he said in awe.

The same children were featured throughout; a dark-haired boy and a freckle-faced girl, playing in the sunlight, running through fields, rolling down hills, as a dark-haired woman stood watchfully over them.

'That's my wife,' Radcliffe said, pointing to the woman in the blue-flowered dress. 'And these are my children.'

'I didn't know you have . . .' Nick said, their eyes meeting, cutting him off mid-sentence as his own pain reflected back at him. The pain of a loss so deep it leaves you as nothing but an empty core.

'Memories,' Radcliffe said, blinking back the tears. 'That's all I've left. But I didn't bring you here for sympathy. I wanted to show you because I'm not some paedophile downloading images of children. I just paint them.'

It was true. 'I . . . I had no idea you were an artist,' Nick said, shame washing over him.

'We don't all wear berets and carry easels,' Radcliffe said, gesturing to the framed photograph taking centre stage on the wall. This was not a painting, but a photo of long ago. Nick recognised the family, or at least one of the members. It was Radcliffe with the woman and children from the paintings. But Radcliffe had grown a beard and had gained several lines on his face since then. 'I had an art exhibition and was meant to join them in Thailand the next day. Petra loved to travel. She insisted we travel long-haul with the kids instead of the usual Costa Brava holiday. It was tiring, but it opened their minds.' Radcliffe dropped his gaze from the photo, and turned to Nick. 'I lost them all in one fell swoop, because of my selfishness.'

'How?' Nick said.

'A tsunami. They were on the beach when it happened. They didn't stand a chance.' Radcliffe cleared his throat as his voice broke.

'I'm sorry,' Nick said. 'But what has this to do with Abigail?'

'Nothing. But do you think I'd put another person through my pain?' Radcliffe said. 'I lost my family ten years ago, but I can't let go of them. Not yet. But my paintings, they lack life essence. I can't paint my children from memory any more. So I spend time in the company of other people's children . . . but not the way you think. It helps me to paint. I have photos on my computer. Your DCI knows they're innocent, but he doesn't care. All of these children, they help keep mine alive.'

Nick's eyes fell on a painting of the boy and girl in a field of sunflowers. 'This was painted from the photo of Abigail and Olivia, wasn't it?'

Radcliffe nodded sadly. 'Yes. There were a pile of photos on the table and I took one. I'm sorry. I miss my kids. I don't want their memory to die.'

As Radcliffe broke down, Nick could see he was telling the truth. It was like looking at himself, in ten years' time. He couldn't allow himself to end up like this. His daughter's disappearance had to be resolved.

'Don't you know *anything* about Abigail?'

Radcliffe swabbed his tears with his sleeve. 'Haven't you been listening to a word I've said? I wouldn't wish this pain on another living soul. I should have been with my family that day. If I had been, I could have got them to safety. It's my fault they're dead.'

Nick could barely believe what he had heard. The police investigation was totally misleading, and DCI Anderson was at the forefront of it. He had heard the man was a bully, and sailed close to the wind when it came to getting what he wanted to push him further up the ladder of promotion. But to purposely mislead him . . . he almost killed this man. Radcliffe lit a dim lamp in the living room and handed him a small glass of whisky.

'Here. It'll take the edge off.'

'Are you not having one yourself?' Nick said.

'No.' He said, switching off the harsh bulb overhead. 'If I start, I may never stop.'

The men talked until dawn broke and the sun began to filter through the curtains. Nick didn't have to believe him. The fact that the man had suffered a loss may have driven him to take his daughter. But all of his senses told him that Radcliffe was telling the truth. He was just grateful he had discovered this before things went any further. Red welts were beginning to come up on Radcliffe's neck and Nick dropped his gaze to the floor.

'Don't do anything stupid,' Nick said, remembering Radcliffe's whispers as he wrapped the cable around his neck. 'There's been enough loss. You've got to find a way of carrying on, because that's what your family would have wanted.'

Radcliffe stared through deadened eyes. 'I'm moving away when all this is dealt with. There's no point in staying any more. The newspapers have taken care of that.'

Nick drained the last of his whisky and laid the glass on the fireplace. 'But you can talk to the papers. We can sort this out.'

'I don't want to live here any more. Haven will be tainted by this forever. It's why I moved away from my last address. It may have happened thousands of miles away, but their deaths might as well have been on my doorstep.' Radcliffe sighed. 'I don't know. Maybe it's time I went back to my family and friends. At least they understand me there.'

Nick stared blindly at the floor, at a complete loss for what to say. He had a missing child. How do you comfort a man who has lost his entire family?

As if reading his mind, Radcliffe spoke. 'I know you and Joanna have your ups and downs, but take my advice and keep her close. Be there for Olivia as a family. I used to row with Petra all the time. We argued the last time we spoke. What I'd give for one more day with her, just to say I'm sorry. I should have seen what was important, instead of staying behind for work.'

'You probably wouldn't be alive today if you had.'

'Exactly,' Radcliffe said.

Nick left the house with a heavy heart. How could he have gone so wrong? And who could he trust? So far, the only person that had been honest with him was DC Knight. He needed to get his life back on track. Then he needed to speak to Jennifer Knight.

CHAPTER FIFTY-THREE

Five Days Gone

Nick's disclosure about visiting Radcliffe's home was enough to make Jennifer squirt a double dose of hand sanitiser on the palms of her hands. It was frightening to think that DCI Anderson would go so far as to mislead the team. His insinuations about Radcliffe weren't illegal, but it was certainly immoral in her eyes, and she wondered if he had been responsible for leaking the story of his arrest to the press. Twisting an investigation to get a result was relatively unknown in Haven, and she began to feel uncomfortable under his leadership.

She thought of Radcliffe, and the pain he must have endured to torture himself, creating painting after painting. It almost made her glad she didn't have children. Her relationship with Will was moving at such a rapid pace it made her nervous. She wasn't familiar with having such a steady, reliable influence in her life. She was used to making her own way, looking out for herself. Almost losing Will had frightened her to death. To leave herself open to such potential pain when she had already been through so much already . . . Splatters of rain began to fall on her hair and face, shaking her out of her thoughts.

That morning in briefing she had been met with a cool reception by her colleagues as she protested Radcliffe's innocence. She had been sharply put in her place by DCI Anderson telling her that Radcliffe was far from eliminated; that although his van had come back clean from forensics, it was just a setback in their line of investigation. She could tell by his disapproving tone that he would seek to have her removed from the family, if he hadn't already. She blinked away the rain as her phone rang in her pocket. She could stay outside for a while. Nick's parents returned with the local priest for more prayers, persistence apparently being one of their qualities. She was in no hurry to interrupt. Taking shelter in the cow shed, she took the call. It was DI Cole. She explained about Nick's visit, without incriminating him. Radcliffe's motives for speaking to children were a lot less damning when his past was revealed. Ethan sighed, not sounding altogether surprised.

'I've heard DCI Anderson can be creative with the truth. He's already been on the phone. He wants you out of there, he thinks you're doing more harm than good.'

Jennifer balled her fist. 'If doing more harm than good means stopping an innocent man getting charged for murder, then I must be in the wrong job. Whose side are we on?'

'That's just it, though, isn't it? He doesn't believe Radcliffe is innocent. He's currently organising searches for all the properties where Radcliffe's worked. I've bought you another day. Break it to the family tomorrow. Anything could happen between now and then.'

'Do you think it will?'

Jennifer listened to him suck on a cigarette and exhale the smoke. It was a private habit. She liked Ethan because he was guarded. Just like her.

'You want my honest opinion? I think you're our best hope. You've got to do as much as you can in the next twenty-four hours to find Abigail. DCI Anderson is gunning for you, Jennifer. The last thing I want is to see you transferred somewhere obscure for going against his wishes.'

'You don't think it will come to that, do you?'

'I won't let you go . . . not without a fight.'

It didn't inspire her with confidence. But her job was the least of her worries. So far, her gut instincts had let her down. The search on Joanna's father's property had drawn a blank. So had her trip to the well. Even her communications with Olivia had dried up. But she wasn't giving up. Twenty-four hours. That's all the time she had left.

CHAPTER FIFTY-FOUR

Joanna

Joanna couldn't remember the last time she had felt true solitude. Being alone in the house was a novelty. Olivia was in school, Fiona had gone to the shops, and Nick was God knows where.

She found herself leaning against the cutlery drawer. It slid slowly on the rollers as it opened to reveal the knives Fiona used for chopping the ingredients for her wholesome stews. Beside them lay the boning knife, long, sharp and sleek, glinting in the soft afternoon sun. She imagined the cold steel smooth against her skin, cutting her flesh, the pain taking everything away. Olivia's face appeared in her mind's eye, and she slammed the door shut. Not today. She would not harm herself today. She needed to get outside; her thoughts were too big for the confines of the house.

Trees flanked her path as she walked the dried mud path that led to the river. The pure country air invaded her senses, and she raised her hand to swipe away a fly. A light breeze ruffled the leaves, producing a shushing sound, as if to ease the thoughts circling in her brain. Spring had finally arrived, and she welcomed the heat of the sun on her face. She rarely went for walks. To be truthful, she had never liked the countryside. When they first moved in, it was a novelty. Nick hired a JCB to tear down some of the more neglected outbuildings. He sat in the cab wearing faded jeans and a T-shirt, his arms rippling as he controlled the machine. She had watched, mesmerised, as the powerful jaws butted the shed walls and they fell with ease as if they were made of cardboard. He shook the dust out of his hair and she followed him into the hay barn, teasing him until they had sex on top of the bales of straw. The smell of the straw tearing into her thighs was a bittersweet memory. It was the last time they had been intimate. He was slipping away from her, back to Matt. She could not let that happen.

Her ankle bent as she stumbled over a chunk of dried mud, disturbed from footsteps of previous searchers. She rubbed her heel, already reddening from the dusty patent shoes. Balancing on her toe, she shook out the crumbles of soil. Her perfume was sweet and flowery, and responsible for attracting the insects that were gathering around her head in a cloud. She hated insects, especially spiders. So did Abigail. When they first moved in, Nick would have to make a grand gesture of checking everywhere to ensure there were none lurking under her bed or over the wardrobe. Then Joanna would tuck her daughters in at night, closing her eyes as they pulled her in for a cuddle. Abigail was such a thoughtful child, presenting her with a newly plucked bouquet from the weeds that bordered the stone wall outside her home. She used to call dandelions 'fluffy flowers', and would pick them for her on the days she looked sad. They were kept in a jam jar on the window sill in the kitchen. The jam jar was always full.

Joanna's breath shuddered and she realised she was crying. Then it occurred to her that she had every right to cry, so she allowed the tears to flow, releasing the tightness in her chest, which had grown to unbearable levels. She kept walking, the warm breeze cooling her tears as they dripped past her jawline. She walked until she didn't know where she was any more.

She missed the city, the background hustle and bustle all hours of the day and night. She missed the scream of police sirens, the shouts of drunken revellers as they poured out of the clubs, and the refuse lorries at 6 a.m. as they reversed on the streets, the *beep*

beep signalling dawn. At least there, she was never alone with her thoughts. She wondered for the hundredth time why she had to go and change everything. Coming back to Haven had been a mistake. She had hoped that Abigail's disappearance would at least bring them closer together, but all it did was drive an even bigger wedge between them. If she had researched the internet, she would have discovered that most couples split up after the loss of a child.

The sweet tangy smell of rapeseed rose around her and she knew she had reached the outskirts of the river. No need to panic, she knew exactly where she was now. The path was still well trampled, and all she had to do was follow it back home. She wiped her face with her fingers, staining her thumbs with mascara. Poking her fingers in her pocket, she pulled out a tissue to blow her nose. It occurred to her that the person fronting the hate campaign could be watching her right now. Any moment they could reach out and touch her. They could carry out their threat to hurt her, and there would be nobody to hear her scream. She imagined a hooded figure jumping from the bushes and pinning her to the hard dusty ground. His breath coming fast and thick, carrying a sour smell. Alcohol perhaps, or cannabis. Strong hands punching her in the face, tugging at her clothes. She would let them. She wouldn't put up a fight because, as they said, it was all she deserved. She would lay there, lifeless, until they had finished with her, and later on she would stagger home, limping and bleeding to . . . to what? A cold reception. Because nobody would believe her. They would probably think she had punched herself, or torn her own clothes. She had cried wolf before. There was no reason to think she wouldn't do it again. But what if she persisted? Gave a statement to the police? Published her story? Would she get some sympathy then? Her mind raced through the possibilities. Evidence. They would need evidence of an attack. Bruising. Bleeding. No. That would not do at all. The shriek of a woodland creature made her jump in her skin, and she spun on her feet, picking her way through the path, half trotting, half running home. Just what was wrong with her? Cold fear stabbed her heart. Her mind was unravelling, and there was nothing she could do about it.

CHAPTER FIFTY-FIVE

Diary Entry

People say you should never underestimate the love a parent has for a child. But I've never been on the receiving end, at least not at Abigail's age. Sometimes I can hear her in the ether, calling out in the dark. My mind becomes tortured with her pleas, and I turn the other way, but her voice still filters through. I hope when all this is over that the cries stop. Such things would drive a sane person mad. A cold chill overcomes me as I imagine spending the rest of my life listening to her pleading to come home. At least Olivia is quiet. Sitting there, pathetically sucking her thumb with those big saucer eyes. Sometimes she looks at me and words pass through her expression. *I know.* But as long as she is silent, she is safe.

I may be able to shrug off her knowing looks, but not the detective. She's from a special department. She can see into your soul. She's acting like she wants to help, but she's not to be trusted. I recognise her kind because I'm an expert in the art of manipulation myself. She's beginning to make me nervous, and I wish she would go away. Given my plans, that's not likely to happen any time soon. Sometimes I look back on this diary and I can barely remember writing the words. It's like there are two sides to me, and that's a frightening prospect. I know that Abigail's cries aren't real, because they're too far away to carry on the wind. Yet, sometimes I look around, to see if anyone else can hear them too. I've been making plans, but I don't know if I'm strong enough to go through with them. If her screams haunt me while she's alive, what will become of me after her death? But it's far too late to back out now. I've stowed away the accelerant and prepared for the fire. This time tomorrow, it will all be over.

CHAPTER FIFTY-SIX

'Come in. Nick told me to expect you,' Matt said, pulling open the door and allowing Jennifer past.

His Lacoste shirt and belted trousers flattered his youthful build, and if Jennifer didn't know what he did for a living she would have guessed him to be quite affluent. A barrister perhaps, or a cosmetic surgeon. Accountancy seemed flat in comparison. Sensible. His auburn hair had been gelled to one side in a trendy style, long on the top with a short back and sides.

Jennifer took a seat on a black leather couch. The flat was the polar opposite to Karen's, although given that Matt, at thirty-five, was ten years older, he had had more time to accumulate his wealth. It was clean and functional, with colourful prints, modern furniture and floor-length curtains. But it was more like a hotel room than a home; something assembled from a catalogue rather than graced with the personal touch.

Pleasantries over, Jennifer set to work and took a witness statement, covering the new information which had come to light. A widescreen television pictured an image of a soldier frozen in battle as his *Call of Duty* game was paused. The statement was brief, as Matt had already covered most of it in his interview. They began with his relationship with the family, how long he had lived in Haven, and general background details. It did not take long to get to the crux of the matter. Jennifer's long slim fingers tapped the statement into the keyboard of her new laptop. The force was finally going electronic, and it was an improvement on the traditional paper forms that sometimes went astray.

'So you're telling me that you've been in an intimate relationship with Nick for five years before he met Joanna, and reignited your relationship recently, your most recent encounter being the day Abigail went missing?'

Matt raised an eyebrow. 'We've met since then, but that was our most recent sexual encounter, yes.'

Jennifer gave two nods of the head. 'And on the day in question, you were giving him oral sex when Olivia crept in on you and screamed.'

'Yes,' Matt said, a rosy bloom creeping up his cheeks. 'Although it was more of a gasp than a scream.'

Jennifer did not raise her eyes from the statement. Matt's and Nick's affair was mild compared to some of the things she'd heard in her career. 'How did Nick react?' she asked.

Matt clasped his fingers over his knee, dividing his attention between Jennifer and the frozen Xbox game. 'He was horrified. He told me to go, said he'd sort things out with Olivia.'

'How did you feel?' Jennifer said.

'Embarrassed . . .' He emitted a nervous laugh. 'I mean, what kid wants to walk in on that?'

'What happened next?'

'Nick didn't handle it very well. He lost the plot. I told him Olivia looked scared, but he got annoyed, told me it was all my fault, that I shouldn't have come. So I left.'

'When you say he was frightening Olivia, in what way did you mean? Was he shouting at her? Touching her?'

Matt swivelled the ring on his index finger, a silver wedding ring, just like the one on Nick's left hand. When he didn't answer, Jennifer fixed him with a stare.

His voice eventually came, with the cautious tone of someone tackling a very thorny subject.

'He was bending down to her level, and his hands were on her forearms. He wasn't hurting her or anything, she was upset and he was trying to get through to her.'

A question rose in Jennifer's mind. Something that hadn't occurred to her until now.

'How did you know it was Olivia?'

Matt frowned, his eyebrows drawing together as he considered the prospect.

'Abigail's missing, so it had to be her.'

'But how did you *know* it was Olivia and not Abigail that found you?'

Matt shrugged. 'Nick said it was. I can't tell them apart. Why, you don't think . . .'

'No, I'm just asking, nothing more.'

Jennifer chased the thought away as she left Matt's flat. It was an uncomfortable thought, but every avenue had to be explored. The child that had found them in the shed could just as easily have been Abigail. Or they both could have been present. Jennifer had witnessed Nick's temper over the smallest of things. What if he had silenced his daughter for good, with Olivia as a witness? Her heart plummeted as she considered the possibility.

She re-read Matt's account as she sat in her car. He was more comfortable with his sexuality than Nick, and Jennifer got the feeling that Matt was Nick's first male tryst. Matt had been full-on, pressurising Nick to leave his wife, but the more Matt pushed, the further away he seemed to drive Nick, who was haunted by his parents' strict upbringing and narrow-minded views. It was hardly surprising that Nick had begun suffering with insomnia around the time of his affair. With pressure from every angle, stress had taken charge of his body, filling him with doubt and longing in equal measures. But were these longings enough for Nick to kill for? Had Matt wanted them to get caught? Used every ounce of his sexuality to tempt Nick into sex so near his family home? Or perhaps he was so annoyed by Nick's reaction that he had abducted Abigail in a fit of fury himself. How did the old saying go? *It's the quiet ones you have to watch.* Jennifer propped her elbow against the car window. So many possibilities, but so little evidence. Fresh droplets of rain pattered against the foggy windscreen, and her thoughts drifted to Abigail. Lost, afraid, alone. She turned on her wipers, allowing the *swish swish* noise to wash over her. This would not be one of those cases that was left a mystery. She felt it in her bones. Time would provide her with the answers. Abigail had not wandered off or got lost. Someone was lying to her. Someone close to home. And she had just twenty-four hours to find out who.

CHAPTER FIFTY-SEVEN

Jennifer gritted her teeth as she listened in to Joanna's phone call. More interference from DCI Anderson. He was her superior officer, and therefore deserved respect, but right now she couldn't help but be irritated by his call. She steeled herself as she listened in. It was the first time she had heard Joanna raise her voice.

'I've said no and that's it. Olivia's been through enough upset. . . . She hasn't spoken a word since Abigail's disappearance . . . What developments? No . . . No, I did *not* know that.' She shifted the phone to her other ear and threw Jennifer a narrow-eyed stare. 'No, she didn't tell me . . . Well, this has come to a surprise to me. I'll speak to DC Knight, but as I said before, I'm not agreeing to Olivia speaking to anyone else.'

Jennifer groaned. DCI Anderson had told her of Olivia's whispered conversations. He was clutching at straws. The investigation against Radcliffe had collapsed due to lack of forensic evidence, and DCI Anderson was using whatever he could to get a shock response. It's all right for him in his comfortable office, Jennifer thought. I'm the one who has to take the flak. Joanna had barely ended the call before she turned on Jennifer.

'Why didn't you tell me Olivia's been speaking to you?'

'What did he say?' Jennifer replied, trying to dodge the question.

'He said that Olivia's spoken. She said she knows where Abigail is.'

'That's not true,' Jennifer said, aware everyone else had gone quiet. 'Can we talk in the living room?'

Joanna nodded, and briskly led the way.

Jennifer could not fail to notice that Joanna was shedding her old persona, by trying to take control.

'Would you like to explain what's going on? If my daughter's talking, then I have a right to know about it.'

'I'm sorry, I didn't mention it because I didn't want to upset you. Olivia has uttered a few words but she doesn't seem to have any recollection of them afterwards.' What she didn't say was that her superior officers were the ones who had told her to keep it from the family in the first place. Such an admission may have been slightly gratifying, but would have made the police look unprofessional.

'Has she communicated with Abigail?'

Jennifer stared out the window, buying some time as she tried to work out what she was going to say. Word might get around, and she couldn't risk people knowing that Olivia had alluded to Abigail's whereabouts because it could put her in danger. 'Nothing really,' she said, trying to make her voice sound natural. 'At least, nothing which would lead us to Abigail.'

'You should have told me. I am her mother, after all.'

'You're right. I'm sorry. I didn't want to put her under any pressure.'

'Well, your DCI Anderson is. He insinuated I'm a bad mother because I wouldn't allow her to speak to a psychiatrist. He said people would make their own inferences as to why I wouldn't agree.'

Footsteps creaked on the stairs in the hall, and Jennifer kept her voice low. 'He's under a lot of pressure. We all want to find Abigail. I don't think it would do any harm for her to speak to someone.'

'I know I've not always been there for her,' Joanna said, flatly. 'But I'm trying to make up for that now. You can talk to her, but that's it. I don't want any more people in our home.'

'They're taking me out soon, maybe even tomorrow,' Jennifer said, glancing up at the fresh batch of cobwebs clinging to the ceiling. A part of her couldn't wait to be shot of Blackwater Farm. But she had hoped her time there would have ended on a better footing.

Joanna folded her arms in a matter-of-fact manner. 'Then speak to her today.'

Jennifer went straight upstairs to Olivia, and scooted up on the lumpy bed. She pulled a Raggedy Ann doll from under the blanket, and found several other toys tucked away.

'I haven't seen one of these in years,' she said, running her fingers through the doll's red corded hair. 'They're American, you know, you don't tend to see them over here. Was it a gift? Or did your mum pick it up in one of her charity shops?'

Olivia barely glanced up from her Nintendo DS. Teachers said she had got on well in school, although she was yet to speak. Jennifer was painfully aware this was the first Saturday without Abigail, and couldn't begin to comprehend what was going on in her head.

The whirr of the dehumidifier hummed from the back of the room as it drew the damp from the walls. Fiona had the Aga on at full blast again today. It was the beating heart of the house, and the heat it pumped made the place more bearable. The whispers that breathed through the walls had died down to manageable levels. There was only one voice she wanted to hear. Jennifer chatted as Olivia played, the game being paused each time she mentioned ponies, and resumed when she spoke of her father.

'Sweetheart, I know about your daddy's secret. He told me everything. It's okay. You don't need to be scared.'

A *meeep* sound emitted from the DS as the Mario character died, and Olivia pushed her glasses up the bridge of her nose before glancing up.

'I've spoken to Matt, your daddy's friend, too. He said he's sorry. What you saw . . . well, it was wrong. He's not going to come around here any more.'

Silence passed between them as Olivia stared with moon eyes, magnified by the lenses of her glasses.

'I've spoken to your mummy too, about how special you are. I'm different too. But you know that. That's why we're such good friends. You mustn't be afraid. We're all here to help you.'

Olivia slowly nodded in understanding. Her eyes were wary now, like those of a fox about to be lured into a trap with the tempta-tion of food. She wanted help, but was scared of the repercussions when it was accepted. Downstairs people milled about, muffled conversations carried on about expanding the search, and Nick spoke of printing more missing posters, for all the good it would do. Jennifer touched Olivia's shoulder, grateful the little girl didn't flinch.

'Can I speak to Abigail now? I know it hurts, but I really need to speak to her just one more time.'

Olivia snapped the DS game shut before sitting against the pink padded headboard and closing her eyes. It appeared that she had known all along that that's what Jennifer wanted.

Her breathing became shallow, and despite the heat Jennifer felt the stirrings of a cold fog envelop her. But there was something wrong with this communication. There was no simple transition like before. It was strained, and Olivia's face relayed the effort involved as her eyes squeezed shut. Finally, she took a gasp, but the voice was weak, barely a whisper.

'Tell . . . tell Mummy and Daddy I love . . . them. And Olly, tell her . . .' Silence ensued, and it seemed as if the communication was lost. Jennifer held her breath as Abigail struggled to form the words. 'Tell her not . . . to . . . be . . . sad.' The last words were spoken with huge effort, as if granted with a last breath. A trickle of blood lined Jennifer's gum as she realised she had been biting down hard. She swallowed, willing the little girl to come back to her. 'Abigail, we're still looking. We've not given up. Please, tell me anything. Can you hear any sounds? Is it far from the house?'

Olivia's face turned waxen, and her shallow breath made Jennifer's heart quicken. This was not good. It was as if Olivia had swapped places with her sister, and her weakness was taking its toll on Olivia's body. Jennifer's heart lurched as realisation dawned.

'No,' Jennifer whispered, clenching her lifeless hand. 'Come back, Olivia. You come back here right now. Your mummy and daddy, they need you. I know it's hard but, please, come back.'

CHAPTER FIFTY-EIGHT

The healing dog was making an appearance at the care home today. Cedar Homes had a wide range of activities for the elderly. A visit from the priest was another important aspect of Mr Hines's day. He had always hated religion. It was the main reason why his daughter had chosen this home, knowing that as he was forced to sit through daily masses somewhere inside he would suffer, just a little bit. Another push of the knife. But today he was in hospital. He would not be returning to the care home again.

To everyone else the blonde-haired woman looked like a bereft daughter leaning over her father to offer words of comfort. The beep of machines, the stale smell of antiseptic; it was more than he deserved. Soon he would be in the ground, and it could not come quick enough as far as she was concerned. Playing the doting daughter really was beginning to wear thin. Her eyes followed the trail to his IV line, carrying fluids to sustain his life. She imagined injecting poison into the bag of saline, and watching as the cocktail seeped into his withered veins.

'This is your fault,' she whispered. 'You made me do this. She's dead because of you.'

The memories were coming fast now, and she could not stop them. She knew it had been a bad idea, but they had insisted; reliving her childhood would allow her to be free. They were wrong. It made her sick to the core as each memory returned with sensory clarity; his rough hands on her skin, her shame highlighted by the blinding flashes of light. *Click click click* . . . the camera was never satiated, always hungry for more. Her shame felt like grease on her skin, but it was something she could never wash away. Happiness came only in brief moments, when she was made to feel like someone else. Someone good.

Hines snuffled from under the blankets. She lightly placed her hand over his, as a nurse breezed past. Wasn't this what normal daughters were supposed to do? A flare of anger rushed into her chest. How dare he lie there lifeless when he had so much to account for? He had never apologised for ruining her childhood. Not a word, a note, a gesture. Not a flicker of guilt in those steel-blue eyes. Not even when tears streaked down her cheeks. Surely he knew it wasn't normal? At least they didn't have the internet back then. If it were happening now, her face would be plastered all over it; there for the titillation of sick minds to play out their darkest fantasies.

She thought about Abigail, the farm, the car crash that was her life. This was all because of him. Would Abigail's death really cleanse her from all of that? She had thought that being here, seeing the old man so close to death would at least help. All it did was make her feel as hollow as the shell before her. But each breath he took was like a slap in the face. She couldn't bear it, not now her memories had returned. And it was the thought of Abigail's tenth birthday that had sparked it all off. Now, the only way she was going to feel better was to wipe out every reminder.

'Your precious granddaughter is dead,' she spat as she leaned over his sleeping face. 'She's dead and it's all your fault, do you hear me? Think on that, old man, think on that.' She drew away her hand, the touch of his skin making her stomach roll around the cheese sandwich she'd eaten earlier in the day. She raised the back of her hand to her mouth to mask a belch.

She knew what people would say. Photos weren't the same as actually being abused, were they? They were just pictures. Nobody had ever laid a finger on her, not really. It wasn't as if she came to any harm. That's what she told herself. But she was soiled. Dirty. She had to turn her back on the past and put on a brave front. And she could. Once he was gone she could move on with her life. It was a necessary evil. A purging.

She briefly thought of Abigail. It was unfortunate that someone had to be hurt, but there was always Olivia. It wasn't as if they would be childless. People had told her that her lack of empathy was abnormal, her inability to care for others. She looked at the man lying in bed, so helpless now, not the giant he had once been. Had he ever been that big? Or had she carried that since her childhood? He had ignored her tears, laughed at her pleas to stop. The threat of meeting the monsters behind the photos was enough to make her submit. But now she wondered if they had ever really existed. If the monster was just the man behind the lens. Tears pricked her eyes and she wiped them away.

She jumped as the nurse hovered past her, giving her a watery smile as she disguised her distress for daughterly love.

The nurse's voice was soft and sympathetic. 'Your father is comfortable. He's not in any pain. It's his loved ones that suffer, not him.'

Her words were meant as comfort but inside she wanted to laugh. Loved ones? He didn't have any loved ones. His death would be a blessed relief and it couldn't come quick enough. She waited for the nurse to leave before leaning over for one last farewell.

'Why don't you just do us all a favour and die, you old bastard?'

She pinched her handbag between her fingers, clutching it to her chest. To the outside world she was a doting daughter, but she knew what she was. She was the spectre at the feast, waiting for the end. But when he went, all reminders had to go with him. Only then could she get on with her life. She could not live through another tenth birthday. She would erase the day forever. She thought of Abigail and sighed. It was necessary. It was just. But first she had to take care of the monster.

She slipped out of the ward long enough to set off the fire alarm, distracting the staff before returning to the room. It did not take long to slip the pillow over his face; far too gentle a death for such an evil man. She could have waited for nature to take its course, but that would risk him being alive on the day. The plot had come quickly, perhaps her brain ensuring self-survival. Just when she had been on the point of ending it all, the idea of revenge had come. She had thought to herself, what have you got to lose? And it was true. Cold and calm, she had worked it out. All the reminders of the past could be deleted, just like when she rebooted her computer. Delete. Reset. And begin all over again. And if it didn't work, then she could revert to plan B and end it all. Either way, there would be no more pain. Wasn't that all she really wanted?

CHAPTER FIFTY-NINE

Diary Entry

So he's dead. I have played the part of somebody who is suitably upset. The last thing I need is to be implicated, not with everything else going on. Should I have waited? He was so close to the end. But that's precisely why I had to kill him. It's a shame he wasn't awake. I would have loved to see the fear in his eyes as they met mine. I would have returned the same heartless expression he afforded me as a child. He was an evil bastard and I don't feel remorse for killing him. It wasn't just for me, because I'm sure I wasn't the only one. It was for all the victims. It's better that I don't go to the funeral. I'm so close to the edge, I can't trust myself.

Sometimes I look at Olivia and wish it had been her. She turns her face on me and all I can see is accusation staring back. There's no love there. I was foolish to think there would be. I thought perhaps *I* could replace her sister. She didn't need to love me when she had Abigail. But all she does now is wander around like a spirit, as if a gust of wind could just take her away. It would be better if she were dead, then they could be together. But how? A tragic accident? Drowning, looking for her sister? Or falling through the bedroom window that she's always staring out of? But when I try to work things out, my head gets all fuzzy and starts to pound. I cannot act on impulse like before. But . . . nobody has caught me yet. And I'm so very close to the end.

CHAPTER SIXTY

'Why didn't you tell me about your dad?' Nick said, cupping his wife's cheeks in the palms of his hand. 'If I'd have known he was that ill . . .'

'I thought he was getting better,' Joanna said, her eyes glazed as she looked away.

'I'm so sorry,' Jennifer said, wondering how much tragedy one family could endure. But then, there weren't many people living in Haven who hadn't suffered loss of some kind or another. Something she was all too familiar with.

She had not heard the call come through, as she had been distracted with Olivia, shaking her gently in an effort to bring her back to herself. The child had drawn in a sharp breath, allowing Jennifer's heart to return to normal as the blueness left her lips. It prompted Jennifer to embrace her in a hug, apologising for asking her in the first place. Olivia had shrugged and returned to her game. The experience put Jennifer firmly in her place. She wouldn't go risking communications of any kind with Olivia again. For all she knew, she could have been adding to her trauma. She was so desperate to find Abigail that she had ridden roughshod over her sister's feelings, and she felt thoroughly ashamed. But there was no time to dwell on it, as news of Joanna's father had filtered through. Heart problems had plagued his later years, but his death had come as a surprise. He had fallen into the realms of dementia, which had left any line of questioning a fruitless task. Another secret in the lips of the town that held many secrets.

Jennifer sighed. She was close, she could feel it. But Abigail's voice had grown weak. The connection with her sister was dying out. Her staggered words felt like a bad omen. Abigail was letting go, saying her goodbyes.

'Father Murphy called. He's going to come around later to speak to you about the funeral,' Fiona said, laying a mug of sweet tea before Joanna.

'I'm not going,' Joanna said, staring at the swirling tea.

Nick reached across the table and touched her hand. His voice was soft, with none of the harshness of recent days. 'Sweetheart, you healed the rift with my parents, and I want to be there for you now.'

But Joanna responded with a cold, sharp smile. 'He had a funeral plan. It's all paid for. I don't need to get involved.'

'But you were his daughter, you're the head of his family,' Fiona said from behind her, a hint of irritation in her voice. 'Your relations . . . they'll expect to see you.'

'Estranged daughter,' Joanna said, her face pallid, her chest rising as she took deep breaths. 'And the family . . . will get by without me . . . I've not . . . seen them in years.'

Jennifer recognised the beginnings of a panic attack. She had experienced enough of them in the past to pick up on the symptoms. The feeling of dread enveloping you. A tightness to the chest, the air leaving your lungs faster than you could breathe it in. The sense of being dragged into an underwater tide of doom.

Fiona nudged the mug of tea closer, passing a knowing glance to Nick. 'You've had a shock, and you're under a lot of stress. Why don't you take some time to think about . . .'

'I don't need . . . to think about it.' Joanna's breathing regulated, but the usually cool exterior evaporated as she banged her fist on the table, making the tea splash over the rim of the mug. 'I'm not going and that's it. Call the priest. Tell him to arrange it.'

Fiona nodded quietly. 'Fine. I'll do that. By the way, my wages weren't paid in this week. Perhaps you'd like to see to it when you get a moment.'

Joanna rose, regarding her coolly. 'I'll do it today. If anyone calls, I'm going up for a . . .'

'Lie down. Yes, I know,' Fiona said, before throwing the tea down the sink.

Nick followed his wife as she ascended the stairs, his voice trailing behind him as he tried to coax her round. Jennifer joined Fiona at the kitchen counter. Steam rose from the tap as she washed and rinsed the mug.

'That was a bit sharp. Are you okay?'

Fiona gave her a wry grin. 'Sorry. Did I come across really pissed off? I struggle to understand her sometimes.'

Jennifer nodded. 'You don't need to apologise to me. It's only natural that tempers are running high.'

'It's just that . . .' Fiona gave an exasperated sigh and folded her arms. 'Oh, never mind.'

'No, go on,' Jennifer said.

Fiona regarded her cautiously. 'Oh, it's nothing. I didn't mean to snap.'

Jennifer lingered, hoping Fiona would open up about whatever was troubling her. But the moment was lost; Fiona's loyalty lay with Joanna.

'I'll be leaving soon,' Jennifer said. 'They've also scaled back on the search on the woodlands.'

Fiona gently dried the mug in a red checked tea towel. 'I know. What do we do after you go? Just carry on as if Abigail never existed? He'll never stop looking, you know. He'll keep searching, even if it kills him.'

'I don't know,' Jennifer said. 'I think he's strong enough to start again. You'll be given an exit strategy. We won't completely withdraw. But the family can't go on like this either.'

Fiona draped the tea towel on the rail in front of the Aga before turning around. 'Ever since I met Joanna she's been living in a different era. I thought about what you said about trying to get her to open up and I've scheduled a meditation session. Well, I say meditation . . . it's more like a relaxation session, where we talk about what's worrying her. It's worth a try, don't you think?'

'I thought you'd never offer,' Jennifer said.

In any other circumstances, the thought of returning to Haven nick may have been a welcome one. But Jennifer would be returning under a shadow, having let down Abigail and her family. With all her enquiries exhausted, Fiona was quickly becoming the best hope Jennifer still had of finding answers.

CHAPTER SIXTY-ONE

Six Days Gone

Joanna awoke with a start, as she realised she was not alone. For the first time since she could remember, her husband was in bed beside her. Unaccustomed to the warmth of his body, she lay still so as not to waken him, and then realised he wasn't pretending to be asleep like before. He was actually snoring. Sleep had been gifted to her husband at last.

So he had made his decision. They had both come to the edge of the precipice and decided to face what lay ahead together. But for how long? Would he stay with her if the truth was not to his liking? She had given herself to him on their wedding day. She had meant the vows when she said them out loud, even if she had reinvented herself a dozen times over since then.

Today was the eve of her daughters' birthdays. Tomorrow would mark their tenth birthday. And she hadn't done a thing to prepare for it. Gratefully, she had taken up Bob and Wendy's offer of having a small party at their house. It was easy to fall back on the excuse of being too wrapped up in worrying about Abigail to contemplate a celebration. Nick had arranged for the loan pony to come tomorrow evening, and Olivia's presents had consisted of everything horsey. Buying two of everything seemed like a waste of money to Joanna, but such was Nick's blind faith that his Abigail would come home, that he had insisted. Joanna had kept the receipts. The thought of the birthday milestone terrified her. Deep in her psyche, it was the day she had been dreading for a very long time. It carried with it a certain finality. Something was waiting on the horizon. Something bad.

She shifted in the bed, getting near enough to feel her husband's warmth but not so close as to wake him. Each second of his sleep was precious. She turned her head to look at him properly. He smelled of lemon shower gel, and his hair had been washed, his skin recently shaved. A sudden swell of love rose up inside her, an alien feeling, amidst all the anguish and pain. But before she could fix their relationship, she had to fix herself. It made her heart thud in her chest, to think about unleashing years of repressed thoughts. The flashbacks were slippery, like soap in her hands, but there was enough insight to make her skin crawl. What would it be like when the full truth was revealed? Could she live with herself then? Could he? There was only one way to find out.

Her stomach growled. Nick was sleeping; she was hungry. Was this their way of getting back to normality? It was an uncomfortable thought. She couldn't see herself ever moving on from this, no matter how much she tried. But she had to. Because she couldn't keep reinventing herself any more. She had run out of cardboard cut-outs. She had no choice but to explore what she had been hiding all these years, to go into the darkness and embrace it. Even if she found out something dreadful – and it had to be dreadful to have hidden it for so long – she could build upon it, and make a new life for her and Olivia. Hopefully Nick would factor in there, but she could not depend on him – not when he had let her down so far. Slowly, she crept out of the bed they shared. Pushing her feet into her pumps, she made up her mind. Today she would face her demons, and release the secrets she had suppressed for so long.

CHAPTER SIXTY-TWO

Joanna

'Take a deep breath in . . .' Fiona said, over the panpipe music playing in the background. 'And out . . .'

Joanna felt her eyes roll back in her head as she relaxed her body. Fiona's meditation sessions had been a lifesaver, bringing her back from the brink of oblivion. Cutting the tops of her thighs had not been enough to hold back the tide, and Fiona had known her long enough to pick up on her silent anxiety, planning regular sessions to ease the pain. Fiona had counted backwards, bringing her to a happy place, albeit short-lived as memories of the past filtered through. But in a strange sort of way, it helped. Instead of being bombarded with images she did not understand, it was as if Fiona were taking her by the hand, guiding her through the sequence of events behind closed doors.

Fiona meditated with her eyes open, and her gentle voice spoke in a soft lull.

'Relax your shoulders. You're safe here.'

She *was* safe. She trusted Fiona. Her shoulders rose and Fiona spoke again.

'Relax. You're in the garden, Joanna. It's a beautiful summer's day. You can smell the honeysuckle growing on the fence.'

'Yes,' Joanna said.

'Tell me, what are you doing?'

'I'm going to Daddy's workshop,' Joanna said, her tone childish and excitable.

'What age are you?'

Joanna giggled. 'I'm almost ten years old. It's my birthday today.'

'That's right,' Fiona said. They had reached this part many times before, but never any further. 'Why don't you open the door, see what's inside?'

Joanna frowned, clasping her fingers on her lap. 'I can't. It's locked.'

'It's open today. Push down the handle and walk inside.'

Joanna paused, a small gasp leaving her lips. 'It smells funny, and it's dark. I don't like it here, I want to go back.'

Fiona spoke in calm, soothing tones. 'Keep going. You're being really brave. I'm with you, you're safe.'

Joanna frowned, her words stuttering, unsure. 'I . . . I can hear noises.'

'That's okay, Walk towards the noises,' Fiona said, verbally scooting her along.

'There's a red light in one room, with photos hanging up. I don't like them. They're rude.'

'What else do you see?'

'There's another room. The door is closed but there's noises. I . . . I think someone's crying.'

'Just keep walking towards the noise. I'm holding your hand. It's all right, nothing can hurt you now.'

Joanna's frown drew down, her eyes shut tight as her voice weakened. 'I don't want to go through this door. I feel sick, please don't make me.'

'Joanna, it's you crying behind the door. It's always been you. Only by opening it can you let the bad things out, and be free. You want that, don't you?'

'Yes,' Joanna said, her body language a complete contrast to her words. Her fingers were wedged tightly together, her elbows glued to her sides.

Fiona sighed. 'We've been here before, haven't we? Today I want you to open that door. Do it now before the moment passes. Be a brave girl and push it open.'

'Oh . . . okay,' Joanna said, tears trickling down her cheeks.

Fiona dared not speak, and waited as Joanna relived the memory.

'Oh . . . oh no. No no no no . . .' Joanna said, her head in her hands, tears cascading down her cheeks as her body shook.

'Tell me, what do you see?'

'I can't. *Ulp* . . . I'm going to throw up,' Joanna said, gagging as her voice slowly returned to normal.

Fiona's voice grew firm. 'You've come this far. Now tell me, or I'll make you go through the door again and again until you do.'

'No . . . I . . . *ulp* .' Joanna clasped her hand to her mouth, rising from the floor.

'Shh, it's okay. I'm taking you away, Joanna. We're outside now. Take a breath.'

The gagging subsided as Joanna took some deep breaths. The frown lines eased from her face as she relaxed back into her position, cross-legged on the floor.

'I don't feel very well,' she whispered. 'Can't we come back tomorrow?'

But Fiona pushed on, giving her little time to recover. 'You're on the farm. It's the day Abigail went missing. Can you tell me where you are?'

'I'm outside,' she said, wrapping her hands around herself, as if cold.

'Good. Do you see Abigail?'

'Yes. It's her birthday soon.'

'How do you feel about that?'

Joanna frowned. 'I feel bad. I want to make it all go away.'

'How do you do make it go away? Take yourself there. You're with me in the house. Then you have to go outside because your internet signal is playing up, and you need to check your emails on your phone. You walk outside . . .'

'I see Abigail. She's playing hide and seek.'

'Good. What happens next?'

'I . . . I can't remember. Everything's fuzzy.'

'Unlock the memory. You're keeping it hidden because it's causing you too much pain. What happens next?'

'I . . . I . . .' Joanna's hands clenched as she struggled to express the words.

'Go on,' Fiona said firmly. 'Tell me . . . you saw Abigail. What did you do?'

But Joanna clamped a hand to her mouth and scrambled to her feet. She leapt from the room, retching, her legs fizzing with pins and needles as the blood flow returned. Skidding into the bathroom, she made it to the toilet as her stomach heaved, spilling her last meal into the porcelain bowl.

Images of her tenth birthday flashed before her as she swallowed back the burning sensation in her throat. Slowly, she came to ground, feeling as if she had been walking through a nightmare. The images revisited her mind, hazy and disjointed. Was it really true? Was that why she had been hurting herself all this time? And Abigail? Was it possible that she had hurt her little girl?

Joanna cleaned herself up as quickly as she could. Her legs felt like rubber as she walked across the landing, but she would not give in. She grasped the door knob to return to Fiona. She was just about to push the door aside when she heard Fiona's voice.

'DC Knight? It's Fiona. I need to talk to you. No . . . not on the phone. Can I meet you somewhere? . . . Not here. Yes . . .' She sighed, and it sounded as if the weight of her soul was in that exhalation. 'We can't carry on like this.' Fiona's words crumbled into a sob. 'I think I know who killed Abigail.'

CHAPTER SIXTY-THREE

Armed with her exit strategy, Jennifer sat in the car park of the supermarket. A call from Fiona had been the last thing she expected, much less an arranged meeting here. Just as she had suspected, she had been pulled away from the investigation and was to report to Haven police station later that day. She would still see the family, but only to provide brief updates. She no longer had the luxury of chatting to them, or picking up snatched conversations. But Fiona's troubled expression told her it was not over yet.

'I've left Joanna and Olivia back at the house so I won't delay,' Fiona said, sweeping the hair from her eyes. Taking a deep breath, she geared herself up for what she was about to say.

'First, I want you to know that I have come to care for the Duncans. Nick, Joanna, the girls, I love them all. But this family is being ripped apart in the worst possible way and I can't stand by any longer and allow it to happen.'

Jennifer nodded, her heart gearing up a notch. 'I understand. From the first day I came to Blackwater, I could see how much they meant to you. But you're right, they can't keep going on like this. If you've got information, you must disclose it.'

Fiona bowed her head in a reluctant nod. 'I've had my suspicions, but I didn't want to believe it. I . . . I lied in my statement. On the day Abigail disappeared, Joanna left me. It wasn't for long, about twenty minutes. I didn't tell you because I didn't want her to get into trouble.' She looked shiftily at Jennifer, dropping her gaze as an angry glare was returned. 'I'm *sorry*, but she's fragile and I just didn't believe she could have done something like that.'

'And now?' Jennifer said, reining in her annoyance, her mind racing with the possibilities.

'Now I'm convinced she has. But I don't think it was intentional,' Fiona quickly added. 'Joanna's mentally ill. She has been for some time. I've been trying to encourage her to explore her memories, but I've bitten off more than I can chew.' Fiona shifted her weight in the seat of the car. 'Something happened just before her tenth birthday. Something bad. I think her father was sexually abusing her. It escalated on her birthday and it's affected her ever since.'

Jennifer nodded. Nothing shocked her any more, and given Joanna's attitude towards her father, she already had her suspicions.

When Jennifer didn't respond, Fiona continued. 'It's a horrible thought, I know. I thought if we explored her past, it would help us find out what happened. But now . . .'

'Go on,' Jennifer said, an air of unease creeping in.

'Now I'm worried she'll do something stupid. Whatever upset Joanna in the past . . . well, it happened on her tenth birthday.'

'And it's the twins' tenth birthday tomorrow,' Jennifer finished her train of thought.

'Yes,' Fiona said. 'She's always said she sees herself in Abigail. What if she's hidden Abigail away somewhere, to rid herself of the memory? That Jack-in-the-box she talks about, all the stuff from the eighties, they're all part of that bad memory.'

'Can you back up any of this?'

Fiona eased the iPhone from her pocket and laid it on the dashboard of the car. They exchanged a glance before she pressed the play button on the voice recorder app. Jennifer listened, straining to hear past the music in the background. There was no mistaking the connotations as she listened to Joanna's voice.

'Why didn't you tell me this when Radcliffe was arrested?'

'At first I thought I'd be able to regress her, maybe find out where Abigail was and have her returned without Joanna getting arrested. I didn't think she killed her daughter. But now . . . she's getting worse, and I'm worried about Olivia.'

'So your sessions were a way of unlocking the past? You do know you were playing with fire, don't you?' Jennifer said, feeling partially responsible. But encouraging Fiona to get Joanna to open up wasn't the same as advocating full-on regression. She should have known this would happen. A hypnotherapy certificate was one of the things Jennifer had discovered when she completed Fiona's background checks. 'The reason that people block bad memories is because it causes them trauma to recount them. Leading her through her past, especially in such an insistent way, could have caused her serious psychological damage.'

Fiona's voice raised an octave. 'She wouldn't open up to *you*. What choice did I have?'

'Where's Joanna now?' Jennifer asked, checking her watch.

'At home with Olivia and Nick.'

'Did you explain to Nick what was going on?'

'No . . . oh . . . Do you think I should have?'

'You've put her through all that and just left her with Olivia? What if Nick goes out and leaves them alone?' Jennifer grabbed her phone from her pocket and called Nick's number. 'Dammit, no answer.' Turning her key in the ignition, she revved up the car. 'We'd better get back there.'

CHAPTER SIXTY-FOUR

The drive to Blackwater Farm passed in a dusty race down the gravel path, as stones clanked against the side of the car. Jennifer didn't care about her paintwork. She was too busy going over things in her head while Fiona tried again and again to contact Nick.

Jennifer wondered if she should have called a unit to race up there on blues and twos. But where was her justification? Where was the crime? Joanna had lived with the memories of her past for years; it didn't mean to say she would harm anyone now. Or did it? The speed Jennifer was going, they wouldn't have got there any quicker anyway. Jennifer gripped the steering wheel as she patched a call through to her DI, bringing him up to date. The recording did not incriminate Joanna, but it raised concerns, and he would have to be a fool not to take them seriously.

As her car skidded into the yard, Jennifer was relieved to see Olivia's face from the top window, just as she had the first day she arrived. But her expression relayed that something was wrong. The absence of Nick's car made Jennifer's stomach clench as she rushed to the front door of the house.

'Joanna,' she shouted in unison with Fiona, who fumbled with her keys, dropping them twice before finally opening the door.

While Fiona ran into the kitchen, instinct drove Jennifer upstairs. She took them two at a time, grasping the old banister for support as she sped upwards, calling for Joanna and Olivia.

The child appeared on the landing, looking scared and confused. Pointing to the bathroom door, her meaning became clear.

'Is Mummy in there?' Jennifer asked.

The little girl bowed her head in a nod.

'Why don't you go downstairs to Fiona? I'll speak to your mummy,' Jennifer said, adrenaline pumping through her veins. Something was wrong. Very wrong. As Olivia descended the stairs, Jennifer turned her attention to the bathroom door. 'Joanna? Open up, will you?'

No response. She tried the old brass door knob, but it wouldn't open. She gauged it as she gave it a rattle. It wasn't the strongest of locks.

'Joanna, this is the last time I'll ask. Open the door now, or I'll kick it down.'

Silence. She took a couple of steps back before launching her foot at the door and kicking as hard as she could. It shook on its hinges but remained closed. Swearing under her breath, Jennifer quickly assessed the situation. She could wait for assistance to force entry or she could try and gain access now. A thought struck her and she ran to the stairs.

'Fiona, bring me up a fire extinguisher, quickly.'

Just where was Nick when she needed him? She grabbed the extinguisher and ran towards the door, gaining as much momentum as she could. Battering it against the lock, it smashed open, the wood splintering under the force.

'Shit!' Jennifer exclaimed, as she saw Joanna lying naked in a blood-tinged bath. The ends of her hair floated in the water, and a shade of blue had spread across her lips. But her eyes flickered as Fiona screamed from the landing, and Jennifer barked orders, grateful at least that Olivia was downstairs.

'Call an ambulance. Tell them she's slashed her wrists and she's barely conscious.'

Jennifer pushed her fingers onto Joanna's neck until she found the slow throb of her pulse. She turned back to Fiona, unmoving in the hall.

'Fiona did you hear me? Call the ambulance. Call Nick. And keep Olivia away.'

Fiona remained frozen, her face struck in dumb horror.

'Fiona,' Jennifer shouted behind her. 'Do it. Now!'

Jennifer made herself busy, grabbing the towels from the handrail and wrapping them tightly around Joanna's wounds. 'Stay with me, Joanna, everything's going to be all right,' Jennifer soothed, fighting to keep the panic out of her voice. Joanna opened her eyes until they were two puffy slits, the colour rapidly draining from her skin.

'Let me die,' she moaned, her head lolling to one side.

Pulling the plug from the bath, Jennifer gasped at the shock of red blotting through the towels. There was so much blood. But at least the water was warm. It couldn't have happened very long ago. Thick spirals of blood ran down the plughole as Jennifer worked quickly, cloaking Joanna with towels before reapplying pressure on the wounds.

'It was me,' Joanna moaned. 'I killed Abigail. I remember now.'

Fiona's shadow filled the doorway. 'The ambulance is on its way. So is Nick. Is she going to be all right?'

Jennifer turned, her voice clipped. 'Can you keep an eye on Olivia? I need you downstairs to direct the ambulance.'

Jennifer turned her attention back onto Joanna, painfully aware that it could be the last chance she'd get to find out where Abigail was.

'Where is she? Tell me where she is.'

'My father. He used to take pictures. I was his little princess . . .'

'Where is Abigail?'

'She was just like me. I couldn't let it happen again. So I hid her away. I hid it all away. To keep her safe . . . but then I forgot.'

'Where is she, Joanna?' Jennifer said, leaning across the roll-top bath, her face inches from Joanna's.

Sounds of a siren warned that time was running out. Jennifer clamped her hands on the towels as another shock of red bled through.

'I . . . I don't remember,' she murmured, between laboured breaths.

Jennifer gritted her teeth. She was so close to answers, it was painful.

'Where? Where is she? On the farm? In the woods?'

But Joanna just lolled her head from side to side, strings of damp hair clinging to her skin.

'It's too late now.'

'What happened?' Jennifer shouted. 'Please, Joanna!' She wanted to slap her, to shock her back to reality. Joanna could be dying, and she couldn't let her take the secret to the grave.

'No more pictures . . . he can't hurt me now . . .' Joanna said, almost incoherent, as heavy boots pounded up the stairs. Led by Fiona, the paramedics bundled into the bathroom, just as Joanna slipped away.

CHAPTER SIXTY-FIVE

All hell seemed to break loose in the minutes that followed. An inconsolable Nick telephoned Jennifer, agreeing to meet her at the hospital as Fiona and Olivia waited in the family room.

Jennifer surveyed the dried blood on her hands. The need to wash them was overwhelming, and she pumped three dollops of sanitiser foam into her open palms, watching it swirl into a foamy pink. Fiona popped her head out of the family room.

'Has she said anything? Has she said where Abigail is?'

'Not exactly,' Jennifer said, keeping her voice low. 'Is Olivia okay?'

'Oh. Yes,' Fiona said distractedly. 'Do you think I should go back to the house with her?'

'No. Stay here until Nick comes, and you can travel back together. She needs her dad at a time like this.'

Jennifer set her mobile phone on silent. Her earlier update to DI Cole was rushed, and she wondered what he would make of it all. She was not there to babysit, but she could not help but feel this wouldn't have occurred if they had left her there one more day.

She turned to see Nick galloping into the ward, a deathly shade of white.

'Second on the left,' Jennifer said, pointing down the bustling corridor. 'They're treating her now. She's going to be all right.'

Nick nodded, and strode down the corridor to see his wife.

Tears slowly trickled down Fiona's cheeks. 'I can't believe she did that. She's self-harmed before, but never this bad.'

But Jennifer had no time for tears, as her mind worked to process the recent information. She had had her suspicions before, but now things were clicking into place she could not afford to waste a second.

Her phone buzzed in her hand. It was Clarkie, a colleague from the child abuse investigation team. And what he had to say was very interesting indeed. Jennifer pushed the phone back into her pocket. She turned to Fiona, who was still standing at the door.

'Can you let Nick know I'm heading back to the station?' she said. 'I'll be back as soon as I can.'

Fiona nodded, drying her tears with a ragged tissue.

Jennifer strode down the corridor, with Fiona's voice echoing in her ears.

'Where are you going? The car park's the other way.'

'In a minute. There's someone I've got to speak to first.'

Jennifer was back in her car within ten minutes. She had spoken to the matron who cared for Joanna's father during his stay in hospital. She knew something was wrong when Joanna refused to go to the funeral, but never could have imagined the depth of the case. The results of her enquiries were coming in at rapid speed, each one slotting another piece of the jigsaw into place. There was just one more piece to uncover. One more step closer to Abigail. It would come in the form of recovered photos. Everything Joanna said about her father was true. Except for one thing. And it was the greatest betrayal of all.

CHAPTER SIXTY-SIX

'They said you discharged yourself,' Jennifer said, taking a seat across the table from Joanna. Arms in bandages, she looked a hell of a lot better than when she'd seen her last.

'I couldn't stay there any longer,' she said, with a naked expression that took Jennifer aback. This was the real Joanna; frightened, overwhelmed, a little lost girl. 'I . . . I was stupid. I'm sorry. I just wanted everything to go away.'

'Have you accepted any help?' Jennifer said, knowing she couldn't be monitored twenty-four hours a day.

'Yes, they've made a referral to the crisis team, and I've already been in touch. But I told them there's something we need to do first. We need to talk about Abigail.'

'Where's Nick and Olivia?' Jennifer glanced around the room, hoping to spare the child any more upset.

Fiona answered from the doorway as she took off her coat. 'They're upstairs. He bought her a new Nintendo game. You know, trying to take her mind off things.'

Jennifer shuddered as a sudden chill danced down her spine. Left untended, the fire in the Aga had petered out, and it hadn't taken long for the cold to descend.

Jennifer rubbed her forehead, as if to assemble her thoughts. 'You said you took your daughter, to save her the trauma you experienced as a child. What did you mean?'

'I've tried to get the memory back, but I can't. Oh my God . . .' Joanna said, her head in her hands. 'Did I do this? Please tell me I didn't do this.'

'I'm so sorry,' Fiona said, placing a hand on her forearm. 'I had no idea it would come out like this.'

'You should have come to me,' Jennifer said, rising from her chair. 'We could have fixed it. But you give me no choice but to take you down the police station for questioning.'

Joanna nodded. 'I've carried a sense of guilt around for years, but every time it surfaced, I pushed it down even further. You've got to understand, what happened was so horrific . . . I couldn't speak about it, let alone return to it.'

'I wasn't speaking to you, I was speaking to Fiona,' Jennifer said.

'What are you talking about?' Fiona said, suddenly indignant.

Jennifer's lips twisted in disgust. 'Why don't you tell Joanna what really happened on the day of her tenth birthday?'

'She knows. It's not fair to make her relive it again,' she said, glancing furtively at the back door.

'To make *you* relive it, you mean. Joanna wasn't abused by her father. *You* were.'

'No . . . no, you're wrong,' Joanna said. 'It happened to me. Fiona didn't know my father.'

Jennifer shook her head. 'That's what she'd have you imagine. Think about it. Can you really picture what happened to you or are parts of it fuzzy? Your birthday party, the photo session, it was there, yes. But when you try to remember the fine detail . . . it doesn't come. Because it happened to someone else. It happened to her.'

'Fiona? But . . . how?' Joanna said, swivelling her head from one woman to the other.

Jennifer felt her pulse quicken as the prospect of arrest drew near. But she couldn't wait hours for the interview to find her answers. She had to draw them out now.

'What you have is a false memory. You repressed the wicked things your father did. When it started coming out, you didn't know how to handle it. Fiona was there to step in and change history.

Think about it. The eighties music, the spinning top, and the Jack-in-the-box. All reminders of a childhood you wanted to forget.'

Joanna stared at Fiona, agog. 'It can't be true . . . Fiona, why would you torture us like this?'

'Because she's not Fiona. She's your step sister. Isn't that right, Doreen?'

'She's lying,' Fiona – or rather Doreen – said, her voice jittery as she bit hard into the skin around her thumbnail. 'That's the police for you, trying to set everyone else up.' A trickle of blood blotted her bottom lip, but she seemed oblivious to the pain.

'I knew something was wrong when I found Joanna in the bath. The scars you described from her years of self-harm just weren't there. Apart from her wrists, and a few mild cuts on her thigh, there was nothing. It niggled at me. I wondered why you would have lied about something like that? Then I remembered when the psychic came to visit, you said you didn't believe in the paranormal – yet your previous qualifications say differently. Rune stones, tarot cards, you've studied them all. Then I got to thinking about you, and what else you had lied about.'

Fiona's eyes narrowed in contempt, but her lips stayed tightly pressed together.

'No . . .' Joanna said, her mouth gaping open. 'My step sister is dead.'

'That's what she'd have you believe. Doreen had a flatmate, by the name of Fiona Roberts. Everything she said was true. A mother living in Canada, and a diploma in complementary therapies. All belonging to Fiona Roberts. Except that one day she decided she'd had enough, and stepped in front of a train. She was identified by the ID in the pocket of the coat she was wearing . . . Doreen's coat.'

'It can't be . . .' Joanna said, squinting as she approached the woman before her. 'Doreen was overweight, with crooked teeth and blonde hair.'

'She's changed, that's all. Lost weight, fixed her teeth, and dyed her hair a muddy brown. When the police came around to confirm that the woman who died was Doreen, she happily stole Fiona's identity. I traced the ID on the system. It bore an old photo of a chubby-faced woman with blonde hair – much the same as the school photo I found of you both at the age of nine.'

A gasp escaped Joanna's lips as their eyes locked. 'Oh my God. It's you. It's really you.' She stumbled back, grasping the chair for support.

Jennifer nodded, relieved. Police had conducted the usual background checks, but her intense digging had uncovered more than she could ever have imagined.

'It's not true. For fuck's sake, don't listen to her. She's full of shit,' Fiona said, shedding her kindly persona.

Jennifer slid an envelope from her pocket. 'Your stepfather was a keen photographer, wasn't he? Except his hobby was used for the most despicable act, distributing pictures for people just like him.'

'No,' Fiona said, her chin smeared with blood as she bit down harder on her nail. 'The photos were destroyed.'

'Not all of them,' Jennifer said, thankful that her friend in the child abuse investigation team had dropped everything to help her out. 'The police were in possession of quite a few, seized from raids in the local area. I matched some of the images with your school photo.'

She leaned forward to strike her message home. Her voice was low, the words crawling out of her mouth as she revealed the dirty secrets.

'I recognised you from the hospital CCTV too, the night you visited your stepfather. The nurses thought it was Joanna, but it would take more than a blonde wig and a red coat to convince me.'

'No,' Joanna whispered, backing away from them both as the truth was revealed. But Jennifer had to keep the pressure on. It was

Abigail's only chance. 'You set off the fire alarm as a distraction, then you smothered him, didn't you, *Doreen*?' she said, pronouncing her name in a slow drawl. 'How did you do it? A pillow? Your hands? He was a weak man, no harm to anyone. Why didn't you just let him die in peace?' The anger flaring on Fiona's face told her that her words had hit home.

'Because he didn't deserve to live after what he'd done.' She spat the words that had been fermenting on her tongue.

Jennifer had her confession, but she did not take a victory from the shattered life of the woman before her.

'Why? Why would you hurt our little girl?' Joanna screamed.

Fiona's eyes turned as cold as ice. 'Because I had to. The only way to stop the pain is to destroy the memories.'

Joanna threaded her fingers through her hair as it fell from the neatly applied pins onto her shoulders. 'But why take Abigail? This is nothing to do with her.'

'Because you saw! You saw and did nothing!' Fiona screamed, spittle gathering in the corners of her mouth. 'It was *me* behind the studio door, not you. When you found me, I was so relieved to see your face. But instead, you ran away. I waited for help, but you didn't tell a soul.'

Joanna said, backed away, 'I . . . I don't remember.'

'Don't you remember how I used to cut myself when we were kids? While you were messing about with your little scratches, I was slicing into myself with *real* knives.'

Fiona shot up her sleeves to reveal the scars lining her arms. Zebra print patterns and deep cavernous zigzags made Joanna gasp.

'I came to confront you, but you didn't even remember who I was.' A thin, hysterical cackle left her thinning lips. 'Funny, isn't it? I had nothing and here you were, with a boarding school private education, and a swanky business, and an investment in a farm. Then I saw the twins, and the memories came flooding back all over again. Except this time, I had a chance to end it all for good.'

Jennifer took a step towards her, her hands open in a gesture of mock sympathy. She would have liked nothing better than to slap the cold steel handcuffs on the woman for picking on an innocent child. But now was the time for reason.

'Fiona, I know you're hurting, but please . . . tell us where she is. We can get you help. We can end this now.'

Fiona wiped her mouth with the back of her hand, staring at Jennifer with a venomous gaze.

'Want to know what's funny? This wasn't the way it was supposed to be. My plan was to destroy Joanna, not her kids. But when Abigail disappeared, I stayed around to watch her life fall apart. She was so screwed up it was easy to plant the seed that it was her suffering at her father's hands. Seems only fair, don't you think?'

'The sleeping tablets, the Jack-in-the-box . . . that was you?' Joanna said, disbelief evident in her voice.

A hollow laugh resounded in the room. Fiona paced the kitchen like a trapped animal. 'Pushing the sleeping pills was giving you the easy way out. I never thought you'd have the guts to actually slash your wrists.'

Jennifer stepped in. 'And then you thought you'd pick up where Joanna left off, queen of the household.'

'Don't I deserve it? After all I've been through?'

'Where is she, you bitch?' Nick lunged from the doorway, knotting Fiona's jumper under his fists as he lifted her from her feet. 'What have you done with my little girl?'

Fiona's eyes narrowed as they rested on Nick. 'Go back to your boyfriend, faggot.'

'Nick, watch out!' Jennifer shouted, as Fiona wriggled free long enough to grasp a ten-inch blade from the cutlery drawer. The cold flash of steel swished through the air as she lunged at him with the knife, catching his flesh. Nick staggered back in disbelief, as blood seeped through his shirt.

'Mummy?' Olivia's voice filtered through from the hall, making Jennifer's heart leap into her throat. A chilling grin laced Fiona's lips as her eyes crawled over to the hall door.

With two deft movements, Jennifer pounced on her, narrowly missing the blade as she swiped a second time. Gritting her teeth, she clamping both hands on Fiona's wrist, twisting it back until the knife clanged onto the floor. A knee to the stomach winded her long enough to pin her down as Nick caught his breath and joined her in restraining the woman responsible for their misery.

'Olivia, go back to your room,' Joanna said, as the little girl tentatively poked her head through the door. 'It's okay, sweetheart, just go upstairs. I'll be up in a minute.'

'Aw . . . here she is, the little angel,' Fiona said, her eyes wild. 'Are you enjoying being an only child? I would have thought it was right up your str –'

Fiona's words were cut short, as Joanna slapped her hard on the face.

'Where is Abigail? What have you done with my little girl?'

'I've cauterised the wound,' Fiona said, as Jennifer and Nick gripped her tightly in an arm lock. 'It's over.'

Without ceremony, Jennifer recited the caution for the murder of Joanna's father. The other offences could follow up later, particularly regarding Abigail. The uniformed back-up she had requested finally pulled into the drive and assisted her in dragging Fiona to the car, still protesting her innocence. But it did not answer their question. Just where was Abigail? Jennifer pushed her head down as she helped her into the back seat of the car, promising to follow on shortly.

'Please . . . tell me, where have you left her?' Joanna said, pressing her face against the rear passenger window. But Fiona did not look at Joanna. Instead, her glance fell elsewhere. And suddenly everything became clear.

CHAPTER SIXTY-SEVEN

'You've got to make her tell,' Joanna sobbed as Fiona was driven away 'Why won't she tell?'

Jennifer inhaled a deep sigh as she rushed back into the house. The cool air refreshed her mind, and sharpened her judgement. Fiona was never going to tell them where Abigail was. But she knew someone who could. Jennifer exchanged glances with Nick as the truth was laid bare.

'Fiona wasn't responsible for Abigail's disappearance.'

'I don't understand,' Joanna said, her eyes swimming with emotion. She looked to her husband. 'Nick? What's she talking about?'

'No,' Nick whispered, his voice catching in his throat.

But Jennifer's words were strong. Determined. Nick would recover from being sliced with the knife. But the truth Jennifer was about to reveal would leave a much deeper scar.

'There's only one person who knows what happened to Abigail that day, and they're much closer to home.'

Her glance took her to the window, where Fiona had looked just seconds before. Olivia's face was pressed close as her breath fogged the glass, her ghostly features haunted with a dreadful secret. A sluggish, sick feeling descended over Jennifer in preparation for what lay ahead.

Nick shook his head. 'You can't be serious. Not our Olivia.'

She turned to Nick and Joanna, now holding hands, clinging to each other like a raft in a storm.

'You both have to trust me. Let me talk to her alone. I only need to know where she's left her. It's not in anyone's interest to prosecute a child.'

'No . . .' Joanna said. 'She would have told me. Fiona's . . . Doreen's lying. *She's* taken our daughter. Abigail's dead, and it's all my fault.'

Jennifer shook her head. 'You heard her. Fiona's mission was to hurt you, not your daughter. But when Abigail went missing, she just sat back and enjoyed the show. And in the midst of it all, she distorted your memories, filled you full of guilt, and played on your worst fears.' She glanced at the crease of blood seeping through Nick's shirt. 'You'd better get that seen to.'

'It's nothing, just a scratch,' he said, lifting his shirt to reveal a small flesh wound.

Olivia stepped out onto the landing, her mouth pursed. Slowly she descended the stairs, her sandaled feet creaking on the boards with weighty finality.

Jennifer bent down and took her by the hand. The life had left the little girl's eyes, and was replaced by fear.

'There's no need to be scared any more. You're not in any trouble, just tell us where she is,' Jennifer said, not sure why she was whispering, but the softly spoken words felt right for the little girl who had been through so much.

Joanna took a step towards her daughter, and from the corner of her eye Jennifer saw Nick's hand shoot out and still her movement.

Jennifer kept her eyes focused solely on the little girl in front of her.

'Did Fiona frighten you? Is that why you couldn't tell me? Did she say you'd be in trouble?'

Olivia nodded, her big moon eyes filling with tears. She took off her glasses and swiped at her face, then placed them back on the bridge of her nose. Jennifer took her by the hands. Her fingers were cool and stiff, as if a little bit of her was still with Abigail. Somewhere dark. Somewhere cold.

'Sweetheart, listen to me. Fiona was not your friend. She lied because she wanted to hurt your family. I'm a police officer and I tell the truth. Do you understand that?' She was going to say *like your daddy*, but was painfully aware that Olivia's daddy had let her down in the past.

Olivia nodded again, dislodging the tears balancing on her long blonde lashes. They trickled down her cheeks and Jennifer thumbed them away from her soft pale skin.

'I promise we'll keep you out of trouble.'

Nick spoke now too, his voice low and gentle. 'She's right. Just tell us where she is, sweetheart. Let's bring your sister home.'

'But she's . . . she's dead.' Olivia blurted out the words, falling into her daddy's arms, burying her head in his shirt. Joanna's legs wobbled, and she clung to the banister, her other hand resting on her husband's back. Jennifer bit her lip. There was no time to spare.

'Olivia, listen to me. I want you to talk me through what happened that day. Can you do that? Show me where she is?'

Olivia straightened up, a hiccup catching in her throat. She nodded grimly, reaching for her hand. 'Outside. Abi's outside.'

Tentatively, they followed Olivia's lead, afraid to speak for fear it would break the spell. I'm walking in a nightmare, Jennifer thought, as Olivia led her past the outhouses to the scrubland at the bottom of the field. Her fingers warmed in the child's grip, but it could not ease the passage of their journey. Their surroundings took on an ugly hue, as they faced their path with dread. Brown fence posts jutted up like rotting teeth, slanted after years of being battered by the wind. She stared up at the ashen sky, steeling herself for what lay ahead.

Olivia broke the silence, her voice punctuated with sobs. 'We were playing hide and seek. I counted and she hid. I looked in the cow shed and found Daddy . . .'

Jennifer guessed what was to come, but the revelation would be too much for Joanna, whose interference would delay things even further. 'That's okay, Olivia. Tell me about Abigail.'

Olivia nodded. 'I . . . I wanted to talk to her, because I was sad. But Abi wouldn't listen. She said she wanted to play.'

Jennifer began to feel an internal clock ticking down. Precious seconds she could not afford to lose.

'I told her I'd found a better place to play . . . somewhere secret.'

'And you took her there?'

'Yes,' Olivia nodded as she kept walking. 'It's a hole in the ground, it goes way down.'

I'm in the ground with the dirt between my toes. Abigail's haunting words replayed in Jennifer's mind.

Jennifer glanced behind, to see Joanna entwine her fingers tightly around Nick's hand. She couldn't begin to imagine how they felt, but at least they were facing this together. She wanted to run ahead, to ask Olivia exactly where her sister was, but she sensed her reluctance. She could just as quickly turn on her heel and run in the opposite direction, rather than face what lay ahead. Olivia climbed over a rusted gate, into a field far beyond where they were allowed to roam. Fiona most likely allowed them free rein when nobody was looking. Joanna would have to face up to not casting a watchful eye over her girls, but that was something she had a lifetime to contemplate. Jennifer joined Olivia on the other side, and quietly asked Nick to open the gate for the emergency services in case they needed to drive through. She walked ahead with Olivia while Joanna helped her husband lift the old rusted metal out of the way.

'Were you still upset when you got to your secret place?' Jennifer said, taking advantage of their time alone.

Olivia nodded. 'I tried to tell Abi about Daddy *again*, but she wouldn't believe me. I . . . I was mad because she wouldn't listen. She started shouting, and calling me names . . . so I . . . I . . .' Olivia said, her chin wobbling.

'It's okay, you can tell me,' Jennifer said, crouching down to her level.

'I pushed her. I pushed her in the hole.' A sob caught in the little girl's throat. 'I called her, but she didn't answer. I was too scared to talk to Daddy . . .'

'So you told Fiona?' Jennifer said, pre-empting her response.

Olivia nodded. 'But she said it was too late, that Abigail was dead and I killed her. She said if I spoke that I would go to jail. She said there were lots of bad people in jail.'

'Oh, my poor baby,' Joanna said, catching the tail end of her daughter's words. She reached out to touch the back of her head, but drew back as Olivia flinched.

'Fiona said it was all your fault. That you knew. You knew and you didn't care.'

'I swear I didn't. I just felt something was wrong, but didn't know it had anything to do with you. Please, Olivia, that's the truth.'

'I'm sorry but we don't have time for this,' Jennifer said, gazing into the little girl's eyes. 'Can you point out your hiding place, Olivia? We need to get to Abigail.'

'There,' Olivia said, pointing over Jennifer's shoulder. 'She's over there.'

Jennifer turned to follow her gaze – and her heart fell like a stone.

CHAPTER SIXTY-EIGHT

Diary Entry

My sister must have sensed something, because she made an effort to be nice to me. She was home from boarding school, something about a bounced cheque, and payments due. So I thought about my rescue. The only way to stop the monster was for him to be caught in the act. And she was the only person I could allow to find me in that way. But it wasn't as easy as I thought. I left clues, dropped hints. They all went unnoticed. Mother threw herself into planning our joint tenth birthday party, and the night before, she allowed us to open one present each. I tried to forget all the bad stuff, just for one evening, and excitedly tore back the paper. I wanted a Simon game. I got a box of Lego. I hated the stuff, and swallowed back my disappointment. I watched eagerly as Joanna opened hers, hoping she might swap. Her present was gaudy, childish, and she loved it. Round and around she wound the handle of the Jack-in-the-box, the *plink plonk* tune getting on my nerves. All I remember about that day is her playing that infernal tune for hours on end.

Half a pound of tuppenny rice, half a pound of treacle. That's the way the money goes . . . Pop! Goes the weasel.

That night, it replayed in my head as I tried to sleep, intermingling with dreams about a wolf stripping me of my flesh. But the wolf was sleeping in the room next door, and what he had taken was every ounce of my dignity. I climbed out of my bed and stared into the moonlight. And there, in the darkness, I began to hatch a plan.

CHAPTER SIXTY-NINE

'No . . . please, not there,' Jennifer whispered under her breath. Filled with trepidation, she stood on the barren scrubland, pushing back strands of her windswept hair. She faced the little girl, a cold sweat running down her back. Olivia spoke, her eyes wide and unblinking.

'I pushed her down the hole. Except . . .'

Jennifer finished her sentence as she stared at the forked tree on the crown of the hill.

'Except now it's been filled in.'

Olivia nodded solemnly, looking more vulnerable than ever. Jennifer had been right all along. Abigail *had* been in the well. But by the time they found it, it was too late. Fiona had moved her somewhere else.

'What do we do now?' Nick said to his wife. But Joanna's empty expression relayed that she didn't have a clue.

Overhead, a flock of ravens cut through the sky, their iridescent feathers catching flecks of the dying light. Jennifer stood entranced as they swooped and cawed overhead. Her mind cleared, like clouds parting for the sun.

'What was it that Fiona said?' Jennifer searched the passages of her mind. 'Something about not going through another tenth birthday . . .' She grabbed Joanna by the arm so tightly it made her yelp. 'Cast your mind back. I need you to remember that day.'

'I . . . I can't,' Joanna whined, pulling back her bandaged arm. 'It's too confusing, I can't remember.'

'Listen to me,' Jennifer said, facing her head-on. 'If Fiona moved Abigail, then she could still be alive. But we may not have long. She's been waiting until today to get revenge.'

Mouth gaping open, Joanna blinked twice, with no response.

Jennifer fought the impulse to scream. 'Don't you see? She's reliving the past through the twins. You and Doreen shared the same birthday. In her mind, you're Abigail. Please. Tell me what happened that day.'

'My father, he was taking photos . . . bad pictures.' She squeezed her eyes shut, blinking out fat droplets of tears. 'It was the day before my . . . our birthday.'

Jennifer bit her bottom lip, wishing she had attended Joanna's father's house search like she insisted.

'C'mon, there's not a minute to lose,' she said, marching Joanna back to the house.

'Where are we going?' Joanna said, as Nick scooped Olivia into his arms.

'To your dad's house. I know there's tenants there, but if we –'

'He didn't take the photos in the house.' Joanna's words jolted as she tripped over a mound of earth. 'He used his studio.'

'Where's that?' Jennifer said, her frustration rising.

'I can't . . .' Joanna clenched her fists and beat them against the side of her forehead. 'I can't remember,' she sobbed in frustration, her wrist bandages blooming with slices of red.

'Shhh, it's okay, we'll find it,' Jennifer said, gently lowering Joanna's hands from her head. She turned to Nick as she remembered the newspaper clipping that hung on the wall of the briefing room. 'Your father – he used to be in the same photographic club as Joanna's dad. Where did they meet?'

Nick rubbed his chin. 'At the back of the old allotment site. They used a bungalow on the end of the lot. It's derelict now . . . And it's already been searched.'

Jennifer frowned as she recalled the list of searched properties. The bungalow *had* been searched by police when Abigail first went missing. But it hadn't been visited since. It was situated on the far side of the woodlands, a couple of miles from where they stood. Near enough for Fiona to take the child in the middle of the night. Jennifer scanned the horizon, from her vantage point at the crest of the hill. A plume of smoke billowed between the trees, fracturing the landscape. Fiona's words came back to haunt her. *I've cauterised the wound. It's over.* She hadn't understood her at the time, but now the meaning became clear. To cauterise was to burn.

'Shit!' she shouted to Nick, pointing at the smoke. 'We've got to get to the allotment!'

Holding Olivia tightly in his arms, Nick took in the sight of the smoke before bolting down the hill. Jennifer wasted no time in giving chase, leaving Joanna floundering behind.

CHAPTER SEVENTY

Diary Entry

I could not concentrate on my tenth birthday party because I knew what was coming. But I had faith. With my sister to look out for me, everything would be fine. I smiled at her as she opened her presents, and briefly, she smiled back. Yes, I thought, helping myself to a second slice of cake. Everything would be all right.

Then *he* gave me the look. The one that said I had an appointment to keep. By the time the children had left, I was back at the studio 'helping' the man I called Father. But he didn't know I had arranged for a surprise. I had promised Joanna my Space Hopper if she would play a special game of hide and seek. She had burst her own months ago, after she bounced on a rock in the garden. Mine was barely used, and she didn't need to be asked twice.

I unlocked the studio door when he was in the dark room, then took my place in front of the cameras. My eyes were on the door, waiting for my sister to turn up and put a halt to the abuse. Then I heard it . . . the *tap, tap, tap* of her patent shoes as she ran up the path. The door handle groaned as she opened the door. I froze, ready to put my plan into action.

'Please don't,' I pleaded, an instant gush of tears pouring down my face. 'Please, no more.'

'What's wrong with you?' Father said. 'I didn't say you could get dressed.'

'I can't,' I said, making my voice sound as if I was scared stiff. 'Please don't hurt me that way again.'

I knew she was on the other side of the door, and began to pull my clothes back on. Because I knew that, that way, he would come out from behind the camera.

'No,' he said firmly. 'We're not finished yet.' And in a show of brute force, he walked over and yanked off my skirt.

'Not again, please Daddy, not again!' I screamed in anguish, just as the door opened a fraction.

Joanna's young eyes were wide and disbelieving, her face white with shock. It was bad enough that he took photos of me scantily dressed, but I had to make the scenario as bad as I possibly could. It was the only way to get him sent to jail for good. At least, that's what I thought at the time. But Joanna simply withdrew without saying a word. I screamed, I howled, and my father clamped a hand against my mouth, whispering venomous threats, his warm spittle landing on my cheeks. My heart plummeted in my chest. I waited for the police, for Mother, for someone to come. But the camera still flashed, as he took his position behind the lens, mumbling about my outburst.

The sense of betrayal was crippling. Sometimes I would give her a look, imagining it boring right through her. She must have believed he did far worse than take pictures, and yet she did nothing. After minutes of absorbing my stare, she would whine to Mother that I was 'acting weird again', and I would be gifted my mother's disapproval. My special friendship ended.

I couldn't live with her treachery. Self-harming became an obsession, easing the pain and providing an outlet. But even when I showed her my scars, she didn't ask why. She tried to join in, scratching herself in an act of camaraderie. It was pathetic. I hoped the cuts would make me less attractive or, best of all, make the monster stop. But he carried on, covering up the scars with scarves and sheets. Then one day, after my mother discovered me cutting, she packed our bags and we simply upped and left. She never said why. Perhaps she knew all along. So we started again, just the two of us – us and her ever-growing army of cats. I was finally able to shut the door on that chapter of my life. But I knew even then, that one day it would come back to haunt me.

CHAPTER SEVENTY-ONE

Eyes streaming from the wind, Jennifer made it to her car before Nick, who had slowed in his efforts to keep Olivia safe.

'What about Joanna?' Jennifer said, as Nick buckled his daughter into the back seat.

'She's got the Land Rover, she can follow on,' Nick said, his thoughts firmly with Abigail.

The car skidded out of the yard as Nick took over the police radio, requesting control contact the fire services to ascertain if they were aware. But updates were slow to come, due to a factory fire in Lexton taking up all their resources. Cutting through the country lanes, Jennifer eased her foot from the accelerator as she negotiated the hairpin turns. She had a child in the back, and she could not afford another tragedy.

Putting her police driver skills to use, Jennifer took the shortest route to the allotment in the quickest possible time. She prayed that she had been mistaken, that the fire originated from someone burning rubbish in the garden, but given the amount of smoke it was unlikely. The allotment was practically deserted, but Jennifer noticed Fiona had been the last person to return from the hospital. Had she made a detour to the allotment on the way back to Blackwater Farm? She tried to do the maths. It was coming up to half an hour since Fiona had been arrested. Surely the house would have been burnt to the ground by now? But then it was hardly a tinderbox. Left in ruin and neglect, the boarded up building would surely be infused with damp, and the recent downpours of rain would buy them extra time. Devoid of furniture, the most flammable parts of the building would be the wooden window frames and doors. But as the smell of smoke filtered through the car's air vents, Jennifer's optimism faded away.

Parking the car on the edge of the path, she turned to Nick, who was liaising with control regarding back-up.

'Stay here with Olivia, at least until Joanna gets here.'

'Like hell I will,' Nick said, reaching for the door handle. 'That's my daughter in there.'

Jennifer grabbed him firmly by the wrist, her words low and insistent. 'And that's your daughter back there.' She nodded towards the back seat. 'Please, Nick. At least until Joanna comes. Olivia's been through enough. She doesn't need to see this.'

Nick dropped his hand, reluctantly staying to comfort his daughter. The smoke was getting thicker now, and it billowed above the trees. But Jennifer couldn't see its origin. The allotment was set on an acre of ground, some way back from the forest, and surrounded by thick hedges. The bungalow was situated on the edge of the grounds, flanked by two potting sheds and high hedges, with access through a chewed up path. Satisfied that Nick was waiting for back-up, Jennifer sprinted down the path, the bungalow coming into full view when she reached the wooden gate, which led on to the fields.

'No,' Jennifer said in a horrified moan.

Thick black smoke bloomed from each of the windows, licked by flames spiralling out of control. All hope died inside her as she ran through the plots of overgrown land. Discarded wheelbarrows, rusted trowels and empty orange pots lay around the deserted allotment, as if the occupants had simply disappeared. She raced through the debris, towards the burning building. The heat was immense, beating her back and making her eyes stream. She circled the house, trying to find access. But it was no use. Tightly sealed, with accelerant to ignite the flame, it had gone up in a matter of minutes. The fire raged on, having consumed all in its path. And as the ceiling collapsed, she knew it was too late. A sob caught the back of her throat as the words tumbled out to the backdrop of the hissing, spitting fire.

'We're too late.'

But then she heard it. Through the spit of burning timbers, and the rage of the sirens drawing near. Jennifer crept towards the potting shed as she approached the soft whine, praying beyond hope it was not a kitten or a puppy abandoned by its owner.

The door creaked as she pushed it aside, her heart pounding in hope and fear. A bedraggled, soot-stained little girl lay weakly curled in a ball, singed but alive. Dropping to her knees, Jennifer got down beside her. She was weak, pale and thin, but she was alive.

'Abigail,' Jennifer said, the word feeling like magic on her tongue. 'Is it really you?'

For a dreadful moment, she thought of the young man who had accompanied the psychic, how she had thought he was alive too when he had already passed to the other side. She held her breath, waiting for an answer.

CHAPTER SEVENTY-TWO

Diary Entry

Every birthday was a reminder. It stuck in my throat that Joanna would be enjoying cake on the day that marked the anniversary of her betrayal. She had everything I did not. A handsome husband, beautiful twin girls, money, a career. I took in my dingy flat, stinking of stale beer and crawling with vermin. Fresh anger bloomed as the *boom boom boom* of a stereo system vibrated through the walls from next door. I spent a lot of time wondering. It drove me to the brink of suicide.

That night I could not sleep. I paced my tiny room, wondering if I was up for a confrontation. Barefoot and wearing my pyjamas, I took the graffiti-smeared lift to the roof of my block of flats. I remember standing there, gulping the polluted night air as I stared onto the rain-slicked streets below. I lifted my foot, allowing it to dangle over the edge as I played with the thought. It would be so easy to step off and end all my suffering. What was the point in meeting Joanna? It would only remind me just how unfair my life was. But surely someone must pay? I must have stood on that ledge for half an hour, arguing the toss. It was then, with the wind chilling my bones, that I made a pact. I would visit Joanna and repay her betrayal. If it didn't work out, I could come back onto the roof and simply step off. I had nothing to lose.

Fiona killing herself seemed like fate. The silly cow was always mistaking my coat for hers. I knew she wasn't right from the minute I moved in, and I never resisted an opportunity to twist the knife. She was everything I used to be: a fat, ugly loser. I hated every fibre of her being, and enjoyed telling her just how worthless she was. When the police came knocking on our door, I knew what she'd done. She'd been talking about it for days, and I had made no effort to stop her. Taking her identity was an unexpected bonus.

I was seeing this guy named Chaz, a heavy drug user. He was always on the scrounge. I put him to work, using his computer skills to infiltrate Joanna's email account. She was looking for a housekeeper, someone to help manage the twins while she spent more time on the business. She had bought a farm and wanted to convert it into one of those petting zoos where inner-city kids could come and visit. Ever the saint, my sister, when it came to helping others. As long as she was helping herself.

Fiona's CV and references made her sound like Mary Poppins, and I added a few personal details that I knew my sister would like. Shared taste in music, similar political views. I only intended on turning up at her house to challenge her, and I didn't think she would give me her address if she knew who I really was.

So there I was, on her own doorstep, my heart pounding as I prepared to face a sister I hadn't seen in over twenty years. The fact that she didn't remember me took me by complete surprise. There was not a flicker of recognition on her face. Sure, I had lost weight, and dyed my hair to a mousy brown, but I never thought for a second she wouldn't know who I was.

Then I saw Nick. He was even more handsome in the flesh than in the pictures on Facebook. Strong. Kind. Protective. Yet I sensed an unease between them. So when she offered me the job, I said yes. And I hatched a new plan. Killing was too easy – where was the satisfaction in that? It would be far more satisfying to push Joanna out, be the cuckoo in the nest.

Little by little I chipped away at her self-confidence. The so-called meditation sessions were, in reality, hypnosis, and I gently implanted memories of the past, making them her memories, not mine. I enjoyed studying the art of regression in my spare time. Things would go missing, confusing her, making her feel stupid. And I was always on hand with tablets to calm her. Sometimes they ended up in her tea. Messages from her friends were deleted on her phone, bank cards lost. I scratched away at her sanity, gaining strength from her deterioration – and in doing so, I began to feel clean. I was Fiona, not Doreen. I spoke to Nick about Joanna's self-harming, describing the scratches on her arms. Of course they were nothing compared to the chunks of flesh I had torn from my thighs, stomach, and arms. All out of view as I played the perfect keeper of home and family. I drove a wedge between Joanna and Nick. I even pretended to love their children. Mother's cats were better company than those whining brats.

Then came the day that changed everything. Olivia, running in with tear-streaked face. Something had happened to Abigail, and Olivia was scared. Inwardly, I smiled. Whatever it was, I could turn it to my advantage. Olivia approached me when we were alone. She told me everything, and said it was all her fault. Abigail had fallen into a deep hole and she didn't know what to do. She was crying because Abigail's glasses had come off when she fell, and she handed me the frames, asking for my help. I bent down, my face inches from hers, hugging her in mock sympathy. It was too late, I said, as I threw them away. Hadn't she heard about the curse of Haven? Abigail had been swallowed up by the land, and she must leave well alone. She had killed her sister and must be quiet, because if the police found out she would end up in jail. Then she told me about her daddy, and I said people like that couldn't be trusted. This mirrored what her religious grandparents had said many times before. Gay people were wicked, unclean, and destined for Hell. Her face was a picture. I think she actually wet herself. I said I would be her protector. All she had to do was not to speak a word.

CHAPTER SEVENTY-THREE

The first thing Jennifer noticed when she visited Blackwater Farm was the 'Sold' sign staked in the jagged earth. Today's visit was to see how the family was coping in the aftermath of recent events. The week of Abigail's disappearance had been exhausting, and Jennifer had broken all her own rules, experiencing the gamut of emotions as if the little girl were one of her own.

Just like the day she first attended, the wind invaded the yard, raising dust that would settle in her hair. A sliver of a breeze swept through the tubular farm gates, whistling a mournful song. Memories filtered through as it played, and she recalled walking through the churned up yard on her first day, nervous about what lay ahead. For all her reservations about becoming emotionally involved, it had happened anyway.

The house had not changed much since her visit the month before, and she glanced up at the dirty window pane, half expecting Olivia's ashen face to be staring down at her, caught up in the memory of her nightmare. But it was empty, and the whole house had taken on a vacant feel.

She rapped on the door, the heavy metal knocker echoing through the building. There was no Fiona to welcome her in. Despite her evil deeds, the thought saddened her. Reading the woman's diary had given Jennifer a greater understanding of what had driven her to commit her crimes, and the lack of compassion that the woman exhibited towards Abigail and Olivia. Fiona – or Doreen, according to her birth certificate – would not be going anywhere for a very long time.

The family had occupied Jennifer's thoughts since that fateful day, and it was with a heavy heart that she stepped back from the door. Nick's car was on the drive, so they couldn't be too far away. And it was then that she heard it: shouting coming from the back garden. But it was not shouting like before, the long repetitive call of Nick shouting for his daughter, his voice hoarse, his stature hunched. It was the shouts of a family spending time together in the sun.

Jennifer smiled in anticipation as she strode to the back yard, pushing past the small rusted gate to enter what was now the rear paddock. A whoop rose up, followed by peals of laughter. Jennifer smiled to see her aunt Laura's pony being put through his paces by one of the twins, who was laughing with such abandon that it had to be Abigail. Nick and Joanna were standing with their backs turned to Jennifer as they encouraged their daughter to take the jump set up before her, consisting of a pole laid across two barrels on their side. With another resolute whoop, she leaned forward and kicked the pony onwards, popping over the jump without any effort.

'Jennifer!' Olivia cried, running towards her. Pink and fresh-faced, she was positively glowing. Her cheeks had plumped out and she ran towards Jennifer with open arms. Jennifer bent down to return her hug, and was almost knocked off her heels. 'We can do jumps now,' Olivia said, 'come see.'

Nick and Joanna turned to greet her, their smiles soft and genuine. Joanna was no longer draped in vintage wear, but dressed in a red shirt, faded jeans and Hunter wellington boots. Abigail jumped off the panting pony, passing the reins to Olivia before running towards them, flushed with excitement.

'Darling, this is Jennifer, the police lady. You probably don't remember her,' Joanna said, beaming with real emotion.

Abigail's expression suggested she did. 'Of course I remember her, Mummy. I spoke to her, remember?'

Jennifer nodded, remembering how Abigail had come within inches of being burned alive. She placed her hand on Abigail's shoulder, a feeling of contentment warming her from the inside out.

'How are you feeling now?'

'Great!' she squeaked. 'Thank you for the pony. We're getting our own one soon. He's black, with a white stripe. His name is Benji.'

'Ooh, that's exciting. You're very good at it.'

Abigail beamed at the compliment, taking her father's hand.

'We thought it was only fair to buy one of our own,' Nick said, looking better than he had in months. 'I don't think your Toby is able to keep up with their enthusiasm.'

Jennifer looked at the snorting pony and nodded her head in agreement. 'You may have a point, although I'm sure it's not done him any harm.'

'Right,' Nick said, squeezing Abigail's hand. 'You stink of horse. Time for a bath. Olivia, it's your turn to turn the pony out. Make sure he cools down before you let him go.' He touched Jennifer on the arm. 'Pop in for a cuppa before you go. I'm sure the girls would like to talk to you some more.'

Jennifer nodded, grateful for the chance to speak to Joanna alone.

'Two more laps, then walk him off,' she shouted to Olivia, who was smiling widely as she trotted around the paddock.

'I was surprised to see the "Sold" sign outside the house. Are you moving?'

Joanna nodded. 'Not far. We've bought a smallholding, something a bit nearer the town, with an acre of land for the pony. There are too many memories here. It's time to move on.'

Jennifer dug her hands into her jacket pockets, nodding her approval. This family had had enough fresh starts to last a lifetime, and she hoped this would be their final move, for the children's sake if nothing else.

'How are you all?'

'We're so grateful to have Abigail back in our lives . . .' The words faltered on Joanna's breath, and she turned to Jennifer, her eyes wet with tears. 'And to you, for being there when we needed you the most.'

Jennifer recalled Abigail's tale of how she had loosened a nail from the boarded up window and squeezed through after Fiona had lit the fire. Weak and exhausted, she made it to the shed, where Jennifer had found her and draped her jacket over the little girl's shoulders, flooded with relief to find her alive.

'It's wonderful to see them looking so well. No long-term damage?'

'Abigail doesn't remember much of the incident. It was very clever of her, loosening the boarded window.'

'You've got two very special girls,' Jennifer said. She finally understood why Abigail had been so reluctant during their communications to name the person who had pushed her down the well. She had not wanted to get her sister into trouble. 'And Fiona?'

Joanna's face clouded over. 'Fiona's betrayal has not been easy to explain. The girls are both seeing therapists, although I think the pony has provided more therapy than any counselling session. Olivia blames herself, but, as I've told her, Fiona was a very manipulative woman. If she hadn't told Olivia to keep quiet, then we would have found Abigail straight away.'

'It's very sad,' Jennifer said, finding it difficult to feel animosity. 'I read the diary. Very sad indeed.'

'I know. We found it in her bag. She gave me a diary exactly the same, about a month after she arrived. She told me to fill it in to help with the stress. I tried a couple of times, but just ended up with a blank page.' She shook her head as the memory returned. 'I feel sick at the thought of what my father did to her. I knew something was wrong, but I wasn't strong enough to face it.'

'Mmm,' Jennifer mumbled. She had given it plenty of thought since reading the jagged words, strewn across the paper, ingrained into the pages underneath. Fiona, now revealed as Doreen, had viewed Joanna's denial as the ultimate betrayal. To Jennifer, Joanna's response had just been a ten-year-old girl using repression as a method of coping because she was unable to comprehend her father's acts. Just how was Joanna coping with the fact her husband was gay? It was a question Jennifer lacked the courage to ask. And with the investigation complete, it really wasn't her business.

'Look at me, look at me!' Olivia cried to Jennifer, waving as she encouraged the pony to trot in a circle.

'Well done,' Jennifer cheered, before lowering her voice and turning to Joanna. 'What about their telepathic skills? Has there been any further communication between them?'

Joanna looked at her thoughtfully. 'No. Well, not really. We're trying to keep everything low-key. I don't expect the next year or two to be easy, but we'll get through it.'

'I'm sure you will,' Jennifer said, a chill creeping over her as the sun lowered in the sky.

She said her goodbyes to the family, after staying for one last cuppa, and pushed the front door of the house firmly shut on her way out. Her eyes crept back to the cold stone building, and she felt grateful that she did not have to spend any more time within its walls. Adjusting her eyes to the twilight, she walked the lonely path to her car. Evening fell quickly in Haven, and she turned her eyes back to the lands as a mist descended. *Jennifer.* The word was whispered in a haunting voice that only she could hear. Haven was a living, breathing entity of its own. She had felt its presence deep in the soil when she had hung in the damp, dark well, surrounded by rotting bricks and burrowing insects. It had allowed her to escape with her life that day, but she knew that many more incidents lay ahead. And the next time she might not be so lucky.

CHAPTER SEVENTY-FOUR

Diary Entry

I would have given up and gone home, if it weren't for DC Knight. She was a crow on my shoulder, constantly pecking for information. Leaving in the midst of the investigation would have looked very suspicious, so I stuck it out, enjoying watching my so-called sister fall apart. Not that it was easy to keep up the pretence. It took every ounce of my self-control to act natural, and sometimes it felt as if she saw right through me. When the medium came, it was my voice she picked up, pleading with my father to stop his cruel acts. A ghost of a memory that never left me, it made my skin crawl to hear the words out loud. Slowly my love for the house, the land, Nick, it all turned to hate. Joanna and her family needed to die, and take our secrets with them. Now, as I look back, I can see how close I came to getting what I wanted.

But it was a house made of cards. Nick and Joanna weren't the perfect couple, and the twins were strange and wild. The house was crumbling, and filled with something so dark there were times I could barely breathe within its walls. I am not sorry the monster is dead. I'm only sorry they caught me. But without solid proof of murder, I'm confident I'll get off. I'll serve a few years for perverting the course of justice, if that. My prison bed is mildly more comfortable than the one in my grotty flat, and I know how to handle my inmates. I'll get regular meals, cockroach-free. Best of all, I'll have time on my hands. Time to plan the next birthday surprise.

LETTER FROM CAROLINE

I can't quite believe I've finished book three of the DC Knight series already. Each book has stretched the realms of my writing skills, bringing me deep into an imagination I didn't know I possessed. Thank you so much to everyone who has bought, reviewed, shared, tweeted and supported my books. I truly value my readers, and I hope you've enjoyed the various journeys my writing has taken you on. There's lots more to come, so don't forget to subscribe to my newsletter to ensure you are kept updated for each new release:

www.bookouture.com/caroline-mitchell

I'd like to invite you to join me again with my forthcoming novels featuring DS Ruby Preston. She has been standing in the shadows for some time now, waiting for her story to be told. She doesn't always play by the rules, but as she says herself, she's a 'real copper and gets things done'. Based in London, this new crime series is gritty, fast paced, and features some rather dubious characters. I can't wait to introduce you to them.

If you have enjoyed my books I'd love to hear from you, and if you could recommend me to a friend, you would make my day. To me, writing is a form of communication, and it doesn't all have to be one way. My Twitter and Facebook links are below, if you'd like to get in touch.

Until next time,

Caroline

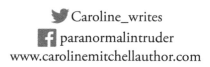

 Caroline_writes
 paranormalintruder
www.carolinemitchellauthor.com

ACKNOWLEDGEMENTS

Coming to the end of a book always feels like a massive accomplishment, but I haven't done it alone. I'd like to thank the fantastic team at Bookouture, in particular publisher extraordinaire Oliver Rhodes and my fairy Godmother Kim Nash, who helped make all my wishes come true in 2015. I also want to give a special shout out to my editor, Keshini Naidoo. I feel very blessed to be working with such an outstanding talent, and a truly lovely lady.

A special mention of gratitude to my author friends, your support has been phenomenal. Thanks to Angie Marsons and her partner Julie Forrest, two truly inspirational (and hilarious) people I feel proud to call my pals. Thanks to Renita D'Silva, Holly Martin, Lindsay J. Pryor, Sue Watson, Mandy Baggot, Christie Barlow, Nigel May, Robert Bryndza, Mel Sherratt (AKA Marcie Steele) and Kelly Rimmer for the giggles, and all the other fab Bookouture authors in our growing team.

To the wonderful bloggers and book clubs who give up their free time to read and promote our books, I owe you a hug for this, and each tweet and Facebook share (we could be some time). A special thanks to Noelle Holten, Lisa Hall, Sean Talbot, Joseph Calleja, Tracy Shephard, Rebecca Pugh, Helen Phifer, and Lisa Cutts for adding sparkle to my year. I could go on, but I'm running out of room! To my police colleagues, and in particular to Nigel Dermott who kindly shared his experiences of leading the police diving team. Your input has been invaluable. To family, friends, and my all important readers, words are not enough to express my gratitude. I hope you continue to enjoy the books I have to offer.

Lightning Source UK Ltd.
Milton Keynes UK
UKHW021306141222
413924UK00023B/543